The Gauntlets of Power

Guardians of the Gold-Rimmed Scroll

BY

W. E. JAMES

A novel by W E JAMES
Edited by ROBERT MATTHEWS
First published by Amazon in 2015
Copyright © 2013 W. E. JAMES. All rights reserved.

No part of this publication may be reproduced, stored in a retrieval system or transmitted, in any form or by any means, electronic, mechanical, photocopying, recording or otherwise, without the prior permission of the copyright holder.

This work is registered with the UK Copyright Service: Registration No: 284672226

ISBN 978-1-5087-0091-3

Authors notes

I'd like to dedicate this book to those that dare to dream, but believe the end is not in sight, there's always a beginning and a end. This book was my dream I hope it is as worthy as yours.

W. E. JAMES

The Gauntlets of Power
Guardians of the Gold-rimmed Scroll

Prologue

Lost beyond the cosmos and the bones of the dead, a gift, a curse in salvation rest.

Forged by hammer at Elohim's request, four kings summoned from the north, south, east and west.

A gift not for killing though governed by strength, bestowed insight and the world was blessed.

A curse, the keys to the inferno's room, a wolf, a spider and a witch to rule.

While Cernos yearns, creation folds, salvation in a prophecy foretold.

When thirteen ride out, evil's destruction is assured, and the age of innocence will be restored.

Act One

The Tale of the Drunken Three-Quarter Elf

Tartarus Leadbottom had had the worst run of luck. It wasn't enough that he had been tricked, robbed and left for dead. He slowly opened his oval eyes and surveyed his surroundings, searching for the stars and the clear blue distant moon in the night sky. But they didn't come into view. Everything was a blur at first, which became clearer as the shapes became sharper, as his mind fully awoke.

There was no moon; it was pitch-black apart from the odd firefly darting past, although he could hear the scurrying of insects and birds in the trees.

He could only see tall grass close to his face, along with the plants and flowers that lit up at night, setting shadows on bushes and tree trunks alike.

It was a dank, cold place which fresh rain never reached.

The trees seemed to be almost without end. Most of the elm trees were over two hundred metres tall, with winding branches. Some of the tree trunks were thicker than a small house.

Whispered voices whistled with the wind rustling through the trees, its terrifyingly eerie, cold breath travelling through flesh and into bone.

The forest was filled with the pungent stench of a battle long since fought. Miles and miles of boggy moors coupled with thick undergrowth stretched as far as the eye could see.

He could feel its hypnotic charms. A captivating force flowed throughout the forest which, although peaceful, was inherently evil.

Tartarus Leadbottom was in no doubt that the Black Forest was a place he would never grow to love.

It had been his short-sightedness that had caused such a catastrophic blunder, he thought to himself. Losing the scroll was unforgiveable. Smaller nations and tribes with paganistic beliefs often relied on happenings in nature to show the will of the gods and had no time for prophets or the followers of Cernos the Fire Lord, who was held back by the gates of inferno. They ridiculed Eben's foresight, written on the parchment.

Beings such as dwarves and elves called their exalted one the giver of life, and the majority —believers in the word of Elohim — were more interested in dreams, prophets and seers. They revered the teachings of Eben.

The scroll had never been read, but he believed it would liberate all. Its safekeeping and secrets were entrusted to the temple of Aafari, the homestead of his spiritual leader.

It would bring immense dishonour to his name if it were known he had lost the scroll. He would be shunned by his people, which for him would be a fate far worse than death.

He reclosed his eyes and rested his head back down onto the muddy soil ... at this moment, he wished he *was* dead.

He considered himself a smart, able-bodied elf. He was young in elven years and still had many years to ripen before he could be called an elgar, the title given to a mature elf.

The task he had been set was not an unreasonable one for an elf of his standing. He was a good hunter and tracker, and was considered in many circles to be a promising warrior. His dabbling in magic was a secret he had kept well hidden; after all, why should the dark elves have all the fun? Not only was it entertaining, but it aided his hunting too.

Normally, Tartarus's suspicious nature would have steered him well clear of the game of arrows, which was similar to archery. But his good looks, a smooth blend of elf and human, together with a mischievous attitude and youthful exuberance, gave him a heightened sense of self-confidence. This had caused him to become competitive to a point where danger was not always fully considered. At times it got him into a lot of trouble; this was one of those times.

He dug his fingers into the soil underneath him, clenching his hands into fists as he shook his head in total disbelief. 'When will I learn life isn't just a game?' he thought.

'Why me?' he murmured, as the sequence of events flashed through his mind. There was only one thing that could have made him think that taking this unholy route was a good idea: burned-barrel ale.

The taste of stale blood and ale in his mouth led him to believe that he had been unconscious for some time. He wiped the dried blood mixed with mud from his lips, while cursing his rotten luck and his human traits.

Elves were not allowed to gamble and were certainly not allowed to drink human ale; the effects were far worse on elves than on humans, a fact that wasn't lost on Tartarus as he gathered all his strength to raise himself off the muddy ground. He could see it all now: the tale of the drunken three-quarter elf. The thought did not amuse him, and he continued to curse his misfortune.

His attackers had thought he was dead. The arrow that had hit him from close range had not been poisonous but it had hurt like hell, having pierced his body armour. He wore a muscle breastplate, neatly concealed by a long, dark, hooded cloak made of leather.

The blow had knocked the wind out of him, which had, in turn, made him fall from his elven horse. Willow was a beautiful animal with a long slender head, spiky mane, and sharper facial features than those of a normal horse.

The fall had rendered him unconscious. Had the arrow struck a little higher he would certainly have been killed; his breastplate offered his neck no protection. The protruding arrow embedded in his vest was an offensive sight. Fortunately, elven bone was extremely strong. There would be a scar but for an elf, or even a three-quarter elf which Tartarus was, it was only a flesh wound and as such would not kill him.

He unclipped his body armour to inspect and tend to the wound the arrow had left. Visibility was poor so he conjured a little spell, by reciting a few words under his breath, to illuminate the area around him.

He uttered the words *'Illustro, lux lucis meus via.'*

As the spell brightened up his surroundings, the full horror of his situation came into view. Vacant eyes stared back at him and he jumped back in shock; the head of one of his companions was within striking distance.

'Vince,' he murmured.

The colour drained from Tartarus's face and his usually warm complexion was replaced with a pale, gaunt look. His eyes searched for his companion's body; the search did not take long. He then found himself shouting the name of his second companion, Asrack, hoping in vain that the same fate had not befallen him. He was about to shout again when he saw Asrack's foot protruding from the shadow of Vince's headless corpse. Before he knew it, he was vomiting uncontrollably.

Tartarus's mind was spinning; his companions were dead, he had lost the scroll, and the horses and provisions were gone. He quickly cleared his head and gathered his thoughts, while covering the lifeless corpses of his friends as best he could. He would have to track down his attackers to regain the scroll and in so doing he could also avenge his friends and alert the wizard to the impending danger. First, though, he would have to find his horse.

He would send word to the wizard, Nikomeades, through a red star, but not until he found his horse or a faster mode of transport. Flares always gave away the sender's position and he wasn't about to give his attackers any hint of his existence or whereabouts.

The light from his spell was fading fast. Looking for tracks, he found Willow's imprint in the mud. From the depth of the hoof marks he could tell that his horse had galloped away. This was good news. The tracks led in the opposite direction to that which his attackers had taken and elven horses were not known to travel far without their rider, their trust and loyalty being nurtured from birth.

Still seething, he made a makeshift torch from broken branches, wrapping leaves mixed with elm-tree gum round the thickest end and, by striking a rough stone against a piece of flint, lit it. Elm gum was known to burn long and steady, with a bright amber flame. Paying the two burial mounds of earth, leaves and twigs his final respects, he set off in the direction of his horse.

*

Prince Edwin lifted his visor before removing his helmet. He had been victorious and now, high up on the battlements, he wanted to savour the moment and survey the glorious scene. He could see fires to the east and his eyes glinted in response; war was his arena and only in war did he truly feel alive. His appetite for battle was insatiable and there was no better sound than that of sword crushing bone, apart, perhaps, from the sound of torture.

He placed his helmet on the parapet's crenel and looked down at the moat. Hot oils still burned brightly. His army had encountered the stiffest resistance there; many a man had been burned to death in this last-ditch attempt to prevent him from taking the citadel. It was to no avail; as always, his might had won in the end. He cast his eyes over the citadel's fortifications. His army looked miniature from this height; the sight amused him.

The city of Athena, which encircled the citadel, was now ravaged by flames. Smoke billowed and embers flickered from the badly damaged buildings and houses that littered the city's streets. His catapults had kept up a constant bombardment once the siege had begun, and he could clearly see the devastation they had caused within the city walls.

The night sky was filled with thick smog. Screams of women and children could be heard amid the chaos. The looting of the city had begun; he produced a wry smile. The duke's men had put up a good fight, and after several days of fighting many had died, on both sides. Prince Edwin felt no remorse; lives were lost in the blink of an eye, and he had blinked away a lot of lives.

On Edwin's left stood an imposing figure, his bodyguard, Baracus. He was a huge, muscular man over seven feet tall. He wore a pair of large spaulders, with barbed rivets, on his upper arm and shoulders. His breast plate bore the crest of a black dragon, with piercing blue eyes. The plates were all made of the same material: a woven metal alloy, stronger than steel. He wore a sturdy leather kilt around his midriff. His heavy, steel-capped boots had crushed many a man under their heels. Baracus was a man of few words, which was exactly how Edwin liked it.

Edwin's trusted captain, Archelaus, stood to his right; he and Archelaus had fought in many campaigns together. Sometimes Edwin thought his captain had more battle lust than he had, but he would normally dismiss this thought because no one could be seen to supersede his authority, not even a loyal companion. Archelaus could see that Edwin's amusement was already waning, so he turned Edwin's attention to a nearby prisoner held by two heavily armoured guards. The captain summoned the two guards over.

'Sire,' he said to Edwin, 'this piece of filth is a captain in the duke's First Battalion.'

'I've heard those men don't talk,' Edwin replied softly.

Archelaus nodded. 'That's why we require your assistance, sire'.

'Come, come now! Bring him forward, 'Prince Edwin said cheerfully, indicating with a finger where he wanted the prisoner placed.

The man, who had already been badly beaten, was brought forward by the guards.

Prisoner 663 had seen much better days, but he was a captain in the duke's First Battalion and no one, but no one, would make him talk. Edwin gave the guards a signal to release the prisoner, and then raised his left arm. The chain mail under his black amour didn't make a sound. The gauntlet on his hand glowed under the smoke-filled sky. Edwin ordered the prisoner to kneel before him. Prisoner 663 refused.

As the glow of the gauntlet intensified the prisoner's fragile legs began to bend, and before he knew it he was kneeling on the cold, stone floor.

'Where's Mandrick?' Edwin barked. 'Where is he? Where's the duke?' he demanded, taking up a closer position in front of the prisoner. Placing his gauntlet on the prisoner's head, he began to read the prisoner's mind and retrieved the information he required.

'Gone!' he shouted, releasing his grip on the prisoner's head. 'I have no weakness now.'

This wasn't good news. It confirmed his worst fears: that the duke had escaped his grasp. This was a pity. Edwin had given Cressida, the sorceress, his word that he would not return home until Mandrick was dead. A tight-lipped smile formed on his face.

'No one escapes my blade, old friend,' he whispered. Archelaus walked forward. 'What should I do with this?' he said with disdain, pointing at the prisoner. Edwin looked at Baracus and then made a slight movement with his head. Baracus marched forwards and kicked the prisoner square in the face. The impact of the blow dropped the prisoner awkwardly on all fours. Baracus lifted his leg again and in one swift motion his boot came slamming down. There was a horrendous sound of skull and bone being crushed against the hard stone floor. Baracus wiped his boot clean.

The Prince and Archelaus had not waited to see the prisoner's demise. They had already departed and were walking along the parapets in the direction of the citadel's main hall. Baracus gave Prisoner 663 one last look, then followed his Prince.

'Gripper Hawkins did well today. I plan to promote him to captain. He leads the men well, and with the heavy infantry position now vacant...' Edwin said, ponderously. 'What do you think? I think he's earned it.'

Archelaus nodded his approval.

'Good, but all the same I think I'll sleep on it. Where is Gripper now?'

'With the group of men guarding Philippoussis, sire.'

'Philippoussis?'

Archelaus nodded. Both men knew that Philippoussis, Edwin's debt collector, was like a bull at a gate and, for that, he was even more hated than they were.

'He's in the vaults making an inventory of Mandrick's most prized assets,' replied Archelaus. 'That's why I sent Gripper to protect ...' – he hesitated before continuing – 'your interests.' Words such as 'ours' and 'yours' had to be chosen carefully around the prince.

'I see,' said Edwin.

'You seem distant. What is troubling you, my Prince? 'he enquired, while handing Edwin his helmet.

'Nothing,' he replied harshly, but then continued in a softer voice. 'I want you to dispatch Silvanus,' he said. 'Kallen has not yet sent word on the progress of his quest for the scroll.' Edwin handed his captain a note. 'Now, your Prince is tired. Take me to Mandrick's bedchamber; we'll talk further in the morning,' instructed Edwin. They walked down a flight of stairs that led to a set of towers on the east wing, adjacent to the courtyard. While they walked Edwin complimented Archelaus on the strategic planning of the battle. The high praise was welcome by the captain, who produced a small devilish grin behind his neatly trimmed beard. Abruptly, he stopped beside a large oak door adorned with numerous gold studs.

'Here are your quarters, sire,' Archelaus stated sharply. The duke's stately quarters had all the pomp and ostentatious splendour that one would expect from a man of Duke Mandrick's rank and standing. There was a huge portrait of the duke, which overlooked a large, oak desk. In the corner of the room stood a jewel-encrusted circular stand, which was adorned by a limestone bust of the duke. A large four-poster bed took centre stage. The back of the chamber opened onto a balcony overlooking the citadel's main courtyard, with a lovely formal garden at its centre.

Edwin surveyed the splendour; it was in keeping with his tastes, although the picture and the bust were not. He walked up to the bust and knocked it off its stand; the impact broke the bust in two. As the head came to a stop at his feet, he laughed. 'Soon, dear friend,' he thought. Archelaus helped him out of his full body armour. The sleek black armour had been made by the sorceress using a magical element called Blur. The result was a suit of armour that allowed him to travel very short distances quickly, a very useful tool in battle. The black armour had given rise to Edwin's nickname of 'The Black Knight'.

The removal of his armour revealed Edwin's pasty whiteness. The skin under his eyes was dark black, as though he were ravished by illness. However, he was far from being ill and actually cultivated this look. The black marks under his eyes were a charcoal pigment, applied to give him a more menacing glare when his helmet was worn. His pallid appearance was the result of virtually living in his armour. He also applied a floury white substance to his skin after bathing. This was an attempt at vanity more than anything else; he believed his complexion made him look significantly more regal.

'Fetch me some women. I'm in need of some female attention,' he said, with a grin. 'Now leave me.' Archelaus turned to face the door and left the room immediately.

In sudden anger, Edwin ripped the large painting of the duke from its carved, gilt frame. It didn't matter how many battles were fought and won, he would never have the power he so desperately craved if his master, the Autocrat, continued to rule. Edwin did not want to be king: he wanted to be the king of kings and have the entire world under his rule. As long as the Autocrat Abandanon, lived, his ambitions would not be fulfilled. The duke had escaped his grasp so far, and that had marred his progress, but by capturing the citadel Edwin's plan was in motion and gaining momentum.

A knock at the chamber door brought Edwin back from his thoughts. He raised his head, looked towards the door and said 'Enter.' Baracus opened the door and replied in a deep voice, 'As requested, sire. 'Two scantily dressed women squeezed past him and entered the chamber. Edwin nodded his approval. As Baracus left the room and closed the heavy wooden door behind him, Edwin smiled; it had been a good day.

*

Brun was one of the last blacksmiths still in the city of Athena; he had kept faith with the Duke of Tyrus which, in hindsight, had been a misguided course of action. Most of his competitors had fled the city weeks ago taking their business elsewhere; they'd taken advantage of the amnesty offered by the Black Knight before his attack on the city. While the battle to hold off the invaders was being fought, business had boomed. In the three weeks before the city had fallen he had made all manner of armour and weapons to aid the duke in the defence of the city; his hands told the story of their toil. Now, held as a prisoner, things did not look good at all. His captors were brutal. He had felt many a hard lash from a metal encrusted whip, and to top it all off he had still not been paid for his services. 'Bloody duke,' he murmured.

The irony was that his own stables had now become his prison, and there was no means of escape. He should know; he had built it with his own hands from the ground up to prevent his livestock from doing just that: escape! The survivors of the siege had been herded like cattle into confined places, such as Brun's workshop and stables.
'What a mess. What good is money now, anyway?' Brun felt true despair. The odds were stacked against his even seeing out the day now that aiding the duke was an offence punishable by death. He wished he had been told this fact earlier. Maybe someone had told him, but knowing his luck the information was probably divulged into his right ear. Brun only had hearing in his left ear; years of working in a noisy workshop had taken their toll.

They had already taken one of his friends, who had not returned. Brun and Captain Cooms of the duke's First Battalion had been good friends for a number of years. When Brun had first arrived in the city of Athena, he was informed that he would need to petition the duke for authority to open a business within the city limits. So, on the second day after his arrival Brun went to the citadel to submit his petition. It was there that he had first met Captain Cooms. It had struck him instantly that the captain's neatly trimmed moustache was in sharp contrast to his furrowed facial features, whose ruggedness was emphasized by a long, diagonal scar under his right eye. This facial ruggedness was a characteristic both men shared.

The captain's fascination with creating unusual weapons was a delight to Brun. He was only too happy to help the captain make weapons, for the right price. Training in hand-to-hand combat and sword-craft was Brun's price, a fee the captain was more than willing to pay. Through this arrangement camaraderie arose and, soon after, a friendship was formed. Brun quickly learned that he was hopeless with a sword, but was formidable with a two-handed war hammer or a set of twin-sided battleaxes. The reason for his failure with a sword eluded him.

Brun's stables were located on the site of the original barn. As Brun's business grew, so did the need for more livestock space. So the barn had been dismantled, its timber recycled and the stables erected in its place. The layout of the building was simple: an area at the front for equipment and grooming or slaughter, then the rest of the building consisted of two rows of seven stables. Each row faced another across a central aisle, which became entombed when the large barn door was closed. Eighty prisoners were now confined within its walls and each stable was a cell housing at least six prisoners at any one time. The guards who patrolled the aisle between the rows of stables were a motley group of heavily armed men led by a Draconian. The Draconians were a brutish race of reptilian-skinned people, who were able to endure the extremely high volcanic temperatures found in Draconia, a region in the Southlands.

Brun looked around the dimly lit stable that had now become his cell. The captain had gone but the stable seemed just as full. There was barely enough room for him to stretch out his legs; the onset of cramp was beginning. It seemed as though he had been confined for an eternity, although it had only been eight hours. This was mainly due to the fact that he had not been given a thing to eat or drink while he had been held, and Brun loved his food. The odour of sweat and manure did nothing to help his feeling of dread and, along with the stale air, it just turned his stomach.

The fact that he had got to speak to the captain at all was fortuitous indeed; once the citadel had fallen, a permanent curfew had been enforced. It was around the same time that Brun's place of work had been commandeered as a prison; anyone caught breaking the Black Knight's curfew was either killed immediately or, if they might be of some use, such as skilled craftsmen, brought to one of these new prisons. Seeing martial law take hold of the city, Brun had tried to flee but was caught. Now he sat quietly in a cramped position, in a poorly lit stable.

The captain had been one of the first to be placed under armed guard inside the stable block. A few hours had passed before Brun had been brought to the stables. Luckily, he was thrown into the pen in which the captain was being held. Cooms had been badly beaten and could hardly speak, but in the little time they spent together Brun gleaned that his friend believed he did not have long to live; they knew Cooms was a captain in the Duke's First Battalion. Cooms had urged Brun to attempt escape, find Duke Mandrick and deliver an urgent message: 'When Edwin kills with the power of light, then can he be killed by the power of steel.'

Almost two hours had passed since the captain had been taken away. Brun pondered Cooms's words. He held his head in his hands; it was difficult to remain upbeat. If he did manage to escape he would try to find the captain's wife, Mary, and tell her Cooms sends his love, and regrets not being able to fulfil his promise to her. Now that was worth his time, he thought; the sentiment wasn't lost on Brun, who had lost touch with his loved ones a long time ago. The message about Edwin did not make any sense, though. Firstly, who the hell was Edwin? Secondly, being a blacksmith he had worked with steel all his life and he knew only too well that its power could kill. Thirdly, if he was able to escape there was no way he would be travelling in the direction of the duke. Although, having said that, the duke did owe him money. Brun's dried lips cracked a small ironic smile: that would be suicide.

The large main door of the stable swung open and a Draconian walked in. Draconians were wider than humans but similar in height. After a brief conversation with one of his counterparts he continued down the aisle shouting, 'Stand up if you're a blacksmith!' Brun froze as he heard the words. The Draconian had already checked a couple of the stables. Brun could hear his footsteps getting ever closer. Suddenly, the steps stopped outside his cell and he heard the familiar clicking sound of the stable door's top half being opened. Gradually, a pair of lizard eyes appeared.

Brun looked up to see another prisoner pointing and grinning at him; an array of yellow broken teeth showed within the prisoner's foul orifice. In that moment Brun wished he had not shared the same cell as the captain. He hoped and prayed that those ugly teeth weren't going to be the last thing he ever saw.

'Are you a blacksmith? 'the Draconian asked Brun in a harsh, hissing voice as he observed the grinning prisoner. Slowly, Brun nodded. 'I said to stand up if you're a blacksmith, so why are you sitting? Stand up! 'he screamed.

Brun's mind was in turmoil. A moment ago he had thought his head was for the chopping block. Now it seemed the prisoner with the foul set of teeth had actually done him a favour. The Draconian was after the blacksmith's hands, not his neck.

They walked away from Brun's workshop at a brisk pace. It had been a long time since the simple act of leaving the stables had filled him with such euphoria.

'We need you to prepare a horse,' the Draconian hissed.

Brun nodded. He had quickly come to realize that the less he spoke to these brutes the less likely it was that he'd taste their fists.

Athena was a broken city; rubble and bodies littered its streets, fires burned freely and the smell of rotting, burned flesh filled the air. Brun held his bound wrists over his face to block out the rancid stench. Arriving at a large barn that was unguarded, they walked in and were immediately confronted by the sight of a large horse. The charger's movement was restricted by a rope tied to its bridle and fastened to a post. Fear was making the horse pull away violently, again and again. Brun lifted his arms up, giving the Draconian a signal to release the bonds around his wrists. The Draconian duly obliged by producing a sharp dagger and running the blade between Brun's wrists, swiftly cutting the rope. Brun turned around and approached the horse, arms aloft just above shoulder height. He had dealt with horses in far worse situations hundreds of times; a poorly fitted horseshoe was like the worst kind of toothache.

Brun quickly calmed the animal down, gently patting her mane. He liked her chestnut coat and she had an endearing little white cloud above her brow. He toyed with the idea of asking the Draconian for her name, but quickly thought better of it.

'Good, Good! 'exclaimed the Draconian. 'I was thinking about eating her. Now, prepare her for the ride.' There was an anvil, a hammer and a small makeshift furnace in the form of an open-top kiln. All the tools and equipment needed for him to prepare the horse had been provided. Picking up a horseshoe, then measuring it up, Brun got to work. He had almost finished preparing the horse, and while completing his task he had made up his mind: there was no way he was going back to his stables for incarceration. He had been left alone with his captors long enough to know that the Draconian might not be missed. He called the creature over.

'I think she's ready, but you'll need to inspect the shoes,' he said, looking at the ground in order to avoid eye contact. Brun was not a good liar. The Draconian stroked the horse and seemed impressed with Brun's work.

'Good job, Ling,' he hissed. Ling, derived from earthling, was the Draconian term for a bowl of cooked human stew. Brun motioned the Draconian to inspect the horse's hind legs. Once the Draconian was in position, Brun put his plan into action. He made a movement as if he were about to lift up the horse's leg to show the Draconian her hoof, then, without warning, he tugged on her mane sharply. The horse's hind legs reared up and smashed into the Draconian's breastplate, cracking it in an instant and sending him flying. The brute landed in a heap, having hit the anvil.

Brun could hear that the Draconian was in a bad way. Quickly checking first to see if anyone had heard the commotion, Brun kneeled over his body to examine the extent of the injuries. The Draconian's breastplate was cracked and that meant his injuries could be extensive and agonizing, but Brun's real concern was the Draconian's raising the alarm and, deciding to put the beast out of his misery, Brun started to pull the Draconian's dagger from its sheath. The top of the hilt was adorned with three circular rings crossing over each other. The outer rim was encrusted with emeralds.

'You there. What are you doing?' The voice startled Brun. 'I said what are you doing with Zog?' Brun looked over his shoulder and saw a shadowy figure in the doorway, peering back at him.

'He's been kicked by the horse,' Brun spurted nervously, hoping he hadn't been caught in the act.

'Let me see,' the man replied sharply, walking in from the shadows, holding a saddle. Brun could now see that the man, who was actually a little smaller than his shadow had suggested, wasn't as big as Brun in size. He had on a chrome-coloured helmet with its visor raised, and a long, black cloak which covered him from the neck down. As the man got closer, Brun removed the dagger completely from its sheath.

The man kneeled down beside Zog, while placing a firm hand on Brun's shoulder. He then gave the blacksmith a slight push to give himself more room. In that moment the man felt a sharp pain and produced a gargled sound that was hardly audible. As he looked down the sight of the three-ringed hilt of the Draconian's dagger greeted him. He tried to call for help, but the air had already escaped from his lungs.

Brun waited for a few seconds, then removed the dagger and rolled him over; he was in need of a disguise and this was it.

The boots fitted perfectly, but he was unhappy with the sleek, black leather britches. It had taken him more than a couple of turns to secure the lock around his waist and the britches were a bit stiff to walk in. Apart from that, the outfit would suffice. On searching the man before removing his clothing, he had found a pouch containing a note to a person named Kallen. It wasn't a name he'd heard before and he only just glanced at the note when something else caught his eye. The emblem of a silver stag was emblazoned across the saddlebag. He had just killed a royal rider. Brun knew that an escape might have gone unnoticed but, sadly, the rider's death would not. No stone would be left unturned in capturing the perpetrator. He looked at the unconscious Draconian sleeping soundly; the dagger was a fair trade. Killing him now would be of little benefit: one death by his hands was enough.

There was no time to waste. Placing the rider's possessions in a holder, he mounted the horse, slammed the helmet's visor down and rode out of the barn. His journey to the main gate was a peaceful affair; everyone seemed to know him or, perhaps, feared the Black Knight enough not to halt his progress. Brun thought to himself, 'This is great. What a perfect escape.' Duke Mandrick was to the east, the fires were to the east, and the Black Knight was raging war in the east. Brun kicked his heels, rode through the main gates, then turned west. Brun was now a fugitive, another person's quarry. He would ride to the lands in the west, to an area the war had long since left. His mind wondered to thoughts of Irons Keep, and his sister Lillian. It had been a very long time since he'd seen her face.

High on the battlements of the citadel, Archelaus watched the royal rider, Silvanus, ride off into the night as directed by Prince Edwin. In a barn far below the battlements, a few hours passed before the Draconian awoke from his slumber, still groggy. Quickly, he got to his feet. His ribs felt sore, so he placed a hand over the bruised area, seeking relief. His palm stopped just above his stomach. Wincing with the pain, and still slightly baffled, he wondered where the horse and blacksmith had gone. Then he spotted Silvanus lying naked on the barn floor in a pool of blood. He was shocked: no one ever touched a royal rider unless they had a death wish. Zog looked down to where his dagger was normally kept, and was mortified to find the space empty. He was the third generation to have carried the weapon; to a Draconian family heirlooms were priceless.
    'That blacksmith is a dead man.' He spat out the words with all the venom he could muster, while going to raise the alarm. He feared the Prince's reaction and he had a sinking feeling that his dagger had been the blacksmith's weapon of choice.

*

Prince Edwin awoke in the large four-poster bed and stretched. Realizing he was still sharing his bed, he called for Baracus. The large wooden door creaked as it swung open and his bodyguard walked in.

'I've done with these.' Edwin looked over his shoulder with disdain at the women in his bed.

'Ladies,' Baracus said in a deep voice. Hurriedly the two women dressed, gathered their belongings and exited the room.

'Now, fetch me Archelaus. War never sleeps, Baracus,' he said with gusto, while still stretching. Baracus returned with the captain, then left.

Once they were alone Archelaus gave Edwin a quick report of the night's events.

'A man has killed the royal rider and escaped with his horse.'

'What, Silvanus is dead?' Edwin's eyes widened. 'A spy?'

'No, we believe it was a blacksmith, named Brun, who committed the act while making his escape, sire,' answered Archelaus.

'A blacksmith?' Edwin nearly choked on the word, slamming his fist down hard on the desk in front of him. 'This blacksmith is a lucky man.' Edwin had learned of Brun's existence when reading the captain's mind. He had planned on having this man found and executed this very morning, and Edwin hated loose ends. This was terrible news. He informed Archelaus at once of his dilemma; Cooms had passed valuable information to the blacksmith. In addition, if the note for Kallen was to fall into the wrong hands, the plot to kill their master, the Autocrat, would be revealed, which would mean certain death for both of them.

'Who have you sent in pursuit?' he asked.

'Zog and a battalion of Draconians, but if that's not to your liking, I can send a few assassins or put a bounty on his head, sire,' replied Archelaus.

'No! The imbecile probably doesn't know what he has in his possession. I'd prefer to keep this between us for now. Let's hope Zog clears this matter up quickly. We've got more pressing matters to attend to,' Edwin said, smiling. 'I want to advance on Ganesha.'

At that point there was a rap on the door and Bararus entered to tell them that General Grumondi Bakunawa was awaiting an audience. At the mention of the general's name Edwin felt uneasy. Grumondi was his brother's man. Keeping the rider's mission hidden may have just got a little bit harder. If Grumondi got involved it would be impossible to keep the matter quiet. Edwin had completely forgotten that Silvanus's father was a man of influence.

The pot-bellied general, whose appearance belied his guile, flanked by two officers, walked briskly into the chamber.

'How did he die?' he barked. His eyes were filled with rage. 'Royal riders have diplomatic immunity.' Without waiting for them to respond he marched towards the set of large windows overlooking the floral gardens. 'Lovely view, Prince,' he said with his back turned to them. He then focused his attentions on Archelaus. 'And where the hell were you sending him, anyway? Silvanus's father is a great friend,' he said sternly.

'I didn't send him anywhere,' Archelaus blurted out, wilting under the pressure of Grumondi's gaze.

'Do you know how embarrassing it is to have a royal rider die on our watch?' the general continued.

'It was not Archelaus's decision, my lord,' Edwin said, interceding, 'He was on an errand for the witch. This was a blatant lie.

Grumondi paced around the room, enraged at the mention of the witch. No one could question Cressida, the sorceress; she only answered to the Autocrat.
Edwin told him that he had sent a group of Draconians on the murderer's trail, hoping that would be enough to ease Grumondi's suspicions. Royal riders rode under a flag of truce so that messages could still be passed between warring factions. The general was a good ally if he was with you, but a formidable opponent if not. He was an astute man and a brilliant tactician; in his mind the attack on Athena was pointless. Attacking a city in the middle of the desert just didn't make any sense, even if that city did sit above a huge reservoir.

The resident duke had been a longstanding ally and Grumondi was sure Prince Edwin was up to no good. Something about Edwin made his skin crawl. Mandrick would have allowed them to use his territory, if he'd been asked. The rumours that the duke had defected, changing allegiances, had no foundation. Mandrick lived the life of a king within the walls of Athena; why would he give that up? With this question in mind, Edwin's brother Edmund had sent Grumondi on a secret assignment to find out what Edwin's true agenda was.

While Edwin was a tough, brutal, battle-hardened warrior, Edmund, on the other hand, was a calm, calculating individual, and a skilful legislator, which was a useful attribute in the southern kingdom of Elohim. Wars, treaties and treachery all went hand in hand; that was the usual way of things in the Southlands. Knowing when not to fight was just as important as knowing when to wage war. Edmund believed his brother's gung-ho approach would eventually backfire; war in faraway lands was one thing, but war in your own courtyard was another matter entirely. Their father's reign was virtually over; King Linus had been gravely ill for a number of years and was now considered a lame-duck king, who would soon be dead.

Edmund, as the older of the two brothers, was first in line for the throne, so had run the state's affairs during his father's illness. His brother, in contrast, had sworn allegiance to the sorceress, Cressida and a mystical figure whose real name was never spoken. He was simply referred to as the Autocrat.

The Senate of the Southern Kings was not pleased with Edwin's pact. Even the Senate's own treaties with the Autocrat, the sorceress, and the king and queen of Draconia, Gog and Magog, were felt to be unholy, but tolerable because they brought peace and prosperity to their lands. When their father died, Edmund would probably have to place his brother under house arrest, or possibly even have him killed to appease the Senate. Edwin just wanted too much power and, although he knew that their twin sisters, the princesses Sicilia and Cilia, would not be happy about losing their adored brother, something would have to be done.

Edwin did not like the idea of the general meddling in his affairs, and he knew his brother would want his man to investigate his activities. Having Grumondi's vigilant eyes watching his every move could draw unwanted attention to his plans. The only reasons for attacking Athena were Mandrick's treaty of truce with the Aafari, and the city's close proximity to the elven Forest of Oaken-Dale. Deep within the vast wooded area was the home of the Aafari elves: the city of Oaken-Crag, a metropolis of walkways and connecting warrens of hollowed-out trees, stone and marble. The beautiful, perfectly balanced structure, with amazing views from its north- and south-facing balconies, was perched on twelve large Elohim ash trees. Six were hollowed-out and had a well-maintained lift system as well as a spiral staircase inside the trunk that went from the ground up to the city floor that surrounded the temple of Aafari. The temple itself consisted of a huge dome complex, with the type of acoustics found in a chapter house and filled with unique gothic-rococo sculptured archways. The stunning stained-glass windows gave off different shades of colour throughout the day. A magnificent building to behold, its connecting walkway to the city was always guarded. The City in the Woods, as it was sometimes called, was kept hidden by a powerful spell, and provided the Aafari with a safe haven away from prying eyes and the world of man.

Three elves had slipped through his forward lines. Edwin's spies were rarely wrong, and he was sure his show of force had caused this reaction. The Aafari would remove the scroll from harm's way if they could: that much was certain. He had sought Kallen's services because he needed to know whether they possessed the scroll or whether they were, in fact, a decoy. He intended paying the city of Oaken-Crag and the Aafari Temple a royal visit. The otherwise impregnable city had one weakness: fire. But as long as the elves felt safe, the scroll would remain concealed. Edwin had a better idea. It was time for the words contained within the scroll to be revealed. One way or another the Forest of Oaken-Dale would feel the fire of the black dragon, the banner and emblem used by Edwin. His brother was next in line for his father's throne and if Edmund became king, Edwin's power would diminish; he was not about to stand idly by and let that happen. There were only four gauntlets of power and one of them belonged to him, a gift from the sorceress when he had pledged his allegiance to the Autocrat's cause.

Their father had been a great warrior and a mighty ruler, having conquered a large part of the Southlands, also known as the Land of Kings, an area filled with an assortment of self-governed kingdoms, tribes and monsters. King Linus, who was prone to minor stints of depression, was struck by an acute bout of the illness shortly after Edwin's birth and never recovered. Slowly, a once brave and mighty king became a broken man, trapped in a spiral which would eventually lead to his demise. Edwin knew what needed to be done; the scroll possessed the knowledge and power to rid the world of his master, the Autocrat of the southern and western kingdoms. If Edwin could manage to obtain all four gauntlets – including the one his master, the Autocrat, possessed – he could rule the world. At that thought his eyes lit up.

'Now that we've taken Athena, what next, my Prince?' asked Grumondi.

'We attack the elven forest,' responded Edwin.

'Is that a joke?' replied the general. 'The Alfari warriors are legendary.'

'We'll burn them out,' said the prince, smiling.

'The Senate will not be pleased,' answered a flustered Grumondi.

'To hell with the Senate,' the prince replied harshly. 'My Master rules.'

Edwin never mentioned the Autocrat by name: no one did.

'Your actions could have catastrophic consequences, my prince: tread carefully.'

'Catastrophic? Winning battles instils pride in our army and our nation, general,' replied Edwin.

Grumondi nodded, asked to be excused, and then left the chamber. Once outside and out of earshot of Baracus, the general conferred with his officers.

'The man is clearly a lunatic. He'll start a third Great War. You,'– Grumondi pointed to the man on his right –'take a couple of men and go after this blacksmith. And you,' –he looked at the man on his left–'get word to Mandrick. I think we need to have a chat with my old friend, the duke.'

Once the door was firmly shut Archelaus gave the prince a look.

'Can we trust him?' asked the captain.

'No. If he gets in our way'– Edwin ran a finger across his own neck –'he's a dead man. Now, prepare the army. I want to be ready to attack the forest on the day of the full eclipse,' he commanded.

'Yes, my Prince.' Archelaus had his orders; he nodded and left the room.

The prince sat on the chair behind the large desk. The blacksmith had derailed his plans. Also, the dwarves had not arrived yet; he knew the city of Denvagar and its riches were nearby, but where exactly? If he found its entrance that would quell the Senate's displeasure for awhile. Kings loved gold, and anyway, while he wore the gauntlet no one would stand in his way to world domination.

*

Brun was on the crest of a wave, having had a very lucky escape. Sweat dripped from his chin while Cloud galloped beneath him; he had given his saviour a name, and with the white cloud above her brow the name fitted like a glove.

The lands of the east were split into three regions. The province of Nagari was known for its subtropical rain-forest climate, a perfect breeding ground for the plants, shrubs and flowers, which were a natural antidote for most ailments in Elohim.
The largest of the three, Ganesha, was a fertile and vibrant land; its lush green meadows always seemed ready to be cultivated. It had large and beautiful forests of redwoods, Pyrenean oaks, Elohim ash and yew trees. Gigantic lakes and picturesque rivers and streams were commonplace. Its nickname was 'the land of life' and the air was tinged with the scent of fruit trees permanently in bloom.

In contrast, Tyrus was an uncultivated, barren wasteland of rock, desert and rugged terrain: a bleak landscape of dried, cracked mud, wild shrubs and oddly shaped cactuses. Only small groups of nomadic tribes and scavengers survived in its wilderness, where the single saving grace was an immense subterranean labyrinth of rivers, lakes and lagoons. It was a two-day ride to the coast and the port of Inari, but Brun planned on getting there in one. The coastal town of Inari was built on the trade of spices and antiquities from the east; the ancient god Inari was thought to bring prosperity to merchants, farmers and traders. Brun had decided that he would continue to use the royal rider's outfit until he was safely off the shores of Tyrus. As far as he was concerned the sea could not come soon enough, for him or his horse.
The costume had probably outlived its usefulness – the royal rider was bound to have been discovered by now – so to continue to wear it wasn't the best plan he'd ever conceived. Nonetheless, as far as improvising went it still had merit; the disguise had already got him through two checkpoints and an army encampment.

Brun looked down at Cloud, who was gasping for air under the midday sun. He would have to stop soon. The horse needed a rest and some water. They both did, but he would get his rest once aboard a vessel bound for pastures new.

On the plains of Tyrus waterholes were hard to come by. He had expected as much and at the last army checkpoint he had filled his four canteens with as much water as they could hold. He presumed that this was the reason behind the Black Knight's attack on the city. Athena was rich in minerals and also in water; the city sat above an enormous natural subterranean reservoir. He found respite from the sun's glare as he rode beside a hilly mound of boulders and rocks. Pulling gently on the reins he slowed the horse to a crawl, then stopped. After dismounting, he dug a small hole with his hands, in the shade, and then poured half a canteen's contents into it. Holding the reins, he directed Cloud to the liquid. They looked at each other in amazement: the water was gone. 'Silly boy' he thought, as he snapped his visor shut before reopening it to feed Cloud with another canteen. He took a deep breath while the horse greedily lapped up the water from the canteen's bottleneck top. Looking around, he found a small, flat boulder to sit on, removed his helmet and made himself comfortable. The relief ebbed into his dust-covered face.

Brun had picked a good spot. The sun's glare was barely visible. He touched Cloud's mane.

'Not long left, girl, not long left,' he whispered to the horse. Since leaving Athena he had ridden through the night. His encounter with the Black Knight's encampment had been a shaky affair. He had seen trolls and all manner of creatures from afar, along with Draconians and the humans.

The Black Knight's army was huge: a ferocious horde of men and beasts. At the encampment, just a few leagues from Athena, he had been asked by a Draconian to stop and dismount from his horse.

'Are you mad?' he had enquired, impersonating the royal rider, without allowing the horse to break stride. He had continued in the direction of the guard house, which led to the rear exit of the encampment and the road to Inari. The Draconian had laid a hand on the horse's rear to curtail his progress. Brun had firmly knocked it away. Brun had felt his heart beating in his mouth for what seemed like an age. He was thankful for the intervention of one of the Black Knight's warriors. As he rode away he could hear the Draconian saying, 'But he smelled bad.'

'Don't you know who that is? Don't hinder him,' the warrior had responded.

The Draconian was indeed correct; Brun had not bathed in days and the unpleasant odour was beginning to inconvenience his own nostrils too. The Black Knight had moved his forward lines in the wake of capturing the citadel. Brun had benefited from this; head only encountered supply wagons and nomadic tribesmen on the road from Athena to Inari, since passing the last checkpoint. Now that he had removed the glare of the sun from his eye line, he could just about make out Inari. It was a slow, gradual descent to the coastal town.

A puff of dust in the distance caught his gaze. By squinting he managed to make out the shape of a wagon. 'More supplies, 'he thought. As the wagon got closer he realized he had made a mistake; it was not just another supply wagon, but a holding pen on wheels. The wagon's metal-rimmed wooden wheels creaked under the weight of the four occupants: two orks, one a driver and one a guard, along with two dwarves, both imprisoned within its rusty metal barred cell.

Orks were grotesque, despicable and repulsive beings whose mucus-covered skin was a dark, muddy-green colour. Tiny, piercing pupils in translucent blood-shot eyes, set in hairless, hawkish faces. They were bilingual, although their own language sounded like a horrid bird shriek. Village folk called them Hawkmen and feared them for their cannibalistic tendencies.

Orks were different from dwarves. They were more closely related to Draconians in spirit; both species hated humans. Dwarves, on the other hand, just wanted to live with dwarves and to hell with everybody else. The prison cart stopped on the path opposite Brun.

'Do you have any water?' asked the ork driving the wagon.

'No,' replied Brun. He only had two canteens left, and was not in a sharing mood.

'One of my prisoners is nearly dead,' said the ork, looking at the very canteens Brun was not willing to part with. 'It is very important that he don't die. The Black Knight himself has requested these dwarves be kept alive,' the ork added bluntly, as though that would sway the argument. It did. Brun got up and walked around his horse to where the canteens were attached to the saddlebags. Looking over Cloud's saddle, he could see that the dwarf's injuries looked fresh. He removed another canteen, then walked towards the wagon.

'What happened to him?' Brun asked in a deliberately unconcerned tone.

'He's got a foul mouth,' replied the driver. The orks both laughed.

'Not anymore,' said the ork guard, in between the bursts of hideous laughter.

As Brun stopped by the wagon it dawned on him that he had forgotten to put his helmet back on before handing the water container over to the driver. The ork guard looked over his companion's back and directly at Brun.

'You're not Silvanus. That's his signet on that saddlebag. Who the hell are you?' demanded the ork.

'I'm his replacement. He fell ill,' Brun replied sternly. Orks only respected being spoken to in this way.

'Fell ill ...'The guard slowly nodded while muttering the words, then started to laugh. Suddenly he shook his head. 'Do you think orks are stupid? All royal riders have their own signet.' The ork was, indeed, correct. When given a commission as a royal rider, you were also given an individual mark. Silvanus's mark was an imprint of a stag.

Before Brun could reply, the orks began to shout, 'You're an impostor!'Brun turned to run for his saddlebag where his sword was kept. In the commotion a beefy arm slipped through the gap between the bars and appeared above the loud-mouthed guard's head. A hand folded into a fist and came crashing down.

'Now you've only got one to deal with, lad,' said a dwarf in a gruff voice, his hands around the ork's throat. Brun didn't need telling twice. He ran to fetch his sword. The hard, dusty surface made running easy, although the pursuing ork was gaining on him with every stride. Brun had a decision to make: should he go for the sword, or reach for the dagger? In an instant, he pulled the dagger from his waistband and swung around. He let the dagger fly from his grip.

The ork saw the dagger take flight. It shimmered under the blazing sun. He made an attempt to avoid it, but it was too late. The blade sat just off-centre between the ork's eyes.

'Good throw, lad!' exclaimed the dwarf, still throttling the remaining life out of the unconscious guard. The ork slumped forwards and the dwarf released his stranglehold. He fumbled around the ork's waistband for the key to his freedom.

'Eureka!' shouted the dwarf as he produced a couple of very large keys on a key ring.

Brun looked at the driver's surprised stare as he reclaimed his dagger. Quickly, he cleaned the blade. Ork's bodies decomposed rapidly; within a few moments the body would become rancid as it deteriorated.

'How's your friend?' asked Brun.

'Dead,' replied the dwarf.

'What do you mean? They said he needed water,' Brun said in disbelief.

'Have you got wax in your ears, boy? He's dead,' the dwarf said, fiddling with the cell lock.

'I'll give you a hand with that,' said Brun. The dwarf handed him the keys, and hurriedly Brun opened the lock.

'Those brutes gave him a terrible going-over,' the dwarf said, in a deep voice tinged with sadness.

'Why? Who was he?' Brun asked while helping his new acquaintance out of the cart.

'His name is Furnus Gilbeard,' he answered; it was too soon to speak of his friend in the past tense. 'He told them that he would take great pleasure in standing over their rotting carcasses … speaking of which, you're in possession of an unfriendly odour, too.' Brun made no response.

'So what's your name, friend?'

'Brun.'

'I'm Ragnarr Morbere,' he replied proudly. 'Which way are you heading, royal rider?' Brun gave him a quizzical look. He wasn't sure if he could trust anyone right now, let alone a broad-shouldered man half his size, with a very large beard.

'As far away as possible,' was his ambiguous answer.

'Well, I'm heading west. Mind if I accompany you until the Port of Inari, friend?' asked Ragnarr.

Brun thought quickly. 'No, not at all,' he answered. They might be looking for a blacksmith, but not one with a dwarf.

Brun removed the pouches and weapons from the fragmented ork's body, and smiled at the sight of gleaming steel. A twin-sided battleaxe with a serrated edge down one side: this was a vision for a warrior's eyes. The other ork also had one in his hand, although the axes were not identical. The other was a dull bronze colour and had a small spearhead, which could be used as a bayonet, pointing out of the top of the axe. Orks knew their steel. The weapons were impressive.

Brun's pouch was bulging. First Silvanus's gold coins, and now the orks' too. He kicked some dust over the orks' decomposed bodies in a poor attempt at masking their smell.

'These are mine,' Brun said, referring to the weapons. Ragnarr nodded, busy taking out equipment from a box under the seat at the front of the cart. He removed an unusual amulet wrapped in a dirty cloth and quickly hid it from view.

'There you are, my beauty,' said Ragnarr. He placed a firm hand on his war hammer. It had an enormous spiked head. 'Never leave home without her,' he said with a stern face. With that he fitted an oddly shaped helmet over his head. Brun got the cart off the path, then unfastened the two horses. He couldn't tell if they were black or brown in the dust. Keeping the stronger of the two, he gave the other a smack on its hind quarter. As he watched it run free the truth dawned on him: he might never be a free man again.

They buried Furnus as best they could. Ragnarr said a few words, and then they had to be on their way.

The dwarf's hands were loosely bound; they had decided that they would pretend he was the rider's prisoner.
 'So, why were they taking you to the prince?' Brun enquired.
 'That's news to me. I thought they were taking me to see Black Knight,' said the dwarf, evading the question.
 'So what does he want with you then?' pressed Brun.
 'The location of the mythical city of Denvagar. And no, I don't know where it is,' he lied. 'Just because I'm a descendant of the Dvergar I'm supposed to know where all the hidden cities and boltholes in Elohim are. And by the way, friend, you ask too many questions,' added the cantankerous dwarf.

Brun thought a friendship might be out of the question with this foul-mouthed fool.
They reached the outskirts of Inari at sunset. Brun decided that he would find a vessel for hire rather than hitching a

ride on one of the Black Knight's ships. He did not want to come into contact with anymore of Silvanus's acquaintances. He planned on keeping the royal rider's horse, having become fond of the chestnut mare.

A once bustling coastal town, Inari was a changed place with the war in the east taking its toll on trade. The roads between Inari and the east were now very dangerous places indeed. The only merchant wagons that braved the treacherous conditions were the ones that hired heavily armed guards to safeguard their cargo.

Once within the town, Brun ditched his outfit. The weighty helmet had become burdensome and smelled of Silvanus's foul breath. They found a good spot, by a pile of rubbish, and the helmet was discarded along with the cloak, and Ragnarr's bonds. Then they made their way through the built-up area of the coastal town as inconspicuously as possible.

The road along the portside was packed with taverns, which is where most horse-trading and haggling went on in Inari. The harbour was filled to the edges with merchant vessels and fishing boats.
  'Let me do the talking. I know this place,' the dwarf said to Brun as they tied up their horses outside the Old Forge Tavern and Inlet, which was the third tavern down the side street. On entry they were greeted by a mixed crowd of merchant traders, fishermen and warriors. Although busy, everyone smiled, but minded their own business. These were dangerous times: spies were everywhere.

Brun found an unoccupied table towards the back of the tavern, while Ragnarr went to work his magic, to find a ship heading west. A wench wearing an apron approached his table.

'Been on the road long, stranger?' she said, eyeing him up.

'You can tell, can you?' Brun asked, with a curious look in his eyes.

'Ah-ha,' she said, nodding and producing a tight smile. 'I'll get you a drink. Mead or ale? And then I'll prepare a room; you're in need of a hot bath. I bet you scrub up well though,' she said with a wink.

'Mead, and make that two please.' The wench gave him a fixed stare.

'It's not for a woman,' Brun replied quickly with a glance at Ragnarr. She smiled and walked away, swinging her hips. It had been awhile since Brun had seen a friendly face. The pretty brunette was in her early thirties, with a full figure, which is just how he liked a lady to be. Brun was no spring chicken himself. 'If I just had more time...' he thought. His pleasant daydream evaporated in an instant when Ragnarr banged the table.

'I've found someone of interest,' the dwarf said loudly, drowning out the sounds of the boisterous tavern. Brun looked at Ragnarr, then at the dwarf's companion; with a slight nod he offered the man a stool.

'I hear you be seeking passage to the port of Abbehale,' said the man.

'Can we have three meads?' shouted Brun at the wench, who rewarded him with a wink.

'I like your style, lad. They serve a mean mead in 'ere. The name's Captain Eylbrich, and I was just telling your friend that I've heard all the "rich" jokes there is.'
Brun introduced himself, but withheld the fact that he didn't like being called 'lad' by a man his own age.

The captain was a relatively handsome man of medium build, with an olive, weathered complexion. His dark, leather tunic was decorated with elaborate embroidery and tablet-woven braids along its neck, hem and wrists.

The wench broke up the conversation when she returned with their drinks. She smiled sweetly as she handed the captain his tankard first. Once their drinks were served she informed Brun that a room was nearly ready for him and his friend so that they could wash off the dust and freshen up. Her words were well chosen and very kind indeed. The whiff was quite overpowering, and she had already had a few harsh words from some of her regular patrons.

'Do you have room for horses? When do you leave?' asked Brun when the wench had left.

'Listen lad, my ship is the fastest of her class in this region,' he replied. This wasn't a boast or an exaggeration. 'And I sail under the flag of the Consortium of Export Merchants. Do I have room for horses?' he chuckled. 'My fee is five gold sovereigns or its equivalent, and there's no room for negotiation. You either got it or you ain't. Which is it, lad?'

'That's a bit rich, Eylbrich,' Brun said with a broad smile. He and the captain burst out laughing.

'And it's an extra coin for the horses. Your friend already told me about them.' Eylbrich looked at Ragnarr, who shrugged his shoulders. He had almost finished his drink and was already trying to get the wench's attention over the noise.

'We'll pay once we're aboard,' the dwarf said, gruffly.

'Good. Then it's agreed. My ship's name is the Peregrine.'

Brun thought the ship's name was a good sign; he knew the birds of prey were fast flying birds, known for their energetic antics.

'She's a little way down the quay. Now, you two need a bath,' Eylbrich said. He then produced a miniature copper hourglass, flipped it over, and passed it to Brun.

'Be on the dock by the time the sand runs out,' he whispered. 'I'll not wait.'

With that, the captain emptied his tankard and rose from his stool. He made his way to the door and was gone. Brun liked the man, and felt Ragnarr had chosen well.

'I'm glad he's gone. I wouldn't have stood a chance with that wench if he'd stayed,' Brun said with a smile.

'You still don't stand a chance,' replied Ragnarr with a stony face. 'She's not into men; she prefers dwarves.' Brun started to laugh, but stopped when he noticed Ragnarr had not joined in.

'Don't you ever laugh, dwarf?' he asked.

'No,' answered Ragnarr.

The wench's return immediately lightened the mood.

'Have you finished those drinks, boys?' she asked. Ragnarr tapped his tankard, producing an empty, hollow sound.

'I'll refill that one once I've shown you to your room. Your baths are ready,' she said. Then, turning to Brun and nodding at his drink, she said, 'You can bring that with you.'

They followed her to the back of the tavern, up a flight of stairs and into a wet room with two tin baths in it. Ragnarr walked up to one of them and touched the water. He gave a scream as he withdrew his scalded fingers.

'That's far too hot. I'll not be cooked in that trough,' he said to the wench.

'Leave her alone. I was about to ask her to tend to our baths while we bathe,' Brun said.

'Sweetie, you ain't got enough gold coins in that pouch for that kind of service,' she said with a smile. With that, she left the room.

Ragnarr poured cold water from an urn into his bath.

'Don't these women know? Dwarves only bathe in lukewarm water,' he said. Brun, who was already in his bath, paid him no attention. The strain of the day was disappearing fast and the hot water caused his skin to tingle as the grime was washed away. Ragnarr, on the other hand, was like a fish out of water, with foam splashing everywhere. It gave a whole new meaning to the term 'bubble bath'.

They paid for the room and thanked the wench. Outside, the night air felt different. Maybe it was just that by removing the grime of their recent experiences everything felt different. Although they were wanted men, you would never have known it from the look on their faces. Ragnarr could see Brun's hair colour for the first time: a vibrant ginger. He commented on its uncommonness. Brun explained that he was not Tyrusian as they unfastened the horses and walked away from the tavern. Brun recounted the story of his escape. Ragnarr was shocked, but was glad he knew the truth; Brun probably had a bounty on his head.

Ragnarr spoke quietly as he informed Brun about his mission.

'It's of the gravest importance,' he started. 'The Dvergar have discovered that the planet is under attack. Someone is stealing a vital mineral, a life-sustaining substance. If supplies are depleted to the point where it can't reproduce itself the planet will die. My task is to find out who is taking it, and why. It's imperative that the information about my mission or my collaborators doesn't fall into the wrong hands. Now that the citadel has fallen the dwarves will probably go to war, and I know where the secret entrance to Denvagar is; Denvagar is where I was born.'

'You lied,' said Brun. He looked shocked.

'Well, I wasn't sure if I could trust you. Do you think I go around telling people I'm on a secret mission?' replied Ragnarr. 'The Black Knight has one of the legendary gauntlets of power in his possession. It gives him certain abilities. He is able to read minds, so it was very fortunate for me that you crossed my path before I was taken to him.' Brun could have sworn that he saw the dwarf break a tiny smile, as he received a friendly pat on the back. They stopped alongside a medium-sized galley ship. Immediately they could see the craft was built for speed; its arched bow curvature had been well carved, and it looked like it was made to cut through waves.

Brun looked for the ship's ram, and was slightly disappointed that it did not have one. Being a metalwork enthusiast, rams always interested him.

'Nope, not impressed,' he muttered as the gangway was lowered.

'Peregrine' was imprinted on the ship's portside in gold lettering. The captain invited them aboard. The ship had three sails: a huge one in its centre; another similarly sized one towards the stern; and a smaller one on the bow, which was predominantly used to aid direction. The merchant vessel had thirty crew members who were busy preparing the ship for the open sea. Once aboard, the captain raised the anchor and set sail. His helmsman guided the vessel out of port.

Brun paid the fare. As the gold sovereign landed in the captain's gloved palm, he noticed that a couple of the coins had the prince's signet on them. As he walked to his cabin he thought he might have made a mistake inviting these characters aboard his ship; he didn't take kindly to spies, and for the reminder of the voyage kept his distance.

The horses were safely pinned below in the holding pens, and as Brun watched the coastal town disappear from the horizon he breathed a sigh of relief. On the dock stood an incensed Draconian; Zog had amazing vision and he could just about make out a person who looked like Brun aboard the ship. He was livid at the fact that this blacksmith had managed to evade capture. He ordered another Draconian to commandeer a vessel; for Zog this pursuit was far from over.

When his man returned he informed Zog that commandeering a ship that could match the speed of the Peregrine might take a little longer than he had first thought. Zog, watching the ship become a silhouette in the fading light, hit the Draconian in the face in pure anger.
    'I'll sort it,' said Rog, one of his more competent fellow Draconians. Zog smiled; he knew they'd be on the way soon.

*

Two weeks of salted beef did not sit well with a man who loved his food, so when the port of Abbehale came into view, the anticipated taste of a real meal filled Brun's palate as childhood memories came flooding back. As though reading his thoughts, Ragnarr broke the silence.

'You know what I like about these parts?' In unison, they both uttered the same response: 'Roasted wild hog and burned-barrel ale.'

'Mmmm,' murmured Ragnarr, giving his stomach a rub. Brun smiled. 'If it's still there, the Hogshead tavern make a delicious wild hog; it's within a day's ride of Irons Keep.'

'It's still there,' answered Ragnarr.

Brun was not surprised at Ragnarr's knowledge of Ebenknesha, as they docked at the region's main harbour in Abbehale. Their time spent on the ship had brought them closer together, and Brun had learned many things about the dwarf. Ragnarr's companion, Furnus, was a blacksmith like himself, and his task had been to obtain information on the lost art of forging gauntlets of power.

They said their goodbyes to the captain and disembarked with the horses, mentally preparing for the long ride ahead. Brun noted that the geography had changed somewhat since he had last seen these shores. Gone was the pretty fishing village of Abbehale. In its place stood an ugly harbour town. Baron Brandon of Brandenburg had flattened the village and built the town in its place when he found he needed a larger port.

'What a waste,' thought Brun as he looked around. The buildings had been built with Arkose sandstone which was cheap to produce, and looked it. It consisted of coarse sand, and no refinement was needed when cutting stone slabs. Its grey-reddish colour was a blot on an otherwise beautiful landscape. Above, on the outskirts of the coastal town in the distance, was another eyesore: surrounded by a fortified castle wall and a moat stood the baron's fortress.

With one look Brun could tell the man had no taste; the colossal structure looked more like a fortified dungeon than the property of a man of wealth. Brandenburg was a cruel man who imposed high taxes and ruled his district with an iron fist. Though life in the town seemed normal enough, the place was on edge; the baron's soldiers were everywhere. They decided it might be safer to stock up on provisions and continue their journey straightaway. Plus, the allure of the spit-roasted hog at the Hogshead tavern had them both drooling.

'Do they still serve it with that sweet plum sauce?' Brun asked the dwarf.

'Don't ask silly questions, lad,' replied Ragnarr, mounting his horse.

'One day that sharp tongue will feel my axe's edge,' Brun said with a grin, mounting Cloud. Then he gave her a nudge, and a trot turned into a gallop. It started to rain as they rode out of Abbehale.

*

Zog and his men had commandeered a vessel and were in hot pursuit, or at least they would have been. The only problem was that the blacksmith's ship was much faster. The Draconian stood on the deck and could see the Peregrine's large sails in the far distance.

'Why can't you catch that ship?' he asked the ship's captain.

'That's the Peregrine. Only a war galley could catch her,' was his reply.

As they reached the waters outside the port of Abbehale, the Peregrine was leaving port. The clouds opened up as the rain poured down. Zog was getting soaked, but all he could think about was getting his dagger back and seeing Brun's head on a plate.

'Stop that ship,' he hissed.

They pulled up alongside the merchant galley.

'Where is he?' shouted Zog.

'Who?' shouted Captain Eylbrich.

'The blacksmith,' Zog replied.

'What blacksmith? We only had two passengers: a dwarf and a warrior from these parts. They've disembarked.'

'Stand aside. I'm coming aboard,' declared Zog.

Hooking up ropes, Zog and two other Draconians swung across to the Peregrine, and then searched the ship. Captain Eylbrich was fuming.

'This is insane. The Consortium of Export Merchants has a treaty with Prince Edwin.

'Not when you're harbouring the murderer of a royal rider,' cried Zog.

'What?' responded the captain; so they weren't the Prince's spies, after all.

'They told me they were heading to the Badlands,' he lied, knowing that Draconians feared the Keltic tribes. 'Now get off my ship!' shouted Eylbrich.

'The Badlands,' Zog said in disbelief. He knew it was a very dangerous place, and the Kelts took no prisoners.

Once Zog's galley had docked at the port of Abbehale, he made his way to the fortress to seek an audience with the Baron of Brandenburg. It was still raining when the Draconian and his battalion reached the baron's fortress, Brandenburg Castle. The gatehouse was strongly fortified with arrow loops and murder holes. The commanding structure towered above the castle wall's fortifications. Hideous gargoyles lined its parapets and just below an ornately shaped shield bore the crest of the blue-eyed black dragon. The rancid moat surrounding the complex was a foul, putrid cesspool, filled with muck, secretions and stale food.

One of the guards on top of the gatehouse addressed the group.
    'Who goes there?'
    'Emissaries of Prince Edwin, requesting an audience with the baron. And be quick about it: I'm getting soaked,' replied Zog. The drawbridge screeched and groaned as it was released and lowered to the ground, and the portcullis was lifted. Heavy chains creaked as the internal winch's counterweights were engaged and the open-mesh metal frame was raised. Once all the Draconians were inside the gatehouse the portcullis slammed shut behind them and they were greeted by heavily armed men who disarmed them before the inner portcullis opened and they entered the compound. It was the first time Zog had been inside Brandenburg Castle and he was impressed with the baron's security: heavily armoured infantry and cavalry were everywhere. He and his men rode past a few of the numerous training sites that littered the grounds on the ride to the fortress. The baron kept his elite troops in tip-top condition.

At the huge arched entrance of the fortress, Zog's Draconians were led away for refreshments while he was escorted to the baron. Baron Brandon of Brandenburg was also a lord of the southern realm, and ruled the lands of the west in Prince Edwin's absence. He behaved like a dictator on a power trip: disgruntled subjects were subjected to summary execution if they voiced their disapproval of his affairs. The stout, black-haired baron was fortunate: a fast metabolism balanced out an excessive eating disorder. An unremarkable face was made memorable by the presence of a large wart on the side of his nose, just above his right nostril.

The baron was in his main hall and in the middle of devouring a delicious honey-drizzled roast pheasant when he was informed of the Draconian's presence.
    'I've been expecting him,' was Brandenburg's reply between mouthfuls of red wine. Gluttony wasn't so much a sin as a pastime for the baron. Zog was led into the fortress's main hall, which was a spacious room with a high ceiling and coats of arms adorning its walls. A long wooden banquet table, which would easily seat fifty, centred the floor space.

At the head of the table sat Brandenburg, scoffing down his food. A few yards behind him stood two of his elite personal guards, dressed in ceremonial armour with gisarmes in hand. The long-shafted weapons with axe-shaped heads loomed above their helmets. The baron looked up as Zog approached.
    'Ah, Zog, I've been expecting you. Do sit down. Pheasant?'

The Draconian nodded and sat down. Brandenburg gave a menacing glare to one of the many servants situated around the room. The woman curtsied and left the hall, returning with a golden roasted pheasant, which she placed in front of Zog. The baron continued to talk with his mouth full of game bird.

'I received word from Edwin by carrier pigeon. This royal rider incident is messy business indeed. I offer you any help at my disposal. What do you need?'

'My quarry travels to the Badlands, accompanied by a dwarf. I must follow them.'

'What? The Badlands? Are you insane?' the baron cried, nearly choking on his food.

'No, I am not joking,' responded Zog. 'My orders were explicit, baron.' Zog then described Brun's appearance.

'I need men to aid their capture and, of course, a guide,' said Zog firmly.

'Those are unconquered lands, dragon-man,' Brandenburg said in a warning tone, referring to the Draconian's scaly skin.

'That's not my concern, baron. I will hunt down this man and bring back his head.' Zog spoke the words with venom.

'Well then, you'll need a note. Baron Crofton Abbehale of Glen-Neath will have to provide you with assistance. His lands border that region,' responded Brandenburg.

Suddenly, the main door swung open. The baron's man of arms, Cuthbert Lockwood, and the alchemist and mage, Azram, walked in. Cuthbert was a man nearing his thirties with a crop of short, sandy-blond hair, blue eyes and a reddish complexion. He was wearing a light chain mail with the hooded section down, a thick leather belt around his waist, and matching thigh-high boots. The mage's dishevelled robe was made up of a mismatch of different patterns and oddly shaped pieces of fabric sown together. The slender, wiry man had his beard tied into two knots below his chin in order to shorten its length.

'Ah, perfect timing, as always, Cuthbert. This Draconian needs a map. Do sit down, you're making me dizzy.' Too much wine was starting to have an effect on the baron; he waved at both men to be seated. More food and wine were brought in.

'A map of where, my liege?' asked Lockwood, now comfortably seated in one of the many chairs with elaborately interlaced backs, with clawed cabriole legs.

'The Badlands,' replied Brandenburg.

'Who's the poor soul travelling there?' said Lockwood, laughing.

'You are,' he replied. Lockwood's laughter stopped in an instant. 'Cuthbert, meet Zog. Zog, meet your guide,' continued the baron, pushing yet more food into his mouth.

Zog nodded while Lockwood swallowed hard, gulping a waft of air.

'You should learn to curtail your tongue, young squire,' remarked Azram, amused.

'How goes the procurement of the kromillium, Azram?' enquired the baron.

'The slaves are working well and the Autocrat's requirements are on schedule, sire.'

'Good. I'll inform the prince of your progress.' He turned to one of his servants.

'Fetch me my writing slope and parchment. I've kept this Draconian waiting long enough.' Once the servant returned, Brandenburg wrote a note to Baron Crofton, dropped wax onto the parchment, and imprinted his signet. Then he handed the note to Zog.

'Crofton Abbehale will be more than willing to help you once he receives this,' the baron assured him.

'I hate that western scum,' said Lockwood.

'Silence,' commanded the baron. 'A royal rider has been murdered and Crofton is still a baron under Prince Edwin's flag. Cuthbert, you will show respect. Now, I have pressing matters to attend to. Azram, stay. Cuthbert, attend to our guest. Zog, happy hunting.'

'I've told you before about that tongue of yours,' whispered Azram as he shook his head. Lockwood and Zog got up and left the room. Once outside Lockwood led Zog back to his battalion.

*

It had been a long and arduous three-day ride to the Hogshead tavern. For most of the journey the Black Forest had haunted their path, looming large as they approached the inlet. Although it was only a day's ride to the Keep, Brun was more than a little saddle-sore. It had been some time since he'd sat in a saddle continuously for this length of time. As a distraction, he told the dwarf of his intentions.

'After I fill my belly, I'm taking up the tavern's hospitality,' he said.

'Who made you king?' replied Ragnarr.

Brun just smiled. Outside the Hogshead they handed the reins of their horses to a stablehand, who took the horses into a large barn situated at the back of the tavern. Brun could smell the aroma of singed pork as they walked into the inlet, and he gave Ragnarr a friendly, jovial slap on the back.

The atmosphere inside the tavern was warm and friendly. At the back, above a huge chimney, sat a row of hogs on spits rotating slowly. Flames singed and charred the flesh. A buxom blonde approached them and took their order.

'It seems busy,' Brun said to the blonde.

'Aye, it's always busy, love,' was her response. Her dialect brought old memories flooding back to Brun.

'I take it from your accent that you're from these parts?' asked Brun.

'Aye, this is my father's place. He's the head chef,' she said with a little smile, and then she went to place their orders.

'So what's your plan after we get to Irons Keep?' Brun asked his companion.

'I'm going to Brigantia, over the border,' replied Ragnarr.

'Keltic soil. Is that wise? Those tribes eat their young,' said Brun.

'Don't believe everything you hear, son. They're good people, just misunderstood.' Brun gave him a puzzled look.

'I have a friend who may be able to help me translate these markings,' said Ragnarr. From an inside pocket he produced a large amulet; the ruby-eye pendant had unusual markings all over it. Brun could tell it was from an ancient civilisation, with his extensive knowledge of metals.

'What is it?' asked Brun.

'I think it's a key,' replied Ragnarr.

The blonde waitress was making her way over to the table, carrying two large tankards that seemed too large for her petite hands. Ragnarr quickly rewrapped the amulet in the cloth and concealed it.

'There you are, boys. Enjoy,' she said, handing them their drinks. 'Your hog will be ready soon.' She turned and walked briskly away to deal with a group of customers who had just entered the establishment. Brun thought the three elves looked like hunters. Ragnarr leaned forward. 'I wonder why they're so far from home?' he asked.

Brun made a discreet movement for one of his battleaxes. Ragnarr tapped him and mouthed a silent 'no'.

'They are Alfari warriors, not bounty hunters. They're from the region of Ganesha. They rarely leave the confines of Oaken-Dale forest. I was just surprised, that's all. I've never seen a dark-haired one before. The Aafari are a blond-haired race,' he informed Brun.

The food arrived and they tucked into a succulent roast hog garnished with a sweet plum sauce. The three elves, Asrack, Tartarus and Vince, were feeling at ease in the cosy tavern. They ordered a round of drinks. Asrack and Vince ordered mead, while Tartarus ordered burned-barrel ale.

'Is that wise?' asked Asrack.

'When in Ebenknesha ...' replied Tartarus. They all laughed. 'Anyway, we're thousands of leagues from home. Who's going to tell on us?'

'Doesn't make it right,' replied Vince sternly.

A few hours passed before the door swung open and an unshaven man, with a patch over his right eye, entered the tavern.

'I don't like the look of that fellow,' observed Ragnarr. Brun was in agreement.

The man was dressed in a brown leather waistcoat over a loose white tunic and tight leather britches. Had a shady aura, but seemed to be getting on swimmingly with the elves. Tartarus was a little bemused by the one-eyed stranger, who offered him and his friends a wager on a game of arrows. Elves are naturally good at archery.

The game of arrows required a circular wooden shield, bolted to a wall through its centre, enabling it to be spun. The shield was split into six segments: a red, a yellow, two white and two black. Hitting red meant getting the maximum score, and black the minimum. Each player was permitted three turns to hit the spinning board with a lead-tipped arrow, shot from a child-like bow. The scores were tallied up. If the result was tied at the end of the game, 'sudden death' would commence, consisting of throw for throw until one player faltered.

So he was slightly mystified when the challenge was made. Tartarus was on his first real assignment, a secret mission of the utmost importance. Had the man with a patched eyed not been on his own, it would have seemed suspicious. As it was, he felt the man was simply being disrespectful: a man with one eye thinking he could beat an elf with two! He decided to teach the man, whose name was Bowen, a lesson. Alfari warriors should be respected, and anyway he'd always intended to have a little fun on this trip.

Observing that a contest was about to take place, a few of the patrons began to lay friendly wagers. One of them started to spin the board. Tartarus rose to his feet and walked with Bowen over to the arrows board. Tartarus stood at the mark, took aim and released. A lead-tipped arrow flew from his bow in the direction of the spinning shield. As it penetrated the red section of the board Tartarus smiled; the lesson had begun. As Brun and Ragnarr watched the black-haired elf stand and take a firm shot some distance from the arrow board, they shook hands on a friendly wager.

Ragnarr, having backed the unsavoury character with the patch, wasn't pleased when the man started to lose very badly, while the elf seemed to win every game.
Though Brun was sure no one could play that badly, he was delighted with the outcome: the bill for his meal and drinks now belonged to the dwarf.

Tartarus was having fun. Taking aim, he released another arrow and hit red again. He turned and gave Bowen a wink. The spirited sport between him and the stranger was gratifying; he'd not lost a game yet. It had been a long trip; he and his companions had been on the road for almost a month, and it would be at least another two weeks' ride before they would reach their destination – the mountain known as Black Forest Summit. It was nice to relax and unwind, although playing arrows wasn't everyone's idea of fun and relaxation. His companions, Vince and Asrack, were happy to just sit and watch.

Between turns, Tartarus had time to reflect. His thoughts wandered between his home and the game. He was missing his mother's comforting face. The roast hog smelled delicious, but nothing could beat her cooking. Anyway, elves only ate fowl and fish; red meat was forbidden. And with an inner smile his best friend, Jacob, returned to his thoughts. He and Jacob would hunt and fish the streams around Oaken-Dale, sometimes with hilarious consequences.

Tartarus took a large swig of ale and swallowed. Another waft of the sweet, tangy aroma passed his nostrils, and there was no denying that the hog roast smelled tasty.

Vince and Asrack were busy in conversation. 'Probably talking about their wives,' mused Tartarus. Asrack was forever calling him a 'mummy's boy'. Although Tartarus was not married yet, he was in love with a Nagari elfette named Eolande. In her company, he was spellbound by her charms and sweet nature. The pretty elfette took his breath away and one day, he promised himself, he would pluck up the courage to declare his true feelings to her, and to her father. Being Aafari meant he would have to ask Eolande's father, a Nagari elgar, before being permitted to court her. Elves had strict rules of conduct governing courtship.

The more Bowen drank, the worse his aim got. Feeling sorry for him, and feeling the effect of the ale, Tartarus called a halt to the game. Bowen informed them that he knew of a short cut through the Black Forest which would knock days off their journey, especially if they were heading near the edge of the Badlands. He could guide them for a reasonable fee and it would help him recoup some of the gold coins he had lost to Tartarus. A shorter journey was a shorter journey so the elves took him up on his offer, although Vince had his reservations. The group gathered their belongings and they left the inn together.

Arrows was a noisy game and always got rowdy when participants drank too much. This was especially true with elves; they just couldn't handle their brew. So Ragnarr was glad of the peace and quiet once Bowen and the elves had finally left the tavern. Brun had left for his room once he had finished his hog. He had downed more than a few tankards of burned-barrel ale during the evening.

Ragnarr looked at the now empty bench where his friend had been sitting. He would need to leave the blacksmith soon. Furnus's death had changed things considerably; Ragnarr would have to assume his friend's role too, unless he could find a forger or metallurgist he could trust. He was also missing his wife and children incessantly. It had been awhile since he had seen their smiling faces, and being reunited with them was uppermost in his thoughts. Having lost his relatives at a very young age still haunted him and so, for Ragnarr, family had always came first. But his mission was so vital that if he failed there'd be no home to go to. Just before the war between the south and the west when he was a boy, his father – a legendary Dvergar craftsman – moved the family to the Southlands, to help build a new fortress for the king. While working, his father had discovered that someone was stealing the mother's milk, an act that would eventually cause the planet to overheat and die.

Kromillium, or mother's milk as the dwarves called it, was an essential ingredient to the planet's continued existence. Kromillium kept the volcanic subterranean lava flows at the right temperature. Low on silicon, potassium and aluminium, kromillium had an extremely high magnesium content, which acted as a coolant. When kromillium died, as all things do, its sediment would fall harmlessly to the bottom of the lava flow where it would harden and become a magnet, which helped maintain the magnetic balance of the planetary core.

One fateful night while Ragnarr was out hunting, a bull-headed beast had burst into his home and killed his whole family; his mother, father, sister and brother had all been slain. By a cruel twist of fate he had seen the oxceian when returning from his hunt; if the creature had known they were his kin, it would have killed him too.
Ragnarr had tried to hide when their eyes had met. Ever since, he had reproached himself for being a coward. He should have fought the beast when he had the chance. Now the opportunity for redemption had long since passed.

He believed it was his cowardice that had caused their deaths, even though when he encountered the beast he had no knowledge of the foul deeds it had already committed. He had thought it strange when the creature had not attacked, but once he reached his homestead the full horror was revealed. The beast had already had its feast. He had caught a glimpse of an unusual scar that ran along the oxceian's muscular forearm which, along with its smell, would never be forgotten. Since that day the weight of the world had been carried on his broad shoulders.

Ragnarr was no oxceian hunter but if he ever clapped eyes on the beast again his tungsten war hammer, reinforced with hardened titanium, would do the talking.
In battle, the double-sided bone-crusher could destroy the strongest helmet or plated armour with just a few blows, and could quickly be reversed to punch holes with its fearsome back spike. Or, better still, inflict the full force of a gauntlet of power on the beast. Now that would be a sight to behold; the tight-lipped dwarf almost formed a smile.

A power crystal in its pure mineral form was a beryl crystal, a colourless gemstone. Such a crystal was found only in volcanic rock restricted to the Archaean age, during the period just after the birth of the planet. It was an extremely rare crystal building block that could be manipulated into virtually any gem or precious stone. Adding certain impurities, such as chromium or iron, in the correct quantity would turn it into emerald or, just as easily, into aquamarine. Due to its rarity wealthy ladies of the time would pay a king's ransom to have pink beryl, a bright pink gemstone similar to a pink-blush diamond.

Ragnarr was an alchemist and however sweet the alluring thought of revenge was, the release from his shame would have to wait. He'd been entrusted with a mission of the utmost importance and he was not a dwarf who shirked his responsibilities. Stigwyn had been quite clear when he had instructed him not to embarrass the king. He felt he had already done so by being captured. Now he had a chance to make amends and he intended to grasp that opportunity with both hands.

He wanted the ancient combination that transformed beryl crystals into power crystals. The crystal needed a conduit to channel its energy. Only one man was known to have perfected the ancient and secret art of fusing alloy correctly with a power crystal and that was the old master craftsman, Algrim, the alchemist. He was a noble and legendary dwarf, who manufactured four powerful gauntlets, able to channel the crystal's strength: the gauntlets of power. Ragnarr and Furnus had hoped to make a fifth. Now, with his friend's death, the task had become much harder. Reluctantly, he acknowledged he would need Brun's help. The burly blacksmith had already been useful. Anyway, he enjoyed the big man's company and, truth be told, he was beginning to be rather fond of him.

Overwhelmed by a large yawn, Ragnarr knew it was time for bed. It had been a long day. With a heavy heart, he lifted his round frame off the bench, giving the buxom blonde a wave as he walked towards his room.

The next morning they were both late risers and weren't sure if it was the effect of too much drink or a warm, firm bed which had assisted their slumber more. They collected their horses. Cloud seemed a little under the weather so Brun gave the mare a rub-down before they continued their journey. He was looking forward to seeing his sister Lillian and her husband Nefanial Bartholomew. It was the day of the winter solstice and his arrival would be a wonderful surprise.

*

A meeting of kings was not uncommon although secret ones were held only when alliances needed to be formed in war. A union of minds, no different from its predecessors, was taking place in a mining shack near the western edge of Oaken-Dale. A couple of elves and dwarves stood guard outside.

Lord Erynion, with his inimitable sideburns, and the Aafari King Jeremiah were sitting on a bench across a wide table from two Denvagar dwarves: King Mortfran Weldig and his compatriot Stigwyn Broadfist.
    'We should have summoned you sooner, Jeremiah. It's been too long but, alas, a crown's commitments weigh heavily,' said Mortfran. He had no sooner spoken than his

mind seemed to wander, but then with a smile that reduced his frown lines, which was hard to make out through his beard's thick undergrowth, he continued, 'I remember when we were pups.'

'Indeed, Mortfran, those were the days,' said the Aafari king as he jostled for a better position on an uncomfortable bench.

'Now we rule kingdoms. And mine is in as much peril as your own,' responded Mortfran, which produced raised eyebrows from the Aafari king.

'I don't know what ails you, but the wolves aren't scratching at your door, Mortfran. I've only come here to seek assurance that you will come to our aid. The Black Knight's army outnumbers my elves by ten to one; these are not favourable odds,' said Jeremiah, whose troubled expression told its own story.

Jeremiah looked at Lord Erynion and then at the modest surroundings. A candle flame flickered in a draught, its glow only partially filling the room. Ale barrels were stacked up in one corner, and an assortment of tools in the other. The smell of drudgery and alcohol hung in the room like layers of cobwebs. What a place in which to try to save his kingdom: the irony struck him hard.

'If we drew them into Oaken-Dale, then maybe we've got a chance,' Jeremiah said. Erynion gave him a slight nod, but he had reservations; a battle with Edwin's horde seemed hopeless, even if using the trees in a forest battle offered an advantage. Erynion's black, high-collared tunic matched his mood and the depressing gloom that he seemed to be constantly fighting. Erynion's faith in the giver of life had long since departed and he was perpetually waiting for a spark that might reignite his belief.

'But there is more to lose than your precious Oaken-Crag, Jeremiah. A third great war is brewing,' said Mortfran. 'In fact, the sad truth is: it's inevitable.'

Lord Erynion, normally meticulous and conscientious, was perplexed by Mortfran's statement; there was nothing more important than Oaken-Crag. Jeremiah, ever watchful, placed a firm grip on Erynion's forearm. Now was not the time for foolish outbursts; they needed the help of the dwarves. Mortfran picked up his tankard and took a swill.

'You will not fight alone, king of the Aafari. On that you have my word. Only after battles are won, are songs of our names sung.' Mortfran lifted his tankard high up in the air, as though already hearing the verses. The sound of armour clinking under his robes could be heard as he took another swig.

'We believe Edwin, son of Linus, attacks you for the gold-rimmed scroll, and the knowledge it contains.'

'He'll never get his hands on it,' Jeremiah replied fervently.

'Why don't you just read it and put us all out of our misery? After all, you are the king,' Mortfran said. 'Do you still have it?' The question received a quizzical glance from both elves.

'Of course we still have it. However, only our high priestess can decide when it can be read,' replied Jeremiah. The dwarf king was known for his bluntness, not his diplomacy. His lack of tact was a trait Jeremiah chose to ignore.

'Well, that's what he's after,' Mortfran said, taking a healthy bite from a red apple. He wiped his lips but juices still managed to trickle down his beard.

'He's clearly deranged,' remarked Erynion, straight-faced. Mortfran nodded in agreement.

'But Edwin's search for conquest is the least of our worries.' Mortfran's frown lines returned as he leaned forward. 'Kromillium is being harvested at an alarming rate. We will aid your cause if you will lend elves to aid ours,' he said firmly.

'Kromillium?' said Jeremiah, turning to Erynion for an explanation. From the look on Lord Erynion's face he inferred that he was not alone in needing more information. He looked back at the brown-hooded dwarves.

'I've not heard of this substance before,' said Erynion, crestfallen at being found wanting.

'Maybe we should have come to you sooner, but we were waiting for news from a couple of dwarves who now seem to have disappeared. My man, Selwyn, here' – he patted his friend's back –'is my spymaster and mineral specialist.' The elves exchanged glances; the introduction seemed odd because all dwarves were mineral specialists. Stigwyn, giving Mortfran a stare, couldn't be bothered to correct his king on the pronunciation of his name, and gave the elves a geology lesson.

'There are different types of minerals, water- or magma-based, and kromillium is the latter. We dig in places others dare not, so we were bound to notice a change to the planet's core temperature. Kromillium is easier to get to from volcanoes and deep caves are just as good as a starting point, I suppose.'

Mortfran nudged his compatriot; the elves seemed lost. So although Stigwyn loved talking about minerals and rocks, he relayed matters more quickly and in layman's terms.

'Mother's milk is the planet's only magma coolant and without it Elohim will combust and implode.' He picked up an apple from a bowl in the centre of the table and put it down then, with a small hammer, smashed it.

'What?' said Jeremiah, caught in a yawn, coughing out bits of apple that had flown into his mouth. 'Can't this substance be substituted?' Stigwyn shook his head.

'So just how much time have we got left to prevent this catastrophe? And how long have you been keeping this under your helmet, Mortfran?' he asked, unimpressed.

'All I know is that time is of the essence and, to be honest, we've known for awhile now. We didn't know who we could trust, but I've told my clan it's time we spoke. You know how protective we dwarves are over our minerals,' responded Mortfran.

'Now, isn't that the truth,' Erynion agreed.

'So, who is taking it?' asked Jeremiah, as though about to stand up.

'Peasants under the influence of the dark arts, I imagine,' replied Stigwyn.

'A workforce of the walking dead,' murmured Erynion, well versed in the southern realm's despicable atrocities.

'Yes, but who they are working for Elohim only knows. Kromillium is toxic if you inhale too much.' Stigwyn reached inside his hooded cloak then placed before them a small glass jar, half full. The white fluid in the jar was flecked with minute gold specks, glittering throughout. 'Kromillium in liquid form,' he said. The elves agreed it could be mistaken for milk.

'We believe the act has something to do with Prince Edwin, although this activity started long before his beginning, so we think he's just an instrument but not the one who plots this path,' said Stigwyn, sighing. Jeremiah looked deep into the dwarf's brown eyes; the tale seemed far-fetched to him.

'It just doesn't make sense. Who would want the planet's destruction?' he asked.

'Edwin is Cressida's puppet, after all. Maybe she has the answer we seek?' Erynion suggested.

'That trollop,' Mortfran said in disgust.

Cressida, the sorceress, had far-reaching influence and most evil plots came with her seal of approval. She was also the queen of the orks and rarely ventured from her lair, deep within the southern realm. The trek over treacherous volcanic terrain would be a difficult one for any army.

'Well, my father always said to slay one dragon at a time,' said Mortfran. 'We must eliminate Edwin first; we've already had one attempt fail. We're led to believe that only his taster died.'

'Maybe if Edwin knew the truth he might change sides?' said Jeremiah. The other three shook their heads.

'No, Edwin must go; he's caused too much heartache,' protested Mortfran firmly.

'One thing is certain: wherever his army treads kromillium is consumed soon after,' Stigwyn added as he dipped two tankards into an ale barrel.

'Well, we need a plan of action that we can bring before the Supreme High Council,' concluded Jeremiah.

'Now you're talking!' the dwarf king said, smiling.

'Our plans are already at an advanced stage. We are ready to wage war.'

Stigwyn passed Mortfran his tankard and they clunked the wooden vessels together; despite the hinged lids froth spilled onto the stone floor.

'Who will stand with us? The west has long been conquered and the north will only fight if they are attacked,' said Jeremiah. 'With the fall of Athena the east is at war too, so you must convince the Ljosalfar to rally the north,' he added; 'the knights of Adalhard have much to answer for.'

'And the west has been under the south's tyrannical thumb for far too long. I'm sure, at a push, they'd rise up; we've got a friend in the Keltic tribes,' the dwarfish king said, beaming. Stigwyn retook his seat.

'I see you've thought this through,' observed Jeremiah. Mortfran nodded cheerfully.

'But no mention of the enchanted?' continued Jeremiah shrewdly.

'Those beings are no more; the Swarm consumed them,' said Mortfran, dismissing the issue flatly, while devouring the rest of the apple, core and all.

Suddenly, there was a rap on the door of the mining shack. Before any of them could answer, the door nearly came off its hinges as it slammed open against the stone inner wall. A stout, unkempt dwarf, whose girth took up the width of the opening, fell into the room with an arrow lodged in his back. He managed to croak out the word 'assassins' as he fell. Behind him the sound of scuffling ensued. The company sprang to their feet. Lord Erynion took the lead, grabbing his egg-shaped shield; instinctively he peered over and looked directly at the entrance. There was no movement. A black abyss glared back now that the evening sun had set.

Mortfran and Stigwyn flipped the wooden table onto its side for cover. Their hooded cloaks were flung away to reveal an array of dwarfish weaponry ideally suited to just this sort of predicament. Jeremiah managed to catch the airtight jar before it hit the ground, while bouncing apples missed his face and his crown slipped from his brow.

'Vargas, how many?' Stigwyn asked the dwarf lying at the foot of the doorway. Vargas held up two fingers. As he did so, his skin turned a ghostly blue. Erynion knew assassins usually travelled in threes, so two would have been no problem normally but, having seen the colour of Vargas's skin, he began to realize that one of the assassins must have been ...
'A Svartalfar,' whispered Jeremiah, kneeling behind Erynion, who was looking at the corpse of Vargas.

Mortfran made a hand signal, which suggested he was about to send Stigwyn outside. Erynion mouthed a silent 'no' and his eyes widened. Then, without making a sound, he slipped three arrows from his quiver, just in case Vargas had miscounted.
Holding two shafts in his mouth, he picked up an apple and threw it at the doorway.
In the blink of an eye the fruit was sent flying. An odious black-shafted arrow extended from its centre; instantly Erynion knew the distance from which their assailant's arrow had been shot, and its trajectory. That was all he needed to know.

'Careful! Those arrows are poisonous!' shouted Stigwyn. The apple was now black and the protruding shaft had crumbled into ash. Aware of the danger, Erynion handed his shield to Jeremiah and, steadying an arrow along his bow, he gave it a practice pull. Then, with a signal, Jeremiah launched another apple. As it hit plump centre Erynion, visualizing exactly where the arrow took flight from, made his move. With a spring and a dive into a death roll, he was out of the room.

Mortfran helped Jeremiah extinguish the remaining candle light. Stigwyn sprang into action; with his short sword and war hammer gripped tightly he followed Erynion. The clang and clatter of his armour, along with his dwarfish roar, rang through the room.
At the doorway, his helmet suddenly went flying and its side plates flapped cold air as a crushing blow struck his middle. It was a crippling strike that would have cut him in two had his armour not taken the impact.

Erynion held his bow firmly and an arrow was released almost immediately, with another one set as he leaped to his feet; the prolonged scream, along with the cracking of branches, told him the archer had probably been subdued. A black arrow vibrated and embedded itself in the ground at his feet, indicating just how close margins between life and death actually were. The duel, although quick, had still been a stiff test. He looked round to see an assassin entering the hut, while another stood above an Alfari elf, with arms aloft ready to inflict a devastating blow.

Erynion's bow sang again and an arrow buried itself in the soft shell at the base of the aggressor's skull. His body lurched forward and fell in a heap. Still in fluid motion, a gargled shriek from inside the mining hut made him remove his remaining arrow shaft from his lips and slip it into the groove on his bow, covering the doorway as he made his approach.

Mortfran, seeing Stigwyn in trouble, raised his war hammer. Jeremiah threw the jar at the attacker and threw back a section of his cloak to free up his sword's hilt. Mortfran rounded the table to confront the masked man. Already white foam was bubbling from his mouth and his screams were enough to stop Mortfran in his tracks. The man seemed intent on throttling himself and, with a last hideous gargle, he keeled over dead. Erynion ran to check that the archers had not being feigning death. As he cleared the glade and entered the woods, he heard someone running away.

Stigwyn, taking a moment to get his breath back, inhaled deeply.

'Didn't I mention that kromillium isn't edible? It's fatal when consumed,' he said with a knowing grin, while still sucking air. Mortfran gave him a hand and helped him back onto his feet. With a groan Stigwyn stretched, still a little dazed. Erynion's call for assistance brought them outside. Jeremiah lit a torch. Sprawled across the patchy grass were an elf, a dwarf and one of the assassins.

'The Svartalfar has escaped, and Dain is hurt, sire,' said Erynion, drawing their attention to the elf he'd just saved.

'There's a faint heartbeat, but it doesn't look good,' Jeremiah said with a shake of his head. The elf was making incoherent noises; he was clearly barely alive. Mortfran scrutinized the injuries; a swollen bump above his left eye, a dislocated shoulder and a broken arm were all treatable, but his real concern was a thin slash along the neckline from an arrow. The poison had only made minimal contact, but a fever was already taking hold.

'This elf may still have a chance,' said Mortfran. 'If you wish him to live, we must take him to my home in Denvagar.'

'Are you sure?' asked Jeremiah, looking at Mortfran then at Dain's broken body.

'If the poison takes full effect there will be only one outcome.'

Jeremiah was deflated. Despite surviving the assassination attempt, there was no way he could leave his High Lord's child. Although they were not related, Dain was like a nephew and his father, Crayfar, like a brother. He tried to delay the decision for a moment.

'How many were there?' he asked Lord Erynion.

'Three, sire,' he replied, pointing to where the Svartalfar had been positioned.

Stigwyn pulled off the assassin's mask to reveal his face.

'I know this man,' he said, while closing the man's eyes. 'I can't place him, but don't worry, it will come to me,' he added quickly, realizing they were waiting for something more tangible.

'By the way, there were three, not two. I think for all your tools, you dwarves could maybe use one of these.' Erynion handed Stigwyn a stargazer. The jest was warranted; Vargas's lapse might have cost them their lives.

'I don't need one of those!' he protested, throwing the leather-bound telescope to the ground.

'All a dwarf needs is a light at the end of his nose,' proclaimed Stigwyn. 'Now that doesn't make sense,' he said, scratching his head and looking puzzled. Mortfran, curious, pressed him to elaborate on what he was implying. Stigwyn explained that this assassin was not one of Prince Edwin's men.

'If you had allowed me to bring my pets here, this would never have happened,' said Jeremiah to the dwarf king.

'Those beasts?' Mortfran shook his head. 'I'm allergic to cats.'

'Prairie Tigers? Where?' said Stigwyn, looking around nervously.

'Do you know who this man is, or not?' Jeremiah asked, hovering his torch closer and noticing the dwarf fumbling with the man's left ear.

'Yes. He's Duke Mandrick's stalwart. Do you see? Do you?' asked Stigwyn in an animated manner. They all looked to see a set of four indelible dots just above the dwarf's finger, behind the man's earlobe. The tattoo stood for 'Action: reaction. Order: chaos.'

'The Order of the Anarchist,' said Erynion.

'We can discuss this matter later, but right now this warrior needs help,' said Mortfran solemnly. Dain was fighting for his life. If the poison was allowed to fester he'd be dead in a couple of days. 'I cannot wait any longer. That black elf may return with more men.' He helped them lift Dain to a sitting position.

'I wouldn't worry. We've got the best physicians in Denvagar,' Stigwyn assured Jeremiah, whose face was etched with apprehension. Crateuas, his warrior-physician, lay dead, and Oaken-Crag was simply too far to travel. Dain required urgent treatment. After a private deliberation between Jeremiah and Lord Erynion it was decided that heading back to the municipality without Crayfar's son wasn't possible, and Jeremiah accepted Mortfran's hospitality.

Down a hill track, the former marble quarry's caves hid a secret route to the legendary city of Denvagar. Lord Erynion went to get the four elven horses from a pen at the back of the hut. Once Dain was ready to be transported the elves mounted their steeds and the dwarves led the way on foot.

'I think I had better let you know,' said Erynion, discreetly, 'that we don't have the gold-rimmed scroll.'

'What?' responded Jeremiah, confused. However his next thought, as Mortfran turned to be greeted by his coy smile, was: would it be wise to tell him the truth?
'Don't worry, I'll send a burial party to tend to our fallen once we get to Denvagar,' announced the dwarf king. Jeremiah nodded gracefully in acknowledgement.

The marble caverns were reached after a short downhill trek. Stigwyn greeted and unsecured two ass-camels.
'Good boys,' he said, patting the beasts. Usually found on the plains of Tyrus, the allocamelous or ass-camel was closely related to the llama. They were widely used as pack animals by dwarves because of their stamina and their ability to retain water. This made them ideal for arduous journeys.

The elves dismounted. The dripping and echoes of water could be heard deep within the caves.
'Are you sure these caves are safe?' enquired the Aafari king. The dwarf turned and smiled and the cavern was lit up by their bright torches, as Stigwyn led the way.
'We know these caves like we know our wives' backsides,' replied Mortfran.
This didn't instil confidence, but with Erynion's firm grip on the reins of Dain's horse, he and Jeremiah followed the dwarves into the airless, cramped space.

*

Tarquin and Flint were on a hunting expedition for furs in the Black Forest. Both young men were amiable, hard-working, honest and trustworthy. Being adopted at birth had far from hindered them; it seemed to spur them on to succeed where others had failed. Tarquin, a handsome, pale-skinned lad, was fair-haired in comparison to Flint, whose hair was a mousy brown colour. They were both of medium build, although Tarquin was a couple of inches taller than his younger brother. Flint had distinctive jade eyes and freckles that spread across both cheeks. He was called cute and mischievous in equal measures. Flint just couldn't help himself if an opportunity arose for a practical yarn or a tall story.

Their homestead was within the confines of a stronghold called Irons Keep, one of the many strongholds scattered on the outskirts of the Black Forest, or the 'vast space of gloom' as the boys called it. They both wanted to travel the world to seek fame and fortune. They didn't believe either would be forthcoming if they stayed in Irons Keep. They had heard the old stories, but they didn't fill them with awe as they once did; the age of innocence was behind them and they could no longer live on dreams alone.

Flint pondered a thought before deciding to share it with Tarquin.

'Why don't we just go? We've helped them for long enough,' he said, referring to their adopted parents. Tarquin ignored him; he wanted to leave just as much as Flint, but now wasn't the time.

'Has a maiden stolen your tongue by any chance?' said Flint, looking for a reply.

'Just leave it, will you?' retorted Tarquin. 'I thought we were here for furs?'

'Yes, we're here for pelts, but we're not getting any younger. I'll be an old man before I see a battle at this rate, Quin,' replied a resigned Flint, with a quizzical look on his face. Tarquin smiled at his brother. 'They'll come, they'll c ...' he began, but suddenly he placed a finger over his mouth and pursed his lips. Flint understood the signal and, without making a sound, he turned to give their horse a blank stare. As if he understood Flint's concern, the animal stopped in its tracks. The packhorse, which looked more like a mule, had been named Rainbow by their father and now followed them religiously. They took him on their expeditions to carry the furs that they caught.

From an early age they had hunted in the Black Forest. Although it was dangerous they needed money to eventually escape the clutches of Irons Keep, and furs meant money. Unusually for humans, they could see in the dead of night; others had commented that it was cat-like, but after years of hunting in the forest their eyesight had acclimatized to the darkness of its nights. Always hunting on foot, Tarquin was pretty good with a bow and arrow, while Flint was a dead aim with a crossbow. Both were handy with short or long swords and with their fists; their father had trained them well.

Flint was slightly off-balance. His weaker foot was in an awkward position, so he replaced his footing. Suddenly, there was the sound of a twig cracking underfoot. He hadn't been careful enough. Tarquin looked at him sternly. Flint acknowledged his brother's disapproval. They both crept forward, Flint being extra-vigilant this time.
They hadn't taken five steps when a gap appeared between two large elm trees. Peering through the gap, they could see movement. Their eyes bulged with excitement. Instantly, they looked at each other and smiled. Tarquin gave Flint a few hand signals which, at first glance, went unnoticed because Flint was too busy rubbing his palms together in

delight, but then, in a flash, he was heading towards Rainbow.

Tarquin just stood absolutely still with a broad smile on his face, which was still present when Flint arrived back by his side and handed him a large pouch stuffed with Rainbow's favourite treats and snacks. He grabbed a handful of the shrubs and walked out of the shadows, through a gap, into the opening where he encountered the objects of his gaze. Three magnificent horses were drinking water from a stream. Their tails, manes and facial features were different from those of other horses he'd seen before. One was a stallion and would fetch a tidy sum; good-quality breeding horses were in high demand, and this one's beauty overwhelmed even him.
Immediately noticing their saddlebags and provision packs, he wondered what fate had befallen their riders. All manner of creatures inhabited the forest, lurking behind every shadow. No matter: that was not their concern, and once re-registered the horses would be legally theirs.

He waited until Flint was on the horses' opposite side before he made his move; he wasn't about to let these beauties escape. Once Flint was in position, he stuck out his hand holding the shrubs and walked forward while making a light clicking sound with his mouth, which horses were known to find endearing. The closest horse to Tarquin had a golden coat with a white mane and tail. It was a gelding and its golden sheen glistened as he approached. Abruptly, the horse raised its head from the stream as though it had smelled his scent and sensed impending danger. Tarquin got within touching distance before the horse reared its head, then trotted a few yards from the stream. Unperturbed, he simply approached the next horse in line, a snowflake-white mare. The horse was not intimidated by his presence. Gently, he stroked its mane. The mare raised her head and was greeted by Rainbow's shrubs. The mare showed her appreciation by rubbing her mane against his neck.

The black stallion, on the other side of the mare, had stopped quenching his thirst and seemed annoyed at Tarquin; its breathing became erratic and rasping. Flint saw his chance and, without confirmation from his brother, headed for the stallion at pace and with a hop and a skip was in the air. The stallion moved deftly out of reach. Flint clipped the horse's saddle on the way down, spun full circle and landed in the stream, getting completely soaked through. Tarquin was still absorbing the moment sometime after they had rounded up the horses.

    'My brother's an idiot,' he declared. 'I had the mare and the others would have followed.' Tarquin shook his head, more in amusement than disbelief. Flint, too busy to listen, was moving around as though doing some form of tribal dance as he tried to keep warm in front of the fire. He dangled his clothes on a stick over the warm flames.

    'If you hadn't been talking so much, we might have caught some furs,' Tarquin said sarcastically, while wrapping an imaginary fur around his body. Flint just closed his eyes, hoping to be free of the humiliation. It was agreed that Flint would be of no use unless he had a good night's rest. The cold had got into his bones. The remedy was simple: wrap up warm in front of a fire with a bowl of garlic and mint-leaf soup. So they threw more logs onto the fire and made camp around its flames.

Rummaging through Rainbow's saddlebag Tarquin removed the ingredients for the soup, then went about creating their meal. If Flint had been feeling a little better he would have told his brother that the soup tasted vile. However, he could feel that it was doing its job. Squeezing his blanket tighter around himself and closing his eyes, he drifted off to sleep.

Tarquin kept watch but after listening to the sounds of the forest and staring into darkness he succumbed to the weight of his eyelids and fell asleep too. The remainder of the night was uneventful. Flint awoke with a big yawn. The effect of the icy bath still ailed him but he felt much better now that his strength had returned and he was pleased he had taken his own advice to have a good night's rest before making the long journey home. Tarquin was still asleep.

'Bloody cheek,' thought Flint. His brother was as fit as a fiddle, whereas he'd been at death's door, or felt as though he had been. He woke Tarquin with a playful kick and was greeted by cursing, obscenities and a stern look. Flint explained that they were now running late and would be hard pushed to make it home for the eclipse.

'I promised our Pip I'd take her to the festival,' Flint said. Their sister, Pippa, loved festivals.

'We'll make it,' said a yawning Tarquin.

'Can't we ride the horses?' The casual request was followed by a cheeky smile; he knew the horses would need to be registered before they could be ridden. This was the law and the law of the land was quite simple; most crimes were punishable by death.

'Are you mad? You know the law,' replied Tarquin.

After feeding their horses they broke camp. Flint conceded that Tarquin may have won this battle, but not the war. They attached their provisions and packs onto the grey mare's saddlebags, before Flint mounted Rainbow. Tarquin's disapproval of Flint's defiance was written all over his face but he did not utter another word. They had been travelling for hours, following a winding path, and the winds were getting cold again. Sunset wasn't far away.

'We're not going to make it,' Flint said bluntly as the light faded.

'The festival goes on for two days. Anyway, it's the winter solstice today. It's supposed to get dark early,' replied Tarquin.

'If you meet a maiden on the night of the full moon it can be most pleasurable.'

'Is that all you ever think about?' said Tarquin, in a huff. 'And wipe that absurd smile off your face,' he scolded.

Busy in conversation, they hadn't noticed that they were being followed or that the gelding was straying into quicksand, having veered from the path. Both were startled when they heard the shrieks of the terrified gelding. Flint was about to dismount when there was a rustling of leaves and out of the gloom came a figure running straight at his brother.

Tarquin and his attacker fell in a heap. Fists flew as both figures slithered around in the mud, seeking the upper hand. Flint reached for his crossbow. Tartarus had been on the trail of his horses for most of the day. He'd picked up the tracks of two humans with a packhorse and had arrived at the brook desperately hoping to see his horse, Willow. He had reared the stallion from foal to adulthood and shared a special bond with the moody steed. When he'd been ordered to have the horse castrated he had refused; he liked the horse's attitude.

Tartarus was glad when he had finally caught a glimpse of the horses through the thick undergrowth but he hadn't made up his mind whether the humans were to be trusted or not. The fact still remained that the forest was a haven for rogues and brigands. All that changed when he saw the gelding in trouble. Instinctively deciding they were enemies, and without a moment's hesitation, he charged at Tarquin who, being on foot, was an easier target. Tartarus struck out with his right fist and was surprised when he was hit with a left-hand punch in return. Now, on the mud in the throngs of a roll, he knew he was in for a fight.

Flint had decided not to shoot the attacker. The tussle amused him; the sight of his brother and the elf wrestling, unable to get their footing in the mud, was hilarious. It didn't take a genius to work out that the horses probably belonged to the stranger and Flint was no thief. Finally, Tartarus got to his feet, exhausted and breathing heavily; he could hear all his horses making frantic noises.
    'And damn, this human wouldn't stay down.'
Tarquin seized his opportunity; his tired and distracted opponent suddenly felt the thud of a firm kick between the thighs. Reeling from the pain, Tartarus was livid. He'd been robbed of the scroll, robbed of his horses, and now this human was trying to rob him of his manhood. With all the energy in his reserves he dived on Tarquin.

On seeing that the elf was raging, Flint got off his horse to stop the fight but was only able to get them into a huddle before they continued the bout. Now, caught in the middle of the fracas, he tried to persuade them to call a halt to the fighting and save the mare. However, all he got for his trouble was a mouth full of mud weed. When a ball of fire suddenly took centre stage its tremendous heat made them all jump back.
Flint quickly checked to see if his clothes were on fire.
Tartarus removed his cloak hurriedly. He'd only just done so

when it was consumed by a flaming orb, which then shot off like a comet in the direction of the sky.

'What the hell was that?' asked Flint, still shaking.

'Yeah, what was that?' Tarquin looked stunned as he pointed at the object in the sky. The brothers each looked at each other as though searching the other's face for the answer. Tartarus, sitting on the ground, was inconsolable. He'd released the flare prematurely. As Aafarians went, he was fast becoming an embarrassment, before he could wallow in self-pity.

The gelding made one last plea for help. All three of them turned in response to the shriek, just in time to see the horse's nostrils disappear from view. They had completely forgotten about the gelding. Quickly, Tarquin jumped into the quagmire, furiously looking for the animal's reins. Flint grabbed him by his ankles. Tartarus would have chuckled at the sight if the horse hadn't been in so much trouble. Quickly, he tied a rope onto Willow then threw the other end to Tarquin, who attached it to the gelding's reins. After a tremendous effort, they pulled the trembling gelding out. While the horse shook the muddy sand off its coat, the three rescuers lay on a patch of grass, panting from the exertion.

Flint gave an exaggerated sigh, then wiped his brow. Tarquin gave him a puzzled look; it was he who had done most of the work. The funny expression caught them all by surprise and suddenly they were laughing hysterically. When they had all calmed down Tartarus, having changed his mind about these characters, introduced himself and told them about the mess he had got himself into. He told them the tale of the scroll and its importance, and what that red thing had been.

The flare intrigued them, since they had never set eyes on one before, but they did not know what to make of their new-found friend. Flint could still feel the heat from the flare and swore the exposure had given him sunburn or, at the very least, a suntan. However, Flint was still glad to finally meet someone who seemed to be able to get themselves into as much trouble as he did.

'We'll help you get it back,' said Flint.

'We don't take kindly to brigands in these parts.' The thought of some action, at long last, was the only image in the young lads' minds. Tarquin explained how they had come by the horses and complimented the elf on his fine animals, although he expressed slight dissatisfaction at the fact that there would be no profit for their efforts. They had, of course, been hoping for a nice sum for the horses. However, after hearing of Tartarus's plight both brothers agreed that if the elf required it, they would provide assistance to him in his quest: fame brought fortune and fortune favoured the brave.

On accepting their offer Tartarus gave them each a horse. Tarquin was given the mare, and Flint the gelding. The premature release of the flare meant that time was now of the essence and his friends, he reflected sadly, would have no need for their horses now. From the sound of it, the ambush would require more armed men and Tarquin suggested they visit their keep to recruit some. Tartarus agreed. They mounted the horses and continued their journey to the stronghold.

*

The Dökkalfar had not always been called by that name. They were different from other elves; their skin was a pale green as though they were permanently ill. The condition was caused by a lack of regular sunlight on the skin. They simply preferred to live in murky, damp places such as caves and caverns. The isolation made them socially inept and selfish; it was imbedded in their nature.

It was only after being expelled from the Supreme High Council over a difference of opinion that the Kalfar, the green elves, were given the name Dökkalfar, which meant dark elves or tainted ones. Since that day, two of the six seats of the Supreme High Council had remained empty. The Svartalfar, the black elves, who had never recognized the council as an authority, also kept away. The Kalfar had disagreed with the Supreme High Council over the use of the dark arts. The Kalfar had argued their case that the power could be controlled; they felt that since the use of the dark arts had become more prevalent within the world of men the only way to defeat the darkness was by being skilled in its ways. The Andvari, the river-dwelling elves and direct descendants of the Kalfar, were in agreement with this proposal.

The Aafari, the Nagari and the Ljosalfar were not, and had argued that it was always better to fight fire with water, the dark arts with the power of light. With a vote of two to three the motion failed. Already swayed by the dark elements, the Kalfar were furious with the decision and swore an oath of revenge against the Aafari, whom they saw as their main opponents in the debate. The Kalfar were barred from the Supreme High Council, the remaining members deciding that violent outbursts of this nature and intent had no place in the council. Only by recanting their oath would the exclusion of the Kalfar be lifted.

Once outside the laws of the Supreme High Council, the leaders of the Kalfarian kingdom tried to harness the power of the darkness, and failed. Corrupted by its power, a malignant seed festered, seeping into the depth of their souls and darkening the colour of their hearts. Their once bright, brown eyes were now replaced by blank milky-blue pupils. Void of empathy they were now cruel, self-indulgent beings. They began to look more like goblins with each passing day and they took extreme pleasure from the discomfort of others.

Kallen had his orders; he was not to return without the scroll. 'That prince is always giving out orders,' he thought. The prince wasn't even fully human. A half-breed, he could tell. The killing of Alfari warriors and bringing the kingdom of Aafari to its knees, those were his true intentions, and those were his orders from the Kalfar High Council. The prince had been easy to manipulate; a whispered word here and there was all it took to get him to attack his own mentor in the pursuit of more power. Power-hungry men were easy to control. Losing their power was all they feared, and Kallen was a master at playing with fear.

Now that Kallen had the scroll there was only one problem: the text was written in a language he had never seen before. Although he should have been riding in the direction of the prince, he needed to read the scroll first. He wasn't about to hand over the secrets contained within the scroll to a mad half-breed without knowing what it was he was giving away. Kallen was from the city of Caldaria, which was in the Kalfarian Mountains, situated in the south-western border of the Southlands. His unattractive appearance was made more hideous by an unsightly left lazy eye that seemed to be resting on his cheekbone. His face was partially concealed by a velvet-hooded cloak, with slits for his large pointed ears.

Kallen and his men had remained hidden within the forest for almost thirty days, when he received word that three elves had taken lodgings at the Hogshead tavern, which was famous for its wild hog and burned-barrel ale. The tavern was under the control of the Baron Brandon of Brandenburg, Prince Edwin's puppet. His mouth filled with a sweet taste as he imagined chewing on the baron's flesh. He had sent one of his men to the tavern to befriend these travellers and trick them into taking a short cut through the forest, where he would be waiting to ambush them. His plan had gone without a hitch and he had killed an Aafari in the process, which had given him a great deal of pleasure.

Kallen's spy, Bowen, had not gathered much information because the elves had been very secretive but, after observing their equipment, Bowen had discovered that they had kit and provisions for an arduous mountain climb. Kallen wondered if Black Forest Summit was where that cunning old man, Nikomeades, had been hiding all these years. It was the only logical explanation. The lands to the west had rolling hills, forests and flat lands but there was only one mountainous range within a moon's ride of their location, and that was the summit. The capture of Nikomeades would be a great feather in his cap, and he might be able to shed more light on the information contained within the scroll. Their food and provisions were low and it was more or less a week's ride to the summit, but it was only a day's ride to Irons Keep.

He knew that riding deeper into the Black Forest and then facing the demanding climb was unwise, especially now that he possessed his prize, the scroll, which rested against his chest. The dangers of the forest were well known to Kallen. He was akin to the things that lurked within it: creatures who sought solace in their own company, but were ready to devour a traveller at a moment's notice. The dark elf had more in common with the inhabitants of the forest than he'd care to admit.

Supplies would be needed for the laborious excursion.
    'Irons Keep it is,' Kallen informed his men.
Irons Keep was of greater significance than other places on the outskirts of the Black Forest because it was within a day's ride of the old ruins of Ebenknesha. The once great city, named after the powerful mage Eben, was the former home of the High King of Elohim. Every four years a constellation of stars, coupled with a full moon, signified the start of the leap year. The kings and rulers of all the civilized tribes would send envoys to Ebenknesha to pay homage and give their tributes to the king of kings. Traditionally, it was a week of celebrations: festivals, shows and feasting. All manner of races would be present to celebrate the rebirth of the planet. These days the festival only lasted two days: the day of the eclipse and the day after. The west had been ravaged by war and only the races of the western plains now came together in this way.

Kallen made camp just outside Irons Keep, while still remaining within cover of the forest. Kallen had been given strict instructions: it was imperative he stayed out of sight. To be seen could endanger the mission if others got wind of the prince's plans.

For this reason he would normally have sent in two men to barter for food and equipment when provisions were low but, unusually for a stronghold, the defences looked weak. His band of misfits were becoming restless and the keep's provisions looked ripe for the picking.

It had been awhile since they had felt the spoils of war line their pockets and he was partial to a spot of pillaging. It would also give his men's morale a welcome boost; good morale made men fight harder. As the sunset, Kallen conjured up a fog-based spell. Suddenly, the keep was engulfed in fog and they attacked. With well-placed arrows, they killed the two sentries guarding the main gate and a sentry in the watchtower before they had a chance to sound the alarm. The guard in the tower had noticed the weird fog but never saw the arrow that hit him full in the chest. All he heard was the thud, before being thrown clear of the lookout tower.

The stronghold was a mismatch of wooden structures and buildings centred round a main square and interlinked through a muddy network of trails and paths. A high fence of spiked logs surrounded the compound. The keep housed mainly agricultural folk and old war veterans. It had most basic provisions through good trading links, although you'd have to go elsewhere for luxurious goods. Over half of the villagers were at the festival and the keep was more like a ghost town compared to the bustling place it normally was. The streets were virtually empty.

Kallen's men were brutal, falling on their victims without warning thanks to the fog. The violence only stopped so that wealth and supplies could be taken. What could not be carried was burned. Those who had not hidden in time were set about mercilessly: men, women and children were all killed, indiscriminately. Some of the villagers fought back once they realized what was happening.

Tarquin and Flint's stepfather, Angus, saw the mist fall on the village. It was not unusual or surprising in the slightest since fog appeared in the flatlands as suddenly as it disappeared but, with all the commotion outside his cottage, he asked his wife to fetch him his broadsword. Once outside, Angus could tell this was no ordinary fog; he could feel the presence of witchcraft. He was about to tell his wife and daughter to hide, but suddenly a rider came galloping out of the mist and crashed through the cottage's outer boundary gate. Once the rider was within range he leaped off his horse onto Angus. Unfortunately for the rider, he landed on Angus's broadsword. Blood spewed from the man's mouth as the farmer used his sturdy boots to dislodge the attacker who was caught on his weapon.

Angus and his wife, Bellamina, were cultivators of the land. Bellamina was now approaching old age but was still slender and very beautiful. Her rosy skin, along with her long, silky, jet-black hair, would gleam under a moonlit sky. Angus was a robust man with a character that was larger than life. His once glorious blond curls were now a drab grey and his square, chiselled chin was filled with a spiky stubble. His clothing was the only clue to his previous occupation as a knight of Adalhard. The last time he wore his spurs and armour, with the Adalhard crest, was the day they met.

By day they tended their lands on the outskirts of the keep and by night they sought refuge within the safety of the compound.

Seeing Angus in trouble his wife told her daughter to hide, grabbed a large rolling pin, and ran outside to help her husband. He was already on his feet and facing another attacker. The ruffian walked past the entrance of the doorway to engage him, not noticing Bellamina as she came rushing out. If he had worn a helmet it may have saved him but he had not, and Bellamina knocked him out cold. She smiled at her husband.

A gap in the fog appeared and, whistling while they travelled, two crossbolts hit the couple almost simultaneously, sending them both to the ground. The bolts penetrated deeply and brought their resistance to an abrupt end. They reached out for each other and held hands tightly in that fleeting moment before death. As Bellamina closed her eyes for the very last time and her rosy complexion faded, on her face was the faintest smile. Angus's face was filled with anger.

Immune to its effect, Kallen walked out of the fog. Dark elves were spell casters and longbows were cumbersome, so crossbows were their preferred weapon. He observed the bodies with only a moment's glance, just as Angus drew his last breath.

'Dead. I never miss,' he thought, stepping over the bodies and through the doorway into the cottage. Making a brief search he stuffed anything valuable into a large, brown, cotton bag. He paused for a moment as a scent entered his nostrils. He followed the scent to its source.

'Yuk,' he said as he opened the door to the pantry. Dairy products were of no interest unless it was stale milk. Kallen's favourite dish was a plate of roasted grass snakes with toadstools, boiled until it was soft and chewy. His belly would always rumble at the mere thought of the meal.

Pippa was trembling, hidden from view inside a cupboard in the pantry. Through a tiny gap between the cupboards doors she could see a man who looked more like a monster from her dreams. Suddenly, he closed the pantry door and was gone.

She breathed a sigh of relief and closed her eyes. Abruptly, the pantry door swung open again, followed by the cupboard doors. Pippa looked up at the dark elf and felt completely petrified.

'Now, now, my pretty, no harm will come to thee,' was all Pippa heard; she closed her eyes as she was shrouded within his robe. On leaving the cottage Kallen kneeled beside Angus with Pippa under his arm, and told her to remove the handsome gold and ruby ring worn by her father. She was unable to fight the flow of tears running freely down both cheeks as she looked at her dead parents. She separated the band from her father's middle finger, which was still warm, and handed it to Kallen.

'One day I'll get that back,' she thought, as the dark elf tightened his grip around the ring. With the virgin firmly in his grip the Dökkalfar walked towards his horse.

In the main square, at the combined butcher's and pastry store, Lillian, the baker's wife, was putting up a good fight. She had been one of the first to realize what was happening. From the store's windows there was normally a clear view of the watch-tower and the main gate of Irons Keep. Even with the fog obscuring her view, she heard the sentry hitting the ground when he was thrown from the lookout tower. She had left her premises to aid the sentry and before she knew it she was under attack.

Fighting valiantly with a slim, long baker's knife, she was nearly felled by a slash from a cutlass along her thigh, which slowed her momentum momentarily, but her large, plump frame was hard to stop. Swarmed by three attackers she lashed out, catching one of the brutes flush on the cheek with her blade. An opening appeared, immediately followed by the flow of gushing blood. Suddenly, Lillian was hit in the stomach with a crossbolt and then another, her white baker's outfit turning crimson as the blood poured from her wounds. Still determined to take one of her attackers with her, she reached out and grabbed hold of one by his helmet, dragging him down while she fell. She plunged her knife into his neck, burying it just below the helmet's chin strap. As she died, Lillian was satisfied that she had taken one of the brutes with her to the afterlife.

Kallen saw a red star shooting towards the sky and immediately knew what it was. He grabbed the horn at his waist and blew it to end the onslaught. The quickness of the act and the swiftness with which it brought a conclusion to the chaos was remarkable; almost instantly his men fell into line and within a matter of moments he and his men were clear of the keep and on the trail of the wizard.

Three men dead and only nine left: maybe the attack hadn't been such a good idea after all; he was far from home and he needed these brutes to complete his task. Looking at his saddlebags, which were full to the brim with stolen items and trinkets, he removed a little black pouch from a concealed pocket within his robe and put the ruby ring inside. He felt that his loot was more than adequate compensation for the men he had lost, and sacrificing the virgin would enhance his dark powers for a short while. Once he was in range of the wizard, she would become very useful. Digging his steel spurs into the side of his horse, causing the animal to squeal in pain, Kallen signalled his men and they followed him into the Black Forest.

*

Gunn-Hilda was hard at work mopping the floor with soapy water while humming to herself.
    'There. Spick and span,' she murmured. She loved Nikomeades dearly but he was such an untidy wizard. She smiled while picturing one of his more colourful moments, such as his attempts to wash the dishes. The dinner was almost ready and she wanted her palace neat and tidy before she served up her feast. Gunn-Hilda was a large, middle-aged lady with a sweet nature. She was always cheerful and although her beauty was fading, it still held its lovely rustic charm. Her long, blonde locks, tucked neatly away in a bun at the back of her head, were complemented by a fair complexion which, when she smiled, revealed two lovely dimples on her cheeks.

She had lived with Nikomeades near the edge of the Black Forest for as long as she could remember. In troubled times he had saved her life and brought her to his mountain retreat, an old farmhouse which had the ambience of a castle within. A small, crude banquet table and a large inglenook fireplace in the main hall were the focal points of an otherwise sparse room. Their home had a cosy feel, especially when the log fire flickered on long winter nights. She loved those evenings the most; just watching the flames after a mouth-watering meal.

The back of the retreat was built into the mountain rock. It had been designed this way to hide the entrance to a tower which had been used as an observatory for mapping the stars in ancient times. The edifice inside the mountain's rocky terrain had been created by the Dvergar, whose craftsmanship was legendary. At its top was a clear view of the sky. The structure was impossible to see from a distance; it just looked like part of the mountain's peak.

Black Forest Summit was about half a mile above sea level and could not be seen from the ground level up, mainly due to the wide and expansive elm treetops. The top of the mountain led to a cliff face with a sheer drop into the sea. A remote hideaway, some distance off a beaten track, was situated on one of the many plateaux that littered the mountain-side, overlooking a vast field of trees.

'Where is he?' Gunn-Hilda asked herself, although in her heart she knew exactly where he was. 'Up that bloody tower again.' She shouted is name, but heard no response.

'Nikomeades,' she shouted again, 'dinner's ready!'

A smile came to her lips; it was the night of the full eclipse and so she had prepared a delicious banquet for them both. She was never one for stargazing: the patience for it eluded her. Burying her head in a recipe book, however, was seventh heaven, and the culinary treats she created were true delights. She loved to cook, and any excuse would do.

Nikomeades was at the top of the tower, gripped by events: ribbons of entangled colours untangling themselves in the heavens. It was a light show like no other. A totality of the moon during the winter solstice on a leap year only happened once a millennium and was a stunning visual display in the night sky, both before and after the actual total eclipse. Suddenly he fell off his stool and his telescope slipped from his grip. A red star had just shot past the periphery of his lens.

The surprisingly bright light had flustered his composure. He wondered if it could really be what he thought he had seen. It had been years since he had last seen one, and questions raced through his mind as he replaced his stool and reclaimed his position. Only the Aafari priestesses contacted him in this way. He placed his telescope over his right eye and refocused on the flare; a red star always meant impending danger and he needed to know how much time he had left before it arrived at his doorstep.

He had lived life as a virtual recluse since the end of the war, which was the same time his king had died. He could hear Gunn-Hilda somewhere in the back of his mind calling him for dinner, but right now there were more pressing matters. Someone was coming and he needed to be ready. Time to dust off those old tricks. Nikomeades didn't need long to read the information contained within the flare because part of the message was incoherent. For this reason he felt sure a priestess had not released it unless under duress, as a ruse or a warning.

There had been a bounty on his head for a very long time and he knew one day someone would come knocking to test his skills for such a large reward, but that did not easily explain away the use of a red star. Quickly checking his instruments, he plotted the latitude and longitude over a large map of Ebenknesha and pinpointed the position of the flare. The location did not surprise him: the Black Forest. His face hardened and an unyielding look replaced a wry smile.

He realized that time was short. His tummy made a rumbling noise. Gingerly, he gave it a rub.

'What's wrong, dear friend?' he whispered. He always followed his gut instinct and firmly believed it was the reason why he was still alive.

The aroma of his dinner wafted through the cracks, teasing his taste buds. He got up off his stool. Only a fool entertained thoughts of this magnitude on an empty stomach. Brain food, as he called it, was a necessity at his age. The years were rapidly catching up with the old mage. It was some consolation, though, that as he got older he also seemed to get wiser. He opened the wooden circular hatch in the centre of the stone floor, shedding light on a staircase leading to ground level, and placed his foot on its step.

'Who sent this message,' he wondered, 'friend, or foe?' Undecided, he whispered a spell to descend.

*

As he left the cover of the trees, Tartarus wondered if the wizard had received his message. However, once clear of the forest's shadow Flint noticed thick smoke floating in the night sky. As though in unison, they saw the horror of a keep in flames.

Flint gave his horse a kick and galloped off in the direction of the compound. The others followed, riding in hot pursuit, aware that danger may still be lurking within. He jumped off his horse in front of the main entrance and ran to the two guards slumped against the outer fence. He quickly checked their necks for a pulse, then looked at Tarquin and shook his head.

Tarquin drew his sword and rode into the keep. Instantaneously he was surrounded by utter carnage. The bodies of acquaintances lay plainly in view. Flames and black smog billowed from buildings. Survivors attempted to put out the fires. An orderly queue to the well had been formed. Buckets went up and down the queue and were passed to and fro as water was frantically splashed onto the flames.

Tarquin's thoughts turned to his loved ones. He prayed to Elohim that his family were safe as he galloped home. Tartarus, on the other hand, did not know what to make of the chaotic scene and seemed to be in a daze. Now he understood why his people rarely travelled to the world of men; its madness was overwhelming. Instead of following Tarquin he went to help the villagers extinguish the blaze. He put out some of the minor fires with a primitive water spell which, to his annoyance, sometimes missed its mark.

Flint returned to the saddle on realizing the guards were beyond help, and rode hard towards home. His thoughts were on his dimple-faced sister. Being a year younger than Tarquin meant that Flint was given the chore of looking after Pippa more so than his older sibling. Pippa had spent most of her young life in his company and was a real tomboy, to which her little jack-knife was testament. Her sweet smile gave the impression that butter wouldn't melt in her mouth but, having grown up with two rough boys, she was shrewder than other girls her age.

Tarquin nearly fell from his horse when he saw the sickening sight of his dead parents, their hands still clasped together, on the muddy ground just outside their cottage. Anguish overcame him and he dropped to his knees, sobbing. In no time at all Flint was placing a firm hand on his brother's shoulder, tears streaming down his face.

'Where's Pippa?' he said, with anger etched on his wet face. Without waiting for a reply he ran inside the cottage. When he returned to the doorway Tarquin saw in his brother's face that there was more bad news.

'Gone. She's gone,' Flint whispered, deflated.

'What do you mean, gone?' asked Tarquin. 'If she's dead, I want to see her body. Where is she?'

'No, Quin, they've taken her,' replied Flint.

'Who's taken her?' asked Tarquin, immediately realizing the stupidity of his question.

'How would I know?' answered Flint, distraught.

'Calm down, you know what Pippa is like,' said Tarquin, his eyes filling up. 'Our sister is more cunning than a fox. She's probably just hiding, waiting for the all-clear.'

'Well, I'm not waiting. I think we should ride back to the main square. Maybe someone has seen her,' suggested Flint, as he removed a couple of blankets from Rainbow to cover his parents. In that brief silence, the faintest breathing could be heard.

'Hang on, I think this one's alive,' Flint said, looking at the attacker who had been knocked out by Bellamina's rolling pin.

'Tie him up and we'll hand him over to the villagers. It looks like he's just unconscious.' Tarquin knew their justice would be swift. Flint bound the man's wrists and ankles quickly, eager to begin the search for Pippa.
They lifted the man and laid him across Rainbow's hind quarters.

'Those knots look tight enough, Flint. Now, let's find Pip. We'll make peace with them later,' observed Tarquin, looking at Flint, then at the blankets now covering his parents.

'You sure he won't escape?' asked Flint, raising a quizzical eyebrow as he lifted the attacker's head by his hair and looked square into the man's murderous, hideous face.

'I'm sure,' answered Tarquin.

Flint tied the horse's reins to a metal post near the cottage's outer fence. Satisfied, they mounted their horses and went to find their sister and the elf. The main square was an open space that centred on a large well. Tartarus was busy helping the villagers put out the fires when he noticed a woman, covered in blood, concealed under a dead attacker.

'Who's that?' he asked a woman, covered in soot, who was standing next to him. 'She doesn't look like a bandit,' he added.

'That's the baker's wife, Lillian. Poor thing, she fought bravely,' replied the villager.

'She's not dead. Elves have a trained eye, sensitive to the slightest change in vibrations,' observed Tartarus proudly. The woman gave him a blank look, completely baffled by his statement.

Proving a point, he marched over to Lillian, slowly rolled the man off her, then checked her neck for a pulse. The rhythm was faint. He looked down at the crossbolts. Stomach wounds would normally provide their victim with a slow, agonizing death. Lillian had only passed out from the excruciating pain. When the attacker had fallen on her he had probably saved her life; his weight would have pushed the crossbolts deeper into the wounds. If he acted swiftly she could still be saved. He got up to fetch help. He didn't see or feel the shadow covering him. Suddenly, he was rocked by a tremendous punch that knocked him off his feet. Once again, through no fault of his own, Tartarus Leadbottom was rendered unconscious.

*

'What the hell was that?' enquired Brun, looking at a red star that had just appeared on the horizon of the Black Forest.

'A warning flare! Isn't that Irons Keep in the distance?' asked Ragnarr. Unexpectedly, the landscape lit up like a lantern. The flare continued climbing and a constellation of stars started their final cosmic dance before the full eclipse. Both could clearly see the stronghold far off in the distance.

'It's on fire,' exclaimed Brun, aghast. There was half a league between them and the keep and, from that moment on, Brun rode as though Cloud had wings. Ragnarr lagged behind slightly, bouncing in his saddle as he tried to keep up, while remaining in control of his steed. Their horses were exhausted by the time they reached the keep and their moans of displeasure persisted until a tug on their reins signalled that the gallop was over.

The dead sentries outside the entrance gave them serious concerns and both feared the worst. Cautiously, they entered the keep. Brun thought his eyes were deceiving him as they locked onto his sister lying dead on the ground, and the elf he'd seen a day or so before standing over her corpse. Well, he wasn't going to let Ragnarr stop him this time. He jumped off Cloud, enraged, and in the blink of an eye he was bearing down on the elf, hitting him so hard across his jaw that Tartarus's feet left the ground. Before he could strike another blow he was accosted by a charcoal-faced woman.

'You've knocked him out, you brute,' she scolded.

'Lillian.' Brun blurted out his sister's name.

'He was just checking to see if she was alive.'

The word 'alive' rang in Brun's head and diminished his appetite for the elf's blood. Looking to see if his sister was still alive, his anger changed to delight when he discovered that the elf had, indeed, been correct.

Tarquin and Flint rode up on their horses.

'You there. What happen to him?' Tarquin asked Brun, while pointing at Tartarus, who now lay in the mud beside Lillian.

'I thought he'd just killed my sister, but I think he may have just saved her life. Give us a hand, boys. We need to get them out of the cold.'

'Our homestead is unscathed. We can take them there,' suggested Tarquin.

Ragnarr walked up to Flint, who was still inconsolable, and tapped him on his legs.

'What troubles you, friend?' he asked.

'We can't find our sister,' replied a dejected Flint.

'They took her with them. I saw her with a really ugly elf, or maybe it was a goblin,' said the sooty-faced, pig-tailed brunette, who was now helping with Lillian's care.

'Pale pastel-green and blank milky-blue pupils?' asked Ragnarr, describing a Dökkalfar. She nodded.

'Are you sure, Myrtle?' asked Flint. She nodded again.

'He shot Lillian, of course. I'm sure of it,' said the middle-aged widow.

'Our parents were killed with crossbolts. Let me have a look at those bolts,' responded Tarquin, peering over.

'There's plenty of time for that later, lad,' said Brun.

'Sounds like a dark elf to me,' said Ragnarr.

'What does that mean?' asked Tarquin.

'It means that your sister is in grave danger, son, and at first light we had better give chase.' Ragnarr wasn't about to tell the boys that Dökkalfar sacrificed young virgins; he knew this information would cause them great distress.

'First light? We should give chase now! No one knows the forest better than us,' Flint declared.

'Our quarry is a dangerous breed and we'll need many men to save your sister,' the dwarf replied, with a grunt.

'Then first light it is. Anyway, we need to tend to the wounded,' Brun announced, taking charge.

Although Tarquin was in agreement, he didn't understand Ragnarr's agitation; after all, it wasn't his sister who was missing. Tarquin took a dislike to this character, displeased with his lack of compassion. Brun, noticing the change in the boy's facial features, walked up to Tarquin and whispered to him.

'Don't worry, lad. He's like that with everyone. He doesn't mean any harm by it. I think it's old age,' he said, with a wink. With the aid of a few other survivors they placed Lillian and Tartarus on stretchers.

Tarquin informed the group that they had captured an attacker who was bound, gagged and lying across their horse. This helped lighten the mood as they made their way to his father's cottage. The winter solstice, the shortest day in Ebenknesha, occurred at the end of the year. Stellar eclipses were less predictable, occurring when the planet casts its shadow upon the moon as it passes between it and the sun.

The effort to put out the fires and tend to the injured meant that everyone was caught unawares by the full eclipse. The keep and the surrounding areas were plunged into darkness by a blackened sky and, as if by magic, all the remaining fires within the stronghold were extinguished. A stillness fell over the land, and an invisible breath of pure fresh air refreshed as it passed by. Elohim's kingdom was being cleansed; the planet's rebirth had begun its final cycle.

The totality of the shrouded moon lasted only a little longer than one can hold a breath before, gradually, the celestial symbol reappeared. As the shadow passed, a purple shimmering glow changed into a luminescent light that clashed with the shine of a bright, blue moon. The light flickered across the western plains, covering the landscape in unusual reddish silhouettes. Not all eclipses occurred at night but the ones that did were truly breathtaking. The leap year and glittery effect of a full moon, combined with a total eclipse during the winter solstice, only occurred in Ebenknesha every thousand years. Apart from Myrtle, none of the inhabitants of Irons Keep had any knowledge of its true significance.

Flint's face softened briefly, his distress taken away by the solace contained within its beauty, and along with the others he was left speechless by the spectacle.

*

When Tartarus next awoke he was lying in a nice warm bed. Brun was standing over him with a sombre look on his face.

'I'm very sorry. If it hadn't been for your quick thinking my sister would be dead now. By the way, my name is Brun.' Tartarus nearly jumped out of bed.

'Is she alive?' he asked, and immediately fell back on the bed in a dizzy spell.

'Steady on, friend. I pack a mean punch,' Brun said sympathetically, passing the elf a hot herbal tea. The room was a small, simple room with a bed, bedside cabinet, table and chair. Looking through the window, Brun explained that when he had entered the keep the first thing he had seen was Tartarus standing over his sister's body. 'At that point the red mist descended, lad, and my mind was bent on revenge.' Tartarus opened his eyes widely.

'The scroll,' he said, as he sat up sharply, reaching out an arm to Brun to steady himself.

'Gather your strength, young elf. The boys have already told us about your plight and after an attack on defenceless women and children, there's more than a few who will aid your cause.' He paused to watch Tartarus take a sip of the brew. 'So does it taste better than burned-barrel ale?' he asked, chuckling. 'Ragnarr says that stuff can put hairs on a maid's chest but it's great for a sore head, so I'm told.'

Tartarus cracked a tight smile.

'Myrtle said she saw a man with a patched eye, wearing a frilled white tunic. Does that ring a bell? I'm sure you left the tavern with him?'

'Bowen,' replied Tartarus between gritted teeth.

'Well, now our quarry has a name. Now drink up, lad. There's work to be done.' Brun looked down and tapped the battleaxe at his side.

The elf polished off the liquid and handed the drinking bowl to Brun, who poured more hot tea. With a knock on the door Flint popped his head through the partly open gap.

'Is he up yet?' he asked, with a smile directed at Tartarus. 'Are you enjoying my bed?'

'Are you sure it's not mine?' replied Tartarus jovially, with the drinking bowl at the base of his lip.

'I'm sure, so don't get too comfortable,' Flint said, grinning. 'Ain't he told you yet? We've caught one of them and the villagers want to hang him, but the dwarf ...'

'The dwarf? What dwarf? And who undressed me?' Tartarus gave the blacksmith a quizzical look as he held out his clothes.

'That was Myrtle you were talking to,' said Flint. 'I think she's taken a liking to you,' he added with a smirk. Tartarus just rolled his eyes.

'I forgot that you haven't met Ragnarr yet. Well, once he heard about the scroll he suggested we question the brigand first. We were waiting for you,' continued Flint.

'Well, I still feel a little groggy but we've wasted enough time already,' Tartarus said as he got out of bed. Brun filled in the missing blanks about Lillian's care.

'My companion, Ragnarr, knows a trick or two with that kind of injury,' he said.

'So do I,' Tartarus responded, shaking his head then looking at Brun. 'I know a spell that will seal those wounds and aid her recovery. Where is she?'

'She's in the guest room,' answered Flint.

'Take me to her before we speak to this thief,' said Tartarus.

Once Tartarus was fully dressed, he and Brun followed Flint to the guest room. The guest quarters were slightly more spacious in size than the room Tartarus had slept in. On entering the room a lady, who introduced herself as Edith, the butcher's wife, was in the process of keeping Lillian's forehead moist and cool with a damp cloth.

'She's a strong girl, your sister,' she said to Brun with an encouraging smile. 'And you, young man,' she said, looking at Tartarus, 'I heard about your heroics.'

'You're most kind,' replied Tartarus. Walking up alongside her, he looked at Lillian, lying still in the bed, and held her hand for a moment while whispering words into her ear.

'This spell may cause her some discomfort,' he said, 'but trust me, it's worth it.' Gently lifting the blanket so that her abdomen could be seen, he removed the dressing and revealed a large leaf with herbs, nuts and berries contained within its fold. He handed the item to Brun. All eyes turned to the two slits, still weeping blood.

'Stand back,' Tartarus said as he placed his palm directly over her wounds. In the elven language he muttered the words, *'solvo vestri mens vacuus poena, plantois res universus iterum,'* repeatedly under his breath, until his pupils turned a milky blue and a radiant light glowed beneath his palm.

The smell of singed flesh filled the room as magic wove the frayed flesh together, leaving two minute scars. The glow dissipated and Tartarus raised his hand.

'All done,' he said with a smile. The butcher's wife stood transfixed in awe.

'Are you a mage?' she asked.

'He's an Alfari warrior,' replied Flint proudly.

'But what about her thigh?' she questioned.

'We cannot waste magic. Those wounds were fatal. That one is not,' Tartarus replied courteously. Once outside the room Flint told Tartarus of his parents' fate and about his sister's disappearance.

'A dark elf,' Tartarus thought to himself. Suddenly, it all made sense. The Dökkalfar and the Aafari were sworn enemies, so the ambush had been a ruse to steal the scroll.

'Dark elves are depraved beings. We must leave at once,' Tartarus informed the others, in no mood to be argued with.

'But what about the brigand?' enquired Brun.

'We'll bring him with us.'

'Feelings are running high, lad. Somehow, I don't think ...' Brun shook his head. 'No, not even if you offered them all the ale in Ebenknesha. Those villagers would still want his blood.'

'He's right, you know. They won't stand for it,' agreed Flint.

'We'll see,' Tartarus said, confidently. He was a hero now, and heroic deeds were usually paid in kind.

They walked through the main living quarters, out the back of the cottage and down a garden path that led to a weatherbeaten shed. Inside a brigand lay on the shack's cold floor, in front of Ragnarr and Tarquin, with his wrists and ankles still bound. Flint acknowledged his own handiwork.

'At last,' exclaimed Ragnarr, rubbing his thumb against his index finger, which was an indication of his eagerness to begin the interrogation.

'We're taking him with us,' declared Flint.

'We're what?' barked Ragnarr.

'So I take it you've not told them what the Dökkalfar do to virgins?' asked Tartarus. Everyone looked at the dwarf, who just shrugged his shoulders, unrepentant.

'She's probably dead already,' he said, 'and so our task is simple. We must find out as much information as possible about our quarry. Dark elves don't travel this far west for nothing.' Then he gave the brigand a kick. The loud thud reverberated in the overcrowded shed.

'I think we would all like to know the truth, Ragnarr Morbere,' demanded Brun sternly.

'Very well,' the dwarf said reluctantly. 'They sacrifice virgins to make their dark magic stronger but I, for one, will not let this act go unavenged.' He banged his chest loudly. 'And he's got the answers we seek.' He pointed a finger at Kallen's man, gagged on the floor.

Tarquin did not doubt the dwarf's intentions but if there was even the remotest chance that Pippa was still alive then that chance would have to be taken and that was enough to kick him into action. He gave Flint a nod and together they lifted their captive off the floor. Flint cut the bond from the man's ankles. As they left the barn Tartarus took a quick glance at the dwarf. The scroll was of the utmost importance and the question of whether this dwarf could be trusted preyed on his mind.

*

Outside in the main square dawn had just broken. Many of the villagers who had returned early from the ruins and the celebrations were busy in deep and heated conversation. A wiry figure, Nefanial Bartholomew, was absolutely livid. Ruffians attacking the keep on such a sacred day was blasphemy and, along with the sacrilege, the fact that his wife may never bear children required swift justice. Even the little things like having the words 'Bartholomew &Sons' on the front of his bakery store were now in question. Most of the villagers were of the same ilk. The only problem was that Nefanial wanted to go much further. If Baron Brandon of Brandenburg could not protect them then his head should roll too.

Brandenburg was one of the three barons who ruled the lands of the west, in Prince Edwin's name. Along with Baron Crofton Abbehale of Glen-Neath and Baron Syracuse Bargelmir of Daginhale, the Baron Brandon of Brandenburg controlled all of Abbehale and a large part of Ebenknesha. The village chief, an old war veteran named Gwillym, was not impressed with the prospect of going to war. The west had fared poorly in its last encounter with the south and there was no natural leader to rally behind. The Earl of Abbehale, now a baron, was a true descendent of the western realm. A cruel twist of fortune had banished the earl from his lands. The former earl, a turncoat, having sided with the Autocrat against his king, was outwitted by a love potion and duped into believing he was in love with the king's beautiful wife, Desiree, a subtropical beauty from the land of Ganesha. He was convinced that only the removal of his king would allow his love to bloom, and his appalling treachery had turned the battle in the Autocrat's favour at the decisive moment.

Led to believe his action would secure his lands, and her affection, it was a shock for him to find, when the potion's effects wore off, that she was dead, that he'd been stripped of his title and then ordered to govern the western border between Ebenknesha and the Badlands. His castle was the first line of defence against Keltic tribes that had never been conquered.

The earl had died from a broken heart, knowing he had caused the deaths of his king and queen and great sorrow to his people. Now his son, Baron Crofton Abbehale of Glen-Neath, had signed a pact and it was common knowledge he did not want or care for it. A role that entailed being the southern kingdom's lap dog was repugnant and his father's awful transgression was a heavy burden to bear. To betray your king was the worst crime imaginable to a royalist. Beneath his family's crest and coat of arms, the motto read:

> *Pro Rex rgis quod Terra nos operor nostrum officium men of Abbehale.*
> *Stabilis ut nostrum causa nostrum terra mos nunquam cado.*
> *Intus Elohim bona nostrum brevis nostrum Rex rgis mos rudo.*

Translated, it meant:

> For king and country we do our duty, the men of Abbehale.
> Steadfastly loyal to our cause, our lands will never fall.
> With Elohim's blessings on our shores, our king will roar.

The motto was irrevocably tainted, the words now empty and hollow. It was believed the new baron wanted to restore the honour of his family's crest and reputation. However, Crofton's army was not big enough to take on the Black Knight's horde, let alone the barons of the western lands.

Gwillym, deep in thought, decided that even with Crofton's help their plan was still full of holes.

'Nefanial, we've got no proof that Brandenburg had a hand in this incident. Let's just pursue and capture the culprits. War is very messy. Why bring it on ourselves?' said Gwillym. Nefanial, ever the alarmist, was stirring up the crowd and in a defiant mood.

'War is messy, but so is having women and children slaughtered and that greedy pig Brandenburg is always up to no good. I'm sure he's mixed up in all this,' he replied, raising a cheer from the crowd.

'All I'm saying is that if the baron is not involved then lives could be lost for nothing.'

'Lives have already been lost. Look around you. We're about to light the funeral pyres,' Nefanial retorted. The arrival of Tartarus and the brigand brought an abrupt end to the conversation, as villagers with menacing eyes turned on the prisoner.

'The hero,' said Nefanial, going to shake Tartarus's hand. 'How can I ever repay you? You saved my wife's life.'

'I need men to pursue these brigands.' They all looked at the brute in Tarquin's custody.

'So many wanted to travel, we've had to draw lots. We all want a piece of them,' replied Nefanial.

'And I'll need a horse for him,' said Tartarus, pointing at his prisoner. The crowd was in uproar and Tartarus went from hero to zero. Gwillym was the first to put forward his objection.

'Listen, son. Unless there's been a vote I'm still in charge of this keep's affairs.'

'Let the boy speak, Gwill,' Nefanial said, willing to listen.

'We need to leave now if we have any chance of saving Pippa,' said Tartarus.

'Well, you go but he's staying put,' replied Gwillym sharply.

'I have a solution,' said Nefanial. 'You there, tell us what you know and we'll set you free.'

For a moment the brigand, with numerous scars adorning his face, remained silent, but then the prospect of freedom loosened his tongue.

'There's nothing much to tell. Kallen said we needed some supplies to hunt down some wizard. At first I thought we were following the orders of some prince or king. We were told to take a scroll from him,' he said, pointing at Tartarus. 'But that's all I know. Kallen only really talks to Patch.'

'Bowen?' asked Tartarus. The dishevelled man nodded.

'Who's Kallen?' asked Tarquin.

'An elf,' answered the brigand. Tartarus slapped him square across the cheek.

'A Dökkalfar,' hissed Tartarus, his face screwed up in anger. Brun was slightly puzzled. He was sure he had come across the name Kallen, or perhaps Kellen. He wasn't sure, but then it dawned on him: the note carried by the royal rider. Hurriedly, he searched his saddle bag for the pouch that contained the letter.

'You're sure there's nothing more you can tell us?' Nefanial asked, pressing the prisoner.

'No, that's it,' was his reply.

'Well, that's that then, Gwillym!' he shouted. The large war veteran made his way through the crowd.

'But you said I'd be freed?' said the captive. Nefanial gave the man a blank look.

'Yes, to not kill again. Now take him,' commanded Gwillym.
With that the prisoner was removed from Tarquin's custody and before long was swinging from a gallows in front of the

stronghold. A hearty cheer arose, a signal of the villagers' fortitude.

Brun had found Kallen's message and handed it to his brother-in-law, who read the message aloud: 'Kallen, how goes your procurement of the scroll? Our pact proceeds as planned. I will attack the Forest of Oaken-Dale in a matter of weeks.'
There were gasps from the crowd once it was confirmed that the attack was connected to Brandenburg.

'This is all the proof we need,' proclaimed Nefanial, holding the note aloft. 'Do you see it? Prince Edwin's mark below the script,' he added, handing the note to Gwillym.

'Hey, I'm from the Forest of Oaken-Dale,' Tartarus said, shocked by what he'd heard.

'Well, I've had it awhile now lad,' Brun replied sadly. The amount of time he had kept the item in his possession meant there was no course of action that could possibly have prevented the attack. He placed a big arm over the young elf's shoulders. As all saw Tartarus lower his head, it struck Nefanial that Gwillym was right: war is, indeed, messy. The evidence was indisputable. The mercenaries were part of the prince's private army and this newly acquired knowledge implicated Brandenburg. Myrtle's ruddy face glowed as she gave Tartarus a wink before voicing her opinion. He returned her wink with a pleasant, tight-lipped smile, although his heart belonged to another. A blue-eyed elfette occupied his thoughts; after what he'd just heard he feared for her safety.

'Gwill, are you going to stand for this? I almost died,' said Myrtle. She put her hands on her waist and her chest expanded as she took a deep breath. 'You're a lot of things, Gwillym, but I never thought you were a coward.' Her statement was vocally acknowledged by some of the crowd.

Gwillym, not amused by the lack of confidence in his abilities and having made up his mind, cleared his throat and spoke in a loud voice.

'This meeting is over. I'll ride to Brimstone Keep and arrange a meeting with the other keep leaders. The leaders must speak with one voice if our ideals are to be reached, but first we'll light the pyres.' Then Gwillym handed the royal rider's note to Brun.

'Guard this well. It may yet save your life.' Brun nodded and tucked it away.

The dead had been laid out on separate funeral pyres ready for their ceremonial cremation. Gwillym said a few words on behalf of the fallen and then he told the crowd to stand well back before he lit the base of each pyre, one after another, as a light drum roll followed his steps. Nefanial had recruited seven men to accompany Tartarus, Ragnarr, Brun, Tarquin and Flint on the quest to save Pippa and reclaim the scroll. He lined the men up and introduced them to Tartarus and Ragnarr.

'This is Rex, Calhoun, Barnaby, Daniel, Sidney, or Sid for short, and Randolph. Him on the end, that's Reece.' The men duly nodded. Tarquin and Flint waited around long enough to pay their last respects, deciding not to speak on their parents' behalf; that luxury would come when the dark elf was dead. They rode on before the flames consumed their parents.

Flanked by a couple of well-armed men, the village chief left the square. Tartarus and twelve men rode away from the keep. A few villagers came to see them off. Some thought thirteen to be an unlucky number. However, Myrtle did not share those superstitious views and, handkerchief in hand, she waved them off. It wasn't time, yet, to reveal her true identity for the action of one the prophecies had only just begun. She took one last look as they disappeared under the cover of the woods and wondered how many of them would return. Elohim's salvation was in their hands.

Act Two

The Quest for the Gold-rimmed Scroll

Although Pippa's tears were real, she was not as timid as she would have her captors believe. The 'innocent little girl' act was essential. Riding on the back of Kallen's horse had been an extremely uncomfortable experience and one made even more unbearable by what she had witnessed. So Pippa was happy when they stopped to make camp. She knew that the further they rode from Irons Keep the harder it would be for her brothers to find her, if they were even alive.

Flint was supposed to have taken her to the Ruin's festival. Her brother was the worst at timekeeping, but she trusted her instincts and intuition that they were both still safe. Suddenly, a fresh tear ran down her cheek; she loved the boys but her parents had been her entire world. Her captors believed the forest had scared the little girl and they took immense pleasure from the idea. After countless forays and sorties into the forest with her brothers, her fear for the domain had long since departed and she was much more accustomed to the surroundings than her actions implied. The performance had achieved its purpose. She was now slumped against a large elm tree, her bonds only loosely fastened, and she had not been searched. Pippa was just inching to remove her jack-knife from a concealed compartment in the top part of her boot.

The goat-leather boots, below calf-height, were stuffed with straw, mainly to protect the sole from rugged terrain, but also for extra warmth in the winter months. Some children latch onto an item that gives them inner peace and a will to succeed. Pippa was no different. For her, this object was a straw hat that Bellamina had made for her, and with all these strangers in her midst the hat was sorely missed. Woven from grass reeds, full of small holes and its colour fading, the hat was still by far the most treasured item she possessed, and when worn would obscure her curly blonde locks from view.

Pippa's dimpled face was covered with tiny little freckles, all over her nose and across both cheeks, which were the exact same colour as her hazel eyes. She was of average height for a girl of her age and in the company of her peers she was a feisty little madam. Calmly, she waited for the disgusting pigs to go to sleep; since they had made camp the brutes had been drinking and feasting non-stop. Pippa was not planning on sharing her company with these brigands any longer than necessary. Although they were under cover of the forest they all felt the eclipse; the brief darkness followed by the cool, fresh breeze was infectious. Even Kallen's motley crew were in high spirits as they guzzled down looted ale, while one of them played a mouth organ.

Pippa watched as the hooded dark elf approached.
    'Your father, who was he?' he demanded.
    'Just a simple farmer, sir.' Kallen was curious; a simple farmer could never afford a ring of such wealth. Maybe the brat was lying. It was the second time in a matter of days he had come across these same markings, and Kallen did not believe in coincidences. His beliefs lay in the principles of darkness and its eternal battle against the zest of life. Everything happens for a reason and when the signs were read correctly it was extremely beneficial.

'I've been examining your father's ring. Where did he get it from?' he asked.

She looked up at him with wet, red eyes, shook her head and whispered, 'I don't know.'

'This ring,' said Kallen, holding it up, 'shares the same strange markings with another item in my possession.' Pippa saw the plush ruby gleam in the light of the camp-fire.

'I don't know where he got it from. I'm only ten,' she murmured.

'Do you have brothers and sisters?' demanded Kallen. She shook her head. 'No, sir. I do not,' she whispered, her voice barely audible between the fake sobs.

'Don't lie to me child. I feed on lies.' He fixed her with a menacing glare that she found unable to resist.

'I've got two brothers,' she blurted out, then pouted her lips. She wanted to add, 'and when they get here, you're dead', but she remained tight-lipped.

'This little one might need extra vigilance,' Kallen thought, as he held her for a moment longer within his gaze before walking away. Her father may have held vital information about the gold-rimmed scroll; his ruby ring and the scroll shared similar markings. If any of the girl's siblings came looking for her, before their inevitable death, they would be probed and interrogated for the answers Kallen wanted. Her father was definitely a farmer, that much was certain. So how did he come by such a valuable item? It could have easily been through an opportunistic set of circumstances, but maybe by solving this riddle he'd be a little closer to unravelling the secret of the scroll.

Capturing the wizard would not be easy. Nikomeades was well versed in the principles of light and, being one of the last of the enchanted, he had been born with the ability to cast spells from his twelfth birthday. When using sleight of hand the enchanted were deadly. Large spells required intricate hand movements and took longer to propel towards the chosen target, but these astrophysical beings were different. The size of the spell did not matter and their hand speed enabled them to cast spells at an alarming rate. They were vulnerable if overcome with exhaustion, which would only occur when an excessive number of spells were cast without the chance for recuperation. In this state they could be captured, and restrained with the use of a mouth harness that prevented the tongue from casting spells. Thumb cuffs, crude iron contraptions that crossed both thumbs behind the victim's back, were used to restrict hand movement.

In ancient time ropes had been used to bind spell casters in this way, but with time ropes had been proven to be a less effective method than the practice in use today.
For this reason eliminating, rather than capturing, was a far better option because if an enchanted one escaped there were usually ramifications. That reminded Kallen: without sacrificing the girl, capturing the wizard would be an extremely hard task. He did not care for his men, but all the same he had better put a guard on the girl. If she escaped a lot of his men would die, for without the blood sacrifice his dark powers would not have the strength to overwhelm this wizard, and in any case he might still have need of his men. When he was attacking Irons Keep he had seen a red flare, and only the Aafari Priestess or the Alfari warriors use them. Kallen knew it was probably the latter, so the elves he had killed were probably being tracked or maybe shadowed by another group of Alfari. He walked over to Bowen, to have a word about his suspicions.

Bowen and a couple of men were cavorting around the camp-fire; one of the brigands, named Darrel, who was wearing a leather tunic, was pulling funny faces. The other man, named Goreham, was laughing in response. He wore a blood-stained shirt under a long brown waistcoat.

'Patch, tell us again about how you hoodwinked those elves,' requested Darrel. Bowen, retelling the anecdote, made the actual events sound more comical.

'I made those Alfari elves believe I was drunk,' said Bowen, laughing. 'Me, drunk? I used to be a sailor and I drink like a fish! I lost this for cheating at arrows,' he said, smiling and lifting up the patch covering his left eye to reveal a vacant space. It was clearly a badge of honour. 'This is what you get when you can't stop winning.' He turned to face Pippa, who gasped at the sight. When he turned back to face his two companions his demeanour had changed. A look of disgust had replaced a face full of merriment and the laughter stopped abruptly.

'Now,' said Bowen, 'why don't you tell us all why Lord Kallen had to kill a middle-age wench, on your behalf? She only had a cutting knife. Can't you two handle your women?' Without waiting for an answer he continued, 'You two don't know your armpit from your elbow.' Goreham pointed to his armpit and said, 'This is my armpit. 'As his fingers touched his armpit he looked like he was impersonating a monkey.

'I rest my case,' said Bowen, smirking.

'Are you mocking us?' asked Darrel, unclipping the top button of his leather tunic.

'Why do you ask?' said Bowen, his face hardening.

'Just answer the question and you'll find out soon enough. We mercenaries are lovers of women and killers of men, 'Darrel replied through gritted teeth, reaching for his sword.

'Silence,' said Kallen, bringing the confrontation to an end. Immediately voices were hushed throughout the makeshift camp before Kallen cleared his throat and continued: 'Patch, put a guard on that girl and I want a sentry posted. We don't want uninvited guests, now do we? And once you've done that, I want a word.' Bowen dipped his chin, and then looked at the brigands who had been discourteous to him moments ago. Glum, ominous looks covered both their faces as Bowen barked out Kallen's orders, pointing at each one in turn.

'You two, you're on sentry duty and you're on girl duty,' shouted Bowen. The men responded with grunts and moans as Bowen walked off. They looked at each other.

'Now why did you have to go and upset him?' asked Goreham.

'So you think I planned that we be put on watch? Do me a favour and lay off the ale. I don't know what type of mercenary you are, but I'm not going to let a one-eyed man push me around,' replied Darrel as soon as Bowen was out of earshot.

Kallen spoke to Bowen about the ring, the flare and the little girl's brothers.

'I want them taken alive if they're stupid enough to cross our path,' he informed Bowen. Then the dark elf made his excuses. Using magic was tiring. The fog-based apparition was not a complicated spell but maintaining it took mental fortitude and a brief period of rest was needed. He made his way to a section of the camp away from the fire and sought a damp location in which to sleep. The drinking and frolicking continued for a few hours more. It was nearer dawn than night when the last man tumbled to the ground, shattered from alcohol-fuelled antics.

A once-fierce camp-fire was approaching extinction; its bright gleam had dimmed as its logs turned to ash and flames smouldered. Pippa had kept a watchful eye on the whole scene. Darrel, having been assigned to guard her, had locked her in his gaze.

His beady eyes and greasy skin were as unnerving as his gaze. Luckily, he too was eventually taken by tiredness and with everyone in the camp fast asleep the opportunity she had been waiting for had arrived. Without a moment's hesitation she removed her knife from her boot. The jack-knife was in excellent condition and the hairline crack running across its wooden handle simply gave it character. The folded weapon revealed a sharply pointed blade when opened.

Pippa's hands were bound and freeing the blade was difficult. After a couple of flicks had not helped, Pippa used her mouth to release the blade from its handle. Then, putting the handle in her mouth and biting down hard, she rubbed the rope along the blade's sharp edge.

'Stop that.' Pippa froze.

'I saw you,' said Darrel. Pippa looked at the guard, unable to move.

'You're a cheat and a liar,' he continued, but as he spoke saliva dribbled down his cheek, his eyes re-closed and snoring followed. Relieved, Pippa realized he had been talking in his sleep. She quickly cut through the rope around her wrists and ankles, then stood up awkwardly. Once Pippa was sure none of her captors had awoken, she crept around the tree on her tiptoes. Then she lifted her feet and ran as fast as her little legs could carry her.

Kallen awoke to a camp in turmoil. 'Patch!' he shouted. Bowen came running over.

'Yes, my lord?'

'What's all the commotion?' asked Kallen. 'I like peace when I sleep.'

'The girl's gone.'

'What?' Kallen wiped the sleep from his eyes as he got to his feet. His anger was clear for all to see. 'I thought I told you to guard her.'

'I did. I put Darrel on her, and Goreham on sentry duty, and both fell asleep, my lord,' explained an apologetic Bowen.

'Call them over.'

As Darrel and Goreham stood before him, Kallen pondered whether he should kill them. Dereliction of duty was a serious transgression. However, he decided that he couldn't afford to cut his army down in size, especially now the girl had escaped. He gave them each a volley of vicious blows to their faces. Both men, with cut and bruised faces, were ordered from sight. Kallen now knew the names of his first volunteers if he encountered the wizard.

'Should I send them after her?' asked Bowen.

'No, she's probably long gone and time is of the essence. If I don't send word to Prince Edwin soon, he may get worried and send us help: help we don't need,' replied Kallen, giving Bowen a knowing look.

'The Order of the Anarchists?' said Bowen. Kallen nodded. 'Maybe,' he said.

The Order of the Anarchists was a band of ruthless assassins, whose motto was: every action has a reaction; after chaos there is order.

'Ready the horses. We leave at once,' Kallen commanded.

'Yes, my lord,' said Bowen, going about his task.

*

Tartarus and his band of men rode into the Black Forest and immediately a bright morning sky was reduced to a shadowy light as the treetops became the new skyline. Although revenge is always bittersweet, hanging the brigand meant they were all in a buoyant mood when they left the compound.

Ragnarr confessed to the others that even though he was a dwarf, and was supposed to like dark places, the forest gave him the creeps. This brought a half-hearted laugh from the group; everyone knew humans did not inhabit the area of forest they were travelling through to reach the summit.
'Don't worry, I'll protect you, 'said Brun, as a joke.

Nefanial, curious as to what kind of elf his men were being led by, rode up alongside Tartarus.
'Your name,' he said, 'it's very unusual. Where does it originate from?'
'I'm from the land of Ganesha, which borders Tyrus,' responded Tartarus.
'Ah. Tyrus: Tartarus. I get it. Never been there, I'm afraid,' said Nefanial. Without explaining in too much detail Tartarus talked about his homeland and its beauty, its tranquillity, and about the dangers. He explained that he was one part human and spoke about being an Alfari warrior, with all that it entailed.
'So you're not married, I take it?' asked Nefanial.
'No, never.' Tartarus raised an eyebrow.

'Don't worry, it's not a proposal,' said Nefanial, laughing and tapping the gold band on his finger. He liked men who spoke with a free tongue and one look at Tartarus told him that his newfound friend would find a suitable spouse soon enough. Nefanial gave the elf a hearty slap on the back and a warm smile.

'Women love a man fresh from a quest. I should know: I wasn't always a baker with a wife,' Nefanial said with a wink, as he slowed his horse to rejoin the men he had recruited, who were at the back of the line.

Flint and Tarquin rode alongside each other in the convoy.

'So, what do you think we can expect on this quest?' Flint asked his brother.

'All I can really hope for is that we save Pippa,' Tarquin replied sharply.

'Don't worry, we'll save our Pip all right,' said Flint. The thought of a real adventure had been unimaginable a day or so ago.

'So what's changed your mood?' asked Tarquin.

'We would have felt her passing,' said Flint. 'If you don't mind, I'll have an answer to my question, please?'

'What question?' replied Tarquin, fed up with his brother's persistence.

'I'll tell you what I expect on this quest,' said Flint, seemingly oblivious to his brother. 'Wild times, women and songs, with fame and fortune to boot.'

'Listen, Flint, a quest always goes hand in hand with unspeakable danger, so keep your wits about you,' replied Tarquin, with a stern look. A small smile then broke the ice and Flint reciprocated.

They had been riding for a couple of hours when Tartarus heard the sound of barking some way off in the distance, to the left of their position and away from the trail he was following. With a hand signal he brought the men to a halt.

'Can you hear that?' he asked Brun.

'Yes, I can lad, even with one bad ear.' Tartarus did not know how to take his answer. 'A mutt doesn't bark like that for nothing. What do you think, lad?' Brun continued. Ragnarr rode up to the front of the convoy.

'Why are we stopping?' he asked.

'I can hear a dog barking, in that direction,' said Tartarus, pointing to the left of their position.

'Is it in the direction of the Dökkalfar's trail?' Ragnarr asked.

'No.'

'Elves are daft,' Ragnarr responded.

'Well, I've already decided we're going to investigate. I'll leave no stone unturned.'

'What?' asked Ragnarr, gruffly. 'Did I sign up for a sightseeing tour? No, I did not. We need to keep going.'

'Five of us should be enough,' said Tarquin.

'And you can wait with the others; they might need protecting,' added Brun, which brought a little chuckle from the group. Tartarus took charge.

'Nefanial, grab one of your men.'

Nefanial gave Calhoun, his shop assistant, a nod.

'Tarquin, Brun, you're with me. Flint and Ragnarr, wait with the others,' commanded the elf.

Before Flint could voice his disapproval, the five of them galloped off in the direction of the growls. Once they had disappeared in the entanglement of trees and bushes, the dwarf had a change of heart.

'On reflection, I think six is a safer number than five in these parts. You wait here, sonny. I'll be right back.'

'I ain't your sonny,' replied Rex, annoyed.

With a flick of his reins Ragnarr had followed the party into the trees. Some distance from Tartarus's group, in a boggy meadow alongside a brook, a Daginhale terrier was barking wildly at a water nymph. Each attempt by the minthe to gain a foothold on the bank was met by ferocious snaps from the dog. The terrier had almond-shaped eyes and its fleecy hair and tasselled ears resembled those of a lamb. Its coat had a silvery blue sheen. Smart problem-solvers, and unequalled water dogs, the breed's disposition made them good swimmers, and agile enough to make acute turns when they ran at speed.

However, the terrier was not the water nymph's intended victim, for her eyes were fixed on the young girl lying on the bank. The nymph's hypnotic melody and suggestive whispering had already subdued the girl, holding her in a sleepless trance. Unable to move or even scream out, Pippa was completely helpless. Tired and thirsty, she had been enticed by the sound of running water and had gone to investigate. Once at the murky stream's bank she was overwhelmed by a sweet melody that seemed to soothe her troubles away. Comforting images of her parents calling to her filled her mind and before she knew what was happening, it was too late. With the ability to control her muscles gone, she lost her balance and fell to the ground. The nymph, eager to have her prize, had revealed herself, and although Pippa's field of vision was somewhat restricted she could see the minthe's skin change from being shiny and scaly to being just like that of a human as the malevolent creature edged out of the water. She had pale flesh and engaging deep-blue eyes. Her voluptuous body was covered from the neck down with tiny glands.

As the minthe edged ever closer, for the first time in her young life Pippa knew true fear and what it felt like to be caught in a spider's sticky web. The water nymph, or minthe as they were called, looked like mermaids without the tailed legs normally associated with that species, and were usually found in forest pools and waterfalls.

These striking songstresses had beautiful low-pitched voices that echoed and hummed over the water's surface, the unusual tones initiating dream-like states in unsuspecting travellers lured through illusions of riches or loved ones. These mysterious beings then dragged their prey into the water, pulling them down to its murky depths, and as the last breath of air escaped their lungs their soul was purged from the dying body. A nymph's preferred victim was always a child. The young were more susceptible to their will and the essence of the innocent provided more sustenance.

Pippa was thanking her lucky stars; she would have already been in the water if it hadn't been for the terrier, who had defended her stoutly for over an hour. She wondered how long it would be willing to continue protecting her without having a meal. Although the clever dog had stolen sips of water from the stream between stints of defending the bank from the nymph's advances, it could not go without food forever. If help did not come soon Pippa knew she was doomed.

Tartarus was the first to reach the brook, closely followed by the others.

    'A stream witch!' exclaimed Nefanial.

    'Pippa!' shouted Tarquin, initially in joy; but fear soon set in on his seeing the predicament his sister was in.

'Stay well back. I'll deal with this wench,' proclaimed Nefanial, jumping off his horse and running at the creature with sword in hand.

'He's a brave one all right,' commented Tartarus, reaching for his bow.

'Aye, he is,' responded Brun, proud of his brother-in-law.

Nefanial realized pretty quickly that vanquishing the witch would not be as easy as he first thought. After a couple of sweeping strokes from his blade struck nothing but thin air, he turned and said, 'Hey, I may need a hand here.'

Calhoun duly ran to give aid as Brun got off Cloud to enter the fray. The minthe raised her voice and a blast of her full vocal range stunned them all. Tarquin, who was already having difficulty reviving his sister, shouted at the terrier that had now turned on him, snarling and nipping at his heels. Stopped in his tracks by the inviting, intoxicating tones coming from the witch's dark-green lips he turned, only to be frozen by an illusion. A vision of such beauty he had never seen. The overwhelming allure of her apparition and her words drew him deeper and his sword slipped from his hand. In that moment Tarquin knew he was trapped and he remembered why he never stepped foot in this part of the woods.

Nefanial had also realized his own folly. He now lay rigid on the ground in front of the minthe, with Calhoun comatose beside him. Slowly, it dawned on the baker that he seemed to be moving away from his companion, and he swore his feet were wet. Brun watched in horror, unable to move and powerless to help as the creature gradually dragged his brother-in-law into the murky stream. Tartarus, too, was starting to bend to the minthe's will. Still sitting on his stallion, he was slowly moving in the creature's direction. The first two arrows shot at the nymph seemed to disappear and reappear as though they flew straight through her. And he just did not understand why she was starting to look so much like his beautiful Eolande.

Ragnarr, on clearing the small meadow, saw the trouble his friends were in, and shouted at them.

'By Algrim, cover your ears! She's a taker of souls. Her instrument is the vessel of your destruction.' He rode up to Tartarus and gave the elf a nudge.

'What are you gawking at? Use a spell. The water, direct it at the water,' urged Ragnarr. With his hands over his ears Tartarus uttered a spell.

'Al-La-Rar-Far-Congelo-Profusum.'
The water around the brook immediately froze and with a mighty swing Ragnarr's war hammer took flight. Its spiked head hit the minthe and shattered her into a million shards of ice.

Nefanial, up to his middle in frozen water, gave the dwarf an intense look.

'Sweet Elohim, Ragnarr. Do your companions ever last long?' he asked, touching the top of his head.

'I don't lip-read and I can't hear a thing, so let me remove these things,' the dwarf shouted as he pulled the battle-buds out of his ears.

'How did you know I was going to duck?' asked Nefanial.

'Like me, you're married,' replied Ragnarr, stony faced.

'I can't feel my legs,' said Nefanial, looking down at the solid block of ice that had been a stream only a few moments ago.

'If you ever save my life, I'll just say thanks too,' the dwarf continued, but no one was listening.

'Take my hand, boss,' suggested Calhoun. After a brief attempt, he turned to the others and said, 'I think he's stuck.'

Pippa and Tarquin were not paying any attention to the aftermath. They were in the throes of a family reunion.

'Don't you be changing the water back,' warned Ragnarr.

'Why not?' asked Brun.

'She lives in the water. If the water returns, so will she,' he answered.

'What should I do? We need to get him out before he loses his legs,' asked Tartarus.

'Sand, my boy, sand,' said Ragnarr.
Tartarus turned the area around Nefanial's legs to sand and Calhoun helped him out.

'We've wasted enough time here. The girl is safe now so let's rejoin the others,' continued Ragnarr.

'I think it best the whole group sticks together next time,' suggested Brun, still visibly shaken.

'What about this mutt?' asked Tarquin.

'Get rid of him,' retorted Ragnarr, moving towards the dog to shoo him away.

'I want to keep him. He saved my life,' said Pippa, looking up at her brother, her eyes pleading.

'I think your sister has found a new friend,' said Tartarus, as everyone looked to see Pippa cuddling and stroking the adorable terrier.

'Can I keep him, Quin? Please,' she said. Her brother nodded and smiled.

Ragnarr shrugged his shoulders.

'Well, you'd better keep it away from me and I think you should all count yourselves fortunate that I followed you,' he announced. 'A minthe's sole purpose is to claim souls. Some say Cressida was one of those.'

The short ride back to Flint and the others was without incident. Flint ran to greet them and helped Pippa off Tarquin's horse. He gave her a huge hug before giving Tarquin a hearty pat on the back.

'That's enough of that. We need to press on,' urged Ragnarr.

'Hang on, what about our sister?' asked Flint.

'Sorry, lad. We can't take her back now. She'll have to come with us. Anyway, we need the manpower.'

'Is this dwarf crazy?' asked Flint, as he kicked a small rock and immediately grimaced as pain shot up his right leg.

'Who among us is battle-hardened?' responded Ragnarr. Nefanial and the old veteran Rex raised their hands. Ragnarr continued, 'And who among us is willing to take Pippa back to Irons Keep?' Swiftly, both put their hands down. No one else put theirs up.

'Not even you, boy?' Ragnarr asked, looking at Flint. 'Well, that's settles it,' he concluded.

Tartarus agreed, although he was not willing to air his views. Upsetting the apple cart by angering his newfound friends, Flint and Tarquin, was out of the question; but the dwarf was right. The mission had just had its first success and compared to the perils that awaited them, hidden within the Black Forest, it was one of those rare moments in which to smile – but not to get complacent. Keeping the group together was the right move. Pippa's escape could easily be a ploy to split up the coalition. They mounted their horses and continued.

Pippa was given the task of riding Rainbow, which was one of her favourite pastimes, so she mounted the horse with glee. As she rode alongside her brothers, she was extremely glad the dwarf had spoken up on her behalf. If he had not she would have voiced her objection, having no intention of returning home. Kallen had her father's ring and Pippa wanted it back. Flint rode next to his sister. She was deep in thought. He reached into a large bag tied to his saddle.

'I think this belongs to you?' he said with a smile. In his hand was Pippa's grass reed straw hat.

*

Prince Edwin was in his private quarters within his encampment on the outskirts of Oaken-Dale Forest. The Geneshian mountain range was within sight and the two mountains, named the Geneshian Peaks, loomed large in the distance. Through the gully between the two mountains lay the entrance to Oaken-Crag, the home of the Aafarians and the many wonderful tribes and beasts that inhabited the forest's beautiful scenery. The smoke from the fires in the encampment filled the bright sky and the sounds of preparations for war could be heard from miles around.

The prince's private quarters were located in an enormous black, satin tent, with gold corner arches and trimmings. The royally decorated tent was split into three connecting compartments: the prince's sleeping quarters, a washing and dressing area, and a spacious living section which was mainly used for eating and entertaining guests. The prince's stalwart helped him into his black armour. The stalwart was a middle-aged man, of slim build, with a mop of black hair that matched his dark attire.

Edwin stood in front of a large oval mirror admiring his ghostly pale complexion. The battle for Oaken-Crag was about to commence and strategically his battle plan was sound; his captain had seen to that. The armour tightened uncomfortably around his chest. His face contorted and he turned and hit his stalwart firmly across the face. Instantly, a dark bruise appeared on the man's cheek.

'Careful,' said Edwin harshly. His stalwart nodded and continued fastening the armour. Inwardly, Edwin smiled. Soon another part of the jigsaw would be firmly in place, with the added bonus that the sound of screaming elves would soon be ringing in his ears.

Archelaus made his way past the ork guards at the entrance to Edwin's quarters and entered the tent.

'Sire?'

'I'm in here. This stalwart is an imbecile. Help me with my armour,' responded the prince. Archelaus acknowledged Baracus with a slight nod before entering the dressing room area.

'Leave us,' said Edwin, and the stalwart left. 'They don't make slaves like they used to,' Edwin continued.

'Why the guards? Isn't Baracus enough?' enquired the captain.

'My quarters are to be guarded at all times,' Edwin replied, quietly but sharply. 'You can never be too careful, Archelaus. The Senate of Kings is loyal to my father but I hear they tire of me.'

Archelaus buckled the remaining straps. He was aware that the death of Edwin's previous wine taster was a concern. Archelaus attached a black velvet cloak by clipping a circular gold clasp, which depicted the black dragon emblem, around the prince's neck. Once this was done the obtrusive silver buckles were concealed.

'You look impressive as always, sire.'

'Indeed,' replied Edwin, as they both looked into the gilt-edged mirror.

'So what brings you to my tent?' enquired Edwin as he picked up his helmet.

'The generals have gathered in the campaign tent to await your orders, sire.' Edwin pondered this. The orks had still not delivered the Denvagar dwarves. Cressida's creatures could not be trusted; they loved eating their prisoners too much.

At the back of his mind he knew he should have sent a Draconian battalion to escort these dwarves. At lease those brutes listen, and soon the southern generals would become restless if the king's ransom he had promised their masters remained out of reach.

'Generals,' said Edwin, rolling his eyes. 'Always eager for gore.' Edwin followed Archelaus into the tent's main area.

'Baracus, hand me the box,' commanded Edwin, his voice unusually deep for a man of his size. Baracus picked up a small, simple, unvarnished rectangular wooden box which looked like a miniature coffin in the bodyguard's large hand. Once the box was in the prince's hand, a key released the latch and the top sprang opened to reveal a satin-lined inlaid box, which contained one of the four gauntlets of power. The reddish steel of the gauntlet gleamed even in the subdued light of the tent. The emerald power crystal flickered, encased in an elaborately carved metal mesh that was protruding from the top of the gauntlet. As the prince slid his left hand into the glove, the surge of power was visible in his demeanour.

'Archelaus, lead the way,' said Price Edwin.

Outside a vast array of tents of different shapes and sizes lay in their wake, beneath the midday sun. Two carriages arrived. Archelaus boarded one while Edwin and Baracus boarded the other. With reins in hand the captain motioned the horse to start the procession, and Edwin's carriage followed. As he passed his men shouts of 'Hail the Black Knight!' rang out until the words became a chorus. His barbarism and brutality were legendary among them, and he revelled in their admiration.

They stopped outside a large domed marquee in the centre of the encampment. As the prince entered the boisterous crowd was suddenly silenced. A Draconian general, named Cog, walked forward, bowed and hissed to Edwin, 'We await your orders, my Prince.'

'I take it you're all familiar with Archelaus's plan?' asked Edwin nonchalantly.

Most of the generals murmured their approval, but General Bakunawa did not. In fact, the plump-faced general was visibly enraged.

'Edwin, you can still stop this madness. It will mean certain war with the east,' he declared.

'What?' responded Edwin. 'Simply pack up and leave? Do you think war is cheap? Look around you, general. We're already at war with the east; they just don't know it yet. But today they will.' His smile was cruel.

'And what news have you on the capture of the royal rider's murderer? Silvanus's passing cannot be allowed to go unpunished.'

At the mention of the name Edwin's smile disappeared and he seemed uneasy. General Rutland, standing just behind Grumondi, voiced his concerns too.

'I agree with Grumondi. We were promised the culprit's head and you promised our kings mountains of gold. As yet, we have seen nothing, and now you'd have us start another great war.'

'Not scared of a couple of elves are you?' ridiculed Edwin. Rutland's cheeks brightened.

'The Senate would have not agreed to this. Yet here we are, following a mongrel prince who obeys a harlot witch, ruled by an autocratic king we must all fear,' he protested, his voice rising in panic. 'Well, I'll tell you what I do fear for is my sanity,' he concluded.

'Curb your tongue, Rutland,' Archelaus said as he reached for his dagger.

'General Rutland to you, boy,' Rutland retorted.

'Leave him be, Archelaus. We can all speak freely here. We're among friends,' said Edwin.

'If it wasn't for your brother Edmund we would have never have entered this unholy alliance with this,' Rutland continued.

'That's enough. You've made your point, general,' said Grumondi. Fearing that he knew what his ally was about to do, he placed a firm hand on the man's shoulder, but Rutland shook it off.

'No, Grumondi, let me speak. The king of the Low Lands rules me; this Abandanon does not.'

As Rutland spoke the Autocrat's name, voices were hushed inside the tent and slowly a space appeared around Rutland as the other generals drew back. Suddenly, thunder could be heard outside the tent and there was a flash of lightening. A small grey cloud formed directly above the domed marquee. Three black harbingers emerged from the cloud and flew into the tent. There were gasps of horror from the generals as the creature came into view.

The fearsome harpies, with red eyes, pointed beaks and razor-sharp talons, swirled around the crowded tent as men threw up their hands to protect their faces. The harpies fixed on General Rutland and a knowing look appeared on Edwin's face. Rutland drew his sword and screamed:

'Help me! Help me!' The words sounded hollow, muffled by the harpies' shrieks. Rutland reached out for his friends but general after general pushed him away. Even Grumondi moved away and watched as the general was dragged kicking and screaming from the tent by two of the harbingers. The hooked talons cut deep into the general's flesh. The other creature tore at Rutland's stomach and its blade-like teeth cut through the skin as though it were paper. Soon, the creature was feasting on Rutland's innards.

A few of the generals looked away; there was nothing they could do. Others rejoiced in Rutland's misery. The creatures lifted him up, tore him apart and devoured him in mid-air. Pieces of flesh fell to the ground and onto the generals standing beneath.

Their task over, the harbingers flew back into the cloud as it began to dissipate.

'Now that's how to make an entrance,' said Edwin. 'Does anyone else want to voice any objections, or opinions on my master's actions?'

Everyone in the tent was silent.

'Good. Shall we continue? I want Oaken-Crag razed to the ground. I want the east to fear my master and grovel at his feet.'

Edwin took his position at the head of a large circular table and studied a map of Tyrus and Ganesha. He pointed at their position.

'Our plan is simple. We will bombard the landscape with my catapults, forcing them to come out into the open and fight. Then we'll trap them between here and here' – Edwin pointed at the Geneshian Peaks on the map –'but if this plan fails, then we'll just burn everything in our way, cutting a path to the doors of Oaken-Crag before we knock it off its hinges. If the Aafarians do not swear allegiance to the Autocrat and the southern lands they will die. Gentleman, you have your orders. Now, let us feast.' There was a brief pause.

'Rutland was a good man, slightly misguided perhaps, but all the same, he will be missed.' With that, Edwin clapped his hand and a banquet of exotic foods was brought into the tent. The culinary treats were for his generals; the spicy food served in the east played havoc with his stomach. So he just sat back and watched.

'Mongrel indeed,' thought Edwin as his generals demolished the feast. The Autocrat's love for volcanoes was fine by him; he'd give the swine mountains all right; just as long as he was allowed to feed on kingdoms he couldn't care less, and Oaken-Crag was next.

*

The deterioration of Oaken-Dale's northern frontier was all too apparent. The lyrebirds' crescendo of alluring calls could no longer be heard. The sight of the ever-present tree lilies, the so-called grey-breasted, yellow-bellied flycatchers, was becoming rarer and rarer, but most telling of all was the missing ruckus from the fur-faced monkeys who normally made such a noise when foraging in bushes before heading for the treetops, where they would get up to all sorts of mischief. The deer and fowl had migrated to more tranquil regions of the densely wooded area; instinctively, they felt the prevailing winds, like a forest fire swirling, about to ravage their home, but in this case the coming inferno would be inflicted by humans raining boulders from above.

Less colourful, and perhaps less intuitive, creatures such as the bulligores, which looked like a cross between an elephant and a hippo, stayed and continued to graze. The Geneshian prairie tigers, with their distinctive white stripes, the guardians of Oaken-Dale, continued to prowl. The good-natured, agricultural Aafari folk, who dwelled outside the elven city, had noticed the visible change the moment Edwin's army had erected an encampment just below the valley, between the Geneshian Peaks. As soon as the Alfari scouts reported the encampment, spies were dispatched.

Behind the Aafari temple's impressive arched doors was the Alfari High Lord, Elgar Crayfar, with his flowing grey locks and protruding pointed ears. He wore a tunic with quilted arms, and a long, velvet fur-lined cloak which matched a neat pair of ankle boots. The dark grey outfit with elaborate silver patterns looked elegant. Crayfar, like so many elves, had style, taste and grace. Similarly attired, though in brown, were three elgar Alfari warriors, all of the rank of lugar. The lines of age had started to show on the face of the High Lord.

Passing a couple of Callidora guards they entered the marbled courtyard. A group of priestesses was sitting round a fountain, the centrepiece of which was a life-size statue of Kleodora on a carved pedestal with water cascading from its base. One of them got up, approached and greeted them with a bow.
 'Hello, Elgar Crayfar,' she smiled.
 'Greetings, sister. We seek counsel with the high priestess.'
 'She's in a meeting, my lord, with Duke Mandrick,' she replied softly.
 'Good, I need to speak to him too. Can you take me to her?'
They followed the priestess, who was dressed in a hooded white robe with gold trimmings, through a large, domed hall with stained-glass windows, then into a corridor that led to an ornate golden door.

The sentries were females with scant body armour covering their torsos. Immensely beautiful, they were armed only with a staff and elongated dagger which belied their deadly effectiveness in battle. Trained in the hidden arts, their stealth and close-range combat abilities were renowned throughout the east. They were warriors of the Order of the Callidora, named in honour of Kleodora, the first high priestess of Aafari. The order was charged with guarding the sacred scrolls and other archives which were kept away from prying eyes.

One of sentries tapped the floor three times with her staff and the golden doors opened inwards to reveal a number of guests and two more Callidora warriors. The chamber was stunning. Its floor was split into two levels separated by two steps. The elevated section was smaller with an arched, wooded door to its rear and a solitary gold bowl on a thin circular stand which was full to the brim with a honey-coloured liquid, used in rituals and for bestowing blessings. Beside the bowl stood the high priestess in all her majestic splendour. A golden headdress flowed into her bright blonde hair which partially covered the large angular collars of a divine, white gown. The priestess led the group in and announced the arrival of the High Lord of the Alfari. Then she bowed to the high priestess and left.

The high priestess was always a celestial prophet. The role of matriarch of the religious order was one for which there was no training. A celestial prophet was born with the abilities required. She addressed the group.

'As always, Crayfar, your presence pleases me, although these are troubling times. How is the king? I know you have his ear,' she said, smiling. Everyone knew Lord Erynion, was King Jeremiah's favourite; not Crayfar.

King Jeremiah was head of state, but her rank equalled his in certain matters relating to the rule of law. On issues such as war, both had to agree, even though those battles were fought and led by the king.

'We expect him to return soon and, as always, he sends his greetings,' replied Crayfar politely.

'Lugar Badhron, Arvellon,' – the high priestess nodded to them both – 'and how is your wife, Lugar Richon. Isn't she due soon?'

'We don't have time for these niceties,' said Mandrick, as impatient as ever. He looked at his aide; the soldier's facial expression mirrored his own. Crayfar, not one to hold his tongue, gave him a very harsh look, before he spoke.

'We always have time for these things, Duke. Unlike you, we do not belong to a race of barbarians.'

'Mellow your words, High Lord. This is a house of the Giver of Life, is it not?' the high priestess asked. Her voice, though quiet, seemed to fill the entire room. 'Have you forgotten we have a pact with the duke?' she continued, although it was clearly more a statement than a question.

'She is well, thank you,' Richon interjected hesitantly. Crayfar shot his lugar a look.

'Where are my manners?' he said, as he walked forward and lowered his head. Ekaterina, the high priestess, reached out her hand from her elevated position and he placed a gentle kiss upon it.

Mandrick, flustered, stood steadfast; he held ceremony in high regard but all this posturing was too much. He had seen at firsthand what Edwin's horde was capable of. The results were too ugly to comprehend; the large-scale slaughter of the innocent. He interrupted again.

'We must abandon the city and flee deeper into the forest where we can mount a resistance campaign, your highness. I still have many men at my disposal and if we send word to all the tribes to rally at Galatea, we can still save the day. Only the White City can raise an army that can match his. What say you?'

'Leave Oaken-Dale? Never. We will fight until the very last Alfari has stopped breathing,' Crayfar responded sharply, disgusted by the mere suggestion.

'That is why the decision to go to war is not taken only by the male elves of our clan, High Lord. Arrogance in battle has lost many wars,' said Ekaterina, in no mood to have her authority undermined.

'I know his intent; he seeks our servitude or our annihilation. There is no compromise with this man. He is possessed by the will to conquer,' Mandrick informed them.

'And you should know. You trained him,' whispered Arvellon. Crayfar looked over his shoulder, amused by the truthful comment.

'Now, what is the king's wish?' asked Ekaterina.

'He seeks your approval to take up arms against this Edwin, the transgressor.' Crayfar answered, putting his hands behind his back.

'Have you seen what awaits you, old friend?' Mandrick knew how brave the Alfari were; battle was in their blood. Crayfar just grunted, then spoke directly to Ekaterina.

'My lugars have brought word: war is imminent. We can cower like feeble beings or stand and fight.' His posture was commanding as he spoke the words. Then, looking across at the handsome duke, he lowered his voice, and continued, 'We must move the gold-rimmed scrolls and plan a surprise attack. Richon can lead the evacuation.'

'Can he now?' replied Ekaterina, displeased by Crayfar's presumptuousness.

'I have spoken at length with Mandrick and, indeed, this Black Knight needs to be stopped. But if it's as grave as we all fear then your action may be no more than a mission to safeguard our escape. So make sure, High Lord, the warriors have a clear route to give ground. I will not sign away the lives of elves merely to preserve mine,' Ekaterina added firmly.

Crayfar bowed.

'Inform the king and the council that you have my permission and my blessing.'

Badhron handed a small chrome cylinder to Crayfar, who pulled out a rolled parchment from within, which he passed to Ekaterina. Her lady-in-waiting brought forward a box that contained her mark and the high priestess placed her seal on the document.

'Give this to the council,' commanded Crayfar as he returned the tube to his lugar. As Badhron left the room Arvellon whispered to Richon.

'So, its war then.' Richon nodded, a grim expression on his face.

The high priestess was helped down from the elevated platform by her lady-in-waiting. As they clasped hands Ekaterina stumbled; the mental burden of holding the spell keeping Oaken-Crag invisible was taking its toll on her. Both man and elf went to her aid but, with resilience, she raised her palm.

'Come, let us take refreshment while we discuss our exodus,' she said wearily, looking at the duke and the High Lord in turn. They followed Ekaterina through an arched doorway which led to an informal glass-domed sitting area, overlooking the forest.

The high priestess's successor, formally known as the shekhinah, was an elf named Maya. She and a Nagari elfette, Eolande, took up seats round a marble table. Mandrick and Crayfar also sat. Their subordinates stood.

'I had planned on riding immediately for Galatea, your highness. I'm still willing to leave a small force behind to slow the prince's progress. I had the perfect man for the role; he was to discover Edwin's weakness before rejoining me to lead my resistance, but now I fear Cooms has been captured. He would have sent word by now.'

'His weakness?' Crayfar said, pricking up his ears.

'I needed to know how to rid me of his wimps. Edwin is in possession of a gauntlet of power, is he not?' questioned Mandrick. This information was greeted by a subdued gasp from the elves.

'We've not meddled in the affairs of men for far too long. The gauntlets were made to bring peace to the realms of Elohim,' Crayfar responded, still digesting the intelligence. The high priestess was in agreement; a man with such power would be difficult to depose.

'This changes everything,' said Ekaterina. 'Crayfar advised the king, on his return, to follow Duke Mandrick, with the royal household and half the army. My Callidora and Richon's forces will remove our archives and citizens. Then they can meet up with you at the White City once our people are safe. I cannot go until all have left, so Maya will go in my stead.'

'But what about Tartarus?' said Eolande.

'Who?' snapped Mandrick.

'He is a greenhorn under Lord Erynion's tutelage,' answered Crayfar. 'Why do you ask, Eolande?' Even with her tanned complexion rosy cheeks instantly appeared.

'Well, I like him,' she responded, looking at the floor. They all laughed.

'You're brave warrior will be fine,' said Ekaterina, smiling at Eolande to ease her fears. 'I've sent him to see a dear friend of mine, who will take great care of him.'

'I wondered where that naughty three-quarter elf had been hiding,' added Richon, laughing.

'I say, is he short?' asked Mandrick, which brought more fits of laugher.

'Why are you not coming with us, holy mother?' interrupted Maya. The endearing young blond elfette was only twelve years old, so the upheaval and turmoil were obviously overwhelming, but everyone knew the answer was connected to the fire crystal that held the city's visibility shield in place. The high priestess continued.

'As Maya's guardian, you must escort our people and guide them through the fire caves to Nagari.' Eolande smiled and said, 'It will be so with your blessing, for I love Maya like a sister.' Her violet eyes glowed and the two elfettes embraced.

'I take it by "archives" you mean the scroll?' asked Crayfar. Ekaterina neither lied nor told the truth.

'That's not your concern,' she replied sharply.

'Very well,' said Crayfar, getting to his feet. 'Duke, Ekaterina, if there is nothing more I will take my leave. The king must have a report of this meeting.'

In fact, King Jeremiah and his son should have returned by now. It was too early to divulge this information and cause alarm, although if he did not receive word soon troops would have to be sent. The elves feared nothing, but an army led by a dangerous tyrant wielding such a destructive weapon might have devastating repercussions for Oaken-Crag. Rarely had the Alfari been defeated in battle, and Crayfar knew it was the calm before the storm, during which the decisions were made that won and lost wars. He did not approve of Mandrick and Ekaterina's defeatist mindset but Crayfar knew that complacency would be disastrous.

*

The Murumendi mountain range, bordering Tyrus and Ganesha, was a beautiful rugged expanse of wild terrain with an elegant magnificence. The seemingly identical rocky mountains, Mari and Sugaar, were named after weather gods. Legend had it that their last act was to turn themselves into the Geneshian Peaks to watch over Mount Lurbira, a dormant volcano bordering Oaken-Dale and the lands of Nagari.

The pinnacles of Meditation and Solace, so named by the Aafari, could only be seen on the clearest of days. Pilgrims would brave the treacherous climb to the summits where, in a cloud-like haven, they would feel closer to old deities.

Below, in the lush valley's meadow, the gateway to the forest was a hive of activity where the flags and banners of the Southern Alliance flapped and flickered in the breeze. A long line of large, skin-covered drums thundered as the horde moved as one, row upon row of battalions and brigades heavily armed with gruesome weaponry. Charcoal fires burned in cauldrons on wheels; a foreboding smog floated above the men, half-men, monsters and beasts. Fire-hounds were contained in wagons with iron bars; the vile four-legged hunchbacked fiends snarled and snapped at anything that moved. Woolly mammoths, especially bred for war, with huge curved tusks and covered in chainmail, were ridden by Draconians and archers. Signal men stood at the ready to relay their master's orders.

Massive rolling monstrosities, built for the sole purpose of demoralizing the enemy, creaked and groaned. Trebuchets, alongside catapults and ballistas, trampled the earth underfoot in a three-pronged approach worthy of any conquering army. Although Cressida's mage, Balthazar, had located Oaken-Crag, he had not been able to remove the invisibility spell, much to Edwin's annoyance. Ekaterina's mental defences had proven impenetrable. Balthazar's attempts to remove the spell screening the city had met with failure, but at least the location had been pinpointed and Edwin knew that would have to suffice.

The generals had followed Archelaus's battle formation precisely in anticipation of Edwin's signal to attack. Even General Bakunawa was toeing the line; his heavy cavalry and infantry were primed to carry out his orders at a moment's notice. He still felt uneasy about the whole sordid affair, given that Mandrick was still in hiding and his men were unable to ascertain whether or not the duke was a traitor. These enquiries would have to wait; the safety of his men in battle was paramount now.
He could see that the men under Edmund's banner were ready for battle. The general's second-in-command, Captain Molton Montfort, was an excellent officer and tactician. He gave Grumondi a reassuring smile. The clean-shaven, fair-haired young man rode alongside Grumondi on a stunning black horse whose coat sparkled. Humorous and popular, Molton always seemed relaxed in his saddle. Grumondi admired Molton; although he was from a family of considerable wealth he was not a buyer of men, but a leader of them.

Leading the attack were General Rutland's troops; his men would pay a heavy price for the general's indiscretion. After the general's death Grumondi had asked if Rutland's troops could merge with his own. However, the request was denied. Edwin said that he wanted to set an example among his generals. Grumondi, however, believed the real reason was that the prince was in no mood to bolster Grumondi's numbers.

Edwin, standing beside Archelaus and General Cog, had an ideal view of the valley and was taking pride in his captain's strategic planning while he assessed his troops' movements on the map.

'It starts tonight,' the prince proclaimed, looking at Balthazar whose motiveless expression said nothing. Edwin's irritability was unrivalled. In fact, Balthazar was sure narcissism ran in the prince's family because his father was just the same, but his orders from Queen Cressida were clear. He was to aid Edwin and observe, nothing more: so he would do just that.

Whereas most wizards looked as though they were suffering from malnutrition, Balthazar looked more like a jovial baron, with fat fingers and a plump middle. He cultivated this deceptive look which disguised his true character.

Balthazar realized that he should be paying more attention. He'd been distracted by pondering the question of whether Edwin actually knew that Linus wasn't his real father. It was the only reason he was afforded such privileges in Cressida's hierarchy although he was without the full backing of her army. He caught the last part of Edwin's sentence as a stalwart moved a stone figure of a catapult across the map.

'We will wake them from their slumber,' said Edwin. 'Thanks to Balthazar the elves have no place to hide.' Edwin turned to his captain.

'Archelaus, are the catapults are in position?'

His captain nodded.

'My Draconians will serve you well, high prince,' General Cog assured Edwin, slamming his forearm across his chest in a gesture of loyalty. Then, with an informal bow, Archelaus and the reptilian warrior left.

Balthazar approached Edwin.

'May I have a quiet word?'

Edwin lowered his ear to meet the mage's lips.
'Might I remind you not to stray too far from your path, my prince. Our task is to retrieve the other two gauntlets of power. The killing of elves is an unnecessary delay in achieving our objectives. Be warned; Cressida is not known for her patience.' Balthazar whispered the last part softly with a lingering gaze. Edwin looked at Bararus and chuckled to conceal his trepidation. He knew the sorceress's immense power could not be treated lightly.

Immediately he dismissed the mage, who turned to leave and bumped into Archelaus returning in a hurry.
'I think we're under attack,' the captain stated in disbelief. Balthazar just shook his head and just stared at the prince like one would a petulant child. A cloud of arrows filled the horizon as the Alfari rode out of the forest to meet Edwin's horde.
Mounted on stallions, they were as silent as a fog enveloping a field. The smell of elven metal and oiled leather was the only indication of their presence. Arvellon's cavalry, unflinching in the face of overwhelming odds, fell upon the invaders, some of whom were already screaming, injured by the arrows that had fallen from the sky.

Crayfar had ordered his elves to strike fear through Edwin's ranks and the rousing speech had succeeded; his warriors were unleashing a furious attack. Without a figurehead Rutland's troops cut forlorn figures on the battle-field. The Alfari set about them mercilessly and with brutal efficiency. Some jumped off their horses to take on two, or even three, southerners; dazzling swordplay resulted in scattered body parts and pools of blood.

On horseback, under the cover of the trees, observing Edwin's troops advance, were High Lord Crayfar and Arvellon. The delayed assault had been initiated once the party sent to search for the king had returned with bad news. Crateuas was dead. Lord Erynion, along with Crayfar's son, Dain, and King Jeremiah, were missing, probably kidnapped. The dwarves were nowhere to be seen. Crayfar had warned against a meeting at such a critical time, the discussion becoming heated once he had suggested the notion was brash and reckless. King Jeremiah had erupted, forcing Crayfar to retract his words. However, with a regretful satisfaction, it appeared he'd been proven right.

Arvellon's brigade, led by Captain Durion, was cutting a swathe through men and running rings round the confused infantry, although a few of the elves had fallen and been killed. Durion, who normally commanded five hundred Alfari, had double that number at his disposal now. The elves were lightly armed with bows and arrows, basket-hilted swords and munga blades that were strapped to their saddles. The ancient metal weapons had a curved, serrated back section and a separate spike above the handle. They could be used in hand-to-hand combat or for throwing.

    'Your elves do you proud and Durion leads them well,' said Crayfar, observing the captain's actions.
    'I should be with them,' protested Arvellon solemnly and taking no comfort from the High Lord's words.
    'With our forces so fragmented I need you by my side. When we retreat, they will pursue and be taught a lesson,' Crayfar replied, coldly.

With the king's disappearance Oaken-Dale was in turmoil. In its entire existence it had not witnessed a mass departure on this scale. The evacuation, supervised by Lugar Richon and his three captains, was a logistical nightmare compounded by the profound sadness felt by the people leaving the city that had been a place of safety for aeons. With the Aafari High Council still in two minds on whether to follow Mandrick or go through the fire cave to Nagari, Crayfar's resolve was truly being tested. But he was an elf of steely determination. With Jeremiah missing he was the last line of defence for all that he held precious and dear, and he would fight to the bitter end to protect it. He had to force himself to push thoughts of his missing son to the back of his mind.

Crayfar raised his right hand to signal Arvellon's cavalry to withdraw and a blue star was released. As the flare twinkled over the field in the dwindling sunlight Durion's horn sounded the retreat. Those fighting on the ground whistled for their stallions and, mounting them, were whisked away followed by another volley of covering arrows which aided their escape, while inflicting more damage and injury on the enemy. The area in which they were to make their stand had been picked for the closeness of its trees, which became denser with each passing step. Durion directed the riders to the designated spot.

Crayfar knew that not having a man by his side who understood the enemy intimately was a huge disadvantage. Mandrick's departure had been a blow. True to his word, though, the duke had left a group of battled-hardened warriors, led by a brute of a man named Hal Stone, who all looked cumbersome and inept.

'The bigger they are, the harder they fall,' thought Crayfar under his chrome helmet with the golden bird-of-paradise crest.

The Alfari preferred to fight alone but, in this instance, they needed the numbers. If Mandrick had faith in this man, Crayfar decided, then so would he. Hal's black-haired, wiry sidekick seemed like a man to be feared, with his menacing stare and collection of unusual throwing daggers which was concealed under a leather riding coat. This gave Crayfar reason to be more optimistic. He hoped, alongside his elves, that the duke's men, carrying the burden of losing Athena to Edwin, would cover themselves in glory this time.

Edwin's horde, realizing the Alfari were retreating, let out an enormous cheer, the noise shaking the very earth where Crayfar's horse stood.

'Do you hear? Do you? They think we've given up,' said Crayfar, directing his infantry into a crouched position. The cavalry, led by Durion, rode past at pace and continued on. With the moment approaching, he motioned his elves and the duke's men to be still.

'Silence now.' The order was given in a hushed voice while the decoy could be heard moving away.

Edwin knew the familiar roar from his men was the sound of victory, and revelled in it.

'By killing elves we weaken the east,' he said triumphantly, directing the words at a loitering Balthazar, who hadn't moved from his position since being told they were under attack.

'Ready my horse and signal the men to hunt them down,' he commanded.

Given the signal to chase, the rest of Rutland's battered battalion ran into the forest with victorious shouts. Grumondi, with rein in hand, was transfixed. He knew these beings had guts but he did not expect this; on seeing the

Alfari surrender their position so easily he knew it must be a ruse. Why ride off when you're winning? He told Captain Montfort to ride up with a battalion, so sure was he that the men sent into Oaken-Dale would not return.

'Do not follow them into the forest. I believe it to be a trap,' he told his captain, before Molton rounded up the best and the brightest to follow him to the front.

General Cog had the same hunch, but took a different approach and sent a battalion of heavy infantry into the forest to reinforce Rutland's men. As Edwin horse's was brought forward, along with Archelaus's, both men were wondering why the generals hadn't sent in the light cavalry. Heavy against light would be suicide.

*

The High Lord watched as Captain Morcion sat ready with the second wave of Arvellon's light brigade, poised waiting for their turn to shine, with the moment nearly at hand. However, next to enter the fray was Jeremiah's Tiger Division with Lugar Badhron at the helm in the king's absence. The division consisted of trained Geneshian prairie tigers accompanied by handlers armed with weapons and nets.

The honey-coloured animals with white stripes had sharp maxillary canine teeth which extended from their mouths even when shut.

Marauding through the forest in pursuit of the Alfari, Rutland's men were running full-pelt, closely followed by the Draconians. None had noticed the trees getting thicker until they hit a wall of tangled branches and white mist. Suddenly, their war cries were drowned out by the feline's growls.

'Release the beasts!' shouted Badhron, and their handlers unlatched their collars. Encountering the muscular predators must have been a shock to the system. The Tiger Division roared to life, with teeth cutting bone and metal to ribbons.

'Run for your lives!' was the foremost shout as Rutland's men broke ranks and fled towards the oncoming Draconian battalion.

Crayfar shouted at Hal to enter the fray.

'Do not let them escape,' he commanded. Mandrick's men sprang into action, having been sprayed with a pheromone that prevented them from being attacked by the tigers. Hal, trading swords with a Draconian, had a near-miss when one of the big cats leaped on the Draconian, who swung his sword at him as the tiger dragged him away. Hal just picked up the dragon-man's fallen sword and turned around to find someone else about to attack him. He set his sights on one of Rutland's men, but before he could engage him a blade came out of nowhere and buried itself in the man's chest.

His kill count still at zero, Hal was in no mood for anymore interruptions and rushed in, tackling a man before delivering the death blow. Crayfar, watching, noted the man's impressive strength and skill. After a short time the carnage was over, with the remaining Draconians finally falling prey to elven blades and arrows. The elves moved forwards to retake their position and right on cue Durion returned with the first wave. If the Alfari warriors were an orchestra, the High Lord would be the perfect conductor, moving his troops with timing and purpose. Signalling the Alfari archers in the trees to let their arrows take flight, he gave Morcion the gesture he'd been waiting for. With a flick of his heels, the captain left the cover of leaves and branches and went out into the open expanse with a thousand elves on horseback behind him.

Edwin looked up at a sky rapidly filling with distant stars as the sun finally set and was replaced by a fierce blue moon. The flames of hand-held torches became the main source of light. In the time that passed since the roar of victory rang out over the valley, murmuring and muttering had replaced the cheerful mood as it became clear that the troops sent into the forest were not coming back.

It seemed ludicrous, but from just one counter-attack he'd managed to lose three battalions. Edwin cursed the devious, ingenious elves. Suddenly, a glint from above caught his eye.

'Arrows!' he shouted, and shields were instantly raised again as another volley filled the darkened sky, blotting out the moon and the stars.

Led by Morcion, the second wave of Arvellon's light cavalry galloped towards their foe for the honour of their kin. For some that was the moment to acknowledge a compatriot, maybe for the last time before the heat of battle. Their task was to cause more mayhem and confusion while trying to disable Edwin's siege weaponry. The only flaw was that this time it wasn't a surprise attack. Bursts of light flashed as Balthazar conjured up a spell that unseated elven riders.

The prince was ready and he rode to confront the enemy. He rode, like a man possessed, directly at the Alfari cavalry. He seemed to be impervious to their arrows. They bounced off his breastplate, the shape of which constantly shifted thanks to the magical element that distorted the armour's edges. Archelaus and the warriors followed him stride for stride, their weapons drawn.

With the time close at hand to engage the southern tribes head on, Morcion split formation for a two-pronged attack. The captain's group made a beeline for the catapults while his son, Mort, led the other group into the melee. Mort had got his position through hard work and one day might even surpass his father's exploits as an Alfari warrior. His endeavours were respected by his seniors and subordinates alike. The well-groomed elf was much liked among the females in the municipality.

Edwin pulled his double-handed broadsword from its sheath. He swung the weapon and cut down the Alfari as easily as cutting through butter. The elves were dropping like flies. The Draconians and Molton's men were well versed in the art of open warfare and inflicted heavy casualties on their enemies.

Crayfar looked on in horror as elves he had known from being little ones fell from their horses to oblivion. His plan was unravelling before his eyes and Morcion was making no inroads against the orks. Durion insisted he be sent back into the fold but Crayfar refused, sticking rigidly to his plan.

'We must hold firm and give Morcion more time to breach the orks' defences. Those siege weapons must be destroyed.'

'But they are being slaughtered out there,' said Arvellon, revolted by the sickening sight.

'We must hold our nerve. The survival of Oaken-Dale is at stake,' insisted the High Lord.

'Send Durion in again or give the order to withdraw,' said Arvellon in a direct challenge. He knew he was overstepping the mark. However, neither King Jeremiah nor Ekaterina would ever stand idly by and let elves die needlessly. Every attempt to breach the lines of orks guarding the siege weapons was met with stiff opposition. Morcion's elves had only managed to disable one catapult before the Ballista's crossbolts tore through them, wiping out his ranks.

Although Morcion was an excellent horseman, even he could see they had bitten off more than they could chew. His warriors were in deep, deep trouble and Edwin's ork infantry began to charge with pikes.

'Can't they see we cannot break through?' said Morcion to Jacob, the greenhorn who had found himself beside his captain in the midst of the orks' onslaught. Jacob, angered by the savagery, was more concerned about getting revenge than merely surviving.

'I just wish the king was here,' was his courteous response as he released an arrow into the horde.

In the chaos, Mort saw his chance. Riding at an angle that was obscured from Edwin's view, unblinking and with elbows pointed outwards, he charged with the aim of dethroning the prince. At the vital moment Archelaus shouted a warning that alerted Edwin to Mort's looming presence. Before he was able to swing his sword in the elf's direction, Mort lunged at the prince's neck, the armour's only weak spot.

Edwin released his reins to raise his gauntlet and deflected the blade. Then, with all the might he could summon, he discharged a black pulsar blast from his ornate weapon, hitting Mort full in the chest. Its intensity crushed the elf's rib cage and left Mort mortally wounded as his horse galloped off in the direction of the forest. Severely weakened, Edwin signalled to his warriors, who closed ranks around him.

Mort's act of gallantry raised the elves' spirits and the Alfaris' attack intensified. Chimes of steel rang out. General Cog rallied his troops and the Draconians pushed the second wave back.

Having seen Morcion's son fall, Crayfar gave the signal to withdraw. At the sight of another celestial flare, a hail of arrows was released and the elves retreated again, although this time no one followed. Molton stood firm on his mount and the southern tribes held their line. Edwin observed the captain's stance. He, too, was in no mood to lose more men to Oaken-Dale this night.

Bodies of Alfari warriors and their horses littered the meadow and the sounds of those who were dying filled the air. Edwin was glad the elves had missed a trick by not sending out another attack. With his energy depleted the horde was in disarray without their figurehead. He was in two minds as he tried to decide whether to send in the hellhounds or to use his siege machinery.

After deliberating with Archelaus, the decision was made and he called for Morkpork, his kennel master. The ork appeared wearing a hideous grin.

'You called, my lord,' said the bald-headed cretin. He was armed with a whip and a choke-hold collar attached to a wooden pole, which was weirdly similar to the leather collar around his neck.

'Send in the dogs,' ordered Edwin with a morbid pleasure.

'I'll need a fresh scent, my lord,' the ork said, eager to please.

'Look around you,' Archelaus responded flatly. The carts containing the hell-hounds were rolled to the edge of the forest and Morkpork, with his orks, gave the dogs the scent and watched them fight over the fabric before opening the gates one by one. The hounds disappeared into Oaken-Dale.

On his return Morcion was inconsolable. The grief-stricken warrior had nearly fallen from his stallion when he saw his son absorb the full blast from the gauntlet. Jacob, ever alert, had helped him back into his stirrups and escorted his superior back to relative safety. Mort had been brought back from the battlefield, but the warrior physicians immediately knew there was nothing they could do. Through rasping breaths, the elf called for his father. Morcion kneeled beside his son and removed the elf's helmet.

'I'm here, Mort, I'm here.' Morcion's words seemed to give his son some comfort.

'I was trying to make you proud.' Mort looked up at his father with spent eyes.

'I know, my son. Not a day has gone by that I haven't been proud of you.'

Morcion manage a brave smile as the tears flowed. Mort had already slipped into unconsciousness and died where he lay, in his father's arms.

Durion offered his friend a consoling embrace. The passing of any elf was sorrowful, but one so young and well liked was an extremely bitter pill to swallow. Crayfar could see

Morcion was a broken elf when the second wave returned, but there was no time to console his captain. He could see that the brigade was not being pursued. He called over Hal Stone, then pointed at the orks standing beside the cages.

'What are they?' he asked.

'Beats me,' responded Hal. Then he looked over at his men. 'Jared,' he called, and his sidekick walked over. 'Jared, the High Lord wants to know what those things are.'

The eagle-eyed knife-thrower was a mute from birth, so with a few quick hand gestures he explained to Hal what they were.

'Barbaric! He wouldn't?' said Hal, shocked. 'They're surmas in those cages,' he informed Crayfar, 'and if he's about to release them, then we're off.' Jared nodded in agreement.

'What?' asked Crayfar.

'Hell-hounds. Let me be clear: our mission is to ambush Edwin's army where he is weakest in order to slow his progress, and we can't do that if we're dead,' replied Hal, with a resigned look.

'Cowards,' muttered Crayfar under his breath, but he could see from the look on his face that Arvellon thought Hal was right. Hal had overheard the word but before he could react the sound of hounds howling and barking reverberated around them, the demon pack inching ever closer.

Hal, with an expression that spoke volumes, whispered, 'Too late,' and shouted this men to arm themselves. Crayfar followed suit. The baying and yowling became almost deafening and, being downwind, they could smell the tainted air of the foul hounds. Arvellon was still livid at the High Lord's decision not to back up his brigade. It was clear to him that Durion should have been sent back into the fold, which would have allowed them to save more lives.

Looking at his depleted ranks, Durion suggested respectfully that Crayfar sound the retreat. His ruse had failed, and continued dithering would only get more elves killed.
The High Lord conceded the point and Badhron was ordered to lead the withdrawal.
Suddenly hell hounds were upon the Alfari, dragging them from their saddles and, in packs, were systematically picking them off. Noticing that his own men weren't their intended target Hal allowed them to aid the fight. Jared producing two daggers with a cheeky smile, then began his task with relish.

Badhron didn't wait for another command. Seeing the carnage, he gave the order to release the tigers again. Their powerful hind legs propelled them forward into an almighty collision with the hounds and, with eyes fixed on their prey, they tore through the onslaught. The shrieks and yelps emanating from the forest gave away the elves' position.
 'Now load the siege weapons and aim at the dogs!' shouted Archelaus.
 'What?' yelled Morkpork. 'What about my hell-hounds?'
 'Those that survive will be worthy of our cause,' replied Edwin bluntly.
Morkpork grunted and walked away despondently. He wasn't buying any of that crap.

The catapults were loaded up with steel ball bearings and the large trebuchets with massive rocks covered in elm oil. The contraptions whistled loudly when released, as though full of life. The devastation was inevitable once the hail had begun. Ball bearings tore through the forest and hot oils and molten metal fell from the burning boulders. Morkpork's hell-hounds continued to attack, spurred on by the flames. Jeremiah's Tiger Division was still up for the challenge. With Alfari dropping all around them Arvellon was fuming at the carnage.

'Is this what you call a victory? The council will hear of your arrogance!' he shouted as a boulder flew past Crayfar and swept him from his horse, crushing him to death. Although still in a state of shock, Morcion retrieved Arvellon's broken body in the chaos and, placing his lugar on a horse, rode away from the bombardment. With the loss of such a vital warrior the High Lord was crestfallen. He spurred his horse and, alongside Hal, rode for dear life. Crayfar knew Arvellon had been right.

*

Some time had passed since the incident with the minthe. Tartarus had to admit he had seen much better days. He was experiencing a dreariness that felt suffocating. He could hear the rain and the periodic rumble of thunder. Although he felt uneasy by its grumblings, the lighting was obscured from view and that was probably a good thing since it would have added to his cheerlessness. He was thousands of leagues from the beauty of Oaken-Dale and wondered why Lord Erynion had put him forward for this dangerous mission. He'd been knocked out twice and still he was no closer to regaining the scroll.

There were things to be thankful for, though, such as meeting the boys and finding their sister. That had been a touch of good fortune; he hoped for more of the same. Pippa's account of Kallen and his men could prove invaluable. A girl in the clutches of a dark elf; he shook his head and smiled. The effect her presence had on the group, especially on Tarquin and Flint, seemed to alleviate the pain of losing their parents. The Black Forest was a scary place at the best of times and he was glad to be accompanied by people who were comfortable with its surroundings. Ragnarr's rapport with the blacksmith, and his constant mood swings, were a source of great entertainment. As for bravery, Nefanial had that in spades. He recalled the moment the man had taken a run at the witch, and smiled again.

Tartarus wondered how Jacob and Eolande were faring. Tears of joy came into his eyes when he thought of Jacob and his infectious laughter. Thoughts of Eolande stirred him in other ways; her sculptured features, warm complexion and firm but slender form always gave him goosebumps. The royal rider's note worried him greatly, but fretting about Oaken-Crag would not help him or anyone else so he did his best to suppress the feelings. To remain vigilant took fortitude and most Alfari elgars thought he lacked this quality. Tartarus was determined to prove them wrong. Returning without delivering the scroll was not an option.

His new-found friends inspired confidence in himself and helped to build an inner belief that obstacles could be overcome. From Pippa's description it seemed that Kallen would be a fearsome opponent, but growing up in Oaken-Dale forest made him just as tough. In a way he resented not being treated as an equal. Not everyone accepted him with open arms; being only a quarter human was, at times, a hindrance, and its beneficial points sometimes went unseen. Tartarus believed that his human attributes accelerated his development and made him an even better elf; his teachers disagreed.

'Your humanity will get you killed one day, greenhorn,' he had been told. The words evoked painful memories because they referred to his father's demise.

'Steady on, young pup.' Rex rode up alongside Tartarus. 'Thinking too much?' he said with a knowing look. 'I like to keep an open mind and a clear head on a quest; you'd be wise to follow my lead.'

'How did you guess?' enquired Tartarus.

'When you've been around as long as I have then you'll know,' answered Rex.

The ambiguous response left Tartarus even more baffled.

'What does that mean?' he asked.

'The weight of the world cannot be carried alone, for its burden will break the bearer in two. A wise man once taught me that,' replied the weather-beaten veteran.

'You're trying to remind me to spread the load?' Tartarus acknowledged the insight with a courteous smile.

'You've got it. This part of the forest will play tricks on your mind, so remember – clear thoughts,' Rex said solemnly.

The forest's silence closed in on them once they left the main trail. Spiky bramble bushes tore, like claws, at their clothes and unsettled the horses. A feeling of dread hung, like a lingering smell, on layers of mist and a mixture of sour, fusty air filled their lungs. The earth under hoof was soft, slowing their progress.

'Be careful where the horses tread. There are quagmires everywhere,' warned Ragnarr. Brun looked down at Cloud's hooves just to check, with a hand firmly placed on his serrated bladed axe. Nefanial looked at his men then tapped Calhoun on the arm, warning him to be mindful. There was no need to warn his assistant; he was still shaken by previous events and his eyes roamed the forest feverishly.

Pippa, although weary of the environment, was still as enthusiastic as Flint about the expedition and the marshy wooded area could not dampen her spirit. Wearing her straw hat she patted Rainbow's mane, then looked up at her siblings with a fondness rarely seen. Her protector pounced on all paws gleefully by her side. She had named the Daginhale terrier Angus, after her father. Ragnarr, riding alongside Brun, was going through a list of creatures they may encounter lurking in the forest.

'There are ogres, parasitic fairies and a lair where huge two-headed serpents slither. We've already met a witch, although she was a water nymph,' he rambled. Brun wasn't paying much attention; he was watching a pair of very large eyes observing them through the trees.

'So what's that, then?' he asked the dwarf.

'They're supposed to be extinct,' said Ragnarr, his expression changing as he pulled on his reins.

'Not in these parts they're not,' said Brun.

'It's a three-legged solar bird,' Ragnarr replied still shocked. The lizard–bird hybrid had a tail that was considered to be a third leg.

'It looks hungry. They're not dangerous, are they?' Brun asked in what he hoped was an offhand way.

'They can be if there are ...' Suddenly more eyes appeared from either side; the low-pitched squawking and the rustling of leaves were unnerving. Angus started to growl.

'Be still now,' requested Pippa, which seemed to settle him down.

Tartarus looked at the others for answers. All eyes fell on Ragnarr.

'When I say ride, ride like your lives depend upon it,' instructed the dwarf.

Flint positioned his horse beside Pippa's and chuckled.

'Well, you did say you wanted chicken, Pip.'

'Oh, Flint, will you ever grow up?' The joke was badly timed and in poor taste.

'No,' he said with a serious face, and gave her a wink.

Tarquin made sure the rope attached to Rainbow's bridle was secure; there was no way on Elohim he was letting his sister out of his sight again. Nefanial gave his men the signal to draw their swords. As they slowed to a crawl the lizard-tailed birds attacked. chaos of flapping and high-pitched shrieking ensued. The birds had bright yellow eyes, jagged beaks and dull brown feathers with rainbow tips. They were carnivores and they saw the convoy as their next feast. Tartarus decided that a spell was needed and muttered under his breath, *'Permissum suum exsisto incendia, incendia, incendia.'* A fire apparition emanated from his finger tips, deflecting the attack long enough to give them a head start.

'Ride,' shouted Ragnarr. Riding blindly through bushes and around trees meant that Kallen's trail was lost, but at that the moment the only clear thought was for survival. Tartarus led the way. One of Nefanial's men, Randolph, was pounced on and, losing his balance, fell in a heap. Screams followed as he was eaten alive. Tartarus, alongside Rex, rode as hard as he could, the sickening screams spurring him on.

'Can't we make a stand and fight?' asked Nefanial, shouting over the noise.

'Too many,' shouted Ragnarr.

Brun clenched his teeth and his tight grip on Cloud's reins turned his knuckles white.

'Solar birds, indeed,' he thought, as he guided Cloud through the dark forest. He looked at his axe but dared not reach for it. His stability was too important. Ragnarr, bobbing alongside, was fighting to regain his poise at every turn and wished he was onboard his war-rhino. He could ride his pet with war hammer in hand and these pesky birds needed swatting. Reece was riding one-handed, flapping one arm furiously in an attempt to shake a bird off his wrist.

Half hopping, half flying, the birds snapped at their heels and were not giving up on their meal. A few were trampled under the horses' hooves. Flint was slashing his sword through the air, catching the odd one in flight, while trying to retain his speed. Angus was having a horrid time, his fleece bloody, but the terrier was giving as good as he got. Tartarus rounded a few more trees and a knoll with a cave entrance became visible. He headed straight for it.

'There,' he shouted, 'we'll make our stand there.'
Rex nodded in agreement. As they closed in on the opening the birds stopped chasing.

'That's unusual,' commented Ragnarr. 'I don't think going into that cave is a good idea.'

'But they've stopped chasing us, 'said Flint, out of breath and glad Pippa had come through the ordeal unscathed. Tarquin, also breathing hard, looked at Pippa then pinched her cheek with a smile.

'Get off, Tarquin,' she said, returning his smile. Tarquin shook his head in amazement.
'Nothing scares our Pip.'

Brun looked at Ragnarr.
'Well, if you want to you can wait out here,' he told the dwarf.
Both turned to see Randolph's horse gallop past without its rider. Nefanial shook his head. In his grief, he told himself that his recruit knew the risks.

The cave looked tranquil enough, although they were aware that this may not be the case. The noxious smell of rotting, decaying flesh was a warning. Water dripped from the cave's roof, extinguishing their torches. The echo could be heard ringing far off in the distance.
'Keep your wits about you,' said Rex, as he held his wrist over his nostrils to mask the smell. No sooner had he spoken the words than they encountered a sticky substance that emitted a luminous, transparent blue light as soon as it made contact with the group.
'I think this stuff is some sort of web,' Ragnarr said, still sulking about the decision to enter the cave. He tried to relight his torch but found his movement somewhat restricted by the web.
'And what, by Elohim, is this blue light?' asked Nefanial.
'Some sort of presence detector, I imagine,' said Tarquin; it reminded him of laying down trip-wires.
'Can anyone else hear that noise?' asked Pippa. Everyone listened intently. Tartarus nodded.
'Unholy inferno!' shouted Calhoun as the sound of scurrying insects became louder.

'You're not afraid of spiders are you, boy?' whispered Rex over his shoulder.
The tearful assistant answered, 'Yes.'

Black, hairy spiders with numerous tiny, red eyes filled the cavern, scaling the walls and swarming over the floor. In seconds they had completely encircled them and begun to spray more webs. Tartarus went to cast a spell but, being covered from the neck down, found that he couldn't.
'We need fire!' shouted Ragnarr, still trying to light his torch.

The web seemed to have a drowsy effect, but it didn't bother the horses or Angus, who was barking loudly and attacking at will.
'I think now might be a good time for some magic!' shouted Flint, his horse rearing to avoid the spray.
'I can't. There must be a spell inhibiter close by,' said Tartarus.
'That doesn't sound good,' said Nefanial, with a raised eyebrow.
Having seen Randolph fall, both Barnaby and Daniel swallowed hard, looking at each other and wondering who would be next.
'I think we should dismount and squash these bugs,' suggested Brun.
'Are you crazy? The floor is covered with them,' snapped Ragnarr.

Before they could comprehend the magnitude of their predicament, their energy ebbed away and they were entombed like mummies, falling with a thud from their horses.

The spiders cleared the space around them and then half-human male spiders entered the chamber.

'Queen Arachna will be pleased,' one of the spiders hissed.

'That doesn't sound good,' Nefanial said just as he, along with the others, was dragged into a labyrinth of connecting tunnels. Not long afterwards they all succumbed to the power of the web and were sleeping soundly.

*

The normality of day-to-day life had still not returned to Irons Keep. The heavens were grumbling and behind the log fences, rain and sweat poured off the industrious villagers who were busy repairing their homes. Under the master carpenter's expert guidance the rejuvenation was in full swing. The noise of hammering rang out constantly. It was hard work and their only salvation was knowing that men had been sent to seek revenge.

Though impoverished by Brandenburg's taxes their zeal remained intact and anger inevitably ran deep while they all awaited news of retribution. The flurry and bustle could be heard when Lockwood, Zog and his battalion galloped up to the main gate. They were greeted by the sight of the brigand swinging from the gallows.

'You there, why is that man swinging and what's that infernal racket? I can't hear myself think,' Lockwood demanded, looking down at the sentry. The sentry gave him a nonchalant look; before he had seen this man, he thought the lizards were going to attack.

'Where's Gwillym?' asked Lockwood impatiently.

'He's on an errand,' answered the sentry suspiciously, ready at a moment's notice to unseat Lockwood from his horse.

'When will he be back?' Lockwood asked sharply. The question was not greeted warmly.

'And you are who?'

'Me? I'm Baron Brandon of Brandenburg's man-at-arms,' Lockwood declared proudly, getting off his horse and unperturbed by the lack of respect. Zog and his Draconians did the same.

'He didn't say when he'd be back,' said the sentry. 'The keep was attacked by bandits, a day or so ago.'

'And he's one of them,' said a second sentry, pointing at the still-fresh corpse, swinging in the wind.

'Oh, I see.' Lockwood recognized the brigand but did not mention it. Zog was on the sentries in a flash.

'Really? Did any of them look like this?' He unrolled a parchment with a crude drawing of Brun. 'I've been told he's travelling with a dwarf.' Both sentries gave the portrait a quick glance.

'So what's he done then?' asked the second sentry.

'Murdered a royal rider,' hissed Zog.

'Flipping heck! Then I don't think he'd be daft enough to pass through here,' exclaimed the sandy-haired sentry, lifting his chin in the direction of the gallows.

'He's right, his face doesn't look familiar,' added the second sentry.

'He may be one of them, but I couldn't say. We went to the winter solstice celebrations at the ruins of Ebenknesha,' said the first.

'Enough of this chit-chat. Who's in charge then? I need to know if anyone knows where this man was heading,' said Zog.

'That would be Gwillym's cousin, Adrian,' answered the first sentry.

'So where is this Adrian?' demanded Zog, becoming increasingly frustrated by these two sentries.

'That work-shy oddball is probably at the tavern,' whispered the second sentry.

'He's at the tavern, sir,' replied the first sentry. The second sentry then gave the command to open the gate, revealing a keep in ruins. Zog rued crossing paths with this accursed blacksmith. In the days and weeks of pursuing his quarry, he was slowly beginning to admire the man's ability to evade capture. However, he never lost sight of the fact that Silvanus was a friend, and the loss of his stolen heirloom was incalculable. Anyway, if he did not return with Brun's head on a plate he was sure his own head would take its place.

Since landing on the shores of Abbehale the blacksmith had vanished. The western lands were kingless, lawless and filled with peasants; a perfect breeding ground in which to hide. Going by his misfortune so far, the mission to apprehend Brun may have become more difficult if he was indeed one of these brigands. Unlike the weather he was accustomed to, where the sky was a reddish colour from the sulphur in the atmosphere and the twisting flames of firenados reached skywards, here the skies constantly opened up and he hated the rain. Droplets slid off his leathery skin as he shook the moisture from his face. The blacksmith's day of reckoning would come soon enough.

The sentry led them up a muddy track into the main square and stopped outside a tavern with waist-high wooden railings as a barrier along its porch. A long redwood bar separated the bartender from his patrons. The Iron Mead was the stronghold's only tavern.

'That's him in the middle, sir.' The sentry pointed at Gwillym's cousin, Adrian, who was sitting with two villagers seemingly subdued by the euphoria of a drunken stupor.

'You're sure that's him?' asked Zog with a sceptical expression. Lockwood was bemused too. 'He looks more like a shaman.' The sentry grunted. Zog ordered Rog, his sergeant, to take his battalion and search the village. Then, flanked by two Draconians, he followed Lockwood into the tavern.

Adrian was one hundred percent gay, and proud of it. Keeping it in the closet was the last thing on his mind. He would even go as far as to flaunt the fact, much to Gwillym's displeasure. His flamboyant personality ruffled the feathers of more than a few of the villagers, but on the whole the majority loved his eccentric nature. The dressmaker's audacious designs stayed in his scrapbook and he drank heavily because he wasn't fulfilling his true potential. He was dressed in a black velvet tunic with tights and pointed felt boots. He wore silver rings on each finger, including his thumbs. Long yellow, frizzy hair covered high cheek bones.

'You there, are you the chief's regent? I'm Cuthbert Lockwood, Brandenburg's man-at-arms.'

Adrian raised his head from his tankard and burped. He looked at his two companions, then at the two Lockwoods standing in front of him, and said playfully, 'I could be. Why? Which one of you wants to know?' Lockwood walked forward, pushing tables out of his path, followed by Zog.

'We haven't got time for your jests. The sentry has just pointed you out,' said Lockwood, pulling his sword from its sheath. In the blink of an eye its pointed edge was propping up Adrian's chin. Zog was impressed.

'Calm down. There's no need to be aggressive. I'm Adrian,' he said with a hapless grin, gingerly moving the blade away from his face before waving his arm to the bartender. 'Virgil, fetch my new friends a drink.'

Adrian looked at Zog.

'I like your outfit. Very nice,' he said coyly.

'We're not here to buy or sell dresses,' replied Zog firmly.

'Pity,' said Adrian. 'I'd make you a fine outfit.' He smiled at his companions, and presented Zog with a stool. He had a thing about muscles and the Draconian was bulging all over. The offer was not accepted.

'Suit yourself, friend,' said Adrian, withdrawing the stool. Lockwood looked at Adrian's companions.

'Leave us,' he commanded.

'Now hang on a moment. That's no way to speak to my guests,' interjected Adrian. Lockwood's face contorted in anger. Adrian raised his eyelids and reluctantly uttered the words, 'Very well'. The men gave the southerner a harsh look as they vacated their stools without saying goodbye.

The dressmaker's flirtatious eyes were making Zog feel uneasy so he nudged Lockwood to pursue their lines of inquiry. Adrian, amused, revelled in the Draconian's visible discomfort. The man-at-arms pulled one of the now vacant stools over and sat down, while Zog stood.

'So where is your cousin anyway?' Lockwood was curious and thought a bit of prying wouldn't go amiss.

'Gone to recruit men to chase down the men who attacked us, and report the incident to the baron of course. After all, this is his land,' Adrian answered, aware that Lockwood was fishing.

'Do you know why they attacked?'

'All I know is that we suffered a heavy loss: nineteen dead and many injured.'

Zog handed Lockwood the parchment.

'This man is wanted for murder. Have you seen him?' asked Lockwood.

'No, alas. He's just my type,' Adrian said, sighing and handing the parchment back. He lifted his tankard to his mouth and took a hearty swig.

Adrian knew exactly who the person on the parchment was. Brun was a friend. This man and his dragon battalion were not. If this Lockwood character thought the alcohol would loosen his lips he was sadly mistaken. Prince Edwin's intercepted message was clear. The fortified stronghold had become a pawn in the prince's twisted game. Lillian, still lying gravely ill, was testament to that. The indications were that Lockwood was not aware of Brun's connection to the village, and that was the way Adrian wanted it to remain.

Gwillym was alert to the fact that Brandenburg may send men to gather information and, after a quiet word, Adrian was only too happy to send anyone asking questions on a merry dance. He wasn't sure what would give him more satisfaction: seeing Prince Edwin, or Brandenburg swinging alongside the brigand on the gallows. He savoured that thought for a moment. Virgil rounded the bar and placed three tankards on the table. Adrian smiled.

'Great minds think alike. I was about to ask you for a refill.' The burly man acknowledged him with a wink.

'Bartender, have you seen this man?' asked Lockwood.

'No, not in these parts,' replied Virgil, picking up the empty tankards.

'So he wasn't one of the men who attacked this keep?' asked Lockwood, wiping the froth from his lips.

'Might be. I wouldn't know. I was at the ...'

'The ruins,' said Lockwood, finishing the sentence for him. Adrian nodded.

'I was there too,' he added cheerfully.

'This is a waste of time,' said Zog, clearly annoyed.

'I know,' agreed Lockwood, looking up to the heavens, where his eyes found only the tavern's wooden ceiling. 'Look here,' he continued, 'someone must know something.'

In response to Rog's uncompromising search methods a few of the villagers had started to congregate outside the tavern, wondering why these Draconians were here so soon after the keep was ransacked. With the prospect of another soil invasion, pitchforks were at the ready. As the crowd grew their grumblings got louder and more animated.

'What's wrong with them?' asked Lockwood.

'What do you expect? It's only a matter of days since we were raided and now dragon-men search our village for a man we know nothing about,' said Adrian. The boisterous disposition of the villagers seemed to unsettle Zog, who was acutely aware that he had insufficient manpower to deal with a rowdy crowd of this size, and if they decided to lynch them their death would be inevitable.

'Where are the baron's men when we need them?' one villager jeered.

'We pay our taxes. It's only right that we receive protection!' shouted another.

Lockwood got to his feet, turned to them and nodded as though he was moved by their plight.

'We're here to address your concerns,' he said, trying to sound as though he shared their sentiments, but inwardly he vehemently disagreed. His personal view was that the western tribes were vermin and he couldn't care less if they were slaughtered. When tackling the crowd he had made eye contact with one of Brandenburg's moles. The difficulty was how to amalgamate the spy's information with his own without revealing the mole's identity.

'He's right. It's all in hand,' said Adrian, authoritatively. 'Now go back to work,' he added, attempting to quell the fire in their bellies. The villagers did not disperse but stood firm.

'So, who was present when the attack took place?' Lockwood asked the crowd, in no mood to speak to anyone else that had been to the ruins. Adrian had him just where he wanted him.

'Myrtle was. Maybe she knows.' He signalled the sentry. 'Call Myrtle over,' he ordered.

Myrtle, escorted by the sentry, walked in, removed her apron and threw it onto the adjacent table.

'And what do these men want?' she asked, clearly annoyed. 'I was about to prepare a meal for Lillian when I caught wind of all this commotion.' Adrian gave her a look; talk of Brun's sister was definitely a bad idea.

'Who's Lillian?' demanded Lockwood.

'The baker's wife. She's under the weather,' Myrtle replied. 'Now, I haven't got all day, so what do you want with me?' Adrian explained, and they showed her the parchment. She squinted at it.

'Maybe he was one of them,' she said. 'I can't be sure. There was so much fog. I do remember a goblin-looking creature named Kallen and a man with a patch over an eye.'

Adrian noticed the slip of the tongue. So did Lockwood.
'Did they say where they were heading?' asked Zog.
She turned to face the reptilian.
'I overheard them say they were going to sell their wares to the Kelts if that helps.'
'So how do you know the creature's name?' the man-at-arms asked shrewdly.
Myrtle, realizing her mistake, backtracked quickly.
'Must have heard them call his name, I suppose.'

Although he could not prove it, Lockwood was sure the hag was lying. The man swinging by his neck was one of Kallen's men and, if he wasn't mistaken, that would mean the prince had Silvanus killed, if he believed this woman's account. Just why would Edwin have the Draconian pursue his own men, and why would the blacksmith and a dwarf be riding with a dark elf for that matter? That just didn't make any sense. The Dökkalfar and the Denvagar were not natural bedfellows. Even for Lockwood it was all getting confusing. Hiding out in the Keltic lands? From his last reports Kallen was in the Black Forest. Unless Prince Edwin had a secret pact with the Kelts that his baron did not know about. No. He had to believe she was lying.
Brandenburg had sworn him to secrecy; Kallen's activities were to be overlooked.

Zog had heard enough. All this dithering was squandering time. She was the second person to say his quarry was heading for the Keltic lands and there was no smoke without fire.

'We're leaving,' he announced.

Lockwood's thought processes had reached a different conclusion. He followed Zog out, but stopped by the porch railings to address the crowd while Zog continued walking towards his horse.

'Friends, your grievances will be better addressed if you write them down in notes, which I will deliver in person. Remember, the baron is known for his short fuse so choose your words wisely,' advised Lockwood.

Myrtle's face was a picture. Adrian noted Lockwood's strange behaviour. Hurriedly, a few of the villagers got scribbling before individually handing their notes to the baron's man. Unsurprisingly, the clouds opened up as the crowd escorted the battalion to the main entrance.

The gate slammed shut and the sound of repairing resumed.

'How do you think that went?' asked Adrian.

'Only time will tell, Adrian,' replied Myrtle, getting soaked.

Licking the water from his lips, he placed an arm around her chubby frame.

'Let's hope they meet the Kelts,' he laughed. Myrtle didn't join in.

'We've got a spy in our midst,' she whispered. His face turned deadly serious and he nodded.

'I know.'

As Irons Keep faded into the distance, Lockwood shared some of his suspicions with Zog.

'The hag was lying. Your man can't be with Kallen.'

'And how do you know?'

'I can't say, but believe me I'm sure.'

That was not the answer Zog was looking for and he was having none of it.

'I've met two people both saying the same thing. If you're scared of these Kelts, say so.' The other Draconians laughed.

'Do I look it?' said Lockwood, his face hardening. 'All I'm saying is that Kallen's in the Black Forest.'

'No more keeps, no more forests. Your baron has ordered you to be my guide. Now take me to the Baron Crofton Abbehale or leave. I can find my own way, if need be,' replied Zog, having trouble keeping his temper in check.

'No. When we get to Glen-Neath I'll send word to the baron to destroy that keep. Something is amiss there for some reason. They're lying through their teeth and this note will prove it.' Discarding the rest of the villagers' messages, he kept one and tucked it into his pocket.

*

'Ragnarr wake up,' whispered Brun. 'Wake up.'
Feeling groggy, the dwarf rolled his eyes to focus. He was about to shout out but, seeing Arachna's spiky leg, he decided to hold his breath. The domed mausoleum was dimly lit but Ragnarr could see that the tightly packed mud walls were covered with carved depictions of heroic deeds and lined with lavishly woven tapestries in extravagant colours. A large, inlaid sarcophagus was at the back of the tomb, which was undoubtedly Arachna's bed. Over it hung a wall carving of the spider queen in all her splendour. To its left, a treasure trove of victims' valuable possessions was

piled high at the entrance of a connecting tomb. A cocktail of stale air was a clear indication that they were a long way from an exit.

Apart from being a mausoleum, the area was set up as though Arachna believed she was more human than spider. The queen's female form – half black widow, half homosapiens – had little spikes running along her spine and two human arms were supplemented by six prickly legs spewing from her torso. Black hair flowed to just above the small of her back. She moved pryingly between her prisoners, akin to an inquisitive spider. The large insect eyes on her beautiful, gaunt face seemed wrong.

'Guests, guests, I have guests,' she hissed from behind fanged teeth.

'Pray tell, what sorcery is this?' asked Nefanial, completely bamboozled. Having awoken from unconsciousness he was surprised to find he was still locked in this hellish dream.

'Silence, I think I'll eat you first,' she said, pressing her clawed tarsi against his chest.

'You'll do what?' retorted Nefanial, despite the queen's intimidating aura. He had been lost to fear a long time ago and she didn't scare him. Arachna did not entertain him with a response.

'One of you is a spell caster. Is it you?' she asked, looking at Tartarus. Her eyes were like a stained-glass window mirroring the same image on each shard. He saw his reflection in them and was horrified to see that from the neck downwards he was bound up tight; even his feet had been covered.

Tartarus glanced past her and noticed a large ruby set in an ornately patterned gold holder on a pedestal, and instantly he knew what it was; Ekaterina had a similar one.

The queen was no fool and she knew that in order to protect her lair the spell caster must be killed. She could not sense magic; that's what her ruby was for. Still she looked over her captives individually as though she could detect the presence of magic.

'A girl,' she purred, stroking Pippa's face with her leg then gently kicking off her hat. 'A special girl,' she said, her sensitive hairs detecting Pippa's potential strength.

Pippa closed her eyes. With her jack-knife in hand she was quietly attempting to cut her bonds.

'Stop wriggling. Your sustenance will last longer than the others,' the queen said, amused.

'Leave her alone,' shouted Tarquin.

Arachna gave a small smirk. Human meat was a delicacy when digested slowly and she planned on gorging herself on their flesh. In a flash, Arachna stooped over him.

'Tell me, boy, who is she to you? You bear no resemblance to each other.'

Tarquin fixed her with a cold stare.

'What do you care?'

'If you tell me who among you is the spell caster, I'll set her free,' hissed the queen, revelling in Tarquin's discomfort. His blank expression gave nothing away. Tightly wrapped in webbing, her rancid breath was making it even more difficult for him to breathe.

'Worthless humans. When Cressida opens the gates to inferno our time will come and then your kind will know true pain. Pity that you'll be long since dead.' Her hideous hiss was menacingly cruel. At the mention of the sorceress's name Ragnarr felt an urge to be sick. The prophecy about the nymph, the spider and the wolf resonated, but he had never before believed it to be true.

'Free me and I'll tell you!' shouted Flint. Though the others voiced their disapproval Tartarus did not. He trusted Flint not to reveal his identity; he knew it was a ruse. He just wasn't sure if it was foolhardy, or well thought out.

The queen ran a claw along Flint's bonds and the cocoon fell apart. Seizing his chance and knowing that failure was not an option he rose and took aim. A bolt flew from his crossbow and headed straight for Arachna. Even at such close range, the agility and speed at which she moved meant the arrow missed. The spider hissed, spitting strands of web in Flint's direction. With the nimble feet of a hunter he managed to dodge the web.

'Shoot the ruby, the ruby!' shouted Tartarus, wishing he was able to point. Flint's eyes scoured the room for the object, his arm moving in tandem. Setting his sights on the glowing target, this time he did not miss. The impact cracked the gem stone and a shimmering green mist seeped out. Arachna let out a scream of dread that reverberated around the chamber, her deafening cry waking up Daniel and Reece. With absolute hatred etched on her face she charged at Flint, who in turn pivoted on his heels, and the queen slid past. She scaled the wall using her tiny leg-hairs for grip. If Flint was worried it didn't show. He released another shaft just as Arachna sprang off the wall. Tartarus was already on his feet, his first spell freeing him from his bonds and the second directed at Arachna. The mini-explosion momentarily threw Flint off his feet. Although severely singed the queen managed to scamper from the chamber, screaming for her guards. Flint freed Barnaby, who helped liberate the others, while Tartarus guarded the entrance.

'*Ego excito vox perussi incendia,*' muttered Tartarus, releasing another fireball at Arachna. Somehow she avoided it and slipped into a connecting tunnel out of view.

'I can't keep this up all day,' he said in a panic. With the spider calling for reinforcements he knew she would be back.

'Cal, check that room for an exit,' directed Nefanial, still shaking off web.

'Sidney, Tarquin, find something to barricade the entrance with.' He pointed at Tartarus's position.

'Incendia.' The elf targeted one of the guards, crippling him with a magical blast.

Calhoun ran to the other opening, which was packed to the rafters with previous victims' personal effects, and tried to peer over. Then he called to Nefanial and shook his head. If there was an escape route, he couldn't see it. By accident, his foot nudged the pile and an item near the top bounced down, hitting a crown that rolled out of the entrance, landing at his feet. He reached down to pick it up, immediately noticing its Keltic markings.

'Hurry up, Cal, we need a hand here. Forget that old crown. We need weapons.' Calhoun looked up at Nefanial and back at the crown. Although it was plain, he could tell that once cleaned it would gleam. He decided to keep it.

Having seen Calhoun shake his head Nefanial, who, along with Rex and Brun, stood by Tartarus's side, informed him that they were looking at the only route to freedom. The news produced a grimace. Pippa's main concerns were Rainbow and Angus's health, and she asked Tarquin about the horse and her pet.

'How do I know?' he asked, abruptly. 'Sorry. We'll find them, Pip.' He, too, had an affinity with Rainbow and the terrier had saved her life. Caught up in the moment, he wished he hadn't been harsh with her but, as though she understood, she smiled and gently squeezed his hand.

Looking into the next chamber, Brun could see the sprawling legs of half-human male spiders, with shields and spears, being marshalled by Arachna.

'There's an army out there. There's no way we're getting through them,' Brun said, disheartened. Rex was in agreement.

'It doesn't look good, lad.' Even Nefanial had to admit the signs were ominous. Although Tartarus put on a brave face, inwardly he was doleful. His magic could probably save some, but not all, of his companions.

'This might not be the only escape route. I bet you'll be glad I brought this,' said Ragnarr, pulling out a petri dish which contained a yellow substance from his pocket.

'What is that?' asked Tartarus, fascinated by the gooey organism in a cylindrical glass tub.

'Slime mould, and it solve mazes,' he replied, as though a chance to escape was still within his grasp. 'If you dig tunnels it's impractical to leave home without it.'

'And we all know who loves digging tunnels,' added Rex. Ragnarr nodded.

'Solves mazes?' Tartarus repeated, baffled. 'How does it do that?'

Ragnarr took a few paces back, opened the dish, and asked Pippa to blow on the mould for good luck. Then, pouring half of the slime out, he quickly put the dish back in his pocket. The mould hit the floor, split into two globules that expanded in an erratic line, and began to seek out clear air.

'Watch and learn,' Ragnarr declared proudly. 'Once it finds the exit its point of origin will start to retract.' One globule of mould headed straight past them at speed and went into the adjoining chamber then disappeared down a tunnel. The other went through Ragnarr's legs in the opposite direction.

'That's good, there's another exit,' said the dwarf confidently as he looked between his legs. The others gave him a quizzical stare.

'Slime mould never lies,' Ragnarr assured them.

Calhoun seemed horrified as he watched the mould bear down on the sarcophagus.

'I think it's heading for the coffin,' he said aghast.

'I'm not getting into that,' screamed Pippa with eyes wide open.

'Don't worry, Pip, I'll protect you.' Flint kneeled down and gave her a hug to allay her fears.

'Blimey, that stuff moves fast,' commented Nefanial, observing the slime mould reaching the black marbled coffin in no time at all.

'That's what's good about it,' was Ragnarr's response.

Tarquin tapped Tartarus, enquiring about their horses. He was right: without their mounts the quest was doomed.

'I know,' replied Tartarus, 'but we haven't got time to find them before that thing retracts.'

'But we need our horses,' insisted Tarquin.

'Well, we'll just have to come back and get them.' Tartarus stood his ground. Sentimentality and irrationality had no place in a spiders' cave.

'We must save ourselves first,' he stated, sweat dripping from his hair onto his face. Foolish decisions had already cost him dearly; Asrack and Vince were testament to that. Nefanial grabbed them in a huddle. This wasn't the time to be fighting each other. He looked them both in the

eye. It was a long shot but he believed he had an ace up his sleeve. Having trained his mare to obey a whistle, she'd come – if she was still alive, and that was a very big if – and hopefully with the other horses as well. Tartarus returned the glare; it was speculative to say the least.
Tarquin just seemed to be happy with any sort of plan. The baker pursed his lips and, with a tiny chrome flute, played a short tune.

Calhoun watched the slime mould go round the sarcophagus and enter a crack in the wall behind it.
'Hey, boss, I think this wall is a fake wall!' he shouted.
'Well, don't just stand there; break it down. Reece, Daniel, give him a hand,' directed Nefanial. Then he blew his whistle again.
'You don't really have faith in that?' enquired Tartarus.
'Oh, you've got to have faith in something, Tartarus,' said Nefanial.
Rex, who was watching the spiders' movements, was getting worried.
'I think they're getting ready to attack. If we're going to do something, then we'd better do it quickly,' he warned.

Unbeknown to Tartarus, those melodies were a call of impending danger, and it hadn't fallen on deaf ears. Their horses, led by Willow, had put up such a valiant fight, sporadically raining down hooves while charging. They had activated a stand-off, with neither horse nor spider willing to advance. Nefanial's mare's ears pricked up on hearing the whistle and she went to her master's aid. Angus continued to bark; his attacks had become intermittent, as though he, too, had drawn an invisible line in the sand that they were not permitted to cross. The terrier didn't know what to make of the yellow fungus that crossed his path. Nevertheless, picking up a familiar scent, he and the other horses followed the dark brown mare down into the spiders' warren.

If there was the remotest chance of being reunited with Pippa then Angus was willing to take it.

Calhoun, Daniel and Reece were positively beaming, having broken through the depiction of Arachna to reveal a huge tunnel.

'I think that queen is very crafty,' said Calhoun. The others nodded.

'Where's Sid disappeared to?' Nefanial asked, looking around. 'Calhoun, where's Sidney?'

'He's in there,' responded his assistant, referring to the tomb.

'Well, tell him to get his ass out here.'

The sound of rummaging stopped. Sidney, having heard his name being called, didn't need telling twice and he appeared with a large bag filled with various items slung over his shoulder. They were all wondering how he was managing to carry that amount on such a slender frame.

'Hey, have you lot forgotten this is a quest?' asked the black sheep of Irons Keep. Flint laughed. Nefanial was about to object when Brun smiled at his brother-in-law.

'Leave the lad be. You never know, it may come in handy,' he whispered.

Suddenly, Arachna ordered her spiders to attack. Sid put the bag down and ran to join the others. Rex shouted 'Duck!' as spears flew into the chamber. With each step Arachna's

horde closed in on the entrance. They were unafraid to die for their queen.
Flint loaded his crossbow and let loose. Tartarus felt dizzy as he released another spell.

'Steady on, tiger. You don't look well,' observed Rex.

The mention of tigers seemed to give Tartarus renewed vigour; the sound of a Geneshian prairie tiger's roar filled his mind. Nefanial's men were collecting the spiders' spears and returning them with gusto. Then a sound Pippa had been longing to hear came to her ears. Barking echoed from the connecting tunnel.
Pippa's eyes filled up as she smiled.

'I can hear Angus,' she said with sheer delight. Tartarus was happier to hear the stride pattern of Willow among the chaos.

'Come on, boy!' he shouted.

Leading the procession, Angus entered the connecting chamber first, closely followed by the dark brown mare, Willow. Cloud came next, along with the others, crushing a path through Arachna's troops, and jumping over the barricade. Rainbow was at the rear. Ragnarr picked up the ruby. Brun gave him a stern stare.

'Well, you never know when a cracked ruby will come in handy,' the dwarf said, sheepishly. Brun could have sworn Ragnarr smiled. With no time to spare they mounted the horses, glad to be reunited but knowing the nightmare was far from over. Pippa, still hugging Angus, was lifted off the ground and placed in Rainbow's saddle by Tarquin. Tartarus nominated himself, Flint and Brun to stay behind and give the group time to get a head start.

'You'll need more than three?' said Ragnarr.

'If Tartarus can keep that up a little longer we'll make it,' assured Brun.

Nefanial gave him a pat and followed Ragnarr into the tunnel. The blacksmith then turned to defend the entrance.

The spiders that had reached the barricade felt the might of Brun's axes and Flint's lead-tipped shafts whizz through the air. Tartarus released an oil spell which had the spiders slipping over themselves. Flint was rapidly running out of arrow bolts, and his face showed concern. Brun, aware of the predicament, swung his axes just above the makeshift defence holding Arachna's horde at bay. After a couple more spells, Tartarus admitted he was spent. Just before they were engulfed by the spiders, Brun pushed him towards his horse. The ride through the tunnel seemed like an age. Pippa, riding behind her brother, wasn't fazed by the dark. Since she'd been kidnapped, the world she'd inhabited had been a place of complete darkness sprinkled with periodic rays of light. Being condemned to the forest's gloom, and now this tunnel, gave her plenty of time to reflect. Kallen, and her father's ring, had run through her thoughts many times.

She wondered why her parents had to die at the hands of such a hideous being. The dark elf had shattered her paradise forever and his demise was now her only desire. In a strange way she felt safe riding Rainbow, and the terrier by her side made her feel even more at ease. Although fearful for Flint, Pippa was sure the elf would take care of him. They neared the exit and the forest light, although dim, appeared bright to them, and they were thankful to inhale the dank, fusty air. Nefanial could hear the spiders giving chase. He had stationed his men just before the exit with spears in hand, waiting for Brun, Flint and Tartarus to ride past before caving in the tunnel.

'Do you think they're going to make it?' asked Reece.

'Of course not. That's the last you'll see of them,' replied Ragnarr, although the question hadn't been directed at him. As a light drew closer, Calhoun shouted,

'There they are!'

The three rode past and, after a quick head count, Nefanial gave the order. Earth and lumps of mud tumbled down. A spider, targeting Calhoun, hissed, 'For the Queen,' and threw a spear aimed at the assistant. Nefanial watched the spear in flight.

'Not on my watch!' he shouted as he slammed the spear to the ground within touching distance of Calhoun's back, just as the tunnel caved in. Having all reached the other side, they breathed a collective sigh of relief.

'I wonder why no one's ever mentioned these networks of mounds before?' asked Reece, thinking out loud. Everyone knew the answer. Nefanial just shook his head and sighed. Nevertheless, he was right to ask the question. They were completely surrounded by a swamp and the knolls looked very similar to one they had entered. On the bright side, though, Black Forest Summit was partially in view.

*

Crofton Abbehale swivelled in his spinning chair, trying to ease the monotony and failing miserably. Since being commissioned to watch the Keltic lands for an attack that never seemed to materialize, his enthusiasm had diminished considerably. Being one of the few remaining trade routes to the frontier, Glen-Neath saw a constant stream of wagons from the west leave its northern gate, groaning under the weight of furs and elm-tree oil, only to return creaking with a different cargo onboard such as sought-after rugs, pottery, precious metals and assortments of gems. Still, for the baron, it was worse than counting sheep. He felt for the men charged to monitor the movements of the wagons. There were endless battle drills and inspections, too. The boredom was intolerable.

He was hard-pressed to find anything aesthetically pleasing, and the lustre in his eyes had waned. Even his relationship with Kennice was tame in comparison to what he had hoped for. She was no flagon of fine wine that matured and got better with age. Although his mind told him different his union was a sham, devoid of love. Her beauty, her flawless perfection, had turned out to be only skin-deep, and his ability to ignite his wife's passion had seemingly slipped through his fingers a long time ago. When she had whispered those magical words, 'I do,' it had been the happiest day of his life. If contentment was determined by smiles, his happiness had been immeasurable in the beginning. Her captivating allure and her charm were infectious, though these days it was used less on him than others. Alas, for better or for worse, he would stay the course. Reminiscing, a subtle smile passed his lips.

The baron's only saving grace here was the scenery. If there was ever a room to die in, this was it. His stateroom's dual aspect meant he could look at his territory and the free western lands of the Kelts simultaneously. The landscape was breathtaking; no painting could do justice to the stateroom's views. There were birds of prey, stags, deer, and the sacred Keltic wildebeest to look at. There were lush meadows against a backdrop of rolling hills. The leaves of the wild maple trees were turning golden with the onset of autumn. He closed his eyes and imagined the fields of gold.

In the spring and summer months, against his better judgement, he would hunt game on the lands. Galloping on his horse, with the wind lashing his skin, he could absorb the beauty of the environment. These moments gave meaning to his existence. Crofton was afflicted with bouts of depression. His father's demise had been a terrible blow, and now he was shackled to the town and not permitted to travel more than a day's ride from its boundary lines. Glen-Neath was home but it felt more like a prison. Unbeknown to his people his baronage came with a high price. He was distrusted by his southern peers, and the decree was to prevent any delusions of grandeur from taking hold. Crofton longed for the days when he'd be able to rove free, like he did when he was an impulsive, reckless, impetuous young buck and the only title he owned was that of the baron's son.

A baron's son; even now the name left a bitter taste. He was an earl's son and the last of his royal lineage. The sins of his father remained like a lead weight around his neck. So even if the west were as free as the lands he now watched, he could never be king. The Ebenesian Knights of the Order of Eben were long gone but his army, made up of westerners from various tribes, was the last bastion of western chivalry. By proclamation of the Autocrat associating with, or being, a knight was forbidden, the brotherhood having been outlawed after the war against the south. Those who had survived the final battle were hunted down, rounded up and summarily put to death.

The Order's seal and regalia were never exhibited, but Crofton had managed to resurrect their beliefs in part, choosing the most loyal of his men to keep the fallen knights' beliefs alive. They met and jousted in secret. Despite this, by comparison to the other barons' armies, his force was smaller, and without a credible army and gauntlet of power the west would remain under the rule of the south.

Nestled on the side of a hill, Glen-Neath originally started life as a fort and monastery overlooking the stunning Loch-Neath, bordering both regions before it was enclosed behind an impressive stone wall. The Kelts called the lake Tengdamooir, meaning lake of pearls or mother's pearl. The baron had seen the pinkish, almond-shaped silhouettes covering its surface at first hand; in the moonlight the shapes were more pronounced.

His father had made great strides in taking the black-market town of Glen-Neath from a backwater settlement to a thriving town and now the baron was continuing his work. It had been a good harvest and the grain house was full to the brim with wheat, barley and oats. There were more than enough provisions for the winter months. Despite the daily threat of war, normal life continued and the population increased. He was instructed to stem the tide of the illegal racketeering, but for the sake of the men, women and children under his stewardship he allowed the trade to continue unchallenged.

Glen-Neath was larger in diameter than most border fortress towns and there were two main gates on opposing sides of the fort. Outside the south gate the growth continued; settlers seemed to be drawn to the way of life and a flea market had sprung up. A second boundary wall, with a gatehouse entrance and turrets, was nearing completion some distance from his castle: it was to be Glen-Neath's first line of defence. Opposite was his chamber of commerce and an abbey, still under construction. A quarter of his castle temporarily housed the Church of Elohim, though Crofton didn't feel in need of absolution.

A knock on the door distracted him from his thoughts.
'Enter,' he ordered.
Zog and Lockwood were escorted into the staterooms.
'Messengers from Brandenburg, your liege,' the footman announced.
'Messengers? I am not expecting any message,' he replied, slightly perturbed.
The baron had never seen a Draconian before, but he had heard plenty of stories. As for Cuthbert, he knew the man well and had never liked him.
'And your name, sir?' he asked.
'It's in this,' responded Zog, handing him Brandenburg's sealed envelope.
'And I'm here under orders of the High Lord Prince Edwin, not the baron,' he corrected.

After reading the note Crofton slammed his fist on his marble desk.
'This is an outrage!' he declared, getting to his feet.
Lockwood went to hand Crofton the parchment.
'This is what he looks like.'
Crofton waved him away.
'Details, details. We can deal with that later. Have you shown it to my guards at the barbican and southgate

gatehouse?' Lockwood nodded. The baron tugged on his waistcoat and looked at his footman.

'At last some action, Eric. Ready my horse and a riding party. We leave at once,' he ordered. Inwardly, he was smiling; the ride might free him from the rut he was in.

'But, baron, won't taking so many men be considered an act of war?' asked Lockwood just as Millard, Crofton's Captain of the Guards, walked through the doorway.

'What could be an act of war?' asked Millard, puzzled. 'I heard you had guests, my liege. Lockwood.' Millard then acknowledged Zog with a courteous nod.

'Give me a moment,' said Crofton before resuming his conversation with Lockwood.

'Do you think the Kelts will be petrified at the sight of a mere twenty or so men? You've delivered him,' – Crofton nodded at Zog –'you can now return to Brandenburg.'

'Don't they recognize our laws?' asked Lockwood, not taking the hint.

'No, but the protection afforded to a royal rider is acknowledged everywhere.'

'A royal rider, my liege?' asked Millard, removing his helmet and straightening up his mop of dark brown hair.

'Yes. Silvanus has been murdered,' responded the baron, clearly flustered by his captain's constant interruptions. The footman returned.

'Your squire is tending to your horse, my lord.' Crofton dipped his head.

'Maybe a smaller party is required for such a delicate matter, baron?' suggested Lockwood. His idea was greeted with raised eyebrows.

'We're safer with higher numbers. Now, are you in or out?'

For the first time in awhile an honest smile passed Zog lips.
'My thoughts exactly.' Crofton's decisive attitude appealed to Zog.
'Yes, I'm in,' replied Lockwood, sharply.
'That settles it then,' the baron said, with a firm smile. 'Is there anything else?'
'Yes, I have received word that the keeps are planning a revolt, though it is still in its early stages. I want Gwillym, of Irons Keep, detained. We passed his stronghold on the way here. Bowen, with a number of men, ransacked it, killing many,' said Lockwood, taking great care not to mention Kallen's name. Fortunately, Zog was only interested in Brun.
'Bowen? Are you sure? That's my wife's messenger,' replied Crofton, shocked. Reluctantly, Lockwood nodded.
'I'm sure.'
'Have you got proof?' asked the baron. Lockwood passed him the spy's note. The baron's eyes gradually widened as he read it.
'I know this Gwillym. He was in my father's army. This is tricky; he'll want Bowen's head,' said the baron.
'Well, he doesn't have to worry. Once I inform my lord of the trouble Bowen has caused I'm sure Brandenburg will be only too happy to accommodate that request. Stirring up a hornets' nest for supplies and wares is in nobody's interest.'
'Agreed,' Crofton replied sternly.
'That said, what's to be done with this rabble-rouser?' asked Lockwood.
'These chieftains are predictable. They're probably meeting at Brimstone Keep as we speak. Millard will take a few men to Brimstone. If he's present they'll detain him. In all honesty, the other chieftains will dissuade him. They know what renewed conflict would mean,' said the baron.

All this talk and no action was making Zog's stomach churn, and its rumble brought the conversation to an end. Lockwood and Millard gave Zog a discerning look.

'Are you hungry?' asked Crofton, surprised by the ferocity of the noise. 'I didn't think. You both must be famished. Eric, take them to my banquet hall and feed them.' He looked at Lockwood. 'It will be a dangerous trek,' he said.

'Gentleman,' said the footman, ushering them away. The corridor guard pulled the door shut. After only a moment's hesitation, the captain did not mince his words.

'I've heard those Draconians are savages and as for the southerner, I don't trust him.'

'I've heard those stories too,' Crofton responded. 'As for Lockwood, the man's a fool and there's nothing more dangerous.'

'So why escort them?'

Crofton handed him Brandenburg's message. Millard digested the note.

'Do you want me to come with you? We can send Wilfred in my stead to pick up this chieftain,' he suggested, returning the envelope.

'No, I'll take Wilfred. I feel your talents will best serve me here,' Crofton replied, looking pensive.

The door swung open, startling them both. Standing there was Kennice, smiling. Cascades of brown hair curled around her neck. Her outfit, which incorporated a black lace corset, was stunning.

'Don't you ever knock?' said Crofton, giving the corridor guard a frosty glare.

'No,' she replied, playfully. 'A merchant has just shown Isa and me the most exquisite pink-blush diamond I've ever seen.'

Kennice was positively beaming, while Isadora giggled.
'Until the next one,' thought Millard. Her beauty held no sway for him. He could not understand why Crofton wasted his time on this southern trollop when he could have his pick of more suitable western wives.
'I'm busy,' said Crofton. Millard smiled.
'No, you're not,' she said, looking into his eyes, and once he returned her gaze she turned to Isadora.
'I've got to have it, 'said Kennice. Isadora nodded gleefully in agreement.
'Will you excuse us, Millard,' she said, locking arms with her husband and leading him from the room.
'Make sure Wilfred's ready to ride.' Crofton cut a forlorn figure as he walked between the two taller ladies, and his order was swallowed up by the corridor.
'Yes, baron,' replied Millard.

Sometime later Wilfred greeted Crofton on the stone steps leading to the courtyard and stables.
'My liege, the men are ready.'
'I'm not,' responded Crofton, ruefully.

Kennice was taxing, especially when accompanied by Isadora, her cousin. Of course, she had got her wish with the pink-blush diamond which was now warming her middle finger. However, he waved his irritation away. It did not matter if his advances were not welcomed; he still loved her dearly.
'Pardon?' said Wilfred.
'I jest,' said Crofton, smiling.

At the bottom of the steps ten of his men, along with Lockwood, Zog, and his battalion were seated in their saddles awaiting his arrival. Hardly acknowledging his men's salutes, he marched with purpose to the squire tending his white mare and ordered the gate to be opened and the drawbridge lowered.

The signal was given and with Wilfred taking the lead they rode over the moat into the fortified fort and town. In the fading light Crofton took a last look at the castle's high walls as it receded from view. Its night fires were lit, their flicker seemingly giving life to the leering gargoyles along its parapets. As they approached the north gate's gatehouse Zog noticed it bore no similarities to that of southgate. From a bygone age, the north gate was still a pendulum rolling gate, under a winch, in the shape of a shield and with a bladed edge; if caught underneath when it shut you'd simply be cut in two.

The company galloped under the archway, unimpeded, towards the short hill descent and the bridge that crossed Loch-Neath. They passed over the border which was marked only by a solitary purple and orange ribbon; hearts fluttered with trepidation as the forbidden realm was entered. On the Keltic plain of Asseconia there was no escape from the dramatic temperature change that took place once the sunset. With the cold seeping through his fleece lining Crofton tucked in his chin while tightening the collars of his long sheepskin coat. Riding in the dead of night was usually easy for Draconians who were blessed with incredible vision but, without tree cover from the blustery conditions, even their visibility was poor and the pace was slow. At first Crofton was willing to continue on regardless, but then decided that the welfare of his men far outweighed the capture of one. Settling on a grove of trees to shield them from the biting wind, he told Wilfred to stop and make camp.

*

Waking up to a sunny sky and rolling countryside must have been a dream come true. Even Lockwood was touched by the views as the next few days passed by without incident. Making camp at nights and riding by day they headed in the direction of Brigantia, bordering the region of Asseconia, making for the stone of ages, the Kelt's ancestral home. They were unaware they were being watched.

On route the few Kelts they happened upon refused to talk, saying only that Crofton would have to speak with someone of authority because his business was not their concern. Not discouraged by their coldness, on the third day they crossed paths with a merchant on his way back to Glen-Neath and got directions to a Keltic encampment close by.

Crofton chose four of his men, suitably skilled, to help him locate the site. The Kelts they had encountered so far were convinced the Draconians were demons. Giving Wilfred the order to keep the group in check, he and the men left. Unbeknown to the baron, Glen-Neath was constantly being spied upon by Keltic scouts looking for any suspicious movement. They were so in tune with their habitat they could tell how many riders approached their position simply by putting an ear to the ground and the horses' hooves sounded, to them, like a volcano about to erupt. Every time Crofton had ridden on their territory the Kelts chose to ignore his carelessness. A baron prancing about with a few of his men wasn't worth spilling ale over and any scout bringing such a trivial matter to Taliesin's attention would be given short shrift. This time, though, it was different because the invaders rode under a flag of truce with the baron's colours below.

Word spread like wildfire straight through the open entrance of the Keltic king's tent, landing at his feet.

'Rise, Eldrun,' commanded Taliesin as his brother, Druce, placed his palms onto the scout's shoulders to help him stand. With the messaged delivered Eldrun went. An invading army of twenty-five men was not a reassuring development even though the number of men involved was laughable.

'I told you it was a bad idea letting this bringer of death, Sucellos, roam free hunting fowl,' said Druce, his voice deep and aggressive.

'Calm yourself, brother. Has not peace and prosperity reigned under Aghamore's guidance and that of the Circle of Druids? We have wives and children. Would you trade their happiness for war?' answered Taliesin. As always, the king's words were full of wisdom.

'First they roam, then they want talks. This is always the way of things,' Druce said. 'They murdered Iden,' he continued, disgusted by the idea of talks. What was there to talk about? For him the answer was simple: nothing.

'You wish to rule in my stead?' Taliesin asked.

'Taliesin, my loyalty to you is unquestionable. Why do you mock me?' replied Druce, hurt. The king smiled.

'Don't worry. Any proposal will be refused and he and his troops will be told to leave. I remember Iden too,' he said in a reassuring tone.

'So why doesn't this baron just send a royal rider to request parley?' asked Druce.

Taliesin had to admit his brother was right; it did seem unusual that a rider had not been dispatched. Distracted by a gust of wind he looked at the tent's entrance just as its flap closed shut. There stood Bollymore Tumbleweed returning from his hunt.

'Greetings,' the Denvagar dwarf announced as he marched boldly into Taliesin's spacious tent. The brothers looked at each other.

'What's wrong with you two?' Bollymore asked with a grin. 'I've had a wonderful few moons away from here. Don't tell me I've come back at a bad time?'

The brothers smiled and greeted the dwarf with warm embraces.

'As always, Bollymore, you're a remover of gloom,' Taliesin said, grinning cheerfully and patting the dwarf on his back.

'It's good to see you too,' he replied with equal enthusiasm.

'So, how was your hunt?' enquired the king.

'It was a very good hunt. My cart is full of pelts and I have news,' said Bollymore, beaming.

'So have I,' said the king.

'Me first. I've found another mineral mine and I'm sure this one possesses the ninety-third element,' he said, nodding to show his conviction.

Sceptical, Taliesin smiled; the ninety-third element of the cosmos was the aging dwarf's dream, but everyone knew there were only ninety-two elements. Yet, for some reason, the dwarf was certain there was one more.

'Come, share our fire and take a load off your feet. The women are preparing a feast and you must join us. Aghamore is visiting the village,' said Taliesin.

'You don't have to ask me twice, but don't keep me guessing. Tell me your news,' said Bollymore.

'Crofton,' said Druce in response.

'What's he gone and done now? Don't tell me he's upset the Asseconians? I suppose allowing him to hunt birds on their land was bound to ruffle a few feathers,' he said, smiling at his own pun.

'No, he's riding on our land under a flag of truce,' continued Taliesin.

'Then he just wants to talk. That's not worth delaying dinner for. I wouldn't worry. Crofton has no love for his southern masters. He probably wants to negotiate a trade deal. Remember his wife has expensive taste.'

'A puppet is still a puppet,' said Druce, unconvinced.

'He's touchy this evening,' said the dwarf, pulling a face.

'Bollymore is right. We have nothing to fear,' added Taliesin.

'They only respect battle-hardened warriors. We need to remind them, brother, what Kelts are capable of,' said Druce in a defiant mood.

'You may be right,' said the king.

With a cabinet void of souvenirs and no notable notches on his blade to confirm conquests Taliesin, kin of Iden, had not matched his ancestors' greatness, won through battle. He was, however, more careful to maintain the harmonious tribal reign that Iden had created. He tried to govern fairly and promoted the ideal of strength in unity, while affording the individual to live as freely as the birds in the trees; the only requirement was being available in times of crisis. For centuries tribe had attacked tribe and the weak perished. Then Iden, a warrior from an insignificant tribe from the highlands of Glandomirum, conquered the others and brought them together. From each defeated tribe a rock the height of two men was ordered to be brought to the temple ruins of Harshada, known as the heart of Brigantia, to create the stone of ages.

The structure, astronomically aligned with the sunrise of the summer and winter solstices, was a beacon to Anu, the goddess of fertility, prosperity, comfort and health. Each rock was marked with an etching of the deity worshipped by the tribe who had surrendered it. A druid from each clan was invited to commune and the Circle of Druids was formed. Through their counsel and Iden's foresight the blood lust ceased. The Circles of Druids continued beyond Iden's lifetime and thus his legacy was born and its philosophy was carried through into Taliesin's rule. The peace made with the Autocrat was not to be breached under any circumstances. If the frail agreement was jeopardized the outcome would be war. Boys had become men under Taliesin's reign without engaging in any significant combat; weapons were only used in re-enactments and plays, or on outsiders. Disputes were settled decisively by the druid of the village. Only the king was allowed to impose a sentence of death, and only for the gravest of crimes.

Trade flourished, although Kelts measured wealth by the size of a man's heart and not the weight of his lockbox. Luxuries and riches had not altered their nomadic way of life. With wagons always at the ready beside their tents, the village was able to relocate at a moment's notice and that made them difficult to defeat. The canopy housing the banquet was modest in comparison with the impressive feast of fruits, vegetables, cold cuts and roasted meats, flagons of wine, jugs of cider and barrels of ale. Over the meal the matter of Crofton's incursion was discussed. Druce and Bollymore sat alongside Taliesin, surrounded by friendly faces. On the opposite side was Aghamore, the guest of the younger female druid, Nemetona, the druid of Taliesin's tribe.

'There's nothing to it. You'll have to send a representative before you can discuss this matter with the Circle of Druids,' Bollymore said between mouthfuls, keeping his voice low and looking in Aghamore's direction. The unkempt druid raised an eyebrow and returned the dwarf's gaze before turning back to Nemetona, who was asking him a question.

'I think you're right, but what do you suggest?' pressed Taliesin.

'Well, he's only a baron. Send his equivalent. That's what I'd do,' said Bollymore.

'We think alike, dwarf.'

'We do?' replied Bollymore, confused.

'Yes and I've got the perfect man for the task.' Bollymore's drink missed his mouth as he waited with bated breath.

'Druce,' continued the king, 'send your scout, Eldrun, to see Lluddrum. Talabriga isn't too far from where they were last seen. I want this westerner watched but tell Lluddrum he is not to intervene. I'm sending Halwn to negotiate on my behalf and we'll see what this Crofton wants.' With his mind made up, his decision was final. For a moment Bollymore thought the king was going to suggest he meet the baron. Wiping his top lip, he took a swig of cider and nodded in agreement.

'Later, Tal. The women are about to dance,' replied Druce.

Druce loved nothing more than red wine, a delicious spread and the added bonus of folk music and Keltic dancing. He gave his brother a sheepish grin. The food and drink were cleared away then six women, in traditional Keltic dress and crowns of woven flowers, entered, holding hands. Given permission by Taliesin the musicians began to play a lively tune. The sound of flutes, fiddles and pipes filled the tent. The Kelts clapped along to the music as the dancing took place. Bollymore sighed contentedly, rubbing his full stomach, and sat back to enjoy the show.

Thoughts of entertainment were a million miles away for Crofton. Daylight had dwindled away before the group returned, having been sent on a wild goose chase. Saddle sore and weary, Crofton rode back into camp. The area he'd been directed to had recently been abandoned. The sweet smell of roasting meat was very welcome; his nostrils tingled and he licked his dry lips. Suddenly, filled with an awful dread, Crofton looked visibly ill as he realized they were roasting wildebeest. Wilfred was summoned immediately. Conscious of his baron's ashen appearance, Wilfred answered the question before Crofton could ask it.

'They were already cooking it before I could put a stop to it.' Crofton looked at his man-at-arms in disbelief.

'Did you allow them to go hunting on their own?' he asked, about to dismount but changing his mind.

'Yes, but I spoke to Lockwood about my concerns first.'

'You did what?' Crofton leaned down and hit him across the jaw. 'Your concerns? Have you no brains? You share the same rank and I left you in charge.'
Wilfred's discomfort was clear to see.

'Pack up now. We're leaving,' Crofton continued.
'To go where, my liege?'

'Glen-Neath,' replied the baron sternly.

Wilfred turned to carry out the order. Zog had to admit the beast slain by Rog was a treat to eat. He and his Draconians sat in a huddle, polishing off the wildebeest.

'The baron says we've got to go back now,' said Wilfred.

'Back?' said Zog. 'Back where? Is he suffering from prairie sickness?'

'What's all the fuss about?' asked Lockwood, walking out of his tent.

'What's all the fuss about?' echoed Crofton. 'The Kelts believe that wildebeest are the spawn of Arawn and eating them brings famine.'

Zog stopped eating and swallowed hard. Draconians knew the horned god by the name of Cernos, a deity with far-reaching antlers.

'Fortunately for us we will not be here to explain why we defiled a sacred beast on their lands, under a banner of parley,' said Crofton adamantly.

'Riders!' shouted Wilfred.
Clouds of chalk could be seen on the horizon, indicating only one thing.

'To your horses, men,' ordered Crofton.

'But don't we want to talk to them?' asked Lockwood. Zog nodded.

'Get on your horse, man! Your companions have turned us from the hunters into the hunted,' said Crofton, with a sour expression.

'Can we outrun them?' asked Lockwood worried, reaching for his horse's bridle.

'How should I know?' replied the baron. Zog's battalion, having discarded their plates, were hurriedly mounting horses and vacating the camp, creating a dust cloud of their own in the process.

The Keltic chief Lluddrum, expecting Halwn's arrival and having received Taliesin's instructions, kept his warriors a safe distance away to observe the baron's activities without being spotted. Admittedly the Keltic king's order was greeted with condemnation, creating an atmosphere of resentment and causing dissent throughout Lluddrum's tribe. Asseconia was the largest region of the Badlands and linked Brigantia to the rocky region of Glandomirum. So the plains of Asseconia, a thousand leagues away from the forests and grassy hillocks of Brigantia, were kept in check by the rowdy and passionate Circle of Druids, led by the staunchest of Iden theorists, the revered Aghamore the Wise. Although Taliesin was widely respected, in the eyes of the Asseconians he had not proven his worth as a warrior. His Glandomirian bloodline linked him to Iden and paved the way for his succession. However, allowing a feudal lord onto Keltic soil was bad enough, and no warrior king would have the stomach to stand idly by and let the Draconians roam free.

The decision to follow Taliesin's instructions changed once Lluddrum's son Varden got involved. The handsome dark-haired warrior, with a thick, curvy moustache, was a younger version of his father. He threw a blackened wildebeest's horns to the earth and informed Lluddrum that a spawn of Arawn had been found mutilated. They performed the rite of passing and doused the creature's remains with elm-tree oil before Toran and Ronan cremated the remains. Varden shared the belief held by most Kelts that the sacred wildebeest were not to be touched.

In the face of this desecration the chieftain, reluctantly, yielded to the will of his men and gave strict instructions that the baron was to be brought back alive.

'Do with the rest as you will,' he commanded. Varden, Toran and Ronan rode out. Descending the hill like a pack of wild men, their deafening shrieks sent shivers down the spines of the Draconians; they knew that in a battle the Kelts would target them first. The speed at which the Kelts covered the ground was incredible, whether on horseback or on foot. Their hunger for combat spurred them on. Wilfred vainly attempted to galvanize his men to go faster, but they were already riding flat-out.

'How many are there?' shouted Crofton with the wind on his back.

'Over a hundred,' replied Lockwood, stealing a glimpse at the shadow closing in. 'We won't outride them in the open. They're gaining on us.' He swallowed.

Zog had got up to speed with the leading group.

'Your orders, baron?' he demanded.

'Beyond those hills there's a wooded area. If my recollection serves me well, we may evade capture there.' Secretly, Crofton wondered whether they could make it; he knew the mission had become one of survival, though he would not say it. The fanatic pace of the pursuing Kelts seemed ominous.

'Kill all those with wildebeest breath!' shouted Ronan.

'My father wants the baron taken alive,' warned Varden, riding alongside.

On reaching the hill's base, Varden watched Crofton's men ascending the mound and gave Toran a hand gesture to take a few Kelts, through a valley shortcut, to the torrent on the opposite side of the hill, while the rest continued their pursuit.

With the climb so treacherous in the dark Crofton breathed a sigh of relief on seeing the Kelts stop. He'd been stuck in his saddle for most of the day and this relentless chase through the Keltic countryside was gruelling. They galloped to the hill's crest, where Crofton's woods came into view. The hazards of the hill's descent and a rapidly flowing river awaited them before relative safety could be theirs.

'We've got to cross that stream!' shouted Crofton, exhausted. He marched his mare across a marshy meadow and into the water. Zog looked at the torrent and heard the sounds made by his horse; he knew his apprehension was shared. Wilfred and the baron were already knee-deep in the water, while Lockwood and Rog hesitantly followed. The command 'Attack!' rang out. The Kelts, led by Toran, emerged from their shortcut and the group found themselves avoiding arrows. Zog saw an arrow whistle past, miraculously missing Rog's shield. It hit Crofton in his lower back. Crofton instinctively looked down at the arrow-head protruding from his side. Suddenly, his horse was being hit above its hind leg, and reared up. With a momentary lapse of concentration his grip slipped and he was thrown into the stream head first. His foot caught in his stirrups and prevented the current from dragging him downriver.

On impact with the water he collided with floating debris before bobbing back to the surface, motionless. Wilfred called the men on the bank to arms as he went to the baron's aid but with his approach the white mare bolted and quickly vanished in the dark. The men and Draconians on the bank fought off the first onslaught directed by Toran. Varden, with more Kelts, closed in fast. Lockwood and Rog continued trudging across the rapids to the other side.

'Where are you two going?' shouted Wilfred.

'Crofton's dead,' retorted Lockwood.

The two men standing beside Wilfred looked at their friends in the midst of battle, and at the Kelts. Gripped by self-preservation they spoke out.

'Will, we can't find the baron if we're all dead.'

'Cowards. Have you no shame?' replied Wilfred, his stony face not revealing that he, too, was in two minds. They were heavily outnumbered and common sense prevailed, although he would have preferred to fight rather than run. Taking a last look at the solitary soul fighting bravely among the stench of death, he led his men away. Zog knew it was hopeless but he wasn't going down without taking as many Kelts with him to the afterlife as possible.

'Where's Toran?' asked Varden, riding into the thick of it and watching Zog staunchly defend the space around him. The clash of steel and brute force presented a feeble stalemate; it was only a matter of time before the Draconians' resistance failed.

'He and a few of the men went after the baron and five escaped across the river!' shouted a warrior standing nearby.

'As for the demon, I want him taken alive. He fights well and may well prove to be a valuable prize,' said Varden, admiring Zog's agility.

'I'd sooner kill him,' grunted Ronan, openly questioning Virden's authority.

'No. I will not return to my father empty-handed.'

With a nod from Ronan, a net was thrown over Zog who, while trying to escape, suffered a blow to the temple that rendered him unconscious. Toran and a couple of riders appeared from the darkness.

'Where's the baron?' asked Ronan.

Toran shrugged. 'Drowned or hiding,' he replied.

'I told you to watch him, 'said Varden in a raised voice.

'What do we care if he lives or dies?' Toran asked, dismissively.

'My father cares!' shouted Varden.

'We can come back at first light for your baron,' Toran retorted.

'He's not my baron!' Varden yelled.

Concealed within the folds of the trees Lockwood, Rog, Wilfred and Crofton's men were watching the Kelts argue among themselves before disappearing into the gully with Zog and the baron's horse. Wilfred wanted them to continue searching but Lockwood refused. In the morning the forest would be full of warriors wanting their hides, and having the baron's horse in their possession eliminated any belief that Crofton may still be alive. Such a blatant transgression over an oversize boar was an act of war. Crofton was a baron of the southern realm, and their power was determined by deeds. Brandenburg would have to be notified at once. So as soon as the trail was clear Lockwood was going to ride back and not stop until he crossed the bridge to Glen-Neath, and all he wanted to know was who was coming too.

*

The marsh was no picnic even for seasoned warriors, so for our courageous heroes it must have seemed hellish. Stopping to free themselves from the remaining sticky web, they were elated at having come through the ordeal intact. Even Ragnarr's grumpy quibbles were quelled and they all enjoyed some of Nefanial's cold cuts and bread. Though the group was still mourning Randolph's loss, they were starting to have belief in their abilities as a unit and they saw the episode as a rite of passage. However, such thoughts offered little in the way of a respite, with the gloom of a swamp full of dying trees beckoning.

Spending time with the humans, away from his Aafari kin, was rubbing off on the three-quarter elf in more ways than he'd care to admit. An Alfari warrior would not go into battle so unprepared. Caught up in the hysteria of wanting to regain the scroll, he hadn't discussed a plan of attack or taken into consideration what spells he would have to use to tackle Kallen who, from the sound of things, was a master of the dark arts. Bravado would only get him so far before it got him killed. Lord Erynion had often told him so.

Trudging through the muddy waters alongside Rex, Tartarus looked unrecognizable. He was covered in drying mud, waist-deep in soily sludge. He was still feeling a little bit peckish, having passed on the cold cuts and only eaten bread. Not even Ragnarr was able to say how long they had been comatose in Arachna's lair and time was of the essence, so cooking up a more fulfilling meal would have to wait. Although a grumbling belly was saying otherwise, nothing could dampen his spirits. Reciting a few of his more useful spells to himself he was oblivious to the friends around him. His intuition told him the scroll was close and that the time to get serious had arrived. With the business of escaping the spiders put to one side, he was more determined than ever to complete his goal. He was spurred on by seeing the summit, even though his view was obscured by trees. If he had to kill witches, slay dragons and cross quagmires, so be it. Gone was the elf who felt sorry for himself. The glint in his eye that had not been present since he played arrows in the Hogshead tavern returned. Oaken-Crag was where his soul belonged, and to see the forest again he knew what must be done.

He took a look to check on how the others were faring. The decision had been made to pull the horses through the swamp rather than to ride them. The practicalities of the task meant Pippa was exempt. Ragnarr had flatly refused; at his height he'd be drowning and, once seated in his saddle, would not budge. Flint seemed happy enough tugging Rainbow's reins, as well as those of his mare. No one was taking the serenity of the swamp for granted, though all seemed locked within their own thoughts except for Ragnarr, who whistled. Being a blacksmith, Brun guided his and Ragnarr's horse through the swamp easily. It was the rancid smell that had him perturbed, and he joined Pippa in bobbing heads to Ragnarr's melody to distract himself.

It was the first time the Denvagarian had seemed remotely happy, and the moment was definitely worth a smile. The rugged veteran gave Tartarus a quizzical look.
    'I'm fine Rex,' said Tartarus with a smile, pointing him in the dwarf's direction.
Rex turned to see the dwarf in motion and smiled too.
    'I shall call you Ragnarr the Whistler,' teased Rex. Ragnarr continued regardless; it was a tune he whistled to his children before he put them to bed, and in a small way it

transported him back home. Rex and Tartarus shared a look as they continued to lead the way.

'Keep your wits about you. I don't like the look or the smell of this section of swamp,' said Nefanial. He raised his concerns even though they were nearing the exit of the swamp. Nothing living had crossed their path in a while; even the fireflies and water rats seemed to stop visiting and, apart from Ragnarr's harmonic fluctuations, it was eerily quiet.

Tarquin gave his brother an encouraging smile. As hunters they had noticed a subtle change in the environment, and the absence of birdsong was always a telltale sign that something bad maybe lying in wait. Nevertheless, neither mentioned birds, just in case the solar birds reared their beaks once more. Pippa, oblivious, continued to stroke Angus's head to calm her agitated pet. Calhoun, at the rear, thought he saw something moving in the swamp's murky waters and shared his suspicions with Sid.

'Did you see that, Sid?' Calhoun asked, his words barely a whisper. Too busy wondering how he was going to spend his newfound wealth, Sid shook his head, putting it down to paranoia.

'You need to man up, Cal,' he chuckled.

'That's easy for you to say, but I've seen things in this forest that no man should see.' Sid was about to laugh when something brushed past him.

'Hang on. I think you're right.' Both men drew their swords.

'Nefanial,' shouted Sid to the baker positioned two horses in front.

'What, boy?' replied Nefanial, still harbouring a grudge over Sid's antics in the lair.

'There's something here,' responded Sid.

'Nonsense. There's no treasure for you here, boy,' he retorted, irritated.

'No. We're not alone,' Calhoun said anxiously. With movements in the water becoming more erratic both men shared a look.

'What was that?' asked Nefanial, blinking as if his vision was blurred. He drew his sword in a panic. At the mention of not being alone the rest had armed themselves and minds were now on high alert. Ragnarr's entertaining whistle was also giving pleasure to an unwanted guest. Angus started barking and Pippa screamed. She and Barnaby were the only ones who saw the vines latch onto Ragnarr's leg before dragging him from his saddle. A gasp followed the splashing and the dwarf disappeared. With events happening so quickly, Ragnarr hadn't had time to react. Even Brun, close by, had been slow off the mark, and Barnaby still stood frozen in his tracks.

'Where's he gone?' enquired Nefanial.

'Who?' murmured Barnaby in a state of shock.

'Ragnarr. Who else?'

'I saw something reach up and grab him, but I haven't got a clue what it was,' replied Barnaby, dumbfounded. His answer shed no light on matters. As he stood scratching his head Ragnarr suddenly resurfaced and shouted, 'Help me!' before submerging with a mouth full of swamp water. Brun and Barnaby were pulled along too, as the vines began to drag them in.

'What's going on?' asked Tartarus.

At first Nefanial had been puzzled by what was attacking the group, but now he knew for certain and clammed up. Ragnarr had also figured it out because he was being dragged towards the plant's orifices. Swamp traps consumed their prey quickly, using their many vines to snag food. Rex quickly surveyed their surroundings.

    'There!' he shouted, pointing to the marshy bank.

    'What is that?' Tartarus squinted.

Lying in the swamp, protruding from its bank, was the base of a swamp trap whose dull green leaves were covered in a vibrant assortment of corpse lilies. The enormous red flower was spattered in little brown spots. Reliant on its carrion-eating flies and beetles for pollen, the swamp trap released a rancid aroma of decay. On seven thick but slender hairless stalks that emanated from the plant's circular centre were snapping lobes, swooning like cobras. Its red surface was densely covered in white glandular hairs that secreted sticky mucus at the slightest vibration. Stiff tentacles meshed together once shut; there was no possible route of escape for anyone caught.

Rex was surprised that he, one of the taller members of the group, had not spotted the camouflaged carnivorous flower sooner.

    'What is that?' Tartarus asked again.

    'It's a tipitiwichet,' Rex said, hurriedly.

    'A tipiti– what?' asked Tartarus, mystified.

    'Exactly,' replied Rex. There was no time for explanations.

    'You must be joking. We've got to get out of this swamp!' shouted Flint as the quagmire began to come alive with vines. The trap, sensing blood and the group's insecurities, propelled even more tentacles in their direction. Brun, with his battleaxes, made quick work of the vines around his legs. Ragnarr was still struggling to free himself, but Barnaby was in worse trouble: a vine had wrapped itself around his neck and was blocking his wind pipe.

'We've got to help him!' shouted Nefanial, turning to see his men still seated on their horses. Tipitiwichets were the stuff of old wives' tales, and none of his men wanted to be devoured slowly. 'Get off those horses. They need our help,' continued Nefanial. His order fell on deaf ears.

'Get those provisions to that marshy bank and out of this swamp. Rex, Brun, Tarquin, you're with me!' barked Tartarus. Nefanial refused.

'I'm coming too.'

'Very well then,' Tartarus agreed, as the others were led away by Flint to seek the safety of the bank. Brun, with Tartarus's help, managed to free Ragnarr after a colossal tussle during which they fought off waves of shooting vines while inching closer and closer to the swarm trap's lobes.

Nefanial's grip on Barnaby's tunic slipped and he and Tarquin watched helplessly as Barnaby was pulled further away. Without a thought for his own safety Nefanial waded after him, though it was to no avail; he reached Barnaby in time to witness him being entombed within one of the lobes. Rex and Brun followed Nefanial's lead, while an angered Tartarus looked to Ragnarr for advice.

'How do we defeat this thing?' he asked.

'We've got to flee!' yelled Ragnarr.

'And leave him?' Tartarus pointed at Barnaby.

'Yes,' responded the dwarf.

'Well, I fear no plant. I only fear ore,' shouted the blacksmith defiantly, as he swung his axe. Nefanial, encouraged by his brother-in-law's gusto, was caught unawares by a lobe looming overhead and was gobbled up as well.

'We can still save them. Its digestive cycle is extremely slow, but we've got to act now, 'said Rex, ducking a lobe's advances.

For the first time Tartarus's naivety really struck him; he was at a loss on what action to take. Releasing a spell would endanger Nefanial and Barnaby and he dare not take the risk. Against the backdrop of forest and oddly coloured shrubs the seven lobes waved supreme. Flint, marshalling the others, wasn't resting on his laurels now that Pippa was safe. Calhoun was charged to look after her, along with Sid, who was more interested in staying with the provisions and his gold. So with Reece and Daniel, he went to help his brother and Tartarus. They decided to attack the Tipitiwichet from its rear to try to evade the vines.

Their efforts were in vain; almost immediately they too were snagged. Vines were wrapped tightly round their legs and ankles, pulling them to the ground. All three were dragged along, frantically chopping at their bonds. Brun, alongside Rex, had cut a path through the vines and were now cutting chunks out of the rosette base, with each hefty stroke seeming to weaken the trap.

'That's it!' shouted Rex, as Brun exposed the tipitiwichet's nervous system, a network of blood-filled arteries. Pinpointing the best spot, he took aim and cleaved the heart of it. After two almighty blows, the nightmare ceased. Black blood filled the remaining cavity and the group battled to save Nefanial and Barnaby before they drowned as the deceased lobes landed in the swamp.

With a few swings of Ragnarr's war hammer and Brun's axes they were quickly freed. Nefanial was only a little the worse for wear and covered in mucilage. Barnaby, though, was comatose with a weak pulse, and in a seriously bad way. His only real chance for survival rested on them finding the wizard; his condition was beyond the expertise or Ragnarr or

Tartarus. After their ordeal the rest of the journey to the summit, with Barnaby tied to his horse, picked up pace now that there was firm ground beneath the horses' hooves. Flint and Tarquin noticed fresh tracks, unnaturally broken branches and torn fabric.

'This is recent,' Tarquin said to Tartarus. The gap between them and Kallen had vastly decreased; the first bit of good news in awhile. The group was brought to a halt when Tartarus noticed horses through a glade clearing and they dismounted.

Kallen was having trouble dispelling the idea of capturing such a highly valued opponent, even though he knew it was a foolish thought. Below Nikomeades' hidden plateau, one of his men was instructed to remain with the horses. The climb looked too steep for animals of their size and so the provisions were carried on backs. The soggy terrain, a mixture of grass and slippery moss, was treacherous and the ropes stolen from Irons Keep were needed.

Kallen marshalled his men. Having guided them away from the worst of the Black Forest's deadlier offerings, with the aid of his dark senses, he wasn't about to let his attention slip so close to the finishing line. Although there was no way of avoiding the solar birds he could cast a spell to subdue their advances just long enough for him and his men to pass. He smiled at that thought. Anyone following would have great difficulty getting past those ravenous fiends. Goreham and Darrel, both at the rear, were arguing among themselves and blaming each other; both were sure they had not given their mark to this and the deeper they trekked into the forest's murk the more soul-destroying it became. Unlike the Dökkalfar, they were not immune to the forest's emotive imagery of ghosts and spirits, appearing from nowhere and issuing infernal whisperings to lead them astray. Even if they survived they would have nightmares for life. Anyway, mercenaries believed in gold and women, not quests for parchments and mages.

Bowen led the way, alongside Kallen. They needed their full concentration. One of the men was already in an early grave; he had not paid full attention to the hazardous climb and had been hit by falling rock. He was thrown into the misty abyss, screaming as he descended. They reached the first of the numerous plateaus that littered the summit's peak. Kallen ordered his men to arm themselves. The first plateau's vast and thick grassy meadow was sprinkled with a variety of muddy rocky hillocks and the odd tree. Megalithic rocks and large boulders in between wild unkempt bushes littered their path. Off to the right of their position a steep climb continued to another plateau. Kallen pointed them in that direction.

Below, the pursuing group made quick work of the man watching Kallen's horses.
    'What do we do about these horses?' asked Flint, with Sid searching the dead brigands' belongings.
    'Secure them. We'll come back for them,' replied Tarquin.
Flint smiled.
    'So, I suppose we've got to climb now?' said Pippa, eager to be let loose on the summit.
    'What is it with children and climbing?' said Ragnarr. Tartarus informed them that Ekaterina, his high priestess, had provided him with a safer and quicker route to the first plateau, and from her description they were not far from its entrance. They followed Tartarus round the mountain's base. The three-quarter elf smiled as the description he'd been given came into view. Then, without warning, he

marched them into a wall of branches and leaves and on the other side an ancient cave appeared. Ragnarr noted its familiarity and patted the upward tunnel's wall, marvelling at its workmanship.

'My people built this,' he stated in admiration, though surprised; it had been constructed well before his time.

If Kallen thought he was going to catch the wizard unawares and use it as an advantage, Tartarus's flare had put paid to that. Nikomeades had heeded the warning and was ready to protect his home and Gunn-Hilda. One of the last of the enchanted, he stood ready to dish out the punishment and retribution that any attempt to capture him merited. His eyes glowed with a fury none had previously witnessed as their clash commenced. Immediately, men ducked for cover as spells whizzed overhead.

Nikomeades revelled in conjuring spells to thwart his foes' challenge. However, after the initial surprise Kallen had gathered his composure and the scene was set.
Whatever he threw at Nikomeades was returned in equal measure as, one by one, his men were eliminated. Though Kallen recognized that these beings were renowned, this encounter had far exceeded his expectations and he knew if a weak spot wasn't found soon he, too, would become part of the enchanter's fable. Seeing another of his men fall, he released a furious attack with a complex flurry, combining a water, fire and earth spell. However, once more the wizard, dispelling the cobwebs of rustiness, and with the pronunciation of spells coming thick and fast to his tongue, obliterated Kallen's spell.

Bowen, with Goreham and Darrel, hid behind a large boulder. Though Bowen was waiting for an opportunity to pounce, the other two just wanted to escape. Ordered to face the mage, they were stuck to the rock like moss, having already considered this wizard to be too powerful for them. Nikomeades slammed his staff into the earth, releasing a shockwave that threw the remaining men to the ground; even the three hidden behind the rock were not immune. Kallen grabbed the closest man to him, sucked his life force to enhance his powers, and discarded the man's withered body.

Still he was no match for the enchanted.

'The Autocrat could never have sent you. How pathetic!' bellowed the aging mage, as Tartarus's group cleared the horizon and made a beeline for the skirmish.

'Dark elf, how many more men will you send to their doom before you concede?' asked Nikomeades, surprised at his opponent's lack of endeavour.

'Give us the scroll!' shouted Tartarus at Bowen, with an arrow aimed at his chest.

'What scroll?' asked Nikomeades, halting the onslaught for a moment.

'The gold-rimmed scroll,' replied Tartarus.

'The scriptures of Eben?' whispered Nikomeades.

'I think so,' said Tartarus, retracting his bow then jumping off Willow. At the sight of reinforcements Goreham and Darrel dropped their weaponry.

'Leave them to us, old man,' said Nefanial. 'Now, which one of you attacked my wife?' Brun stood beside him, axe in hand. Both Goreham and Darrel pointed at each other, although they didn't know who he was talking about.

'Leave the one with the patch to me,' said Tartarus, following Ragnarr into the fray. The battle intensified as swords clashed.

Nikomeades was left scratching his head; this group, with a little girl and two men waiting in the distance, were actually helping him. Tartarus cornered Bowen and both man and elf smiled, with swords in hand.

'We meet again Alfari, although I really thought you'd be a rotting corpse by now,' said Bowen. 'How are your friends, by the way?'

'You talk a lot for a dead man,' replied Tartarus, with Vince and Asrack firmly in his thoughts. In anger, he charged. Bowen stepped aside, their swords touched and, with a deft manoeuvre, he lunged. Tartarus avoided it with a spin. The ring of steel sounded as neither gave ground.

For a brigand, Bowen's repertoire was impressive and a series of vicious attacks had Tartarus watching his own footwork, as well as the swordplay. He hit back with a counterthrust, aiming for Bowen's cheek. Bowen parried the attack and retaliated with a volley that brought Tartarus to one knee, but quickly the elf regained his footing. Both man and elf breathed deeply, ready to attack and moving in a circular motion. Tartarus acknowledged Bowen's ability with a nod, which was greeted with a chuckle.

'I will not die by your hand,' declared Bowen, resuming the duel. He caught Tartarus across the thigh and chest and then tried another manoeuvre, but this time Tartarus was waiting for it and when the elf spun he took Bowen's head with him, cleaving it clear of the man's shoulders. The dull sound of his head hitting the earth was followed by a thud, as Bowen fell to his knees.

'Not by my hand, but by my elven steel,' said Tartarus. He turned to face Kallen. 'Now, to regain the scroll,' he whispered, sweetened by the taste of revenge.

In the confusion Kallen, having been confronted by Calhoun, managed to twist the assistant into a chokehold. With the remaining men dead or captured, they surrounded the dark elf. Kallen's hideous contorted features grinned back at them.

'So, these are your brothers,' he said, marking the two young men's faces as they stood beside Pippa. In turn she screwed up her face; her parents had brought her up not to hate. The dark elf made that extremely difficult, but she was determined he would not sully their memory.

'Let him go and we'll let you live,' lied Nefanial.
'You can't let him live!' shouted Flint.
'We're not letting him go anywhere,' Ragnarr assured him.
'Release him and hand over the scroll, Dökkalfar,' commanded Nikomeades.

The brothers aimed their weapons at Kallen as Tartarus delivered the ultimatum.

'Quick and painless, or slow and agonizing. Your choice. You choose,' said Tartarus, eager to carry out either act. Kallen smiled.

'And who's going to kill me? You?' he asked. The sentence was followed up with a repulsive laugh. 'Stay back. Well back,' he ordered. Toying with them, he pressed his dagger so tightly against Calhoun's throat that it drew blood. The group moved forwards while he moved backwards, maintaining the gap. A precipice was to his rear.

'Watch your step!' shouted Nefanial, conscious that he might slip and take Calhoun with him.

'Here's your precious scroll.' Kallen threw the gold-rimmed parchment into the air and pushed Calhoun forward. As everyone looked up, Nefanial reached for his assistant and Kallen disappeared over the cliff.

They ran to the cliff's edge and looked down at the smooth rock-face; all they could see were layers of mist.

'He couldn't have survived that fall,' said Sid.

'You may be mistaken,' said Nikomeades. 'Magic doesn't live in your realm; he probably used a climbing spell.' The wizard's words offered no comfort.

'But what about our father's ring? He said it shared the same markings as that thing,' Pippa said, pointing at the scroll in Tartarus's hand.

'What? Is your father named Angus, by any chance?' enquired Nikomeades.

'Hey, how do you know my father's name?' she said with a curious expression.

'I'll tell you all about that later, but first come and meet Gunn-Hilda. She'll love you,' he said, smiling.

'Who's Gunn-Hilda?' asked Pippa, bluntly.

'Pippa,' scolded Tarquin, giving his sister a stern look.

'It's all right, lad. She's my wife, little one. Those two men who stayed behind – is one of them gravely ill?' asked the wizard. Pippa nodded. 'And if an Alfari stands before me with the gold-rimmed scroll, then we're all in grave danger. We can do the introductions later. It's getting cold now. Follow me and I'll take you to my home.'

Sid was rummaging through Kallen's men's pockets and brought an item to the group's attention.

'I've found something on the headless one,' he announced. 'It's a note from Baron Syracuse of Daginhale. Looks important.'

'Put it away. We'll read it later,' instructed Nefanial.

'What do we do with these two?' asked Ragnarr, ready to free them of the burden.

'They can come too. I'm taking them back to Irons Keep, for the villagers' retribution,' replied Nefanial.

Goreham and Darrel, standing sheepishly among them, swallowed hard. Flint looked at the others in disbelief.
'But what about their horses below?'
'They'll keep, lad. They'll keep,' replied Brun.

Act Three

The Battle of the Longest Dawn

Under dark clouds and in swirling winds Wilfred, exhausted, gripped his reins tightly with numb hands. Visibility was poor and rain lashed against his helmet. His disorientation was becoming unbearable. Watching his horse's footing he galloped on regardless with the knowledge there was not much further to go, a fact he was very thankful for. The ride home had been long and hard. Nearing Glen-Neath, he welcomed the respite its haven would bring. Trailed by his remaining men, who were riding uphill behind Lockwood and Rog, he feared the worst.

Along with the Kelts baying for his blood, the picture of Crofton being hit with an arrow and falling into the river was set on pause. In his mind there was little doubt he had witnessed the baron's demise; seeing his mare was proof enough. Although the town's fires were a comforting vista, knowing that he would have to deliver the news to Millard and Kennice was a less consoling prospect. Though he distrusted the southerner, Lockwood had not spoken in jest; they hadn't stopped at all, not even for water. With the border town in sight, the time for explanations was soon at hand.

Leaving the Keltic realm and stepping forth onto the bridge's thick creaking, wooden planks, even with the whistling wind at points screeching, brought a subdued relief as the ride's tension ebbed away. He knew that the two men alongside him were thinking of a hearty meal and warm bed; he could tell. These images were not shared as he pictured Kennice's face; he searched for words to lessen the blow, but found none. He patted his horse's mane.

The days had flown by since Crofton's departure. Under his liege's leadership life was good and Millard, the baron's iron fist, knew what needed to be done to maintain that order. His stewardship in Abbehale's absence was without incident; he had taken to the task entrusted to him, as he would say, more smoothly than the mechanism of a catapult. In fact, tending to the baroness's needs had been non-existent; dealing with a woman's whims was something Millard was not accustomed to. He and the baron shared the same flaw: a willingness to be free. He had never married, preferring to choose a life as a fighting man and having no stomach to leave a widow behind. It had stood him in good stead but, with age, the need for sons to bear his name was foremost, though he would not bear sons in a subjugated land.
He was no baron and was happy with his title so, being informed that riders approached, he waited eagerly alongside Lucian and a battalion to greet the feudal lord on his return.

On seeing only five riders, and no white mare, he knew the news wasn't good even before Wilfred pulled up his horse under the gateway arches and started babbling, relaying the sequence of events which led up to the baron's disappearance. Ordering Wilfred and the cavaliers to dismount Millard, shaking his head, was astonished to learn that his man-at-arms had let the Draconians eat wildebeest.
    'They did what?' he exclaimed, cursing the fact that Crofton had not taken his advice. Millard looked at Lockwood and Rog, sitting at ease in their saddles, with disgust; they returned his gaze with just as much venom.

'So where's his body? Did you even wait around to search for the baron?' asked Millard, returning his attention to his man-at-arms; he asked as though he already knew the answer.

'Those two refused to continue the search,' replied Wilfred, looking directly at the cavaliers who were trying to avoid eye contact.

'Detain those two,' ordered Lucian, with a wave of his arm, before Millard could respond. Four men came marching forward. 'We will not have cowards in our ranks.' Lucian was known for his strict stance on cowardice, and they were immediately put in irons.

'Don't you think that if the Kelts had killed him, they would have paraded his corpse?' said Millard, while indicating that he wanted the two cavaliers led away.

'Yes, we did,' answered Lockwood. 'The water's current probably prevented that.'

'The water's current, indeed,' responded Millard sarcastically, as he and Lucian shared a look. Brandenburg's man was fortunate that his remit was beyond their authority or he would have been clapped in irons too.

Crofton's captain was confident in his own abilities, yet still relished a chance to prove his worth. He would be dammed if he was going to believe a couple of cowards, or men he disliked, although their conclusions were plausible until conclusive proof was found; Crofton's passing was still too recent for him to accept. There was no natural successor, which would mean his lands would be passed to a southern baron.

'Over my dead body,' Millard thought to himself. If Crofton was indeed dead then the time to rise up against the west's occupation would now need to be brought forward, with the opportunity for success vastly decreasing.

'Come, we can discuss these developments in more detail back at the castle,' he told Lockwood, flatly.

'No. If a baron's been murdered, then the other barons need to be informed and Brandenburg will want that done in person.' Lockwood, having other pressing matters to attend to before he'd be willing to see the back of Glen-Neath, did not have time to waste talking about a dead baron when, clearly, that was a task for kings. 'Please provide us with a packhorse, provisions, and a couple of men to escort us back to Brandenburg Castle. We need to freshen up first, but then we'll be on our way,' he continued, with a courteous nod.

'Very well. At southgate your request will be met,' Millard replied, knowing full well that if Crofton had been killed, allowing them to leave was a very bad idea. With a look, he passed the task to Lucian. The hipparch nodded. Lockwood produced a twisted smile, while Rog just grunted his approval.

'Wilfred, follow me,' instructed Millard and both men remounted. Brandenburg's man-at-arms and Rog took off in the direction of an inlet and tavern that southerners frequented. Along with his battalion, Lucian, the captain and his man-at-arms rode to the castle to give Kennice the tragic news.

'What's our next move?' Wilfred asked hesitantly. Millard gave him a sharp squint.

'Find the baron and never forget you're a knight. We play this charade to remain unseen.' Wilfred nodded, knowing that was probably the reason why he was not being led away to the dungeons as well.

'I'll call a meeting of the order, but first we must raise an army and send a royal rider to sort out this mess before the other barons rally their armies and take action into their own hands. When that happens war is inevitable. For all our sakes, I hope he is alive. We are the first line of defence against the Kelts.'

'They slaughtered our men and the Draconians like cattle, with a ferocity I've rarely seen.'

'There'll be time to speak of this, but now Crofton needs our resolve,' responded Millard. They rode over the drawbridge and headed for the stables where they were greeted by the stable hands who took charge of their horses. Lucian dismissed the battalion then, accompanied by one of his men, went to make the preparations for Lockwood's departure. At the stone steps leading to the main wing Millard questioned a guard.

'Where is the baroness?'

'In her parlour, sir,' said the guard. They ascended the wide steps.

'I don't envy you,' commented the captain. Wilfred's fleeting look was an adequate response.

Kennice, in her boudoir with Isadora and two chambermaids, was still enraptured by her latest acquisition. The four-carat, pink beryl stone, cut in the shape of a heart, was a constant source of volcanic glint. She raised her hand and stretched out her fingers to create more shimmering from her subtle movements. Candlelight flickered and reflected, enhancing the diamond's starlike sparkles.

'Well, he's good for some things, I suppose,' said Isadora, gazing at the ring.

'Undeniably.' Kennice beamed, while giving Isadora a glance that said, 'Not in front of the servants.' She was all too aware of the admiration her husband inspired in the hired help. Isadora frowned, taking the gesture the wrong way; she thought she was being scolded. The baroness smiled.

'Come, let's not end this day on bad terms. You're leaving me soon and I've so enjoyed your company.'

'As I have yours,' replied Isadora.

'Look, you've missed a bit.' Kennice directed her chambermaid to a blemish on her cheek. With an assortment of powdered minerals, delicately mixed with a brush, the patch vanished.

'It's still the wrong shade,' teased Isadora.

'You're just jealous that you're not afforded such luxury,' Kennice retorted mischievously.

'Don't be silly. You should come back with me. I can tell you're bored herein the autumn and winter there's nothing to do here. Don't you miss Solom City and the hills of Calgorium? I remember when we used to ride along the Bay of Angleshore. Tellick has become very powerful within the senate, with this endless war being waged by the Autocrat. You could make Crofton understand.'

Tellick was Kennice's childhood sweetheart. However, Isadora's impish suggestion was quickly dismissed.

'I wonder when my husband will be back?' said Kennice, giggling.

Isadora, with a chambermaid positioned behind tending to her hair, took the hint and produced a tight smile. The maids shared a look.

A knock on the door made the ladies sit up.

'Speak of the devil,' whispered Isadora.

'Enter,' said Kennice, curious. Millard, beside a sheepish Wilfred, entered.

'I left strict instructions that I wasn't to be disturbed,' she said, displeased with the interruption.

'Tell her,' ordered Millard.

'Tell me what? Are you trying my patience?' Wilfred went through the formalities and at the end Kennice was in tears.

'My poor Crofton!' she cried, going for Wilfred. 'Why didn't you protect him?' she demanded, banging her fists against his chest before stopping and sobbing.

Millard gave her hug and assured her he'd do everything in his power to return him to her side. She pushed Millard away.

'Don't you get it? My Crofton's dead. Would you return a dead man to my bed?' Tears streamed down her cheeks. 'Remove yourselves from my sight.' She pointed at Wilfred with bloodshot eyes.

'It's all his fault. Get out, get out now!'

'As you wish, my lady,' muttered Millard, his head dipped. As they withdrew from the room, before the door closed, the chambermaids were told to leave too.

Millard rolled his eyes.

'Did you see those fake tears? Our baroness is a good recitalist.'

'You never liked her. Why?' asked Wilfred, believing her tears to be genuine.

Millard looked at him, but remained tight-lipped, as they marched along a roomy well-lit passage with walls covered in coats of arms.

'You really ripped into him.'

'I had to make it look good; Millard is suspicious of me.'

'Do you blame him?' asked Isadora.

'No, I would be suspicious of me too,' she replied deviously. They both giggled. 'I thought it was my messenger. He is well overdue.'

'Did he have important papers?' asked Isadora.

'That's the problem. I'm not sure. But if my husband is dead then it is of no consequence. Now that I've dismissed the chambermaids you'll have to help me finish powdering my nose. A grieving widow has to look her best, even more so for bed.' She sat back, sinking into the elaborate chair, as Isadora got to her feet.

'With Crofton gone what will become of you?'

'I was placed here to rid the south of him, so my position will remain unchanged,' she leaned forward and whispered. 'I am with child.'

'Did Crofton know?' she asked, nearly dropping the powder brush. Kennice shook her head and murmured directly into Isadora's ear. Isadora opened her eyes wide and pulled a face tinged with crude delight.

'Now, cousin, powder my nose.' Isadora did as she was asked.

News of the baron's absence filtered through to his troops like a bad smell. Glen-Neath was on tenterhooks; every man, woman and child was aware of the facts as Lockwood, accompanied by the Draconian, met their escort and, collecting their provisions from Lucian at the south gate, made ready to continue the journey. Millard was glad to see the back of him. Having Lockwood around could only make matters worse because the order – the brotherhood of Ebenesian Knights – would now have to close ranks. He had chosen to withhold from Lockwood the fact that he had apprehended Gwillym and, far from throwing him in the stockade, felt the chieftain was right to feel aggrieved. So any mention of Gwillym having been seized would have placed him under Lockwood's charge, to be led away to certain death.

'Another wise head in a crisis ... the more the merrier,' thought Millard, walking past two guards stationed outside a large door. He pushed it open.

'I've been here long enough. Where's Crofton? I fought with his father before he became a turncoat,' said Gwillym, visibly flustered.

'Hold your tongue,' ordered Wilfred menacingly. Millard hit him across the chest. The blow winded him temporarily.

'Did I tell you to speak?' Grudgingly, Wilfred answered.

'No.'

'The baron has disappeared. He is presumed dead, in answer to your question,' replied Millard.

'What is that? A jest in poor taste? Without Crofton the west is doomed,' said Gwillym.

'Without a power gauntlet the west is doomed,' commented Wilfred, through gritted teeth, still feeling the effect of the blow.

'Forget about power gauntlets, lad. All you need is heart to rise up against tyranny.' Gwillym looked at Millard. 'So, captain, have you arranged a search party?'

'No. I dare not risk more men on their lands. I'll need to raise an army first.'

'I can help with that. Crofton is well liked among the chieftains.'

'Good.'

'So, what was he doing in the Badlands? Seems like madness to me,' said Gwillym. Millard told him briefly what he needed to know. Gwillym swallowed hard when he was given Brun's description, but said nothing.

'We cornered one of the attackers and we made him talk. Kallen is Edwin's creature, searching for a scroll on his behalf. And the royal rider possessed proof of Edwin's involvement. This is why your baron was ordered to search for this man,' said Gwillym.

'Do my ears deceive me? Proof that Edwin's men attacked your keep?'

The chieftain nodded.

Millard looked at Wilfred, who was just as baffled.

'That southerner! Lockwood never mentioned knowing him. And what's this about a scroll?' the captain asked. Gwillym pleaded ignorance. Millard turned to face his man-at-arms.

'Alexandra is nearby. I'll send word for her to receive our instructions.'

'A rider? Do you think that's wise, even before we've raised an army?' asked Wilfred.

'Well, I think it's wise,' said Gwillym. 'A genuine royal rider can get to the bottom of this mess sooner than you two can. If you march on their land it will be war.'

'I agree,' nodded Millard.

'How sure are you he's dead?' asked Gwillym.

'As sure as chickens lay eggs,' replied Wilfred.

'Without seeing his body? I'm glad you're not one of my men.' Millard gave his man-at-arms a discerning look too.

'All the same, if I only have your word to go on, I'll reserve judgement and await better evidence.'

'You'll what?' Millard blocked Wilfred's attempted lunge, then calmly spoke to Gwillym.

'Lockwood has left so you're free to leave.'

'I'll leave in the morning for Brimstone Keep. You will have your army, but take heed: we teeter on the brink of war and one wrong move will tip us over the edge.'

They understood the significance of his words. Wilfred yawned and went to pat his lips, but stopped when he saw

Millard's glance. Millard's patience was wearing thin. Wilfred's uncivil manner was becoming a hindrance; he needed the chieftain's help.

'It's been a long day.' His words were spoken more in an apologetic tone than as an excuse.

'Too long,' Gwillym concurred.

'I meant no offence,' said Wilfred, in the midst of another yawn.

'None taken. You seem tired, friend.'

'Wilfred, you need a rest. Go,' Millard said sharply. No sooner had his man-at-arms made his excuses to leave than a figure appeared in the doorway, his normally chirpy smile missing.

'You summoned me?'

'Indeed, Eric. Find Alexandra; I have an errand for her.' After a courteous nod, Eric and Wilfred were gone.

'Guards, escort Gwillym to more suitable quarters.'

'Where are my men and my weapons?' asked Gwillym.

'They will be there to meet you. Your weapons you can have when you leave.'

'Very well,' replied Gwillym, as he left with the guards.

Alone with just candlelight and four walls to keep him company, Millard pulled out a chair and sat down. He wondered what this Edwin was up to. It was late and the hour of sleep was creeping up. Pouring a drink, he removed a rolled parchment from a small tube and began to scribble a note for the king. He wondered if he'd see his friend again. If he was being honest, he would miss Crofton barking out his orders. The baron, although bullish at times, was a bloodline inheritance and, knowing him as long as he had, his faith in Crofton's ability to get out of a tight spot still remained.

So the message would demand his return. However, before he could finish it, burning eyes with heavy lids pushed him in only one direction. The quill slipped from his grip and he drifted off to sleep.

The next morning he awoke, in the same position, when Eric shouted.

'Captain, I've been looking for you. Alexandra is in the state room.'

'Tell her I'll be there shortly,' he replied groggily, looking at the empty flagon of berry wine. 'And Eric, get a maiden to fetch me a basin of warm water.'

'Yes, captain.'

Quickly, he finished off the note and read it again. It was precise, to the point, and could not be misconstrued. He knew what the last sentence implied. He re-rolled the parchment then sealed it with the baron's wax seal and put it back into the container, closing the lid. A flag of parley came under the jurisdiction of the Keltic king, and an attack on Crofton under these conditions meant Taliesin either gave the order or, worse, his authority was being seriously undermined. It did not matter. He'd make him understand how dangerous an attack of this nature was, with reason or with force.

A maiden, standing in the doorway with a basin, broke his chain of thought.

'Hello, captain. How are you this morning?' she said with a pleasant smile.

'I'm well, Aoibhe,' he said, clearing the table as she placed the basin before him. He sank his hands into the warm, scented water. The tingle of splashing water on his face revitalized his demeanour. He looked up at Aoibhe standing patiently with a cotton towel over her arm and smiled.

The morning glare streaked across the horizon, accompanied by a gentle breeze that seemed to give the vegetation-covered landscape vibrancy after a night of torrential rain. 'I haven't been in this room for a while. The views are still as breathtaking as I remember,' murmured Alexandra, believing she was in the stateroom with just the footman; but Millard and Lucian had slipped in unnoticed.

'It's the baron's favourite room,' Millard announced. She spun round.

'I don't like to be kept waiting. I am a royal rider and you do not hold a royal title. I've heard the news so I'll make an exception. Why have you requested my presence?'

'To prevent war,' he replied solemnly. She unclipped a hook and opened her cloak to reveal broad shoulders on a slender muscular frame. Eric, standing by her side, was given her trademark black leather cloak. Millard gazed at her admiringly. A rider's swordsmanship was unquestionable but Alexandra's beauty matched her brawn. Flowing black hair complemented her pale and exotic complexion.

'To avert war, close your jaw and start talking,' she said, amused. He told her that he required her to ride to Brigantia to deliver a message to Taliesin, or the Circle of Druids, and to return with the response.

'Why me? Carrier pigeons are faster,' she asked, running her fingers along the marble banquet table before taking a seat. Millard, positioned opposite her, followed suit.

'This is a delicate matter and pigeons can't get the results we seek,' he replied pensively.

'And they can get lost.' They both looked up. 'Shot down or eaten,' Wilfred said as he walked in, rejuvenated after a good night's rest.

'He's right. We're not sure if Taliesin still has control of the region. With Prince Edwin predisposed to fighting in the east, the other barons will use this as an excuse for war in order to gain more territory. I just want Crofton back.'

'I was led to believe he's dead,' Alexandra replied, confused.

'I believe that stance to be premature, my lady.'

'Very well. Where is your message? And I'd prefer to be addressed as royal rider, if you please.' Alexandra got to her feet. Eric returned the cloak and with a flick of her wrist it was in the air, adorning her shoulders and clasped around her neck. Millard handed her the leather-bound tube, which was placed in a sachet.

'I will expect payment on my return. You know the fee.' Millard nodded.

'Eric will escort you to the stables. Take what you need.' She bowed, concealing the sachet away from prying eyes, and then exited the room.

'There goes our last chance for peace,' observed Millard.

'We seek peace but prepare for conflict. How ironic,' replied Lucian, with a slight smile. The contradiction was a paradox commonly associated with war.

'Isn't it just,' agreed Millard.

They were within a stone's throw of hostilities, and against whom was still in doubt.

*

With the morning dew still fresh on the autumn leaves, Taliesin's encampment, bathed in sunlight, was a resourceful hub of endeavour. Stalls had been set up for trade and livestock were being fed, while common Kelts got on with daily chores. The community was reduced in number as many left on hunts. Woodcutters sourcing firewood could be heard in the distance. Away from the bustle, under the Keltic king's banquet tent, a small gathering was taking place. A spread of light refreshments were on offer: fruits, nuts and pastries, mainly being devoured and enjoyed in equal measure by the ruddy-nosed Bollymore. His face was covered in a rainbow of colours.

If Taliesin had been in a different frame of mind the dwarf's appetite would have brought a smile to his face but, deep in thought, even Druce's innocuous quips or his bard's Keltic harp did nothing to lighten his mood. Everyone else was transfixed by the harmonious rendition but he slumped in a chair, sipping on sylvestris wine. It was way too early for the royal ancestral beverage. All the same he drank and his sulkiness was far-reaching as he gripped the gold sun cross that hung loosely round his neck on a crude, thin, brown, leather twine. The item symbolized a correlation between spirits and the earth and, in a way, he sought divine intervention or, at the very least, the sun's affiliation to self-knowledge.

His decision to withhold Crofton's excursion from the Circle of Druids had been made to look a foolish one and he tried to put a brave face on what had preceded. He cast his eyes over his loving wife; her full figure and her face were a picture of tranquillity.

How long would that remain? He refocused on trying to avoid the bloodshed to come. She smiled back, blissfully unaware of the turmoil engulfing her husband. With help from Nemetona, she had arranged this breakfast blessing. The final gathering for Aghamore, the druid departing for Asseconia and onto Gulzar forest, should have been a joyous occasion, but these were not joyous times. Halwn had returned with disastrous news and an unexpected gift. Although the badly beaten Draconian had proven to be invaluable, it was a gift that he did not care for and, after interrogating the demon, his depression was complete.

He had been wrong to think the request for parley was about commerce. The only reason Crofton had ventured onto his land was in pursuit of a rider's murderer, a noble cause, and in these circumstances access would have been granted. This Draconian, named Zog, had been commissioned by Prince Edwin to apprehend this man. Armed with this information, Taliesin deployed scouts to find this blacksmith, accompanied by a dwarf, to perhaps salvage his footing, but word came back quickly; unless they were ghosts they had not stepped forth on Keltic soil, and to compound matters, if his instruction had been followed his head would be clear of this mess.

'How is it that a comfortable chair can feel so uncomfortable?' he thought. He pulled a face; the facts would actually be laughable if the ramifications were not so grave.
The baron was missing, presumed dead. Under a flag of parley, that could only lead to one thing, unless he found a solution. Even if one could be unearthed the opportunity to implement it was fading fast with a sizeable force gathering at Glen-Neath. His spies had sent word that Brandenburg,

too, was amassing a large army as well as Baron Syracuse of Daginhale, and his network of spies were rarely wrong. Druce had expressed his view with his usual no-nonsense approach: no warrior should be afraid of a fight and he was ready to carve his name in the records of folklore. With a begrudging smile Taliesin had approved of the stance; he expected nothing less from his kin's lips. A king's concern was not only about defending and gaining territory. He had nothing to gain from war with the west. The land was downtrodden after years of southern occupation and war started under the clouds of autumn and winter moons was not prudent. The upheaval of an evacuation would be a mammoth task.

The journey to Fog Forest would not be easy and, if this was his wish, he had wasted enough time on delaying the decision. But who would be a king? It was to the druids people turned for insight and guidance; they were the astronomers, diviners, healers, historians, philosophers and keepers of the secrets of the cosmos. Their teachings inspired total obedience from their clans while kings, on the other hand, were blamed for misfortune. In this environment one could feel obsolete though laws were his alone to command, which kept his fires burning.

The bard finished with a low flurry and then Nemetona got to her feet to recite a blessing for Aghamore's journey. Dressed in her traditional garb, a hooded hessian cloak tied tightly around her waist with a beaded belt, she cleared her throat.
    'May the Keltic hills hide you. May her rivers and streams guide you. May the Keltic luck enfold you. May blessings of Iden behold you,' she said while sprinkling earth onto a small piece of cloth. Then, dipping her fingers into a

bowl of water, she let droplets fall onto the shroud. She picked up a metal Keltic knot emblem, its three-pronged spiral said to signify the cycles of life. She raised it up and whispered, 'Anu,' before laying it to rest on the muddy grit. She wrapped it in the cloth before handing it to Aghamore. The group whispered 'Anu' in unison and the blessing was complete.

Unable to hold his tongue any longer Taliesin tried to speak, to tell them that war was coming. It was a vain attempt to alleviate the strain, but nothing came out. His vocal chords deserted him at the vital moment and it seemed that the decision to speak to Aghamore and Nemetona had already been made for him when a Keltic guard ran towards the canopy, shouting.
  'A royal rider approaches!'
At last a respite. Maybe his delay would be justified; the notion of being considered feeble by the Circle was abhorrent. Though others held a surprised expression he, Druce and Bollymore did not. They shared a discreet look.
  'Clear the tent,' ordered Taliesin. He had been expecting Glen-Neath's next move; the problem was, this should have been their first. As the tent started to clear Aghamore, standing firm, demanded an explanation.
  'I knew something was going on,' he said. 'For days you've seemed unhinged and as for the creature from Draconia being held not five yards from here ...' He leaned on his staff, his beard seemingly showing no sign of life as the words were uttered. 'Don't you think it's time we spoke?'
  'We can discuss these matters in private,' said Taliesin.
  'These are not private matters. Warriors coming and going before my very eyes. Even this dwarf knows more

than me.' He looked at the now clean-bearded Bollymore, returning from pouring a pail of water over his face, outwardly bemused at being mentioned.

Aghamore waved his personal guards away.

'I maybe old but I'm not senile. If trouble is brewing nothing must be hidden from the Circle; it's our Circle that makes us strong.' Taliesin's large throne was becoming increasingly more uncomfortable as he glared back at the druid, unable to see his face due to an overhanging hood. Nemetona, mortified by the embarrassment, didn't mince her words.

'I, too, have chosen to overlook proceedings due to the Circle's leader's visit, and as druid of our clan I stand by his words. I have not heard counsel on these matters you wish to bring before him,' she said, visibly disgruntled.

A chagrined Taliesin got to his feet.

'Husband ...' cajoled his wife, surprised at his lack of respect.

'Everything is fine, Arlina. Please leave us.' With a scolding look she did what she was asked.

'Now that it's a little quieter in here, can I have an answer?' Aghamore persisted. Taliesin's face softened as he sought an elucidation, knowing transparency at this late stage was, indeed, warranted.

'Very perceptive. Are these the innuendos you besieged a king with? Let's just see what news the royal rider brings,' replied Druce nonchalantly, coming to his brother's aid.

'This is not a free-for-all,' retorted Aghamore authoritatively. 'And our king's rule is not a subservient reign; his ancestor saw to that,' he said. With a finger pointed firmly at Taliesin he finished with this veiled warning.

'My brother is right, although a little bullish. We'll deal with this stranger first and then, of course, we'll talk,' said Taliesin.

'Agreed,' responded Aghamore. The group looked at each other: two druids, a warrior, a dwarf and a king awaiting the rider's arrival.

Alexandra, with the crest of the raven on her pouch, rode into the camp, dismounted and handed her horse to a grinning Kelt. She was directed to the king's quarters.

'A woman,' Aghamore murmured, as if his eyes were deceiving him. The comment received a discerning look from Nemetona; in Keltic law a woman could be a warrior if she could pass the initiation. Alexandra, having earned her spurs, had been given a royal commission and had proven worthy of that endorsement. It caused raised eyebrows in the male-dominated southern realm, where men frowned upon a woman in such a role; missions to the territory were avoided. Long days and lonely nights, isolation with a constant fear of danger: that was the life of a royal rider. Shrouded in mystery, it was a pompous name for a simple dispatcher. Nevertheless it worked: the vocation was afforded a certain respect, and it paid handsomely.

Alexandra rarely ventured north. The east, considered moderate, accepted her with open arms. The west, although a wasteland after its destruction, still had many unforeseen dangers lurking within its borders and, though her tasks could be arduous at times, few appreciated living by their wits as much as she did. Moments when extraordinary will was needed were the moments the raven lived for. Unlike her male counterparts, her femininity came with empathy so overcoming obstacles for the betterment of peace was an added bonus, though not a motivating factor. These days she was more used to facilitating war. She loved travelling under clear skies and through nice scenery. Breathing fresh air beat the stench from towns and villages. She had decided long ago that she would be nobody's swinging door. With no one to explain her comings and goings to, the lifestyle fitted her ethos and proclivity for freedom perfectly. Being involved without getting involved suited her to a tee.

On her travels, rubbing shoulders with the ruling class was commonplace. Meeting many interesting individuals while coming into contact with numerous different cultures was considered an advantage of the role. Alexandra, being of mixed descent, had an affinity with the variety of cultural differences between races.

'I have a message for Taliesin,' she said in her husky voice.

Taliesin raised a hand and she walked briskly towards him and removed the tube from her pouch. As the druids observed the handover their disapproval was clear to see; writing was forbidden in Keltic culture. Knowledge was stored in different symbols and passed on through word of mouth.

'How many female royal riders are there?' enquired Aghamore.

'Only me,' she replied brusquely. 'I'll wait outside for your reply.'

Taliesin unrolled the parchment and, casting his eyes over its written words, nodded.

The message read:

Taliesin, King of the Kelts.

Crofton has always trusted you to be fair, so your actions seem out of character.

For this reason it is your deeds now on which you will be judged.
We want the baron's remains and his horse returned.
We want the warrior who shot him, along with Kelt who gave the order, handed over.

If the baron is alive, arrangements to discuss his release are to be sent or an attack on Asseconia will be inevitable.

We will find the perpetrators if you will not.

Captain Millard
Acting Baron, Glen-Neath

He took a moment to digest what he'd read. The parchment was a declaration of war in all but name.
    'Who does this Captain Millard think he is? Does he presume me a fool?' said Taliesin, incensed.
    'Millar is a lackey, nothing more,' replied Bollymore.
    'Well, this lackey has high demands. He wants the baron's body along with his horse and if I don't do what he asks, they'll think I had a hand in his death.'
    'Horse?' said Druce, frowning.
    'Yes, a horse,' Taliesin said and shook his head. 'All I got was a damned demon in a cage.' Druce and Bollymore chuckled.
    'It seems like a reasonable request. We're not horse thieves,' said Nemetona.
    'Indeed, so why do they think we've got his horse?' Taliesin looked at his brother.' Has Halwn left yet?' Druce nodded. 'He's on a hunt, brother.' The king shook his head. Shrewdly, Aghamore, who had been patiently taking note of the conversation, decided it was time to intervene.
    'Yes, what about Halwn? Since his return, you've looked glum. Is this Baron Crofton Abbehale of Glen-Neath, by any chance? His lands border mine. Don't you think you should have mentioned this?'

'There will be time for such questions,' replied Druce.

'Have you forgotten I am a druid and leader of the Circle of Druids?' asked Aghamore.

'I will explain my affairs when needs be,' Taliesin said sharply.

'When will you learn? Who do you think keeps Iden's legacy in place? Now tell us what's going on so we can help,' he responded calmly.

Nemetona, still standing by his side, was not so calm. With unkind eyes and biting her tongue, she awaited his decision with bated breath.

Taliesin looked at the druids standing before him, then at his surroundings and at the sunlit sky. The sun was at its brightest: his favourite time of day. Fluorescent rays flickered and meadows, filled with Keltic thistles, produced a hazy glow. He could just about make out the sound of children's laughter. Its resonance always gave him food for thought and the solace, though brief, still seemed to sober him up. War needed to be averted for their sake as much as his, and he admitted it was time for an old hand's support.

'Aghamore, let us go for a walk. The others can wait here,' he commanded.

The druid dipped his head and said 'Let's.' As they walked, the king explained, at length, what had taken place and the druid listened intently. Some distance away from the safety of the encampment they stopped.

'These are troubling matters indeed,' observed Aghamore. 'It is imperative we find Crofton, dead or alive, but you cannot hand Kelts over to this man, Millard. The other clans will be in uproar. It is a double-edged sword.'

'I prefer to call it a poisoned chalice,' Taliesin sighed, with his hands clasped behind his back. 'I fear the brew was already tainted before I drank from it.'

'Too true. You'll look weak to our men if you hand Kelts over to this upstart. His power will be gone soon and that sign of weakness will be enough once the other barons reach Glen-Neath and continue on to our lands. At that point it will be too late.' The druid looked into his eyes. 'They fear us, Taliesin,' he said, placing a hand on the young king's shoulder. 'They always have and they always will. And we will not change that perception,' he concluded.

Taliesin, unconvinced, pulled away. Distracted by a brace of wild horses prancing about in front of them, he shared his misgivings.

'The flatlands of Asseconia will be hard to defend.'

'I wouldn't worry. One of us is worth ten of them.'

'True.'

It was a first time in awhile Taliesin had smiled.

'Now, you must confide in Nemetona more. She believes you to be a fair king. I am old and have chosen her to succeed me. In time she will be as wise as me.' He paused at his own self-praise. 'Is it because she is a woman?'

'Of course not,' answered Taliesin, shaking his head.

'Without your confidence in her this will never come to pass.'

'The Circle could do with a woman's touch at the helm,' the king said. He paused, then continued, 'although she does have a temper.'

'Agreed.' They both smiled.

'What to do, what to do?' murmured the old druid as though lost in thought. 'You must delay him and gather our forces. You never know, this might just be a ruse to make the Autocrat tear up our treaty. I've never trusted these southerners. After all, eating wildebeest is sacrilege. And I wouldn't trust this demon's words. A blacksmith killing a royal rider? Everyone knows that's certain death.' A Kelt ran up to their position.

'Sire, this royal rider grows impatient.'

'Afford her our comforts, but explain these things take time,' Taliesin said firmly. As the warrior ran off, Aghamore continued.

'Tell this Millard you need time to carry out his wishes, that's all. There's no need to evacuate just yet.'

'No, when I leave for Asseconia I'll give that order,' Taliesin agreed.

'Very well. I will go to Gulzar Forest as planned and have my novices and apprentices search it. If he's there we'll find him. I'll have the torrent dragged for his remains. I know this clan well; Lluddrum's lot couldn't care less if he was buried in a ditch,' responded Aghamore.

'When this is all over, the ones responsible for this mess will be flogged,' said Taliesin, barely managing to contain his contempt.

'That would be the least of my worries; they may already be equipped to launch an attack,' said Aghamore.

'If this was pre-planned the barons would already be mobilized and my spies tell me different. They believe we have three full moons. We must be ready a moon sooner.'

'That sounds about right,' responded Aghamore, knowing full well that to raise an army of the size needed to defeat the Kelts would undoubtedly take time, and he moved on swiftly. 'What about his horse and the demon?'

'I need to speak to Halwn. Maybe he has news. I'll keep Zog alive as long as it's advantageous to us. You never know, he may still prove useful. Once he becomes ineffective ... let's just say he wasn't mentioned on the parchment.'

Aghamore nodded, as though that proven he was right about the philistine. Taliesin smiled.

'You are wise to pick Fog Forest as our retreat. The spirits of our fallen warriors are strong there and the doors of Ascidia have never been breached.'

'If truth be told, it hasn't been attacked in these times,' replied the king, mindful of the fact that, of late, the entrance to its ancient halls had not been truly tested.

'If Keltic blood flows through your veins, the fallen will protect you,' said Aghamore.

'Remember I'm not superstitious,' Taliesin reminded him. 'I chose Fog Forest for one reason only: we will be in the grip of winter soon, but its underground caverns remain tepid.'

He turned to absorb the landscape. The first signs of winter were already starting to appear, with the peaks in the distance covered in snow, and it wouldn't be too long before it was under his feet.

'If it was warmer, I would have chosen the hill of Glandomirum.' He paused, as though reminiscing. 'There, we could continue our way of life and fight.'

'Under these skies that journey would kill many, 'said Aghamore. With a shrug Taliesin displayed a pessimistic grimace, which disappeared quickly.

'I must consult with the other clans. Do I have your support?' asked Taliesin.

'I can see why you kept this from me, but that was then and this is now. It must have seemed trivial to begin with: a simple snowball collecting snow as it rolls, but if we don't stop it we'll be engulfed by its avalanche. What say I?' said Aghamore, before reaching out his hand. Taliesin clasped it. Both knew what the gesture implied. 'Now, let's rejoin the others. You have a message to reply to and the day is still young.'

'You are wise indeed, Aghamore,' replied Taliesin, as though his burden had been lifted.

'I know,' replied the druid, with a smile.

As they closed in on the marquee, Bollymore could be overheard saying, 'Not as troubling as war.'

'That much we agree upon, dwarf,' snapped Nemetona.

'Brother,' said Druce, the first to welcome them back.

'I see I'm missing out on a heated debate,' said Taliesin, teasing.

'Sorry, I didn't realize you were there,' Bollymore said, looking surprised.

'Blind, as well as long in the tooth, I see,' said Taliesin, smiling.

'No, I've just got a blocked nose.' Bollymore returned the smile.

'You've been away awhile,' said Nemetona, prying. She acknowledged their return by dipping her head.

'It was needed,' said Aghamore, with a brief stare at her. Taliesin walked past them and sat back in his chair.

'Summon the royal rider,' he ordered a guard. Alexandra, unescorted, strolled in.

'I trust your stay here has been pleasant?' enquired the king.

Alexandra nodded.

'I can only read, so you will have to write my words, and then I will place my seal.' He handed her the parchment. She flipped it over and, reaching inside her pocket, produced a black-feather quill attached to a tiny black marble inkwell.

'What are your words?'

'You came prepared.'

'Always,' she replied, eager to get on. Frivolous formalities irked herewith his words carefully chosen he confessed to having no knowledge of Crofton's whereabouts, insisting the chain of events was not of his making and that he would need time to carry out the captain's requests. Once he was finished, she handed him the parchment and he imprinted his mark, rolled the parchment and slid it back into its tube. With his blessing he handed it over. Alexandra turned and locked it away in her pouch before bidding them good health and leaving.

'That was not a response I expect from a Keltic king,' said his brother.

'I know what I'm doing. This day is not yet old and already I tire of it.'

'But ...'

'Enough, Druce. Now that she's left, I want you to escort Aghamore to Asseconia then make your way to Lluddrum's encampment. I want Crofton's horse found. Take as many men as you need.' He looked at the druid. Aghamore will have a search party sift through the area where he was last seen. I will await Halwn's return. In sixty days I will meet you on the plains of Asseconia.'

'So it's war,' whispered Nemetona.

'Not quite but, all the same, we must be ready to meet this challenge. 'They all agreed.

'Taliesin,' called Arlina in a panic, 'Dale has cut and bruised his knee.'

Taliesin rolled his eyes. 'Bring him here.' Carrying their three-year-old son, she entered. They all looked at the child sobbing.

'Leave us. Druce sent Eldrun to my quarters. I need to send him on an errand.' His brother nodded and left, along with Bollymore and the druids.

Arlina placed Dale in his lap and then began to dress the wound as Taliesin stroked his son's hair and looked at his wife. He felt a whole lot better; their presence reaffirmed that the most important thing in life was family. It was late afternoon when he gave Eldrun his instructions and was informed that Druce and Aghamore were ready to leave. Bollymore, Nemetona and Arlina were among the crowd who gathered to bid a fond farewell to the group of fifty or so warriors and Aghamore, sitting in his chariot. Taliesin patted his brother's horse and locked eyes with his brother.

'Don't worry, we'll sort out the mess this Sucellos has caused,' Druce assured him.

'Be heedful, brother, until we cross paths in sixty days. Now ride,' commanded Taliesin, slapping the horse's hide. Under cheers the convoy moved off. As Taliesin walked away, with Eldrun by his side, he decided that if it was to be war he'd make sure it was the mother of all wars. After all, he was the king of the Kelts.

*

The trek across the Black Forest's mountainous region was like being lost in a labyrinth once the sunset. Though the affliction of darkness had little effect on Tarquin and Flint, the others were severely hampered. However, with light winds and a clear sky, compared to what they had already encountered, it was by far the lesser of those evils and, with hindsight, only a minor irritation.

'Aren't we there yet?' grumbled Ragnarr impatiently. He lifted his helmet to scratch his temple; riding in the dark, with only starlight to guide their way, made little sense.

'It's not much further,' said the wizard, plotting their path, as they reached yet another plateau. The glow of his staff's orb led the way.

'Not much further, not much further,' repeated the dwarf. 'My bottom's been fed too much saddle.'

'Be still. We'll be there soon enough,' replied Brun, not wanting his friend to upset a mage of Nikomeades' abilities. He received in response a sulky and lingering stare as Ragnarr pouted his lips. The brothers laughed.

'Now he's walking us into a wall of bushes,' continued Ragnarr, shaking his head in disbelief.

Tartarus's elation at having regained the scroll was replaced by exhaustion, brought on by malnutrition; the image of a farmhouse coming into view in such an isolated place was a sight for sore elven eyes. A path through the bushes, where before there had been none, seemed to suddenly appear. Nikomeades turned to them and smiled. So, with the realization that his assignment was finally at an end, the notion of putting his feet up was as much a sobering thought as it was a gratifying one. Doubts about his mission were waylaid and its validity certified. With the gold-rimmed scroll back in his possession he sat in his saddle and travelled alongside Nikomeades, who was on foot.

Bar getting his companions replenished and back to Irons Keep, Tartarus viewed his mission as completed and, far from returning as a failure, he could now return to Oaken-Crag with his head held high. He'd be a hero. He'd be Eolande's hero. He gave Willow a hearty pat as he thought that perhaps his fallen friends would fervently disagree, with only Bowen's death to mark their non-existence. In a way they'd be right; his accomplishment came with a bittersweet taste and he hoped he would not come to rue allowing the dark elf to escape.

'We're here. This is my home,' Nikomeades announced proudly.

'We need to get him inside,' responded Tartarus. Barnaby's condition and complexion were worsening visibly. His normally chubby, rosy cheeks were turning a pastel green.

'At last. Doesn't look like something to boast about but it will do, I suppose,' Ragnarr muttered under his breath. 'I thought he was leading us on a merry dance,' he whispered to Brun.

'Don't you trust anyone, dwarf?' asked the blacksmith.

'No. But maybe you,' was his swift response.

Nikomeades directed them to where they could leave their horses then, accompanied by Tartarus, walked to his main door. The wide oak farmhouse door, cut from one tree, was the centrepiece of an inviting entrance.

'You four, you heard the man,' commanded Nefanial, following up on Tartarus's instructions by pointing. Sid, Calhoun, Daniel and Reece dismounted and Flint took their horses.

'Is he going to be all right?' asked Pippa, watching the men lift Barnaby from his horse.

'I'm sure he'll be fine, 'said Rex, looking at Nikomeades who, in turn, nodded.

'Where do you want him?' asked Sid.
Suddenly the door swung inwards and Gunn-Hilda's large frame stood in the arched doorway.

'You took your time,' she said.

'I thought I told you to hide?' returned the mage.

'You knew I couldn't do that,' she said and smiled sheepishly. Nikomeades nodded coolly while marshalling the group in.

'Wipe your feet,' said Gunn-Hilda firmly, with no intention of having her gleaming tiled floor covered in muddy footprints.

'Prepare a feast for my guests. They are tired and, I expect, very hungry.'

He kissed her cheek and smiled.

At the mention of guests Calhoun, carrying Barnaby, stopped in his tracks, greeting the wizard's word with consternation. Any correlation to Arachna and her lair gave him the chills. So vivid was her image that he could still smell her breath.

'Move it. He ain't light!' barked Sidney, his hands barely managing to grip Barnaby's bulky left ankle. Reece, holding the right ankle, just smiled as they continued into the large entrance hall.

'I see why four of you were needed, 'said Nikomeades, stepping back to give them room.

'They do look hungry, especially this one,' said Gunn-Hilda, looking at Tartarus. 'And this one looks ill.' Her gaze turned to ashen-faced Calhoun. 'So will they be staying long?' she asked Nikomeades, turning her nose up at the combination of smells.

'As long as needs be,' replied Nikomeades.

'Well, they'll need to wash, and what about those two with him?' She looked at Nefanial's face.

'You mean these two?' the baker enquired. She nodded. 'Step forward, don't be shy. Smile for the lady.' Nefanial kicked both brigands into the doorway light. Darrel's attempt at a smile was hideous while Gorham, with his face contorted, just groaned.

'They're wanted men and they'll be feeding on scraps,' answered Nefanial as Rex escorted them in.

'So who's been in that swamp?' asked Gunn-Hilda once the main door was shut and the mercenaries, bound, were locked away in the larder.

'They all have. They've had a run with a Tipitiwichet. That's what injured their chubby friend here. Speaking of which' – he touched Barnaby's forehead –'take him to the back, past the main hall and washroom. There's a room with a few small cauldrons and a high flat bench. Lay him on it,' said Nikomeades, holding two conversations at once.

Daniel, Sid, Calhoun and Reece did as they were asked and followed Nefanial through to the corridor that led to the main hall. Pippa seemed to be in a daze, caught by the dim of the internal lights. Gunn-Hilda looked down at her.

'Been awhile since you've seen candlelight?' Pippa replied with a weak smile. 'And who's this? Hello, little one,' Gunn-Hilda said, kneeling to stroke the terrier. 'Does this cute little dog belong to you?' Pippa nodded.

'Yes, his name's Angus.'

'And what's your name?'

'Ah,' said Nikomeades, 'that's Pippa, Bellamina's daughter. Can't you see the resemblance?'

'Now that you mention it, I can.' She reached across and pinched Pippa's cheek. 'What are you doing with these ruffians, child?' she teased. There was a brief pause before Pippa decided to answer.

'Well, I was kidnapped by a dark elf and I escaped. Then Angus and my brother saved me from a minthe. Well, that's what Ragnarr called it. And please don't call me pipsqueak; Flint calls me that and I hate it.' Gunn-Hilda looked at Nikomeades endearingly as she interrupted. 'Well, he'll need feeding,' she said, still stroking Angus. The terrier, in turn, panted, enjoying the attention. 'You two can come with me and let's leave them to help your friend. We need to get you out of those dirty clothes.' Gunn-Hilda tugged at Pippa's sleeve.

'No. I like my clothes,' said Pippa, resisting stubbornly.

Gunn-Hilda shook her head and looked at the little girl with a grubby face and a dropped bottom lip and smiled, revealing her dimples.

'I'm only going to put you in some clean ones while I wash the ones you're wearing.'

'They don't need washing.' Pippa screwed up her face and turned away. Angus followed suit.

'Oh yes they do, young lady.' Gunn-Hilda stood her ground. Cleanliness was next to godliness; how else could one ascend?'There's a washroom at the back, but not all at once, mind you,' she said to the others. She looked at her husband.   'Your newfound friends smell worse than death. I will not cook until they're freshened up or have left.' Gunn-Hilda's demeanour changed as her gaze returned to Pippa. 'Now child, where was I?I think we got off on the wrong foot. Your mother's a friend and if you're here something bad must have happened, so let's get you cleaned up and you can tell me all about it.' Her persuasive second approach did the trick and Pippa wilted under her charm. From the connecting doorway Nefanial called Nikomeades.

'I think they have found the room. I had better go and fix your friend,' Nikomeades said as he disappeared down the corridor.

Tartarus knew what the rest of them were thinking as he took in the hall's inviting but eccentric entrance. A log fire burned in the fireplace and silver ornaments stood on the ledges of the deep-set windows either side of the main door. He removed his cloak and inhaled the wholesome farmhouse air. Being a tree dweller, the familiar scent of mature wood made him want to kick off his boots and freshen up, but Flint was the first to show his hand.

'We'll be in the washroom, won't we Quin?' he said confidently. His brother nodded.

'I think you'll find its age before youth,' said Rex.

'And if it's age before beauty, I think you'll find I'm first,' added Ragnarr, removing his boots.

'Not in human years, dwarf, although I do concede that you're the ugliest among us,' retorted Rex.

'What?' shouted Ragnarr. Brun held the dwarf back as Rex stood firm and clenched his fists. Before things got out of hand Tartarus intervened.

'No one has seniority here. We'll draw straws and the losers can unload and dress down the horses.'

'I was born lucky,' said Ragnarr, pulling one of the long straws and remaining tight-lipped. Tartarus, refastening his cloak, trundled back outside with Tarquin and Flint to tend to the horses. None of them, including him, thought much of his bright idea.

At the other end of the farmhouse, Nikomeades ushered Nefanial's group out of the makeshift treatment room.

'What is it they say about magicians? They never reveal their tricks.' He answered his own question as he closed the door behind him. Nefanial thought it was rude, but said nothing and just told his men to rejoin the others. They unpacked the horses and took turns in getting cleaned up. Tartarus, using a healing spell, took time off his feet to seal his cuts and treated anyone else with similar wounds.

It was sometime later before the wizard re-emerged, rolling down his sleeves and looking buoyant.

'How is he?' enquired Nefanial.

'Ask him,' said the wizard. Barnaby's large frame cleared the doorway. He still looked off-colour but managed to produce a painful grin. 'Your chubby friend will be fine,' Nikomeades declared while steadying Barnaby's step.

'What was wrong with him?' asked Tartarus.

'The mucus of a Tipitiwichet's lobe contains properties that induce a comatose state so that its victim's sustenance can slowly be absorbed. I simply reversed the effects.' He responded as though it was nothing.

With the meal prepared, a horrified Pippa, with pigtails and dressed in an extremely pretty shoulder-length dress, stood with her arms folded.

'Doesn't she look sweet? Just like a young lady of Ebenknesha should look,' said Gunn-Hilda, hovering over her and beaming.

'Actually, I prefer Pippa dressed the way she was when we got here,' replied Flint, unimpressed. He could not see the outfit's practicality for his tomboyish sister. Tarquin, amused by his brother's statement, nodded in agreement. Pippa's eyes lit up. She was glad her brothers were backing her up.

'But I do like what you've done with her hair and you can clearly see those freckles on her face,' continued Flint. Pippa blushed.

'But where's her hat?' asked Tarquin. Gunn-Hilda rolled her eyes as Pippa turned to the side to reveal the hat firmly gripped behind her back.

'We're waiting,' said Nikomeades. The group, sitting round his banqueting table, was beginning to grow restless.

Tarquin and Flint rolled in a large black cauldron on wheels. In it, boiling bubbles burst on the liquid's surface.

'Careful, it's hot,' warned Gunn-Hilda.

'What's in that?' asked Ragnarr. 'I haven't come all this way for just a big bowl of soup, have I?'

'Broth,' answered Gunn-Hilda. 'It's late and it's all I could rustle up with those brigands locked in our larder, but you don't have to eat it.' She paused. Ragnarr assured her he would eat it. 'And before you ask ...no, it hasn't got any meat in it.' She looked at Tartarus, who closed his mouth.

Once they were all seated, the group stood up in turn and, one by one, introduced themselves before retaking their seats. First was Reece, last was Daniel. Barnaby, although making a miraculous recovery, was still too weak to stand. After the introductions, Gunn-Hilda's home-made broth was readily consumed. It was the first time they had eaten a meal, as a group, with a roof above their heads and in cosy surroundings. It was smiles all round. Spoons hit the bottom of bowls. Lips and brows were wiped. While Gunn-Hilda and Pippa cleared up, Tartarus handed the mage the gold-rimmed scroll.

'It's been a very long time since I've seen you,' Nikomeades whispered to the scroll, running his wrinkled palms over its bright-gold band and coloured script. He waved his finger just above its lock. Tartarus looked at him in amazement when it clicked open. 'What are you gawking at, lad? Any wizard worth his salt could have opened this. The real trick is being able to read it.' At this, Tartarus turned bright red, although he put it down to keeping his mischievous nature in check. The notion of using a spell to open it hadn't even entered his mind. Nikomeades didn't stop to notice as he proceeded to unroll the scroll. 'I just don't know anyone from these shores that can. That's always been the problem. I believe that their father's ring holds a clue. We would be foolish to ignore its association. That Dökkalfar may have killed the only man who could have shed light on its link,' he sighed. 'Angus of Adalhard was a friend.'

Tarquin looked at Flint; neither had heard their father mentioned in this way.

'Sounds brave,' whispered Flint to his brother. Nikomeades stood up and, placing a hand on Tartarus's shoulder, summoned his staff. The stick glided from its position beside the fireplace before resting against his palm.

'I believe, from its description, that it maybe more than just a ring. I will consult my books. Nevertheless, we must regain it at all costs.' He looked directly at the brothers. 'Did your father ever talk about it?' They shook their heads. 'Angus was probably saving it for one of you,' he continued, 'but which one and for what reason, I know not. Time will tell.' Nikomeades sauntered to the centre of his banqueting table. His elongated shadow flickered from a tallow-lit polycandelon above his head; its radiance reflected off the arched ceiling. The circular cast-iron chandelier had seven glass cones held aloft by chains that were linked to enamel oblong-shaped discs. It was in a constant perpetual motion from an invisible draft.

Nikomeades addressed the group as a whole.

'A prophecy is about to unfurl and if it is allowed to prevail true evil will sweep these lands. The scroll holds the key to its undoing.'

'That sounds like something that the spider queen mentioned,' said Nefanial.

'Yes, you are correct. The spawn of Cernunnos. It is prophesied that a witch, a spider and a wolf will release the beast from his lair,' replied Nikomeades pensively.

'Well, I've heard enough. I'm ready to go back with our newfound wealth,' announced Sid, standing up and looking around the table for support. 'When Barnaby's ready to travel, that is,' he added.

'Sit back down. Have you got wax in your ears, boy? If evil sweeps these lands what good is wealth?' asked Rex.

'We're not heroes. When we started out only three of us had even seen a battle, let alone been in one. We've completed our task and Irons Keep has its revenge. I say we take our share of the gold and go home. No offence, but we don't owe this elf anything.' Sid retook his seat. Reece and Daniel nodded their agreement.

'I'd say we owe him our lives. Or was it you who saved us in the spider's lair?' asked Brun.

'Go back? There must be a safer route back to Irons Keep,' interjected Calhoun, fretting. He was not ready to face the Black Forest again anytime soon.

'What did you have in mind?' asked Nefanial, wanting to hear the wizard out before he would side with Sid.

'Have you all forgotten there's a young lady present?' Gunn-Hilda was astonished by the type of conversation being held in front of Pippa.

'She has earned the right,' responded Nikomeades sternly. 'And to answer your question,' –he looked at Nefanial – 'I believe our answer lies in the north.'

'What's in the north?' asked Tartarus

'Andorra. It's where their father's from. Its capital is Adalhard.'

'I've heard of the place you speak of but that's thousands of leagues from here and is shrouded in myths and legend,' replied Rex, not convinced.

'Who among you is a seafarer?' Nikomeades asked. The room fell silent. 'None of you?' The mage seemed shocked. Brun looked at Ragnarr and Eylbrich sprang to mind.

'We may know someone who's trustworthy and keeps himself to himself. He docks at Abbehale every couple of weeks, but we're not travelling in that direction, are we?' asked Brun as he and Ragnarr shared a glance.

'I know of the prophecy, but does the scroll contain the knowledge to make gauntlets?' Ragnarr enquired, his mind full of his mission. Nikomeades raised an eyebrow.

'Gauntlets of power? I see, dwarf, that you're well informed.'

'It pays to be,' responded Ragnarr, still undecided on whether to share his insight.

'You two are unusual bedfellows. Tell me, blacksmith, how did you come by your friend?' enquired the mage, shrewdly. Brun retold the story of their first meeting and laughter followed. Then others shared their stories and, over berry wine, for a moment, differences of opinion were forgotten and their troubles were put to one side. Even Tartarus had a sip.

With the fire dying down, Gunn-Hilda and Pippa bid them goodnight and, with Angus leading the way, they followed him out of the hall.

'We've got bigger problems, but I didn't want to scare them,' whispered Ragnarr, once they had left.

'What could be bigger than what has already been whispered around this table?' laughed Rex.

'Let him speak,' said Nikomeades. From his inside pocket Ragnarr pulled out the amulet. Its red facets sparkled, although the unusual markings were no longer such. They shared an uncanny similarity with those on the gold-rimmed scroll.

'What is that?' asked Tartarus. Ragnarr got to his feet, and cleared his throat.

'The key to Algrim's vault,' he replied. Then, before he could be rudely interrupted again, he told them of his mission to make a power gauntlet within Algrim's vault and the reasons for seeking out Bollymore. His bluntness exacerbated the sombre tale.

'So, if that's true, where are the tremors then? Huh? And everyone knows there are only ninety-two elements,' said Calhoun with a sceptical look on his face.

'They'll come near the end and our dwarfish friend is quite right. There are ninety-three elements in the cosmos,' said Nikomeades, astutely connecting the dots. 'Harvesting kromillium, you say? And the dwarves are ready to go to war? Then things are as grave as you say. We face a battle on two fronts, both of which are worth laying down our lives to win.'

'A reign of terror or annihilation,' said Calhoun as he swallowed hard.

'But we're not heroes. What can we do?' asked Sid.

'The lad has a point,' agreed Rex. A few of them murmured and nodded their heads.

'I share your sentiment but when you left Irons Keep you became champions of menthe fate of the planet rests in our hands and doing nothing is not an option,' replied Nikomeades.

As the gravity of their predicament sank in the blood drained from their faces. Tartarus's apprehension loosen his resolve; from the sound of things his mission was far from over and Eolande's vision quickly evaporated.

'There was a better time, believe it or not.' Nikomeades slammed his long wooden staff to the ground and the purple onyx orb, perched on top, emitted a bright glow, as did Nikomeades' eyes. The room's candlelight and firelight dimmed.

'Primordial,' he said firmly. Emanating from the orb, a projection of a spheres suddenly formed under the polycandelon, with images of the cosmos and the past rotating within. Nikomeades then proceeded to give the group a brief history lesson.

In the beginning three realms coexisted: Inferno, ruled by Cernunnos, the horned god; Ljøsalfheimr, the land of magic and the faerie folk; and Middle-Garth –or Midgardhr, as the wizard pronounced it: the world inhabited by humankind. Cernos wished to rule all and the First Great War was fought. Many were slain, on both sides, before Elohim was victorious. The Giver of Life would not slay his brother so, to bring about a cessation of hostilities and forge a long lasting peace, he decreed he would leave the world of man for Elysian Fields, or Folkvang – the plains of the heroic warrior and virtuous king – if the demon lord remained locked within his realm.

The fallen lord agreed. So, with the key to his realm hidden away and the pact made, Elohim left. Ljøsalfheimr merged with Midgardhr and the new realm was renamed after its creator.

The creatures and monsters who did not return to Inferno with their High Lord waged the Second Great War searching for the key. Then Elohim came in a dream to Algrim and told him where the key was and that he should split it in four, but when he broke it into four pieces, one shard was bigger and a better conductor than the others and, thus, was accompanied by the title of king of kings. The gauntlets of power were born and had been made to bring peace to these lands.

'Seems like a fair trade: on one side is peace, on the other side is a key to our destruction,' butted in Tarquin.

'Be still, lad,' said Brun.

'No, he's quite right. Eben, who penned the gold-rimmed scroll, foresaw our downfall and within its teachings is our salvation,' said Nikomeades. 'And only if you have all four gauntlets can you possess the key.' He looked at Tarquin. His features softened as he spoke of the king of kings and then hardened when his words were soured by the treachery that had befallen the kingdom of Ebenknesha. Casting a net into the past, Nikomeades dared to dream; the majestic palace and city came into view, with the white marble gatehouse and fortified wall now laid to waste and only ruins to mark its endeavours.

'Betrayal cuts deeper than anything I know, but hiding from the world this long is unforgivable. You still have skills to offer,' said Ragnarr, unmoved by the theatrics. The sphere disappeared.

'I found peace with Gunn-Hilda,' he said, with pain in his eyes. 'These eyes have seen much bloodshed.'

'You call this peace? My home is being sought. His' – he pointed at Tartarus –'is probably under attack, or worse. The west is under occupation and the east is next.' The dwarf stopped to draw breath and continued, 'All the while our world teeters on the brink of being hurled towards the void of nothingness and your kind, the guardians of us all, are cut down like wheat, hunted by the swarm, their longevity fuelled by the enchanteds' elixir.' Ragnarr slammed his fist against the hard oak table.

'Leave it be,' cut in Brun.

'No, your friend has a point even if I have my reasons. It is time and I'm ready to make amends.' The statement was uttered with a steely determination. 'Prince Edwin did not conceive this plot, of that I'm certain,' Nikomeades continued. 'He seeks the four gauntlets of power, the key to inferno, which is Cressida's doing. Only one being could envisage such an act and one not of this world. Although Cressida may have a hand in this, she desires souls, not the destruction of the planet. We will not mention his name around this table, but I know whom we seek. Alfari, are you with me?' His steer gave Tartarus a fright, but the elf duly nodded.

'We're with the elf,' declared Flint, with a haphazard grin.

'My brother's right. If our father died protecting this secret then, yes, you have our swords.'

'Mine too,' added Rex.

'Good. In a few days when you have rested and regained your strength, we ride for Brigantia, to the heart of the Badlands. And then to the north. Those of you who wish to return to Irons Keep may follow us to the Gulf of Bar-da-Shar. In the fishing port of Boondreigh, I'm sure I can arrange a vessel to take you across the Tay to Damgarden and the fishing hamlet of Henthorpe. I trade with the Kelts there.'

'You trade with the Kelts? Is that wise?' asked Nefanial.

'Do you think I made this berry wine by magic?' The baker nodded.

'I must have made good impression,' said the mage. Smiling, he turned to leave. 'I have no beds, but make yourselves at home. Tartarus, in the morning we will talk more and you will tell me all about Oaken-Crag and Ekaterina. I first met her when she was the shekhinah.'

'Really?' The elf's eyes lit up as he wondered what stories the wizard might share. Then, just as fast, the light dimmed; he had slipped through the Black Knight's forward lines and knew what his Alfari faced. The news would be grim indeed if the royal rider's note was to be believed. His thoughts turned to Jacob; his knowledgeable companion was more a brother than a friend and, knowing him, he was sure the greenhorn would be knee-deep in trouble without Tartarus to keep him on the straight and narrow. Or was it the other way round? He wasn't sure.

'I'm certain there's something I may have missed. There always is, but I'll sleep on it,' said Nikomeades. 'Sleep well.'

'But what about this?' asked Sid as he produced Bowen's pouch. 'It's got a note in it.'

'What does it say, boy?' asked the mage.

'I can't read,' Sid replied, looking embarrassed.

'The Kelts would love you,' responded Nefanial as he grabbed the pouch out of Sid's hand. 'It's marked with the Baron of Daginhale's seal and addressed to someone called Kennice,' he said as he skirted over the parchment. 'Looks like a bit of a love letter. Hang on, it says here that he's pleased to read she is carrying their child and that he is ready with his army, awaiting the news of Crofton's short illness and death. The note says to remember if he sees any signs of her being with child, it will jeopardize their plans. It's from Syracuse. That must be his name,' he said, looking around the table. The others shrugged.

'It doesn't help our cause. We still need the Kelts to fight,' pointed out Ragnarr, while continuing to drink his wine.

'What's this?' Nefanial shook the leather envelope and a flower fell out, landing on the table.

'Don't touch that!' shouted Nikomeades and Ragnarr in unison.

'Why, what is it?' asked Nefanial, as all eyes fell on the dried purple zygomorphic flower. It was shaped like a bell and had a lilac and yellow centre.

'Poison,' answered Nikomeades. 'Its wolf's bane, but its missing the root.'

'No, I think I can see it,' replied Nefanial, peering into the pouch.

'The most poisonous part, and a world of hurt for its intended victim,' Ragnarr said grimly.

'Well this changes everything,' said Nefanial. 'Speaking for me and my men, we will follow you and then we must part ways. I must get this message to our chieftain. If this message doesn't make Crofton fight nothing will and, anyway, those brigands in your larder have an appointment with our hangman.' Nefanial gingerly returned the oval leaf into the pouch with the folded parchment. 'But we will follow you to Bar-da-Shar.' Sid reached out his hand. 'No, I think I'll hold on to this,' said Nefanial.

'Well, if that is your decision then so be it,' muttered Nikomeades. A traitor's son was no concern of his. The heavens and clouds awaited no man, and his favourite pastime was calling. Stars only told their tales at night. He dipped his head and walked in the opposite direction from his sleeping quarters to the wall marking the end of the corridor. There he pushed a discoloured brick and the wall slid away to reveal a small opening. He kneeled, went through the entrance leading to his observatory, then pulled a lever and the wall slid back into place. In front of him was a spiral staircase. There were more than a few things troubling his thoughts and he hoped a spot of stargazing would help unravel those questions. He stole a smile.

It would be a while before he'd get another chance to see the skies above the summit again, if at all.

'Elohim, are you sure about this bunch?' he whispered, and shook his head in disbelief. Four men: the rest were boys. And none knew the twist of fate they were bound to. He tapped his staff on the floor then murmured the levitation incantation.

'No, navi, nare.' He ascended to the top of the tower.

The scroll contained a spell to cause the destroyer's destruction. It was never written to not be read, but was encrypted to prevent evil eyes from obtaining its knowledge. Until he had met his sons this day, he had thought Angus long dead, along with the rest of the Adalhard Knights who had been sent as reinforcement from the north for the beleaguered king of kings. Although Angus had been a regular visitor to the court, he was at a loss to explain the connection with the ring. Perhaps it was a reading vessel? No matter, the task at hand was clear. It was time to lock horns with Abandanon again, but this time he must prevail. He knew that the Autocrat's name was not to be spoken and, for this reason, he'd explain who their quarry was and the colossal struggle they faced later. He lifted the latch of the door to the observatory and smiled as his trusty stool came into view.

In the hall below, Tartarus had found a corner and made a makeshift bed. He looked at the modest furnishings and the picture above the fireplace, of a monk in a simple robe, then at his weary companions. Brun seemed happy enough sharpening his axes. Tarquin and Flint were busy debating with Sid. Ragnarr and Rex were still sitting at the table drinking while Nefanial supervised the sleeping arrangements. He wondered if he would have Nikomeades' patience to stay hidden for all those years and his answer was a resounding: no. As a boy, he'd have been the first to admit he was on one hell of an adventure, but he was coming of age and so that wasn't the whole truth. He was already ruing allowing the dark elf to escape and, in places, even his elven bones ached. He had witnessed true horror, although he had come through it seemingly unscathed. How long would that last? To date his survival was mainly down to luck.

The broth had been good and so would his sleep be tonight, without the fret of a forest full of dangers surrounding him. He looked up over his blanket and was pleased to see Rex relighting a small fire. He recovered his face. Ragnarr had mentioned the swarm. In his younger years the elven mothers would say, 'If you're bad the swarm will get you.' It was a jest in poor taste, and how could he forget the scary stories he and Jacob shared in Oaken-Dale forest around a warm fire, under darkened skies. Those ravenous beings had shared many of his night dreams; at times he had awoken in a cold sweat. He had learned to dispel the apparitions of five humanoids, made up of millions of insects, and, as sleep took told of his thoughts, he hoped the others shared this skill.

*

Tartarus was right to have concerns about his friend; in Oaken-Dale the greenhorn was having a torrid time just staying alive in defence of their municipality. Large areas of the forest were already under the southern realm's control while other sections of its domain were creaking from the effect of flames and food sources were becoming increasingly scarce. Jacob, standing behind Jared, was about to surprise a group of orks. He had made the smartest move he could after the news of Edwin's resistance to the Alfari's surprise attack, and still King Jeremiah had not appeared. Word spread like wildfire that he was probably dead. So, apart from the few who remained guarding the temple and the high priestess, Oaken-Crag was now deserted and at Edwin's mercy.

The Alfari were now defending an empty shell, but with each passing day the Aafari exodus, led by Richon, had a better chance of succeeding. Half the army and the Tiger Division protected the royal family and the council as they headed for Galatea.
The cold hard fact was that they were heavily outnumbered and although the Alfari were brave and skilled, under Crayfar's leadership, they were dropping like flies. The High Lord had taken Arvellon's passing harder than had first been thought and now his guidance was incoherent. With the carnage crushing the world around him and with no natural successor to relieve him of his post, the warrior clan were in disarray.
Jacob Bear-Whistle, on the other hand, had chosen to leave the main force now that Captain Morcion was more interested in suicidal missions than ones of real merit.
So, when the opportunity to leave arose, he jumped at the chance, having been one of the first to volunteer to roam with Hal when Mandrick's man had requested extra warriors.

Jacob and Tartarus had explored the forest surrounding Oaken-Crag extensively and if ever there was an elf who knew every nook of Oaken-Dale, Jacob was that elf. Hal

Stone found his knowledge of the terrain invaluable. Edwin's horde took no prisoners and Hal's orders were the same. The likable son of man – short on formalities, rough around the edges – was similar to Jacob in many ways and that was one of the main reasons why the elf liked his leadership. With an ork in his eye line, he pulled back his bow and awaited Hal's signal to attack.

Under the cover of darkness a fire-fuelled black smog lingered like fog and, entwined with a low-lying mist, it moved slowly through the trees. The usually vivacious forest was sadly silent. Jacob's lungs were filled with the stench of burning flesh, and resisting the temptation to cough while keeping his hand steady was taxing. Sweat poured from his brow, more due to anger than concentration. Positioned behind a tree, Jacob looked dead ahead. In the clearing, upwind, directly in front of them, was a group of twenty or so orks, and an oxceian. Its breath looked like a constant stream of steam coming from its nostrils. They were sitting round a fire. The torso of an Alfari warrior was slowly turning on a spit. Bright flames lashed and flickered, singeing the deceased elf's skin.

'You sure there's enough for all of us? 'asked an ork with an unusually large helmet.

'It's a delicacy. You won't need much,' replied the ork turning the spit.

'That's what you say,' he retorted.

'There will be enough if that giant remains on watch,' said another ork. The orks laughed.

'I've heard they taste good, 'said the ork turning the spit.

'I've never had one, but do we have to cook it?' asked the ork with the large helmet.

'Rotgut said they taste better that way. He even went as far as to say that if I had chance I should marinate it,' he replied. Another ork laughed and said, 'Marinate it? Are you sure? I prefer my flesh raw.'

'Will you lot shut up. I'm hungry, and from the crackling I'm sure it's ready. Or would you prefer burned elf?' responded the short-tempered oxceian. One of the orks, with a hideous hooked nose, produced a pouch containing elven emeralds.

'What do you think I'll get for this?' he asked, raising one of the large gemstones skywards. 'I cut him in half before I prised it from him.' He looked at the body glistening over the fire and laughed. 'Dinner won't need them now.'

Their raucous laughter and treatment of the fallen Alfari made Jacob's skin crawl. The orks were making noise as though the forest held no fear for them. However, he planned to change all that as he tightened his grip around his bow. The oily-skinned cretin attempting to carve up the torso would be first to go. The ork scouts were blissfully unaware they were being watched. When Hal gave the signal, like a pack of wolves stalking prey, they rushed into the fold with a brace of arrows leading their assault. Jacob released his bowstring and the ork turning the spit dined on an arrow's head instead of an elf. After a gargled squeal he fell to the ground with the projectile protruding from the back of his head.

The orks, momentarily stunned by his demise, drew their weapons to repel the attack, but their swords were useless against arrows that hit their mark. Hal's men, alongside Alfari warriors, tore into the hawkmen with deadly efficiency. Hal's hefty sword hissed as he swung it through the air, swishing and swatting the orks like bugs. Jared could take deadly aim with a dagger in a matter of moments and, as a result, many of the orks lay fatally wounded. Their oxceian leader, however, was a different type of foe all together. He possessed an air of invincibility and with a mighty double-fisted blow to the head one of Hal's men fell, his iron helmet offering little protection from the direct hit. An Alfari warrior in his path was next to feel his wrath, as he was lifted and crushed with the oxceian's bare hands, then impaled on its horns before the broken body was discarded. Picking up his sickle-shaped sword and an oxceian's flail – a crude device on a stick with angled spikes used to drag its victims down and forwards –he advanced and snagged an elf with the vicious contraption, before cutting him in two. A few of Hal's men attempted to keep the bull-headed beast at arm's length and prodded him with spears at any given opportunity.

Suddenly, it felt as though the earth shook under his hoofed feet and out of the darkness came a figure, the height of more than two men and a quarter of that across. He was covered in fur from the waist down and carried a heavy spiked club. Seeing their chance to escape the remaining orks tried to make a run for their horses, but were cut down by elven arrows in the process.

'It's a cyclops!' shouted Jacob, as the monstrosity with one large eye entered the fray.

'Finish this!' shouted Hal and, with a nod, Jared threw six daggers at the oxceian, one at each thigh and four at the bull-headed beast's broad muscular chest. Then he charged, taking great care to avoid the creature's lunge with its iron flail. The weapon's claws harmlessly glided over the back of his neck. Then, using his well-placed daggers as steps, he climbed onto the oxceian's shoulders before plunging a dagger in between the beast's neck and shoulder blade, over and over again. The oxceian, screeching in shock and pain, fell.

Men valiantly confronting the cyclops were being clubbed into the air and hurled to the ground. As the Alfari closed in, Jacob, flanked by two elves, slipped his bow into its holder on his back and drew his sword.

'Where did he come from?' he asked Hal. 'I thought they were only used to pull his siege weapons.'

'Beats me,' replied Hal, producing a hapless expression while pulling back his sword arm to launch another attack. Jacob nodded and then, just in time, pushed Hal out of the way. Both narrowly missed being hit by the cyclops's club. Its spike had scraped Jacob's shield as he was flung out of harm's way. The greenhorn looked up but there was no time to acknowledge that the elf who had been on his left a moment ago had not fared well and was rolling on the ground clutching his stomach, holding his innards in, as the cyclops went to finish him off.

The momentary distraction was all Jacob needed; aiming at the creature's heart, with sword in hand he drove his steel. Instinctively, the giant raised a hand to meet it and, from the collision's force, Jacob's sword sank into his thick leathery palm and went straight through his three-fingered hand. The cyclops howled, enraged, and with the sword still firmly lodged, lifted Jacob off the ground by raising his hand. He looked the greenhorn square in the face and roared, exposing the elf to a set of jagged teeth and his putrid breath. Jacob roared back, unmoved, but acutely aware that cyclops had a liking for eating heads. He released his sword hilt, just as he opened his mouth in an attempt to decapitate him. The greenhorn wisely rolled out of reach. Dropping his huge club, he slid out the sword lodged in his hand and threw it away in disgust. Then, with blood gushing from the wound, it continued to attack. Jacob felt the full force of it and was unable to prevent being caught by a tremendous backhand before he could reach for his bow.

The robust blow sent his helmet flying in the opposite direction. The clang of steel revived him. Semi-conscious and with blurred vision, he could see Hal on his backside while men shouted his name. Hal, getting to his feet and seeing Jacob lying in a daze, ran to his aid and managed to deflect a blow aimed for the young elf's chest; its vibration flung him backwards. With the orks all dead, Hal's remaining men and Alfari warriors released a hail of arrows that bounced off the cyclops's thick coarse skin and simply infuriated the creature further. Hal slipped trying to get up and looked to see the cyclops charging towards him. He scampered for a tree close by, just managing to cower behind as the cyclops swung his club. Jacob, back on his feet, wished he had a cross-spear and looked at Jared, who opened his cloak to reveal he was down to his last dagger. Shrewdly, the mute smiled as though, telepathically, he knew what the elf was about to do.

'Hey, smelly, you forgot about me,' the greenhorn said, brazenly, in faerie-folk tongue. His words stopped the brute in his tracks and he turned to see Jacob on his feet, in a wide-legged stance, with an arrow aimed at his head.

'What did you say, little man? Do you think your feeble arrow can pierce my hide?'

'So he talks. No, my plan is to blind you.' Jacob let fly. Then, with all the speed he could muster, he ran at the cyclops as the creature ducked to evade the arrow and, leaping into the air, he gripped the beast's matted hair and flicked himself onto his neck.

Jared's dagger was already in the air and when Jacob's clinched fist opened up against the cyclops's head, only a dagger's hilt remained. He jumped off the beast as it fell stone dead.

'Physician, tend to the wounded,' ordered Hal.

A wiry pale man, lightly armed with a holdall, shouted over his shoulder as he ran towards them.

'How many, captain?' he asked.

'You can start with him.' Hal pointed at the Alfari holding in his stomach. 'Remember, men, take what we need; we won't be here long,' barked Hal. Supplies and weaponry were piled high. The disintegrating corpses of the orks were placed in a separate pile. Hal picked up the pouch of emeralds and tossed it to Jacob.

'They're yours. You've earned them. Hal ran his forearm across his brow. 'That was close. You fight well.' He patted Jacob on the back, with the cyclops lying at their feet, and Jared retrieving his dagger. 'Crayfar could do with more like you. You're sure you don't want to go back?' Jacob shook his head and Jared smiled. 'Good, my men like you by our side. We would be lost without you. Jacob the giant killer has a nice ring to it. 'The broad-shouldered man smiled at his own joke.

'My second name is Bear-Whistle,' retorted the greenhorn, unimpressed.

Jared said the name in sign language and the three of them laughed.

'Well, I'll tell your High Lord of your heroics. After this I fear I'll be seeing him sooner rather than later; that beast has wreaked havoc. How many dead?' he asked Jared. The mute opened both palms, referring to ten. Hal shook his head.

'Remind me: cyclops are off the menu.'

'If he's here.' He looked down at the giant at their feet. 'There must be an encampment nearby; these things need food.'

'Do you wish to attack it?' enquired Jacob.

'No. We are too few in number and I have my orders,' replied Hal.

Jacob was just glad that suicidal missions were off the menu too and put the pouch into an inside pocket close to his chest.

'Yuck! Their supplies are inedible. When are we going to target beings with things worth eating? Orks smell bad and their food is disgusting,' said one of the militia, covered in black ork's blood.

'You know the duke's orders; we're not to go close to Edwin's main force or his encampments and risk capture,' said his captain.

'Maybe we can scavenge some food from Oaken-Crag. The city is deserted,' he replied.

'Booth's got a point. We can't continue to eat this shite,' responded a lightly armoured warrior, with sandy blond hair, named Callum. Hal mulled over the suggestion. Jared, getting his attention with sign language, said, 'It's a good plan; the men can't fight on empty stomachs.'

'And when the city falls we'll have lost the chance,' acknowledged Hal, agreeing with his friend, then looking at Jacob. 'Can your elves take us there?'

'If that is your wish,' replied Jacob.

'It is. Burn the dead and pack up. We're leaving,' he ordered. Hal turned to face Jared. 'Round up their horses.' His sidekick nodded.

The Alfari, writhing in pain, was close to death and called out Jacob's name. The greenhorn looked at the physician, who shook his head. Then he looked directly into the elf's eyes, as sorrow took hold in his. They were virtually the same age, some would say too young to die, but here he stood and the fallen elf lay. He propped up the elf's neck while inspecting his wound. The cyclops's spiked club had torn through his elven amour as though it was parchment and the deep cut, from left to right, was a sickening sight.

'Tell my father I fought bravely.' His voice was barely above a whisper. 'You and I have never seen eye to eye.' The elf attempted to laugh and coughed up blood. 'And your friend, Tartarus.' He stopped breathing and his suffering ceased.

'I will, Orlund,' whispered Jacob, releasing his hand to close lids on still emerald eyes. Not long after, once they had buried the orks in a shallow grave, the group moved on with Jacob leading the way.

*

Edwin's problem was that he craved dominance, and being a mere king was insufficient; in the wake of such an incessant appetite the Alfari were a pitiful hindrance for a man who overindulged on his own self-importance. Many a man would have sleepless nights after the abhorrent acts he had committed, but Edwin slept like an anvil and his serenity was filled with ways to cause more anguish and the joys of torture. The senseless slaughter offered little by way of a guilt trip. In fact, he felt no shame; allowing victims to live or die was real power and the stories of barbecued elves simply made him laugh. Such stories were insignificant yarns for a man destined for greatness; even the northern realm within his sights. It was all just a stepping stone in the face of the ruler he would become; a puppeteer toying with lives, manipulating will.

Edwin had done that since birth and there was no reason to change course now. People needed to be controlled; how else could they be productive if not in servitude to their lord and master? Since being caught unawares by the surprise attack, the battle had only gone one way: his way. After the demoralizing onslaught of his catapult and trebuchet, he had sent, at first light, five Draconian battalions and ork scouts, led by General Cog, to survey the devastation. Closely supported by half his army they had attempted to gain a foothold and, from that moment on, the news had been favourable. In a matter of days the outer edges of Oaken-Dale forest was his and his alone. The fighting, ferocious to begin with, had begun to peter out, just as he had expected, with his horde inflicting heavy casualties on the Alfari's numbers.
News of numerous crushing victories filtered through his encampment on a daily basis and morale was further bolstered with the Tiger Division's retreat, the Aafari king's very own battalion.

So now, with a large swathe of Oaken-Dale under his control, he had been led to believe the Alfari's attacks were actually lacking coherence. Maybe they were lulling him into a false sense of security, saving themselves for a final fanfare. Well, it was just a thought. In truth, he expected as much; one last foray before he extinguished their meagre existence for good. Once news of the Alfari's capitulation spread, his conquest of the east would be assured. Although toppling Galatea would take an extraordinary battle of wills, he was sure the city would fall, having already mapped out its destruction. Now the only thing that eluded him was possession of the scroll; with a grimace he threw his goblet at his tent's entrance. Red wine seeped from its inner gilded lining onto his chamber's grassy surface. His stalwart went to pick it up.

'Leave it,' ordered Edwin.

He looked at Baracus, who hadn't moved from his position. Why wasn't he blessed with his bodyguard's temperament? It was hard to remain calm. If his master got wind of his intention the swarm would be sent. Abandanon's abominations were well versed in the dark arts. The human–insect hybrid was made up of thousands of crustacean's hollowed-out eyes and had a long lizard's tongue. Insect larvae rose constantly to its skin's surface and popped, replenishing its numbers.

The creatures struck fear into the hearts of many.

He had received no word from the dark elf on the procurement of the gold-rimmed scroll and his patience was wearing thin. Brandenburg had informed him of Crofton's disappearance and Zog's probable demise. The blacksmith remained a thorn in his side. That accursed scroll; why had he listened to Kallen and got involved in this foolhardy quest? He knew the answer, but now his own life hung in the balance and nothing should hold such sway over him. If the scroll was still in the city, why were the Alfari defending it so poorly? He sat in his campaign chair. To compound matters, the mythical city of Denvagar was becoming just that, a myth, with each passing day, and of the dwarves who were captured one was dead and the other had escaped. Subsequently, he had issued orders that dwarves were to be taken, and kept, alive until they were brought before him.

If the senate withdrew their support two-thirds of his army would be gone in an instant. Without gold that was a distinct possibility; he could feel their breath on the back of his neck and his ears were burning, a telltale sign that his name was being spoken. Grumondi's grumblings were gaining support. By taking Athena the duke's power base was gone, so seeking his death was of no importance and, with word that the Eastern Alliance was amassing a retaliation force, now was not the time to be wasting lives in a forest. In private, among his generals, there were whispers that the gauntlet, a weapon made for kings, was changing him and not for the better. Who were they to believe he was losing his grip? Nothing could be further from the truth.

If power didn't change you what was the point? To be consumed in its presence until you became the word itself, that was redemption and, in many ways, with haunted envy he shadowed its stench. How could you be alive and not seek its absolution?
It flows through you, coursing through your veins until every sinew within you is compelled to wield its strength; even with degradation chipping away and bequeathed at the detriment of others, a man must be all he can be. That was Edwin's foresight.

His instructions from Cressida were to start a third great war and to retrieve the gauntlets of power; towards that endeavour things were moving nicely. The east was spooked and its waves were no doubt lashing against the northern realm's shores; fear was a wonderful commodity. Men ran and hid at the mere mention of your name, or pledged their loyalty and undying allegiance. Edwin did not recognize those commitments. He had no boundaries; others were simply extensions of himself and you either lived to meet his needs, or you might as well not exist at all. By way of his inheritance, he was given land to cultivate; the solitude had sowed the first seeds of invasion in the young prince's mind. Land could be taken, which others would tend too, if you applied the right pressure. It was while in this exiled obscurity that he conceived a plot to supersede his brother, Edmund, to their father's throne though, admittedly unwittingly, in the scheme of things he had risen above that position; with the Autocrat's dominance the crown was insignificant. He was the Black Knight, a man to be feared, a High Lord of the southern realms, and his designs were more ambitious now.

The senate was jealous of his accord with the witch. Lazy, fat kings with time on their hands: he fed off their invidiousness. Alas, he needed Cressida as much she needed him. It was her glowing endorsement, not that of his father, which gave him status, and that was a point of contention. There was a time when all he really craved most was a father's consideration although, providentially, that time had come to pass.

'May he suffer eternal damnation.' His words, said with venom, were lower than a hum. He had never known a father's love, nor had he known the man of greatness he was said to have been. The bronze statue before him, of King Linus with sword and shield, in all his pomp and glory, had been kept to remind him of his father's fragility. He represented a figure of hate. Maybe the little boy within him had not completely faded away and still yearned for substance.

All Edwin had ever known was a withering, decaying, empty vessel, soon to be no more, a corpse wearing a crown and watching over a dwindling kingdom. A kingdom that should be his! This was his father's gift. From the halls of Angel Lake and across the plains of Blanda, over the Maas Mountains and up to the border towns of Witch Haven and Desert's End was Strong-Holm, his father's domain. In many ways Cressida filled the void his father left bare; even so, he had no intention of following her blindly and ending up like him. His obedience came with one condition: he would aid her cause as long as it suited his and in the process he would finish what Abandanon had not. He would make all the tribes of Elohim bend to his will or be broken. So what if his generals were baffled by his decision to attack the Aafari enclave in pursuit of Mandrick? Cressida wanted the duke's head. Her pike's tip awaited the ornament: that was reason enough. And the eastern cities were full of enough wealth to fill the senate's coffers. He just needed time.

Archelaus walked in and leaned over to pick up the engraved goblet.

'What's there to be angry about? We're winning,' his captain said, smiling and looking at him.

'Save your yarns and get me that gold-rimmed scroll. We're not here to win a forest,' Edwin responded swiftly. He turned to his stalwart to tell him to leave, just as Archelaus stood up. His prince was, indeed, correct. Swamped by the sweet taste of victory, the focus on their true objective was not to be lost. Archelaus's head was also on the chopping block.

'Have men been sent to that volcano yet?' enquired Edwin. Archelaus wiped the goblet's rim then refilled it and handed it to his prince.

'That's the problem. Your will proceeds as planned. We march on the city in a matter of days but we've encountered stiff resistance in the eastern region of the forest, the route leading to Mount Lurbira. They've got groups eliminating our scout network in that region. For some reason, the Alfari don't want us near that area.'

'My knowledge of this landscape is sketchy at best, but I'd hazard a guess and say they're using it as an escape route,' said Edwin.

'Agreed.' His captain nodded. 'Unless the Callidora guards are still in the city, which I doubt, fleeing east is their only option to avoid capture.'

'What about the route to Galatea?' asked Edwin.

'We did not realize they would flee and attempt to cross the Blue Nile. I'd heard these beings were …' – Archelaus half laughed, –'more tough.'

'Odysseus tells me many got through although, fortunately for you, there were no sightings of the Callidora,' said Edwin, his words riling Archelaus who didn't take kindly to another captain jostling for position, stepping on his toes. 'Isn't it the same route Mandrick used?' continued the prince.

'I can assure you that route has now been shut tight,' replied Archelaus.

'Then we must send men to close off this eastern route too,' – Edwin took a sip of his drink – 'and lie in wait.' His cruel smile returned.

'We've got an outpost out there and it hasn't perturbed them.'

'What are you hiding, Alfari?' whispered Edwin, scratching his nose. 'Well, we'll have to double our efforts. I need the eastern sector secured, and not just for the scroll. Once the area around Lurbira is secure, the Autocrat will send one of his swarm to oversee the mining of the mineral. Need I remind you I don't want the swarm meddling in our affairs?' At the mention of the swarm Archelaus's blood curdled. 'Send Eustace with four battalions. His bloodlust for these elves is fierce.'

'As I recall, his father was killed by an elf,' said Archelaus, surprised by the choice. Edwin showed concern.

'Really? I want those females taken alive. Their thoughts must be read.'

'I'll send Rissien to watch over him,' said Archelaus.

'Agreed,' said Edwin, before he summoned him.

The prince looked at his captain and told him to pour himself a drink.

'That reminds me, the swarm will need manpower. Send Morkpork and a few Draconians to one of the local villages, and round up some villagers. He's good at rounding up dogs,' said Edwin. His captain nodded. 'Good. Now, tell me your news while we wait.'

'I bring word from King Ruben,' replied Archelaus, changing the subject.

Edwin sat up.

'Do I get my reinforcements?' he asked impatiently. The king of Borvoria was in Edwin's pocket, and was his eyes and ear in the senate. Archelaus shook his head while filling a goblet.

'He has brought you time, but that is all. Without gold the senate will not budge. They fear an uprising is brewing in the west.'

'Crofton,' said Edwin.

'Indeed.' Archelaus nodded, running his finger along his goblet's rim. It was common knowledge that Edwin wanted to be rid of Crofton's services. However, his disappearance couldn't have happened at a worse time.

'Brandenburg can handle this incident in my absence. He has his instructions,' said Edwin.

'Glen-Neath is the first line of defence against the Kelts. Are you sure that's wise?' Archelaus paused. 'The Autocrat will not be pleased if we lose such a prize.'

'I don't care if he's pleased or not. When I am king of kings the Kelts will bow at my feet,' replied Edwin.

The only prize worth thinking about was his master's vast army at his disposal, and that would not come to pass unless he obtained the scroll. Archelaus gave him a discerning look; empires crumbled when foes were taken lightly.

'Your task is to deal with my whims. Mine is to deal with his,' said Edwin. 'And anyway, the Kelts will not want war. In a dozen or so days it will be winter and their bellies have been nourished on peace.'

'I hope you're right. A war on two fronts could bring the walls of Hockenheim down upon our ears,' Archelaus warned him. Hockenheim was the Autocrat's masonic and symbolic fortress.

'I am right,' Edwin assured him. The tent's flapped entrance was partially pulled open, shedding light on a chamber adorned with artefacts and fine art. A guard bowed, then spoke to Baracus who nodded. The warriors earlier requested were brought in. Eustace stood beside the oxceian, covered in the Black Knight's regalia, and listened intently as his orders were issued. The tall, pale-skinned warrior had deep-set eyes and harsh features. His wispy blond hair was the only ray of light on a man in black armour, already speckled with Alfari blood.

'Remember the Callidora guards possess knowledge that will further our cause and are not to be harmed,' ordered Edwin. Eustace seemed disgruntled by this decision. Edwin raised his eyebrows but said nothing.

'It will be as you wish, High Lord,' replied Rissien.

When Edwin concluded the man and beast were told to wait outside for further instruction.

'I told you.' Archelaus, who still had misgivings, held his gaze.

'He'll be fine, or he'll be dead,' replied Edwin coldly. 'And anyway, there's nothing wrong with hating Alfari,' he added.

'That much we agree on, sire,' said Archelaus.

'I will lead our final assault on Oaken-Dale,' announced Edwin. It was habitual for him to receive the accolades of victory. His captain produced a tight smile. 'I want to see their king grovel at my feet while I ransack his city.' Edwin paused as though in thought. 'Strange there haven't been any sightings of him.'

'An army without a king is an army devoid of morale,' Archelaus noted auspiciously as he refilled Edwin's goblet.

'My thoughts exactly,' Edwin agreed, before taking a large gulp. 'With his Tiger Division on the run, we need more hell hounds to press home our advantage. Have they arrived from Athena yet?'

'They'll be here within the day,' replied his captain.

'Good. I'll get Balthazar to release his bats. We need spies in the sky.' Then, feeling a stitch in his thigh, Edwin stood up to stretch his legs. He looked at Baracus.
'I'm in the mood for some light entertainment. Get one of the guards to get me some servant girls. And tell my stalwart to return.' Baracus gave his master a slight nod and left. 'Is there anything else?' asked Edwin, his eyes searching the captain's features. Archelaus bowed, then went to arrange a raiding party and to address Eustace and Rissien.

Edwin opened the box that contained the gauntlet and the ultimate weapon glowed. Its gilded red metal glinted, as did the deep green emerald. He cast an eye over its ancient dwarfish workmanship before reclosing the lid. Maybe he already had all the Denvagar ingenuity he needed and he was never surer about one thing: power was certainly worth the price.

*

'Who goes there?' said a dwarfish warrior on watch, standing at the foot of a stone archway. On its apex, partially covered by vines, was a carved motif on a plaque. At the centre were the words *'Ffau vagar'*, another name for Denvagar. He looked into the gloom and became aware of the sound of horses and a flicker of light. He was armed with a war hammer and was wearing dwarfish chainmail. A helmet with two horns was strapped under his chin. He was accompanied by a dwarf with a colourful beard with braided tiny ribbons tied throughout. He gripped a broadsword and a tipped spear.

Stigwyn shouted back the password, *'Argeisiwn chofnodiad at 'r blasau chan 'n dadau,'* which in the common tongue meant 'we seek entry to the halls of our fathers'. His torch's glare lit up the tunnel. The warriors smiled as light was shed on Mortfran's face and he uttered the words that granted them entry, *'Chofnodiad ydy 'n ganiataol.'* Immediately, Mortfran sent the dwarf with the braided beard to the village to prepare a cart for Dain. The elf, gripped by fever and cold sweats, was fighting valiantly. Concentrated arnica had been placed on his bruised bump and, once his shoulder had been repositioned, the broken arm was set in a sling. Just like Vargas, the veins around the infection had turned black and his skin a bleak blue as the vile poison slowly dried his insides.

'Your warrior fights his ailment bravely,' Mortfran said warmly.

'He is young and strong-willed,' replied Jeremiah, touching Dain's forehead, concern etched on his face.

'The dark arts,' Mortfran said, sighing. 'Don't worry, Jeremiah, it's not much further to my home,' he assured the elven king. Leaving the damp, eerie shaft and its labyrinth of warrens behind them King Jeremiah and Lord Erynion, alongside Mortfran Weldig and Stigwyn Broadfist, were met by the warmth of Denvagar, as a vast grotto opened before their eyes.

Fresh air brushed against their skin while, underfoot, a lush undulating meadow greeted their step. Far above their heads a rainbow's hue floated, displaying its full array of lucent colours. The humongous cavern was beautifully lit by thousands of crystals embedded in the ceiling and walls.

'How does that work?' asked Erynion, amazed by the visual spectrum. He pulled his horse's reins, with Dain's horse in tow.

'The tiniest rays of light are reflected through minute cracks in the ceiling. Crystals reflect them tenfold and our heavens are illuminated. In daylight it heats water from the lakes and periodically clouds open up. The good thing is you can always tell when it's going to rain and that creates this perfect haven that our forbears first sought. But if you mean that rainbow, that comes after the rain falls,' answered Stigwyn, marching through the meadow.

'Are we still underground?' asked Lord Erynion.

'Did you expect our halls to be bathed in darkness?' asked Mortfran, vexed.

Erynion laughed off the statement.

'If you want paradise you've got to dig for it,' added Stigwyn.

'Well, we Aafari are the opposite.' Jeremiah smiled sympathetically. The fact that dwarves loved to dig was nothing new. Erynion nodded.

Unusual shrubs littered their path as they navigated a trail on foot. There was an eclectic mix of bold colours and shades, like those of the lavender toad-lily, rich in purple tones, with oversized honey bees sucking its nectar. The flame-lily's centres burned brightly above wavy emerald-green edges. Fierce orange bells, covered with black spots, spread their forbidden charm and the unmistakable blood-red desert pea, with its distinctive bulbous black heart, added to an enticing landscape that grew wild and unkempt under the expansion of light. The awesome scene explained why the dwarves would take Denvagar's secrets to the grave. There were many different plateaus of agriculture and dwarves grazing cattle.

In one of these pastures a huge cast-iron door stood ajar, stuck into the rock face beside a tavern and a row of stables. As it came into view Stigwyn pointed the door out.

'It leads to the mines.'

'And what else?' wondered Erynion to himself, ever the suspicious one. It looked more like doors to a fortress than a mine. He could tell his king shared the same view. Children, playing in the field, were the first to greet them as they reached the outskirts of the village. Mortfran picked up a boy and introduced him.

'This is brave Elrimm, named after Algrim,' he announced, pinching the boy's face.

'You remembered my name,' said the dwarfish child, surprised.

'I remember all my subjects by name,' Mortfran replied, with a wink, as he put the lad down.

In the distance, in uniformed rows, were oddly shaped cottages with smoke ringlets coming from their chimneys. Higgledy-piggledy bridges stretched over a network of canals which led to a large lake where boats were anchored and dwarves were busy fishing. As they crossed the main stone bridge, leading towards a bustling market area, shouts of dwarves selling their wares immediately grew quiet as word spread that Mortfran was among them. Shouts of 'hail, our glorious king' soon followed. Delicious aromas teased the elves' palettes and made the hairs in their nostrils tingle. Dwarves loved food and never were these fragrances more prevalent than in the home of their forebears.

Unbeknown to the Alfari, the domed cavern under the desert of Tyrus was just one of many within Denvagar, each supporting livestock, mining, carpentry, masonry, farming, fishing and alchemy: the list was endless. Each district had its own chieftain and name, such as Teallach Ogilvy, and Feara-Coen. They differed in features and demeanour, which distinguished them from other clans. The digger's clan were, on the whole, grumpy types. Other groups were more jovial, such as the brewers and the clans that made things with their hands. The warrior clans, brutal in battle, tended to be farmers in peace time and were normally a good-natured bunch or, let's just say, less aggressive at times: they did tend to drink too much.

With Dain placed on a cart, and Jeremiah and Erynion on horseback, the dwarves led the way on their allocamelouses. They left the picturesque village, following a path along the lake shoreline through to an adjacent smaller cavern. In the next enclave they were greeted by valleys and hills.

Mounted on one of these hillocks, in another huge expanse in the distance, was the hall of Denvagar in all its splendour.

'Is that …?' Erynion asked, seeming shocked.

'Yes.' Mortfran nodded. They rode alongside the symbol of dwarfish unity.

The majestic roofless structure, in the shape of a mausoleum, had glistening gold pillars and a large stone tablet with benches on either side. The monument was kept bright by a perpetual blue flame, above a cylindrical gold dish mounted on a stand. The flame seemed to flicker at times.

'If that flame goes out, all is lost,' Stigwyn said, disheartened by the flame's appearance.

Behind the hill, not too far into the distance, over a small stream, on the other side of a white granite arched bridge, was a fortified whitewashed stone wall.

'Home,' said Mortfran, smiling, as he quickened his pace on his ass-camel.

At first glance it appeared as though there wasn't a door until heavy white semi-arched doors creaked and opened inwards, revealing a dwarfish city that was bustling with dwarves going about their daily chores, oblivious to the world above.

They rode in under the archway; the workmanship was the first thing they noticed as the elves set eyes on a city entirely made of rock, with its different textures of polished surfaces. Dwarves regarded the craft of building as a divine gift, entrusted to them by the exalted one.

'We sleep when we must, live when we can, and eat and drink in between. Those are my laws,' announced the dwarfish king, as he presented a city with dwellings more familiar with a desert town, although instead of sandstone the buildings were made from granite and limestone. It was more in keeping with the macabre, masonic, gothic carving that dwarves were renowned for than the higgledy-piggledy village they had just left. Nevertheless, there was definitely a link with the oasis being found under Tyrus; no wonder their forefathers had chosen to build it this way. It was a sight to behold.

Mortfran clicked his fingers and the ass-camel kneeled on its front two legs so that he could dismount. Dwarves came running forward to tend to their mounts.

'Night and day have no meaning here so, remember, time can get waylaid. I have to attend to a few things to prepare for war so, Stigwyn, we tend to your needs. In a few days you'll meet the other clans at the hall of Denvagar. Once you are set, I'll send word and you'll be escorted to my keep for an audience. Until then, friends. Take care of their friend,' he said to a couple of dwarves, who unclipped the cart and led Dain away.

'War!' cried Mortfran with a twinkle in his eye. Then, surrounded by a number of dwarves, he vanished from sight.

'I wouldn't worry about your elf. In a few days he'll be almost mended. We've got a special oil for broken bones; it's an industrious being's hazard,' said Stigwyn, laughing at his own joke. The elves didn't bite. 'Anyway, once the poison is removed it's like I said,' he concluded. Tailed by two guards, he guided them through the enclave to visit chieftain's quarters. 'The best way to see the city is to explore,'
advised Stigwyn, stopping alongside a flight of wide steps and nodding at the two dwarves who stood guard.

Jeremiah smiled back at the suggestion but was more interested in taking the weight off his feet as he ascended the flight of steps.

'Those guards will go anywhere you go,' said Stigwyn. At the top of the steps was a stone doorway through which was a spacious, lavish sitting area, lightly furnished. Sleeping quarters, at the back, were sectioned off by a red drape on a rail.

The room with slit windows was connected to a washroom. Stigwyn lit the room's torches and the space lit up revealing a doorway, leading to a balcony.

'Here are your quarters. I hope it is agreeable. When Mortfran sends word the guards will escort you to his keep.'

'If you don't mind, tell your king we'll talk tomorrow. I'm in need of a goodnight's rest,' said Jeremiah.

'Very well. I will be here in the morning to tend to your needs,' replied Stigwyn, turning to leave.

'Do you think we can trust them?' asked Erynion once he was sure they were alone.

'As long as we're on the same side.'

'I still think we've been here long enough,' the elf lord said.

'Oaken-Crag is in good hands. I have faith in Crayfar's leadership.'

'The hour is near when the Alfari will be in need of their king.'

'Indeed. However, if I return without an army I will have failed.' Jeremiah unbuckled his sword belt and his scabbard fell. Instinctively, he caught it before it hit the floor. The regal hilt of his sword, gripped against his palm, instilled inner peace. He missed his city in the woods, maybe more than Erynion, but its very existence was at stake.

Jeremiah walked over to the bed provided; it would do, at least until he got his wish.

'When I wake, you can tell me where the gold-rimmed scroll is.'

He removed his tunic then, taking his boots off, he lay on the firm bed and closed his eyes to think. In a few moments he was sleeping soundly. Erynion, turning to reply to his request, smiled and covered him with a blanket. Then he poured himself a drink.

His king was right: they were in need of manpower. The city teetered on the brink.

He was just sceptical that the dwarves could provide the force needed. Although he rarely agreed with Crayfar, he shared the High Lord's misgivings about Jeremiah's stance and devotion to save the kingdom. However, a forlorn mission had been turned on its head.

Just like the rhythmic beat of his heart, nothing was more deserving than the tree stumps of Oaken-Crag, but the ramifications of what had been shared could not be ignored. He took a sip of the berry wine. No matter what path they took, the road ahead was fraught with danger and, in the coming moons, he was convinced it would be the three Alfari warriors with the gold-rimmed scroll that would save them all. He was sure Jeremiah would implode when told of the task entrusted to Asrack, Vince and Tartarus, but that couldn't be helped; the king had a right to know. He was just glad he'd get a good night's rest before the screams started.

In the days that followed the elves explored the city made of pathways, torch-lit alleyways and conduits. It took some getting used to. The main square was in the shape of a cross, with a marble fountain in the centre. It was full of stalls and shop fronts, selling all things from pottery to fish. Dwarves were friendly and their resourceful inventiveness was worth absorbing. They had visited Mortfran numerous times, enquiring about the meeting of the clans and, with the day approaching, as Stigwyn had predicted, Dain was back on his feet and the Svartalfar's poison vanquished.

The warrior was once again ready to aid his king in the defence of his realm. King Jeremiah and Lord Erynion, escorted by the two dwarves, were summoned to the hall of Denvagar on the sixth morning. Reunited with their horses at the main gate, they rode out.

A cold, bare tablet when they had first set eyes on it, the hall was now full of food as an assortment of different clans sat, ready to proceed. The warrior clans of Teallach Ogilvy and Adalgar wore black leather garb. Thin-Ling, a sect of the builders' clan, were in their usual dark green. The groups were represented by Falcow, Alrick and Alwin respectively. Bernd of Feara-Coen and Vilanshaw of Tuath Farquharson sat among other dwarves with a vested interest. Fingolfin, the ageing alchemist of Rock Haven, with a full white beard and wispy eyebrows, was well versed in clan law. He was the Recorder of Denvagar, a position he had held for a number of years.

'I call this meeting to order. Who will speak first?' he asked, slamming a hand-sized rock against the stone tablet. As was the custom, all the dwarves whispered the king's name over and over again until he took the floor. With the gleaming gold crown of Denvagar resting on his brow and wearing a thick fur-collared cloak and patterned gold vambraces that covered his large forearms, Mortfran stood up.

'I've called you all here because a sickness plagues these lands, tearing at its fabric, a sickness that will eventually destroy us all if we allow it to linger unchallenged. I say we must sharpen our axes and test this foe in battle and I put it to a vote.'

There was a subdued silence among the dwarves as he finished his sentence. Then Vilanshaw, a dwarf with a brown flowing beard and wearing a hooded felt cloak, leaned forward.

'If that is the reason we were summoned then who are these strangers in our midst?' he asked.

'I have asked our elven brothers to join us in this battle. This is Jeremiah, son of Isaac, king of the Aafari. This is his aid, Lord Erynion,' said Mortfran.

'From what I hear, it is they who need our aid,' responded Vilanshaw. The dwarves laughed.

'Would you have the scroll fall into the wrong hands?' asked Mortfran, bemused.

'You mock me, when all I do is point out the facts. Is this how you gain our support?' the dwarf said, slamming his drink down.

'You have never supported me, Vilanshaw, and good dwarves have already perished to form this union. I will not stand here and have you ridicule their lives,' retorted Mortfran.

'Remember, my king, a challenge to your throne can be made at any time,' said Vilanshaw.

'Silence!' cried Fingolfin. 'This is not the time for such words, and losing dwarfish lives is not a decision we should take lightly.'

'Well said,' Mortfran responded.

'Well said? When we last convened, Stigwyn here stated he had sent dwarves to, among other things, find the evidence you seek,' – Vilanshaw pointed at Mortfran, – 'and now you want to start a war by defending these elves. The sons of men have always sought our halls. Why give them just cause?'

'I couldn't care less if we help these elves or not,' said Bernd, 'but Vilanshaw has a point; where's the proof we should go to war?'

'Aye. My kin, and Ragnarr, were supposed to bring us proof,' added Alwin.

'And what of these dwarves you've pinned all our hopes on?' asked Vilanshaw.

'Watch your tongue, Vilanshaw. That's my kin you speak ill of,' said Alwin, Furnus's cousin.

'I don't know this Furnus too well, but Ragnarr's disposition is agreeable,' said Bernd, Ragnarr's clan chieftain, jumping to his defence.

'No mention of Bollymore from Tuath Farquharson,' said Alrick. A few of the dwarves laughed.

'Have you forgotten that I banished that old fool?' asked Vilanshaw.

'That's not how I remember it. He said you were the fool,' replied Bernd. The discussion became heated, as it usually did.

'Stigwyn has sent many, and these dwarves have their missions. I have no doubt they will succeed but we cannot wait any longer for word to return with the fall of Athena. These are the darkest of days and we must give aid before the chance to fight is gone,' declared Mortfran, after Fingolfin had regained order.

'Well, I can afford to wait. My clan sleeps in peace. We have no need of war, unlike the other clans that sit at this table. You said you would give us proof and, as yet, I have neither seen nor heard any.' Vilanshaw sat back.

'Proof?' cried Mortfran, enraged. 'Cressida sent her disciples to disembowel me. That should be proof enough.'

'And you expect us to just take your word?'

'Yes, actually I do. Unless you were expecting me to have had the assassin's body dragged before you, I hope this will satisfy your curiosity.' He threw the tattooed skin, cut from the attacker's neck, in Vilanshaw's direction.

Jeremiah and Erynion looked on in surprise at the animosity and hostility.

'No words from the warrior clan?' enquired Fingolfin, baffled by their non-participation. Mortfran gazed at them anxiously. A broad dwarf got to his feet. He was the widely respected chieftain of Teallach Ogilvy, Falcow, son of Finbar. Adorned with his battle paraphernalia and his familiar white-horned black helmet, he spoke from behind a thick black beard.

'If our king says he was attacked then that is proof enough. And if he says it's time to fight then I will cast the first stone. We are warriors; that is our role. There will be a time for words, but now is the time to meet this challenge head on. We have spoken among ourselves and we are all agreed: Mortfran has our swords.' The dwarf banged a clenched fist against his chest and sat down with the other warrior clans' representatives, who were nodding enthusiastically and patting him on his back. Mortfran acknowledge the approval. Vilanshaw, on the other hand, was in no mood to heap such praise on his king.

'Your plans are ill thought through. There's been no mention of the Autocrat and his deadly swarm, and now you want us to defend these elves' – Vilanshaw looked at Jeremiah and Erynion with distain –'when we're safe where we lie, while they keep the knowledge of the scroll all to themselves.' A few chieftains nodded in agreement. 'Not one word of the enchanted, whose powers we'll need if we are to succeed.' He pointed at Mortfran again. 'He hasn't even tried to seek them out. His excuse is that they are no more, which is a blatant ...' Vilanshaw stopped himself before he went too far, but then continued unashamedly, 'and can our wise king tell us if we're even close to making a gauntlet?' He took a swig of his drink, wiped his lips, and half laughed. 'Does he believe our minds to be so forgetful? This was the reason why Ragnarr and Furnus were sent away.' A few more dwarves nodded. 'And is Cressida the one taking the mother's milk or not?'

He looked around the stone tablet as though he was pleading for someone to answer his questions.
    'No, our king guides us poorly and he does not have my vote,' concluded Vilanshaw. Jeremiah had to admit it did not look good. In retrospect he thought the meeting was a foregone conclusion and, as a king in his own right, he should have been given the opportunity to speak. Mortfran had told him beforehand that this was not the Denvagar way but, with the vote drawing near and the decision still in the balance, he wished it wasn't so because it seemed that Vilanshaw was winning the way of words. Traditionally, the king had the final say and, after a calming breath, Mortfran spoke solemnly.
    'This battle is not about us. It never was. It's about our forefathers and our children's children. War is unkind and unjust, but fight we must. Edwin seeks our refuge to fuel his war, while Cressida's zombies dig and mine on conquered soil. And we know what they mine. I, Mortfran, son of Elgar, will not stand idly by. Our soil is rich in minerals and deposits. And we've got enough gold in our vaults to mount an indefinite attack. If I have your vote Edwin's days are numbered,' he declared, looking over the stone tablet at each chieftain in turn. 'Even now, under our gaze, it flickers,' he said, turning to the eternal blue flame behind him. 'This isn't a war of our choosing but, by Algrim, I will see the

flame right.' Mortfran slammed his fist on the cold stone slab. 'On my honour,' he concluded.

Fingolfin stood up, holding a velvet purple bag.
'We've heard our king speak. I put it to a vote: is it war or not?' he said as the bag was passed round. Each chieftain had a wooden tab for 'yes' or 'no' and dropped the tab that indicated his decision into the bag. Fingolfin's count did not take long, with only two tabs marked 'no'. He announced the result, which was greeted with a roar.
'Now go and ready your kin!' cried Mortfran triumphantly. He looked at Vilanshaw's glum, defeated face and acknowledged that he'd need to have him watched; in war any weakness could be exploited tenfold. The chieftains left to inform their clans of the meeting's outcome. Stigwyn pulled Jeremiah aside.
'I hope you weren't worried. The decision was never in doubt. It's very rare we dwarves vote against the dwarf who speaks last.' Then his smile disappeared. 'I've got terrible news. Mortfran has been brought word that your elves have been routed. Edwin descends on your city as we speak. He also sent a horde in pursuit of a handful of Alfari warriors guarding unarmed Aafari who were evacuating east, through Oaken-Dale. Do we ride to Oaken-Crag or ride to their aid?'

Jeremiah looked at Stigwyn, unable to speak; he felt sick to his stomach.

*

In the skies above the forest of Oaken-Dale, carving a path through the trees, Balthazar's fiends soared, following the scent of fleeing Aafari. Between the rapid flutter of webbed skin and short darting spiral dives, far from harmless, with silent intent they glided over the treetops. Linked to the wizard, through sight and sound, his desires controlled their will. Comparable in appearance to giant fruit bats, they had foxlike fur around their heads and were covered in scaly black skin, from the neck down. They littered their route with drool from a permanent snarl, unable to close their mouths full of pointed, sharp teeth that were accustomed to gorging on decomposing flesh. Below their flight, the views were breathtaking: brooks alongside open fields, thick forestation and a forest full of wildlife, roaming free. The black molten mountain of Lurbira, with its smoky white dome, presided over the treetops and dominated the skyline in the distance. Behind it was the tropical climate of Nagari and its hazy skies.

The woodland's wonderment was far from Richon's thought; mounted on his horse, he was shielded from its charms. His thoughts were solely of his wife, who was close to giving birth to their first child, and the mammoth task of getting her and other Aafarians to safety. With fierce yellow silky hair, he was known as the blond general by the elves under his charge and, after Arvellon, he was the highest-ranking lugar.
He had gained his position by relying on instinct and acting accordingly. Richon's inklings were rarely erroneous, so even before a rider approached from the rear to confirm his worst fears, he knew something was wrong. He had tried to pick up the pace at numerous stages, but with a convoy of this size that was extremely difficult. There was no natural path to the fire caves and he had decided to stay off the

main trail to avoid detection. On reflection, maybe speed was a far greater commodity than stealth. At times the exodus virtually came to a standstill. The sweat on his warriors' brows told its own story of the toil of cutting a pathway through the trees to keep carriages and wagons moving forwards. Fortunately, the convoy was in the capable hands of Captains Orchill and Ennis, Daigar (or man-at-arms) Gwindrill, and Elgar Haedirn.

'Report,' ordered Richon, looking through the glare of a midday sun as the Alfari warrior scout pulled up alongside him.

'Crayfar sends you his greetings, my lord. I was sent once we got word that a large group of riders left the Black Knight's encampment heading in your direction. I fear they are a little more than a day's ride to your rear, moving quickly. It's a horde with two objectives: to block your path and to prevent our army having an escape route and regrouping. You must prepare yourselves.'

'Does Crayfar not protect our path?'

'No, he diverted our remaining forces to defend the city.'

'He only sent you?' asked Richon, bemused; he had been at the meeting with Ekaterina and this was not the plan.

'Yes, I was all he was willing to spare. He still believes he can win,' replied the warrior.

'Does he now?' The warrior, steadying his horse, nodded. 'How many are there?' asked the lugar in a low voice tinged with concern.

'They are two to three thousand strong, maybe more, and made up of orks, men and Draconians.'

Richon was shocked but did not show it. Had Crayfar gone mad? The remaining Alfari would be slaughtered and, without rearguard action, it was looking more than likely they would be next. His Alfari would not be able defend the convoy against an army of that size out in the open. However, his thoughts were not for a lesser elf. If he survived the next couple of days he would share his unease with Haedirn. Richon looked over the Alfari warriors lining the route. Nine hundred strong, if that, safeguarding the lives of thousands, and he felt like a bulligore in a pond that was getting smaller.

'We protect the young and the infirm. Has this prince no moral compass?' said Richon.

'I fear they aim to kill us all; they do not take prisoners, my lord.'

'And has no one seen the king?' It was a forlorn question. He, above all, knew Jeremiah would never commit the Alfari to such a reckless course of action.

'No, my lord.'

'Well, now you've delivered your message you may return.'

'I'd prefer not to,' said the scout. 'My wife is somewhere in this convoy.'

'Well then, you're most welcome.' Richon placed a hand the elf's shoulder. 'Daigar, what is your name?'

'Renthel, my lord. Renthel Xantia Copperfield.'

'Well, Renthel, go and say hello to your wife, if you can find her. Then return to my side. You're with me. 'The daigar nodded and rode off. Richon cut short a small smile. He knew the elf's father but this was not the time for idle chit-chat. He immediately ordered his captains to place his warriors on high alert and to focus their attention on an attack from the rear, while he took time to think.

High above, from the branches, nocturnal eyes were scanning the landscape. Balthazar, deep within Oaken-Dale, was lying in wait for an old friend. He gazed upon the Aafari through a black orb and felt a sudden sharp twinge as one of his links was severed. Determined to slow their progress, he plotted his next move.

Richon had decided on a course of action when Captain Ennis rode up.

'There have been reports of bat droppings and numerous sightings of these,' he said, producing a hideous winged creature. 'One of our elves shot it down.'

'This thing is not of this forest,' observed Richon, casting an eye over the flying rodent.

'Look, there!' Ennis pointed upwards behind Richon, who swivelled in his saddle but saw nothing. 'I just saw one watching us.'

'Are you sure?' The captain nodded.

'Defend the convoy,' ordered Richon and, as the word spread, his warriors drew their bows. 'I want you to ride ahead to Mount Lurbira. Take Haedirn and your battalion with you and hold the entrance to the fire caves at all cost. I fear this Black Knight knows our location. Take only the Aafari that travel light. Take the trail we will follow,' ordered Richon.

'What about the shekhinah and the priestesses?'

'Take them with you; if Maya refuses, come and get me.'

Both knew the high priestess-in-waiting was as feisty as she was cute. The handsome elf smiled back his response.

In the middle of the mass hysteria Maya, among priestesses and Callidora protectors, sat on an elven mare and was cradled by Eolande. She displayed indifference to Richon's request.

'My place is with my people,' she said dismissively as Ennis tried to stress the importance of her riding ahead. Eolande smiled at her charge's stubbornness, before she intervened and tried to help.

'If the captain says we must ride ahead, then don't you think we should?' she suggested, leaning over the young elfette's shoulder. Maya turned to face her.

'No, I don't. The army does not control me. My presence gives those I serve strength.' Eolande looked at Ennis and shook her head. He turned and rode away.

The Nargarian looked at the upheaval that encircled her, compounded by the misery on the faces of fleeing Aafari and she understood Maya's stance. The gut-wrenching expressions, from a proud race, being driven from their home were beyond awful and seeing the shekhinah desert them, would only add to the Aafari's plight at a point when despondency seemed rife. Maya, in her own way, was putting a halt to the contagion, which was the role of a high priestess.

Richon had made some tough choices in his lifetime but not allowing his wife to leave with Ennis was the hardest, even though he might well be condemning her and their unborn child to death. The lives of the many outweighed the few and his wife was simply too far with child to travel at the pace required. If his plan was to work they would need Ennis's covering fire. They might make it by nightfall if they pushed hard and only if they took the mountain road, but his desires were still leagues apart from the predicament they faced. Inwardly, he thought it looked grim. He would be exposing them to reduced forest cover and a possible attack from the skies. However, with their position already known, speed was essential, now more than ever. He ordered them to change course.

Ennis rode back, shaking his head, with a resigned look on his face.

'Don't worry. I'll explain it to our young high priestess,' said Richon. The lugar sighed as he rode alongside Ennis, probably for the last time, and wondered if Crayfar knew the effects his decisions were having. Suddenly, Maya screamed.

*

The High Lord stood on the gangway outside the Alfari Academy looking at the lantern-shaped buildings in Oaken-Crag. He could hear the footfall of troop movement. The morning sun's glare breached the forest leaves, stroking his furrowed brow. He was anxious, consumed with uncertainty. His deliberations were not, however, contemplations; since he had long held a belief that the city must hold some form of intrinsic value to Edwin, he decided that no matter what it was he'd fight tooth and nail to keep it from his grasp. The elves' strength lay in the vines and trees, and he intended to exploit that fact. The Battle of the Longest Dawn was about to commence and here, on the familiar Oaken-wood floor, he would make his final stand. No, his ponderings were for Dain, and a hope of making him proud. They were of a father's devotion to duty in the definitive moments ahead.

For him the city's heart was gone without the boy's presence, a void that could never be filled. The feeling was compounded by the sight of deserted promenades and the sounds of his warriors preparing for battle and setting booby traps. All the while the drone of Edwin's drums became more pronounced; the unerring repetition of inevitability enticing fear. Weakness was not given, remaining steadfast in the face of overwhelming odds. Strangely, he felt more alive than he had in a long while and if this was to be his end then there wasn't a spot more deserving. The wood creaked underfoot. He smiled. He would have to get that fixed. His decision had come with dire consequences; Ekaterina was furious and her words still cut deep.

    'How many Alfari faces have you look into lately?' the high priestess had asked, her eyes burning his. 'Your task is to protect our symbol; that symbol lives and breathes in us. How dare you leave Richon so isolated?'

Unashamed, she had removed the displacement spell in defiance. She was deluded; there was no greater glory than dying in defence of your keep and it was they who would look at him when he snatched victory from the jaws of defeat. In any case he had despatched a rider to warn Richon of the threat to his convoy's safety, with reports from scouts about a large force heading in the lugar's direction. With the road to Galatea now shut, he wanted the area around the fire caves preserved as an escape route at all costs, despite not sending Richon more elves to aid him in that endeavour. There were more than enough able-bodied Aafari under his lugar's wing for the task to be completed.

A sudden breeze blew across him and, somehow, it felt different. The breeze before a battle often did, as though it were preparing to whisk away newly departed souls. Some said it was the whisperings of the dead as they waited to greet new friends. He knew better and felt a heightened sense of mortality, with one question pressing for an answer: will what you do on this day make a difference? In the academy behind him elves were trained to dismiss such questions; Alfari always made a difference. Crayfar was ready to repel the sacking of the enclave, with battalions stationed at the two main entrances, Oaken Gate and Elm Gate, and four other entrances primed and prepped, while below a greeting contingent of light cavalry and archers was at the base of the city. His captains had been given their orders and, with Lugar Hirgon's remaining forces lying in wait, well hidden in the forest and ready to attack Edwin's flank, this time he was confident his plan would succeed. The minor defeats so far were but a prequel leading up to this moment. He just hoped his foe believed he was far weaker than he actually was.

His weapon of choice was an inlaid long rapier, a gift from the Ljosalfar, made in the ice caverns of Andorra, with rococo style embellishments along the blade. The agile instrument was an extension of his arm and, in its patterned scabbard, it rested on his hip. Durion joined him. After Arvellon's death he had been thrust into the limelight.

'High Lord, the archers are in position.'
Crayfar looked up towards the higher tiers. Along their rafters arrow heads glinted.

'Is Morcion ready to lead the first attack?'
The captain's response was a grim nod.

'He and Antien are below, awaiting your word, High Lord.'

'Then let it begin.'

Edwin, beside Baracus, was ready for the city of Oaken-Crag to meet its day of reckoning. Wearing his black armour, but without his customary helmet, he mounted his horse.

Archelaus rode alongside him with the generals marshalling row upon row of troops. In front of them were the massive Elohim ash trees on which Oaken-Crag stood. With the displacement spell no more he could see the mythical city although, admittedly, it was too far up for his view to be uninhibited. In the hazy light the city's majestic splendour shone, but its beauty held no sway. After obtaining the information he sought he would gladly see it burn. Balthazar's reported sighting of the Callidora heading for Mount Lurbira could mean only one thing: the scroll had been moved from the temple of Aafari. However, with the wizard still detecting Ekaterina's presence, the slim glimmer of hope was all he needed.

Unlike in the treetops, dawn came slowly to its forest basin, which was still in semi-darkness. Morcion, with a battalion on horseback, crept through the mist. The drums' drone was magnified by the forest's acoustics. He headed towards it, closing in on his target. He held his breath until close enough to taste the horde's stench and then, with warriors' lances fixed, he gave the call to arms and launched the attack. Leading the charge Morcion roared as his lance skewered shields and gristle. His battle cry continued as he drew his sword and deflected a blow with his defensive shield; his foe's blade ran across it and moved away harmlessly. Other Alfari followed suit, riding into the horde under the cover of elven arrows. This time, though, they were not facing the rabble of Rutland's disorganized men. They faced General Cog's elite Draconian troops and the covering arrows bounced off or embedded in Draconian shields. They were awaiting the call before all hell broke loose.

A handful of oxceians were sent in to bolster their ranks; Archelaus had assured the Black Knight there would be no mistakes and, for the elves, no second chances.
The bull-headed men were ferocious warriors and their aggression seemed, in places, to tip the balance. The hissing hum of steel rang out. At close quarters, with munga blades, the Alfari were lethal, cutting through metal chainmail, flesh and onto bone. Archelaus had to admire their effectiveness. Although the Draconians, marshalled by General Cog, were haemorrhaging casualties, they held firm; with heavy ornate curved shields dug into the earth they formed a line to absorb the brunt of Morcion's offensive. Minor skirmishes were taking place to the left and right of Edwin's lines.

A group of elves taking a particular interest in a bull-headed beast steadied their horses and, in the moments that followed for those warriors, it was as though time stood still as they lifted their lances and took aim. A puff of air escaped from their horses' nostrils, from the flick on their reins that caused them to inhale sharply. With ears pricked up and hooves dug into soft terrain, they leaped off the earth at the command to charge again. Up until that point, the oxceian had been one of the main protagonists in reducing the Alfari numbers, inflicting horrific injuries with a dagger and axe and pulling elves from their mounts in a chaotic frenzy. Nevertheless, as the beast lay taking his last breath, a lance protruding from his chest, the outcome was greeted with a silent satisfaction, his death a boost to morale. Morcion acknowledged their valour by raising his sword. Then, by directing them to attack the flank, he probably saved their lives. At a vital moment, when the fighting was at its most intense and although heavily outnumbered, Morcion must have felt they were making inroads. His warriors' bravery shone like a beacon when, under orders, the Draconians gave way to archers poised behind them. In an instant the Alfari were cut down in a hail of dark-feathered quills, arrow heads in the shape of three triangles on top of each other: ork arrows. The howls of pain were instant. Edwin looked on with glee.

Lugar Hirgon and his second, Shi-mith, watched in the woods and could do nothing; they were under strict instructions not to intervene until signalled. The lugar resisted the urge to enter the fold; if the High Lord's plan was to work he must hang fire. The battlefield was suddenly bathed in sunlight with the shift from dawn to morning light, and this seemed to momentarily confuse Edwin's horde in the scattering of leaves and display of chivalry. Antien's archers took advantage of their lapse in concentration, targeting the orks with devastating effect; many were sent flying, their torsos filled with lead. The Alfari were far superior with a bow to their ork counterparts, and it showed.

Then, out of the blinding light, marauding through their battle lines with a gust of wind, were three woolly mammoths with silver chainmail glistening and reflecting the sun's radiance. Alfari screamed and were crushed underfoot while others were felled by the beast's flailing ivory tusks, which left a trail of devastation in their wake. Morcion's warriors were ill-equipped to stop animals of that size, their lead-tipped arrows having little or no effect on the mammoths' armoured helms and trunks.
Antien's archers tried to relieve them of their passengers, but the mounted Draconians were difficult to dislodge. Spears were being hurled from above. They needed cover fast and, with his battalion's efficiency compromised, Morcion was left with no option; he gave the signal to

retreat. Placing his lips to his ram's horn, he blew. Then he turned his horse to follow his warriors and was hit with an arrow in the back, quickly followed by another. He slumped forward in his saddle, dead. The horn slipped from his grasp, having been blown by his lips for the very last time. At the sound of his horn the Alfari warriors attempted to break ranks and retreat back into the city.

Archelaus ordered his flag bearers to signal a battalion of orks to pursue. This time it was the right decision; there was nowhere to run to and nowhere to hide. The kennel master, fresh from collecting dogsbodies for the prince and seeing the Alfari retreat, was eager to release his hell hounds to compound their misery further. The hounds were making an infernal racket, driven feral by the scent of elven blood.

'When do I get my chance?' he asked, anxious to try out the new batch. He stood beside his ork marshal, Rotgut.

'When the High Lord says you do, not until,' replied the ork marshal in a gruff voice. The temperamental hunchbacked ork shrugged dejectedly.

'Don't you feed those dogs?' continued the ork marshal, looking at a hell hound on a lead by Morkpork's side.

'Yes, on our enemy,' said Morkpork with a grin, raising a hand at the dispersing Alfari.

'Point taken,' responded Rotgut, producing a grotesque smile of his own.

The Alfari were in total disarray as they were picked off one by one and dragged from their horses by a mass of orks. Daigar Antien and a number of Alfari attempted a rearguard action. There was nothing they could do about their captain but there were still elves' lives that needed saving. With defensive shields raised, a group of his archers ran forwards, trying to avoid the mammoths' attentions, while others released covering arrows. At the foot of the entrance the bloodletting was relentless as elven steel rang out against Edwin's might. An Alfari warrior, hit in the leg by an arrow, fell in a heap. Antien, close by, went to his aid, managing to get the elf on his feet before the elves closed ranks around him. They remained in a huddle before releasing their horses and running under the trees. The Alfari still outside suffered the horror of having to watch the portcullis slam shut and the tree drawbridge raised, before being caught up by the flood of Edwin's horde. Looking on, Antien, surrounded by the raw fear on the warriors' faces, felt an urge to be sick, and was.

The atrocities they had just witnessed were only the start of things to come and the worst thing was, they knew it. Though they said nothing, more than a few of them were beginning to question Crayfar's leadership. They were not simply firewood to be discarded on a flame.

The three greenhorns, ordered to attack the flank, looked at each other and each, in their own way, acknowledged Mort and Morcion's gallantry. Despondently, the Alfari made their way up to the city floor, among broken warriors and the clank of armour, chainmail and metal. The lift was dropped for the wounded who were winched up by a donkey-powered contrivance. Removing his helmet, Antien approached Crayfar.

'We could not hold them, High Lord,' he said with his head held down in shame.

'Where's Morcion?' The daigar shook his head.

'He did not make it.' Crayfar sighed.

*

Down below, Archelaus's signaller flagged for the ram's hammer to be brought.

'Ah, the witch's hat,' Morkpork said, smiling and looking at the hound who had survived their first encounter with the Alfari. 'Hungry are you, boy? It won't be long now.'

'Shouldn't it be in there with the rest of them?' asked Rotgut, referring to the wagon kennels behind them.

'I calls him lucky,' said Morkpork, patting the beast which, even with a muzzle on, still attempted to bite him. Rotgut shook his head.

Lugar Hirgon, lying in wait, was already making plans to tackle the armoured mammoths, when a siege construction, moving slowly through the horde's centre, caught his attention. It was covered in animal hides and had a wooden base and support beams made from saplings lashed together; immediately he knew what it was.

'Looks like a roof on wheels,' commented Shi-mith beside Captain Solanko.

'It will be Oaken-Crag's end,' responded the lugar. 'The city wasn't built to ward off such an assault.'

'Is he going to give the order for us to intervene or not? I, for one, can't bear watching this any longer. Wasn't that Morcion who fell a moment ago?' asked the captain. 'First the son and then the father.' If a picture can tell a thousand stories, Solanko's face told only one, that of total disgust. In many ways his sentiments were shared. No Alfari should have to endure what they had witnessed. It had been a massacre from start to finish and, in hindsight, Morcion's battalion hadn't stood a chance.

The battering rams were brought to a halt outside both main entrances, their canopies preventing them from being set ablaze and shielding them from arrows and spears launched from above. Its only solid beam was the battering ram's log, reinforced with a massive metal ram's head, slung like a swing from a wheeled frame that made it easier to bash against its target. The vulnerable parts of the shaft were strengthened by metal bands, also attached by chains. Then, like a pendulum in motion, it swung into action, pushed on by Draconian muscle. The whole of Oaken-Crag shook. The vibration was felt in every corner of the enclave as the entrances were pounded open with a foreboding boom of doom. The other entry points were attacked in equal measure with carrying rams and axes. With Edwin's approval, Archelaus set the Tigurini tree climbers from Borvoria on the city's foundations.

With weapons fastened to their backs and hooks attached to hands and feet for digging into bark, they scaled the huge ash trees like a colony of ants. The flag bearer signalled Rotgut. Morkpork smiled.

Hirgon was surprised by the horde's precision and discipline, while Shi-mith was awestruck at how adeptly the Tigurini climbed; they were quick, agile, and highly co-ordinated, with ankles so flexible that their feet could turn at unnatural angles. Very much like wild monkeys, which can walk up trees in much the same way, planting their soles flat against a trunk, allowing them to hold their bodies closer to the trees, reducing the energy it takes to climb. Shi-mith had to concede his ankles would rupture catastrophically at those angles and then just walking would be a labour of love, never mind scaling thick vines and trees on a regular basis. Crayfar ordered the battering rams to be destroyed, but their protective canopies were preventing a sustained attack. Flaming arrows were extinguished by the inflammable hides and larger projectiles simply bounced off.

'Double the guards on Oaken Gate and Elm Gate,' ordered the High Lord, knowing that a breach was imminent. Durion directed a couple of daigars to carry out those orders as warriors with spears ran past them.

'It won't be long before the drawbridges come off their hinges. Once they're inside, signal Lugar Hirgon,' Crayfar said calmly, surrounded by warriors. Durion nodded.

Hal Stone was in no doubt that this was the worst decision he had ever made as he crept through the lower chambers of the deserted marble-laden Aafari temple. Jacob had led them into Oaken-Crag using an unguarded tree. Leaving a man on watch, seven of them had undertaken the climb. When led to the city he had been expecting a more accommodating entry point than the rickety haphazard climb he found himself involved in, though, in Jacob's defence, the plinths of wood to grip onto were actually quite sturdy. When the greenhorn had divulged its location in confidence it had seemed like a good idea: in and out with no one any the wiser. At present, he was just thankful he had made the rest of his men stay behind. All he had to do now was avoid Crayfar and not get embroiled in the battle raging outside.

'At least those tremors haven't stopped yet,' whispered Booth.
Hal looked at Booth, whose foolish suggestion had led him here, but he did not think it worth mentioning.

'All the same, I don't want to be here when the elves surrender,' said Hal.

'We'll never surrender,' responded Jacob, and the elves behind him nodded.

'Very well. When the elves are defeated. Now, where's this food?' Hal looked at Jared, who just raised a sympathetic eyebrow.

'It's this way.' The greenhorn led them along a dimly lit corridor, down a flight of steps, and then disappeared around a corner. As the group rounded it and set eyes on the larder their faces lit up. The spacious room was filled with neatly stacked sacks of grain, fruits, vegetables and dried-out fish, not to mention the confectionary, cheese and raisin sponge cake. It seemed heaven-sent.

'Don't just stand there gawking. Get your sacks filled,' said Hal. Suddenly, the battering rams' vibrations stopped. 'Let's make this quick; that can't be a good sign,' said Hal, concerned. Jacob nodded back with a mouth full of cake, while Callum was already filling his sack.

Outside, howls and snarling shrieks greeted the Alfari, as Morkpork's hell hounds scrambled through the hole in the drawbridge and the mangled portcullis. The warriors within drew their munga blades. Elven steel against snapping jaws should have been no contest, but in such a confined space the starved, ravenous fiends tore them to bits. Orks were sent in behind them to lower the drawbridge. Morkpork followed, screaming instructions. The hounds did not pay him a moment's thought. They had tasted the sweet flesh of Aafari and were fixated. Mounting the stairwell, they trailed the scent. A bright flair shot skywards signalling that all entrances were breached. It was gazed upon for the briefest of moments before they attacked each entry point simultaneously. Under Edwin's flags and banners, on which the black dragon flapped furiously, ork and Draconians were backed up by the bear tribes from the cold, rocky region of Laskardar. These barbarians wore the signet and paraphernalia of the bear and were, in many ways, similar to the Kelts, although they were cave-dwellers. They ran over the fallen drawbridges and, like a flood, poured in.

Grumondi sat on his horse some distance from the force attacking the tree entrances and watched the proceedings with a keen interest. He was looking out for his captain and Edmund's colours. Then, spotting him near Edwin, he smiled. A third wave, lined up alongside other generals of the senate, and their battalions and brigands, held back to maintain a siege ring and as a deterrent in case the Alfari had a few more surprises.

However, Grumondi wasn't buying it. He had Molton detailed with a battalion to flank Edwin, on the pretext of securing historic and ancient texts contain in the Aafari library. Molton's real task was to watch him like a hawk. Grumondi needed to know why Oaken-Crag was so pivotal to Edwin's plans and, by process of elimination, he knew that nothing of importance would be found in the Aafari library. If Edwin was allowing him to send men to secure it, then it stood to reason. That only left the Aafari academy, temple and palace as sources of interest and, truth be told, his investigation had stalled. From the day he left Athena to this point he was none the wiser and to think the blacksmith was still on the loose despite the strength of the southern realm was ludicrous. In addition, his spies informed him that Mandrick was on the road to Galatea, not in the enclave as Edwin would have him believe. Grumondi ordered one of his men to fetch him some water.

Nothing made any sense, although he considered whether it might be a simple matter of the city's wealth. Granted, the senate was on Edwin's back. Pressure was tactfully applied by his brother Edmund. Edwin, however, was more conniving and, knowing the upstart as he did, there was more to this invasion than the prince was willing to admit: he was sure of it. A plot for simple wealth could dupe a short-sighted fool but he was neither foolish nor short-sighted. No, a pursuit of power was Edwin's calling. Yet the question still remained as to whose power he wished to supplant and what he intended to do with it. Grumondi was sure that Edwin was searching for the ultimate power and that he longed to rule in the Autocrat's stead though, however long he deliberated, his conclusions on Edwin's true motives would not hold up under scrutiny. The prince covered his treachery well and, with his inner circle so small, it made obtaining proof of his suspicions extremely difficult. His correspondences, sent to Edmund, had said as much. Though inwardly he dismissed Edwin's whims, soon the Prince Regent would put an end to this war, leaving Grumondi to return to his estate and orchards. Ah, now there was a thought.

The Tigurini climbers, having got onto the gangway, split up into groups and, within different sections of the city, were causing as much mayhem as possible. Tasked with distracting attention from the main force trying to gain entry below, they were succeeding. Crayfar sent warriors to prevent them from getting a stranglehold but nothing could detract from the cries and echoes coming from Oaken Gate tree shaft.
Against the backdrop of Alfari homes and connecting rope bridges Durion, among a company running towards them, drew his munga blade ready for the taste of real action as he sized up a foe. At the same time the Tigurinians were targeted by archers from above. Arrows rained down, the boardwalks quickly becoming a field of quills. The bare-chested tribesmen navigated them skilfully as they

continued into the city with a fighting style akin to a type of acrobatic dance.

Durion approached one of the tribal climbers. The warrior, for his part, snarled and contorted his face as he pulled a thump across his throat, goading the captain onwards while displaying his intentions with erratic swordplay. Knowing a move or two, Durion made mesmerizing patterns of his own with his blades held tightly, splattered with blood from the wounds they had inflicted; the instruments hummed as they glided in his hand. The Tigurinian's vain attempt to counter hit thin air and his next lunge was only a fraction better. He managed to bang his sword against Durion's shield before being swept off his feet by a leg sweep. The captain pounced, pushing his blade deep into the man's solar plexus.

Seeing him at a disadvantage, an opportunistic Tigurini set Durion in his sights. With his sword held high, he gave the captain, on his knees, little time to react with his blade still wedged in the dead climber's chest. The warrior, bearing down, prepared to deliver his blow, and was suddenly hit with an arrow in the nose. He fell on his back.

Durion turned and looked up at his saviour, Antien, who, in a fluid motion, set another arrow and arched back his bow, giving him a quick nod. The tribesmen were no match for seasoned elgar Alfari warriors once they got a grip on restricting the tree climbers' movement. Confining them to small pockets when confronted, the fight was brief unless they were not in greater numbers. Some lost their balance, hit by well-placed arrows, and fell the long drop to their deaths. The Tigurinians who reached the city's higher levels found greater success attacking Alfari archers. The hell hounds stormed over the tree husk's barricaded openings into awaiting Alfari battalions. The hounds were closely followed by Edwin's hordes who ran straight into shields, long spears, and elven arrows. The collision was deafening and was followed by a horrendous halting screech.

Crayfar's captains, marshalling their battalions, absorbed the first wave. Spears were funnelled to the front and the injured were carted to the back. However, the constant stream of ghoulish orks, alongside oxceians, Draconians and Edwin's heavy infantry, had brutish intentions and butchery in their eyes. Directed by Captain Grip Hawkins, nicknamed Gripper, the battle turned in the horde's favour. The lighting speed at which hounds moved caught the elves off balance. No easier to tame out in the open, they moved freely and attacked at will. Then, in response to an unheard whistle blown by Morkpork, the pack disbursed to all parts, some reaching the city's upper tiers and prowling its gangplanks, hunched on hind legs. Some of the archers, in the hope of escaping, tera-glided down to other levels by extending their arm and holding aloft a cape attached to the centre of their lower back.

Edwin and Archelaus stepped over dead bodies, tailed by Baracus, as they entered Oaken Gate. With the lift shaft secure, they boarded and were winched up to city level. With each entrance breached and besieged on six fronts, Crayfar's only saving grace was the arched opening's bottleneck effect, which prevented the ominous mass from engulfing warriors who were already overwhelmed by the sheer numbers. Durion, in the thick of it, marshalling troops, signalled an archer to release Hirgon from his shackles. Oaken-Crag descended into chaos, with orks starting fires and barricades giving way.

The library, having been cleared of its valuable literature, was no more a point of interest to Molton than it was to Edwin. The Aafari were thorough and nothing was left. As Molton reported these facts to Archelaus, Edwin targeted an Alfari, mistakenly believing he was King Jeremiah.

'That's the elf we need to speak to, the one heavily guarded over there.'

He pointed. In the midst of a number of Alfari, with flowing greyish-blond locks and wearing a dark tunic with a long velvet fur-topped cloak, stood Crayfar, screaming orders.

'I see him,' said Archelaus, and told Molton to take his men and make his way to that position.

*

Having seen the signal, Hirgon put the second part of Crayfar's plan in motion, ordering his troops to mobilize. Shi-mith smiled and left with Solanko to join their ranks. The pair, walking off, were indistinguishable apart from their different coloured tunics.

'Don't forget to jump, old friend,' said Shi-mith, his words spoken in jest to lighten the mood.

'Who are you calling old?' the captain responded. Both laughed, more from the need to expel nervous energy than anything else. A brief respite, however rare, was a commodity. Having to constantly fight the stamina-sapping turmoil of knowingly sending elves to their deaths was a burden not without consequence and, for a moment, they revelled in the frivolousness of being an elf with the luxury of time to rejuvenate their mental stability.

Then, given the nod, Solanko went to address a group of Alfari standing patiently beside a herd of bulligore and greeted them with a grim nod. Theirs was an unenviable task of immense danger. He looked at the four warriors standing in front of him. If they could pull off such a bold move, win or lose, their names would be enshrined in Alfari folklore. It was also fitting that the elves before him had all volunteered, as had he.

'You know what we have to do?' said Solanko sternly.

'Yes, captain,' they responded.

'Then Folkvang awaits the ones who fail.'

Once they were safely mounted on bulligores, Shi-mith signalled Hirgon to indicate that they were ready and, with a loud bang that spooked the herd, they were on the move in a sprinting gallop that rapidly descended into a mad dash as the pace gathered momentum. A bulligore on a rampage was a wondrous sight; their wrinkled skin stretched tightly as they trailed the bull of the pack, crushing a path through the woodland habitation. Though docile, a thousand bulligores were a force to be reckoned with.

Solanko and the Alfari warriors, riding in tandem, were tasked to steer the lead bull into Edwin's horde. Riding alongside them, stalking the captain as though their lives depended on it, with horses in tow, were five Alfari, closely followed by Shi-mith who led two battalions on horseback. Into a breadth of scattered trees the stampede thundered on. The deafening noise rose to a mind-boggling crescendo from the footfall of eight thousand galloping hooves. The billow of dust and animals seemingly out of control was a frightening prospect for the warriors scrambling to defend their right flank. One by one, the captain's group jumped off the hippo-faced beasts with Oaken Gate straight ahead. However, as Solanko was about to jump, suddenly the lead bull tripped, fell and slid to a halt. Left with no other option he stayed mounted and guided them in. The warriors alongside on horseback urged the captain to jump, but he would not. Lives depended on these next few moments and, committed to the cause, he gripped his reins even more tightly and roared as the stampede cascaded into the horde.

The impact knocked the woolly mammoths off their feet, throwing the Draconians on board to their death, as it swallowed up swathes of Edwin's army entrenched at Oaken Gate. Shi-mith's battalions, in the wake of the bulligore's devastation, set upon the survivors mercilessly. Even the wounded were bludgeoned with maces.
Solanko, having jumped off in the nick of time, was now fighting a Draconian and an ork at the same time. Known for his ability with a sword, the elgar despatched both foes ruthlessly and in quick concession. Hirgon, having joined the party, directed Shi-mith to retake the gates.

The battle in front of the academy was, with Molton's arrival, fast turning into a last stand for the city, with only the battalions under Durion's command still left intact to hold the invaders at bay and defend the palace. Confronted with the prospect of having to fight, it dawned on Crayfar that Hirgon's rear offensive may not arrive in time.

Sabre cuts from hammer metal were accompanied by fighting so fierce it resulted in the cracking of reinforced breastplates. Enamelled elven helmets were replaced with blood. The High Lord looked on until Molton had killed the last of his bodyguards with a thrust through the heart. With all his guards dead Crayfar, surrounded, found himself backed into a corner.

'Who are you?' demanded Edwin.

Crayfar did not respond, partly due to anger and embarrassment at being caught.

'Your High Lord has spoken, now answer!' cried Archelaus.

'I am the High Lord of the Alfari,' responded Crayfar aggressively.

'Not the king?' said Edwin in disgust. A messenger ran up and informed Edwin that the Laskarians had taken the temple and were awaiting his orders.

'He carries my rank,' volunteered Archelaus eagerly.

'Well, you take care of him then,' replied the prince with disdain as he looked at the aging elf. 'I'll be in the temple if you need me.'

'With pleasure,' replied his captain.

The men surrounding them gave the two combatants plenty of room to manoeuvre and Archelaus motioned the High Lord to draw his sword. Amused by the challenge, Crayfar did just that and the two locked swords. With his captain preoccupied, Edwin signalled Molton to follow him as he continued his procession to the temple. Any minor resistance encountered was waved away by sporadic blasts from his gauntlet, or met by Molton and his battalion's swords.

Ekaterina knew her time had come as the door to her chamber opened inwards. Edwin walked in with Baracus and motioned Molton to wait outside. Grumondi's captain stopped at the entrance with a group of prisoners and a battalion.

'I see I was expected. The high priestess, I presume?' enquired Edwin.

Ekaterina turned to face him and dipped her head.

'I would return the courtesy but, as you can see, it's difficult in armour.' He tapped his breast plate. 'And while we're on the point of pleasantries, I regret to inform you your guards are dead,' he continued while sheathing his sword, stained with blood. 'We asked them nicely, but they wouldn't allow us entry.'

A tear rolled down Ekaterina's pale cheek.

'I know,' she whispered, and then continued. 'Although you were never invited, even now, as you stand before me, you believe you are worthy to step foot inside this temple, a place of enlightenment and peace, when it is so abundantly clear that your warmongering presence is not welcome here.'

Edwin's expression said it all. He knew that, surrounded by all that was Aafari, her resolve would be formidable.

'Just tell me where the gold-rimmed scroll is and I will leave,' he said behind a tight smile.

'Always looking so far ahead that you haven't stopped to realize that what is sought after is not what you seek. The challenges you've set yourself are impossible to achieve. Your search for redemption will fail. Your conduct has already sealed your own fate.' Ekaterina's words of wisdom were a subterfuge to buy her time while she read his thoughts. A glimpse into Edwin's mind was the real reason she had stayed behind, even though the decision was fraught with danger. Her visions of darkness did not bode well for the whole of Elohim. Darkness meant there was no future but this was a secret she had not shared with anyone. It was imperative that she prise from him the information needed to give the planet a fighting chance.

'I will say this only once. Give me the scroll or many more will die,' said Edwin, disgruntled.

'Triumphs do not make a man, dear prince, nor is intuition judged by intentions but by the burdens you help to lift through endurance and selfless sacrifice. But, alas, these are not words of power in your world although they are plentiful in mine. I'm sorry you've travelled all this way; it has all been in vain, for I do not know of what you speak.'

Edwin walked up to Ekaterina, who stood before him in her headdress and flowing gown, then shouted, 'You lie.'

'We have only the truth, for a lie has never happened,' Ekaterina, resenting his words, replied playfully.

'I have had enough of your riddles. Seize her.' Edwin gave Molton a nod, and a battalion of thirty or so men, wearing heavy armour, marched in with Hal, his men, Jacob and two Alfari greenhorns. They were bound by their wrists and were told to kneel.

'As I just stated, many more will die. Baracus, if you please, show her what I mean. Start with the one covered in ork's blood,' he ordered. His large bodyguard took up a position behind Booth then, removing a sheathed dagger from his hip, stabbed him in the back before nonchalantly pushing the body off his blade.

'Every time you choose not to reveal the truth, you will seal their fate,' said Edwin, laughing as he nodded at his bodyguard to kill another. Ekaterina, aghast at Edwin's brutality, was powerless to stop it. Holding the displacement spell in place under Balthazar's bombardment had severely weakened her ability to cast spells and her remaining strength was reserved for an escape. One by one, man and elf were put to death. Each time she was asked to reveal the location of Mandrick and the scroll. Each time she refused, Edwin nodded.

Hal looked at Jared just before his sidekick, too, was stabbed in the back. Then, with only two left, Baracus stood behind Hal. This time, just before he plunged his dagger's blade deep into Stone's back, Molton told him to stop.

'I know this man,' he said. Something had been niggling at him since his capture and now he realized that he recognized him. Edwin was livid at missing out on the satisfaction of seeing life ebb from Hal's face until the captain explained his reasons.

'I fought this man at Athena. He's one of Mandrick's captains.'

'If this is true you can live a little while longer although he has only delayed your execution,' said Edwin, looking at Hal while indicating to Baracus to stand behind Jacob.

'Last, but not least,' said the prince, producing a cruel smile.

'Our love is immeasurable while you are devoid of compassion. Thus our wisdom is endless while you are predetermined and limited.' She looked at Jacob as Edwin gave Baracus a signal, and Jacob was put to death. 'I have read your thoughts, killer of children. Does your Autocrat know that you wish to dethrone him?'

Molton, visibly shocked by her statement, said nothing.

'Let me tell you a little secret. Your day has been marked,' Edwin said incensed. 'So you will not be around to spread that vile rumour.'

Balthazar had disappeared at the start of his offensive and he was the only one with the ability to exorcize Ekaterina's skills. He'd forgotten that she possessed gauntlet-like powers. Nevertheless, words to that effect would not be uttered by her lips again.

He ordered the guards holding her to release her, and then raised his left arm.
It was time for her to reveal her secrets and die. Menacingly, the gauntlet glowed.

'That weapon you wear was not made for evil. You hold days and years in such high regard. To us they are meaningless for life is constant, half son of man. Even now the light you wish to extinguish blooms as part of a circle that cannot be undone by the likes of you, so take my life if you must.' Ekaterina closed her eyes as the gauntlet's glow intensified. When she reopened them it was as though she had just woken up from a dream. One side effect of her ability of foresight was a bout of lethargic wooziness immediately after using it. Ekaterina, regaining her composure, was glad her plan had worked; now she knew his secret, although how much it would help their cause only time will tell.

Edwin's thoughts were a confused muddle. Otherworldly aspirations had been ravaged by a mind predominately consumed with the desire for power. The swarm and Cressida were controlling influences that persistently angered him and his craving to be released from those chains was constant, fragmenting further a disjointed mind devoid of a father's love. There were still too many missing pieces to be sure she had found something of use although Ekaterina now knew he was not the cause of her visions. Yet, there were clues. Images of people mining a mineral and dropping dead, then carts filled with minute white rocks. But what did it mean?
And as for the king, no news was good news. She had found no trace of Jeremiah or Lord Erynion inside Edwin's thoughts which, alas, added to her concerns because, now more than ever, she wondered where they were. However, the high

priestess had more pressing matters at hand and she called to the Callidora guards at her chamber's entrance. They entered.

'Do you know Jacob Bear-Whistle? Both nodded; the greenhorn's mischievous exploits were legendary. 'He's here somewhere, with six others. Find them quickly and bring them to me.' They bowed and left.

*

If Archelaus thought Crayfar was going to be a pushover that belief was dispelled in flashes of brilliance as Crayfar delivered a sword lesson of the highest order. Through no fault of his own Archelaus found himself on the back foot on numerous occasions. The High Lord displayed a guile he had been told to expect, but had not seen until now. The sound of steel sizzled and a flurry of intricate clashes resulted in Archelaus being cut across his cheek, just below his left eye. Blood seeped from the slit. One of his warriors handed him a large bandana to stem its flow.

'You'll pay for that,' said Archelaus.
Crayfar knew he had the beating of this man standing before him with sabre in hand, as blood matted the dark brown beard below the captain's cut. To aid his escape, however, he would have to give ground. In the defence of a retaliatory flurry from Archelaus, while backtracking towards a rope bridge, he saw his chance and seized his moment, knowing full well that the men surrounding him would probably give him room if they believed the captain was on top. Perversely, it worked. Then, as if losing his balance, Crayfar lowered his sword and Archelaus took a swipe which he clumsily evaded before diving off the side of the bridge.

Sheathing his sword and extending his arms, holding onto his cloak like a glider, he floated downwards.

Archelaus, seeing Crayfar fall, presumed he was dead and went to join Edwin in the temple. Durion, powerless to help from his location, watched Crayfar duelling for his life, but once he saw him fall he signalled his warriors to abandon the city. Below, the bulligore charge had given the Alfari a chance which was quickly snuffed out by Grumondi, with the rest of Edwin's army. Solanko, back on his trusted mount, joined Shi-mith in directing their attack as the Alfari were hit by Grumondi's onslaught and the tide turned in the horde's favour once again. Pike men with long spears pinned the elves back as arrows swished through the air. The cries from his battalions were not war crimes and, as wily a campaigner as Hirgon was, he had no more tricks up his sleeve. He knew the battle to save Oaken-Dale was lost. Fortunately Crayfar, landing near Shi-mith and having been given a mount on the back of his horse, rode over to Hirgon's position.

'The city has been taken,' he told the lugar reluctantly, as he mounted his stallion. Then, with a nod, he signalled the retreat.

'Where to?' asked Hirgon.

'We ride for Galatea,' Crayfar responded sullenly.

'But what about Richon?' asked Shi-mith.

'He's on his own,' he replied sternly, kicking his heels and galloping off.

Jacob, escorted into Ekaterina's chamber by her guards, was baffled at being caught in the larder.

'How did you know I was here?' he asked, with a face searching for answers.

'I don't have time to explain. We all have to leave now. The city has fallen,' said Ekaterina. Jacob was even more confused but no one questioned the high priestess. Hal Stone was just glad he had not been asked to return the provisions he'd acquired and an easy route out of the city was a far better plan than the way they came in, of that he was convinced. He could tell Jared was in agreement. Along with her guards, they followed Ekaterina up a couple of steps and through the wooden door behind the stand and basin. Jacob, ever watchful, noticed the sapphire was missing as he followed her up the steps, before seeing that it had reduced in size and was hanging on a chain around her neck. They entered a bland, round room with no other exits and no windows. Ekaterina shut the door, sealing out her chamber's light and subjecting them to claustrophobic darkness.

'This way,' the high priestess said, smiling.

When she reopened the door they were on the forest basin, having exited through a large round tree. Hal and the others looked dumbfounded and bamboozled.

'Where to now?' asked a delighted Jacob.

'My guards will escort us to a secret cavern under the earth,' Ekaterina replied. Hal was about to object, having left Gentle Ben back at the base of the tree they had climbed, when suddenly, with no time to react, they were under attack.
Instantly a Callidora guard, a greenhorn and Callum were dead, while Ekaterina lay mortally wounded with an arrow embedded in her chest. Twenty orks, an oxceian, and Balthazar, camouflaged by a spell, stepped out from behind tree cover.

'Nobody move!' barked Balthazar. 'I knew you'd use your ability of foresight. You were too weak to attempt anything else.' He looked at Ekaterina holding the arrow's shaft, with blood weeping from her wound, and shook his head. Behind him orks with arrows poised stood drooling. 'Didn't you wonder why I wasn't in Edwin's mind? Now that was an oversight.' The elegantly dressed mage laughed cruelly as he walked toward them. 'Seize them,' he ordered.

'*Nemus clausus suum semita,*' muttered Ekaterina, and a tree came crashing down between them and the orks. She reached out her hand to Jacob, who ran to her side, then she pulled the chain and sapphire off her neck and gave it to him; a blue blur, suspended in its centre, began to glow.

'You must find Maya and give this to ...' She closed his hand around the gemstone but did not finish the sentence. 'It contains my memories and Edwin's secret.' She looked at her guard and smiled. 'Ella will take you to my cavern.' The Callidora guard, close to tears, dipped her head. 'Now go,' was Ekaterina's final command.

With her remaining strength she pushed the arrow deeper. If they caught her, the whereabouts of the gold-rimmed scroll would be revealed. Then her hand released his. As her light force dispersed they felt a gentle breeze as though Ekaterina was saying goodbye in her own intimate way. Deep inside Oaken-Crag, a young elfette screamed. Jacob, following Ella, ran away with tears streaming down his face. He did not look back. Ekaterina's last words rang in his ears.

Edwin, entering Ekaterina's chamber with Baracus, was surprised to find it empty.

'Find her,' he ordered. 'Find her now.' Molton was as baffled as the rest of the men. To whom was he referring? 'And someone check that door,' said Edwin. A warrior ran up the steps and slowly opened the arched wooden door. He shook his head.

'It's empty, a prayer room, my lord.'

The mage looked at Ekaterina, a picture of peaceful sleep, and seethed. In the right hands the sapphire was a weapon of immense power and if Cressida knew he'd let it slip through his fat fingers she would be extremely displeased. Having seen at first hand the torment that could result from her displeasure he knew the price of failure.

'Get me her amulet. Leave none alive!' he shouted at the oxceian as he kicked the dirt beside Ekaterina's face. The bull-headed beast nodded and led a hunting party on Hal and Jacob's trail.

Act Four

A Baron's Revenge

Jacob Bare-Whistle returned to the surface from Ekaterina's grotto, after staying confined within its dank space for more than a day. He dropped to his knees when he saw the devastation. Oaken-Crag was gone, burned to a crisp. Ella just stared skywards at where the city should be, unable to move. Jacob, for once, was lost. His home was gone, the king was missing and Ekaterina was dead.

Jared looked at Hal who shook his head as if to say 'we don't have time for this'. With this section of forest now dead there was nowhere to hide and the area would soon be teeming with Edwin's troops on the search for survivors. Hal advised him that they had better get moving. He was helped up by Ella and Gentle Ben who, if they had not run past him when making their escape, might well have been burned to a crisp too. Once Booth and the other greenhorn were out the group trundled off to see how the group left behind had fared. Although Hal was willing to help Jacob, a journey to the fire caves would have to wait. A captain's first duty was to the lives of his men.

*

The entrance to the fire caves, a large cavity cut into the black rock face of Mount Lurbira, was a welcome sight for weary warriors. From this distance its smoky top could only be imagined. The hot, sundrenched day had hindered them once they were out from under the shade, making their task more laborious. With the group riding ahead taking almost a day to cross sixty leagues, it did not bode well for Richon, trailing behind. Captain Ennis got his Alfari to take up a tactical formation called Eaching, where each elf was strategically covered by another. Their killing field was vast with over two acres of clear meadow, flanked on each side by thick forestation.

Haedirn had to tell his elven brethren that they must relinquish their horses because the next part of their route was impassable for larger animals. At first he had a revolt on his hands; watching tearful Aafari say farewell to their horses was the sad part. The council official had strict instructions to lead them through its labyrinth. If anything happened to Ennis or if defeat was imminent he was to lead a group deep into the dark caverns, out of harm's way, before returning to lend a hand. It must have seemed like forever and an age for the captain while he waited patiently and kept watch on the horizon. He first spotted the general's fierce blond hair, though behind him there was a large cloud of dust and he knew it was no sandstorm.

'Alfari, arm yourselves!' cried Ennis.
Richon's wife was in a wagon being tended to by Renthel's wife. The daigar, having rejoined him at the front, had taken it upon himself to keep his general informed of her progress.

'Can you hear that Renthel?' His daigar nodded. 'Then the time has come. You know what to do?'

'I do indeed,' replied Renthel.

With over four to one when counting warriors, Richon admitted their odds were poor. He veered off, turning his attention to the rear. However, he was tasked with getting their people to the Nargarians waiting on the other side of the fire caves and if they could just hold off Edwin's horde for a little while, at least until the wagons made the clearing, then his mission would be a success. Maya had kept Ekaterina's passing a secret, deciding that, at this point, such news would only make matters worse. Richon had put her scream down to a simple temper tantrum. She didn't like the idea of having to go against his wishes, but Ekaterina had taught her well; even in elven society power could become convoluted so there had to be someone that always put the Aafarians first. Anyway, having her in their ranks would make the Alfari warriors protecting them fight that little bit harder.

Although Eolande said nothing she knew the Nargarian was displeased with her decision, especially if it meant Maya was putting her safety at risk. Eolande was annoyed. Why her charge had to be so bull-headed was beyond her. It reminded her of someone she missed incessantly.

'Tartarus Leadbottom, where are you now?' Eolande whispered forlornly to herself. Since Maya's awful scream, her charge's surreptitious nature had come to the fore; Maya's conversations were brief and her answers cut short, though only someone close to her would be able to notice this, as Eolande did. The path they were taking was an unfamiliar one. Her normal route encompassed the Blue Nile so, like everyone else, she was slightly apprehensive, with the future difficult to predict.

Eolande looked at her charge, still believing the little girl had made the wrong choice.

Suddenly, the Callidora guards around Maya became anxious.

'Protect the shekhinah!' one of them cried. Eolande hoped she wasn't about to be proven right.

Eustace, whose pale skin had darkened from exposure to the sun, raised his axe and, with wispy blond hair flailing, he cried out and charged, his oxceian sergeant, Rissien, behind him barking out orders. Richon looked at the approaching cloud of dust and earth. A roar with a limitless crescendo covered the ground, ploughing towards them in a line of grey and black armour, made up of orks, men and beasts. The fleeing Aafari were filled with dread. A horde of over two thousand warriors tore through a valley of trees to exact the Black Knight's reckoning.

On reaching the rear, Richon ordered Captain Orchill to organize the wagon and carts' retreat. Gwindrill and Renthel were told to cover the right and left flank, while Richon was to hold the centre. All round them, under cloudless skies, bats' eyes, reflecting the sun's rays, flickered like fireflies. Perched, sneering, the scaly fiends were waiting on a word.

'Here they come,' shouted Renthel and arrows on strings were pulled back in preparation. Richon swivelled in his saddle to brace himself for the impact. He raised his shield only just in time to deflect an axe.

'Keep carriages and wagons moving forward!' shouted Renthel in the thick of it. Then, with the battle and defence raging, an Alfari warrior broke ranks and headed straight for his general.

'My lord, Gwindrill told me to inform you that riders approach from the left.'

'How many?' shouted back the lugar, while clashing sword against axe with a Draconian.

'I don't know …Too many.'

Richon, shocked at Edwin's intent, stole a quick look to see how Orchill was getting on with the wagons. He caught a glimpse of Orchill pointing and cheering and thought his captain was suffering from sunstroke. Twisting in his saddle to attack the Draconian again he decided that if he didn't order the retreat soon he'd be a ringmaster to a bloodbath, with one third of his army already lying dead. The problem was he could not call a halt until his wife was safe. Suddenly, the sky was full of wings flapping furiously as the bats descended.

Below the Geneshian Peaks Balthazar, back in the main encampment, was inside Edwin's tent.

'Haven't they caught up with them yet?' said Edwin impatiently.

'They're fighting now,' he replied looking into his black orb intently.

'Let me see.' Edwin stood over him. 'It was a very wise choice sending Eustace and Rissien; they work well together,' he added smugly, watching another Alfari being killed. Edwin's favourite saying was 'no one escapes'. Archelaus, standing behind Edwin, rolled his eyes.

'What's that?' said the prince.

'I don't know,' replied Balthazar. Bemused, he looked at Edwin.

'Archelaus, you didn't send more troops, did you? I thought we discussed this.' The captain shook his head. Edwin, scrutinizing the banners of the group approaching, cried, 'Release the bats!' and Balthazar did as he was told.

Looking on, Edwin's cruel smile returned. Although he could not hear the noises, it wasn't hard to imagine the pain inflicted when the bats closed their jaws. Then, in slow motion, he watched an arrow hit a bat that Balthazar had left to observe. The orb's view went blank and the mage winced in pain.

'Get it back,' ordered Edwin, looking at him with disgust.

'I can't. The burden would be too unbearable.' He shook his head and sat with folded arms.

'Get it back, now,' demanded the prince, still looking at the blank mist-filled orb as his gauntlet's glow intensified.

The elf no one was expecting to see came, leading the reinforcement's charge. King Jeremiah, closely followed by Dain and Lord Erynion, was galloping towards them. However, the noise of a stampede was not coming from their horses; it was from the footfall behind them. Riding out of the cover of trees, as though their very lives depended on it, was an army of miniature size and two horned war-rhinos. The Denvagar dwarves, with Mortfran Weldig and Stigwyn Broadfist, were at the helm.

'There. I knew it,' pointed Mortfran, bouncing on his black war-rhino. Erynion looked up, and Jeremiah nodded, drawing his sword.

'Richon's under attack. Dain follow me.'

'Yes, my king.'

In a tree, watching Edwin's horde attack, was a bat and, once it was shot down, without Balthazar controlling them, the other bats attacked everything that moved, including Edwin's men. Then Erynion, targeting the horde's captain, released another arrow. The unfortunate news for Eustace, to which the dead bat could testify, was that Lord Erynion rarely missed.

*

A gust of wind caught in the fabric of a frilly white kite and launched it high into the heavens. Embroidered with yellow-centred, tiny red flowers, it turned one way and then another, twirling on air. The kite was made from two broken branches and one of Gunn-Hilda's old tablecloths. The young girl below, wearing her unmistakable straw hat, harnessed its direction. Her expression was priceless. Her dark-haired brother stood next to her, at times lending a hand. They laughed and smiled together, rekindling moments not dissimilar to when their parents were alive. For them, and the others, the next few days flew by. Barnaby had regained his full health, indicated by rosy cheeks and the resumption of a jovial disposition. Ragnarr was raring to go and his impatient demeanour was a challenge to be around, as was his incorrigible need for them to venture on. Brun, whose fondness for his friend was not in doubt, was the first to admit an eager dwarf was difficult. Brun had plenty to be thankful for; Ragnarr had saved his life a number of times. However, relaxation and recuperation was the order of the day. Hot food and rest were needed for a man, half deaf, who could still feel the steam coming off his feet, and all manner of other places. To add insult to injury the aromas coming from Gunn-Hilda's kitchen were mouth-watering.

Having had Goreham and Darrel removed from her larder Gunn-Hilda, with her extensive knowledge of herbs, and Pippa by her side, cooked up a feast. The delicious meals and sweets went down a storm after weeks of hard bread and cold cuts. Flint and Sid had retrieved the horses, apart from two chargers. The missing horses substantiated the wizard's claims that Kallen may have survived the fall after all. Rex, Reece and Daniel chipped in by collecting firewood, while Tarquin and Calhoun helped with minor repairs. Tartarus and Nikomeades, for their part, seemed preoccupied and were locked away in the observatory for long spells, before the day came when it was time to leave. Nefanial, true to his word, fed his captives scraps and, with the brigands in tow, waving goodbye to Gunn-Hilda, the group seemed happy enough. Even Calhoun, normally jittery, was upbeat and, though it was a close call between her and Ragnarr, Pippa, back in her familiar old threads, was undoubtedly the happiest.

'Come on, Angus,' she called as the terrier enjoyed Gunn-Hilda's attention a little while longer. Then, after a vigorous shake of his fur and leaving a trail of muddy footprints, he followed.

Winter was fast approaching. The temperature dropped and the nights turned cold. The hours of daylight on the summit were shorter. They left at dawn to make the most of the available sunlight. Nikomeades had commandeered one of the horses and knew of a shortcut, down a mountain path, that would take them to the edge of Brigantia. As the wall of trees closed behind them he steered his mount into the headwind of a north-westerly sea breeze, and led the way to a plateau below. The blue skies were strewn with wispy white clouds and brightened by an easterly sunrise. The rocky undulating landscape, covered in a scattering of white snow, was striking. The prospect of crossing such a beautiful setting was a positive one for all concerned although, admittedly, with a fresh layer of snow greeting their step the summit became a different beast altogether.

Passable trails were now treacherous. Paths were littered with hazards beneath.
Off to their left the intimidating Black Forest and its treetops, covering acres of land, dwindled in size as they rode in the opposite direction, towards the sea. Tartarus, for

one, was happy to see the Black Forest fading away as he watched Willow's hooves crushing a path through the snow. He'd lost three companions within its domain, if you included Randolph, and it was only down to blind luck that it hadn't taken more.

The icy breeze they were riding into would be a drain on Willow's stamina but, after many days of rest, he was confident the horse's strength would endure. He delivered pats of encouragement and guidance and his stallion's coat gleamed with the warmth of an autumn morning on his back. He and Willow had travelled many leagues together and would have many more roads to travel before they reached their journey's end. Alongside Nikomeades, who in no short measure he now considered a friend, he ventured on.

In the brief time since delivering the scroll, his understanding of the way of things had significantly increased. Thrust into this crazy domain, his true knowledge of the perils he faced was unknown, so the wizard, having shared his secrets, had unravelled a great many things, opening his eyes about the Autocrat, Cressida, and the south's power structure. Nikomeades had even helped him with his pronunciation of more complex spells, although he was aware that some secrets were still being withheld. When asked if he had any information about Tartarus's human ancestry, Nikomeades had remained tight-lipped, before answering his question with a question.

'Has Ekaterina not spoken of this?' Tartarus shook his head. 'Well then, it's not my place to say,' was his response, even after being pressed.

Recalling his first lesson produced a stiff smile; the mess that was made when he attempted the levitation spell would live long in the memory. He'd probably still be in the air if Nikomeades had not used a spell to get him back down. So, embarrassingly, he had needed to use the stair to get inside the observatory, which was one of the main reasons he'd spent most of his time up there. Although a sour note in his rise to greatness, it made an old man chuckle. At present it was still a wayward spell, unable to master direction while afloat. However, he had conquered many others in the time and, secluded away, gazing at the stars, had continued his life training.

Nikomeades, who believed the scroll would bring harmony and return balance to Elohim, pointed out the role the stars play. Tartarus understood why Ekaterina held Nikomeades in such high esteem and, even though they did not agree on everything, the aging mage's arguments were pretty convincing. Nikomeades knew the burden he bore; a battle with Edwin's horde would only have one outcome. In a way, he had pushed thoughts of his city to those recesses of his mind where he dare not tread, where uncomfortable emotions were kept. In the wizard's company, though, these areas were explored and he was shown tricks to keep his anxiety in check, alleviating the load of having the fate of a kingdom rest on his young elven shoulders.

Oaken-Crag, his home, was under attack and there was nothing he could do about it. Despite being hardened by his experiences, that fact was beginning to haunt him.
Being placed on uncommon ground, with time elapsing, away from familiar faces, was a feeling which, in such a peaceful setting, even more so, bored holes. Resigned to the possibilities and expecting the worse, he turned to hear Tarquin and Flint bickering. His tight smile blossomed into a full one; it reminded him of a phrase Lord Erynion used to

explain life. 'Some things change: some things never change,' was his uncomplicated explanation.

From above, the group trundling through snow looked miniature and insignificant in comparison to the peaks they were about to cross.

'Do you think it was wise to bring all of them?' asked Flint referring to the six horses he had in tow, carrying their provisions and gold.

'Well, Nikomeades said we could sell the ones we don't need at the place he's taking them to.' Tarquin looked at Calhoun riding beside Nefanial.

'All the same, I think it was a bad idea,' said Flint, aware of the fact that the horses were slowing them down.

'So you think we should have left them with Gunn-Hilda, then?' asked Tarquin. For once Flint, left speechless, said nothing as they continued the gradual descent, plateau after plateau, all with their own unique dangers and perils. There was scant wildlife and rarely seen flora.

Pippa, scolding Angus for chasing off a mountain hare, had the others in stitches, with the hound whining at her remarks. Soon after, they were about to enter an area inhabited by thousands of butterflies, where evergreen trees were allowed to grow unhindered and looked like works of art, some growing horizontally with branches shooting upwards at peculiar angles and in unusual shapes. Nikomeades told them to stop and, leaving Tartarus's side, he rode forward. From the swarm blocking their path ahead a group of butterflies flew to meet him and, when close enough, a beautiful blue one, with the pattern of a peacock's tail on its wings, left the group and fluttered towards Nikomeades' hand before delicately landing on his outstretched palm. Watching the wizard, in his fur cloak and a pointed hat, deep in conversation, speaking the language of the faerie folk to an insect, was inexplicably baffling. A few of the men behind Tartarus shared an enquiring glance.

'Hey, you two. Did I tell you that you could speak?' said Rex, hearing Darrel and Goreham sniggering.

'Tartarus, are you sure this wizard hasn't lost his marbles?' asked Nefanial; the act of talking to a butterfly was not a quality he looked for in a leader. Tartarus nodded and smiled.

After a heated discussion Nikomeades looked back.

'They've granted us entry, 'he announced.

'Has he got water on the brain?' Ragnarr asked Brun, who was also worried by the mage's odd behaviour. But before he finished his sentence the wall of butterflies gave way and, ushered onwards by Tartarus, they rode in.

'What was that all about?' he asked Nikomeades quietly.

'They were not happy with sons of Elohim entering their realm. Can you blame them? Men are such destructive beings,' he responded.

'Are they fairies?' asked Pippa curiously, when she pulled up alongside Nikomeades. Her father had told her numerous bedtime stories about butterfly fairies.

'Why yes,' he replied. 'Their form is an illusion to defend them against attack.'
Pippa squinted at the light blue butterfly soaring above her shoulder, trying to imagine what they looked like.

'Oh, I forgot you can't see them yet,' he observed before mouthing a spell.
Ragnarr nearly jumped off his horse as the butterflies transformed into winged beings.

'By Algrim, vermin!' he cried. As far as he was concerned fairies were an abomination; nothing should be shorter than a dwarf. He flailed a fist at one, and then another, instantaneously regretting his actions when the two fairies' handsome faces turned to a dark shade of red as they sprouted fangs. Their emerald-green eyes, altering in shade, were now a menacing black.

'Elivagar, Elderon,' reprimanded the light blue fairy, her words dampening their anger just as they were about to take a chunk out of Ragnarr's arm. They retracted their fanged teeth as the rush of blood rescinded and pale cheeks returned along with their mild manners.

'They're very dangerous if provoked,' said Nikomeades. The light blue fairy nodded and whispered into his ear. 'And those two, Ragnarr Morbere, I'm reliably informed, wear their hearts on their sleeves,' he continued, amused.

'Now, don't you think you should have mentioned that earlier?' protested Ragnarr, still on edge.

All around them fairies flew by, weaving through the air on transparent dragonfly wings. Born hermaphrodites, with pointed ears and long, shaped nails, some took a female form while other chose to be male. The group marvelled at the trees awash with their vibrant colours. The light blue fairy with soft features seemed drawn to Pippa and made a beeline for her, sitting on her shoulder. Pippa giggled at the sensation. The little fairy wasted no time whispering into her ear.

'My name's Pippa. It's nice to meet you too. I haven't met a fairy before,' she said, smiling at her blond-haired fairy friend. Tartarus watched their innocent exchange with warmth as they chatted away. A little while later, heading along the trail and enjoying being among older trees, one in particular shared a memorable moment. A little red squirrel, perched inside the dark, hollowed-out centre of a tree stump, seemed to be sticking its tongue out at them, looking as if it were hopping mad at being disturbed.

'See, not even the animals have respect this far west,' commented Ragnarr.

Pippa and Brun laughed.

'Did you understand what she was saying?' asked Tartarus once the fairy flew away. Pippa smiled and said, 'Yes. She said she is only a princess and that we've already met the queen of the fairies. I told her we had not, but she was adamant. And she said when I'm older I'm going to be very powerful and I must not forget my friends.'

'It is our task to look after you, not the other way round, little one,' said the three-quarter elf.

'No, silly, she was talking about her kind.'

'Then that's good advice,' he replied, playing along, not sure whether she was actually telling the truth. Falling back to speak with Rex, Tartarus wondered what she meant when she said they had already met the queen of the fairies. She couldn't have been …? A mischievous expression covered his face and then he shook his head, dismissing the thought.

At their territory's edge the group said their goodbyes to their newfound friends who, in turn, wished them good journey. Despite the tears in Pippa's eyes, Nikomeades released his enchantment and the fairies returned to their butterfly form. The group were still travelling across the summit, towards the sea, as a midday sun moved to an early evening blur and a radiant orange horizon covered the summit. Nikomeades, with a hand gesture, brought them to a halt looking out over the ocean alongside a sheer drop. They dismounted and joined him on foot. The sea, a world for merchants, warriors and the rich, affected their lives in so many ways, and not always for the better. Those few who had never set eyes on it found their hearts racing as they absorbed the salty sea air, inwardly moved by its mystery, suspense and adventurous effect. To witness such theatre made the group feel blessed. Breathtakingly powerful waves bashed thunderously against a stack of chalk rocks further up the coast, fifty yards out to sea. Known as the Four Fingers or the Hand of Anu, they marked the start of the Keltic Sea, their grassy tops now replaced by snow. There was no way to get across to them even by boat but, all the same, they stopped for a moment just to enjoy the view. They looked down at the stack of rocks that had stood there, since time and memory began, amidst the waves.

The sun was setting and seagulls circled overhead. Eagles skimmed the waves, still fishing, although soon they'd disappear, migrating east to warmer climates. It was moments like these that strengthened their resolve and made what they were trying to preserve all the more worthwhile. Tartarus smiled. He had the same look of bewilderment on his face as when he first set eyes on the sea with Asrack and Vince.

'Brigantia, the heart of the Badlands,' said Nikomeades with a huge smile. They turned to their left, away from the sea, and below, in the fading light, was the gold and green landscape of Brigantia, a light autumn mist veiling its secrets. Way off in the distance, lit fires surrounded the sacred megalith, the stone of ages. They could see the shade of Fog Forest, on the edge of the peninsula, which Nikomeades also pointed out before hurrying them up with the sun setting fast. They all swallowed hard when they saw the route he intended to take.

'This way,' he prompted, assuring them it was safe to take the path at night.

'Are we sure about this?' murmured Calhoun under his breath. Ragnarr, pulling his horse, gave the mage a puzzled look as he gazed at the descending slope that ran alongside the cliff's edge. Taking a quick look over the lip at the uninviting rocks below, with waves lashing against them, did nothing to soothe his apprehension. He glanced at Brun who was already securing his horse for the trip down.

'Of all the routes off this rock, why did he have to pick this one?' he asked his friend, shaking his head. Brun's expression wasn't one of confidence either. Horses on a slippery slope was a recipe for disaster.

'Don't worry, it opens up further down and is protected from snow by the cliff's ledge,' responded Nikomeades, as though he'd overheard him. Throwing salt in front of his step, they followed his lead onto the windy path, two by two, with Flint and Tarquin picking up the slack. The sound of horses' hooves slipping and scraping the gritty terrain set them all on edge.

Encouraged by Tartarus and Pippa, leading the way behind Nikomeades, they stayed close to the rock face while making the descent. Adjacent to the top of the Four Fingers it levelled out and although, at this height, they got splashed from larger waves, the relief was clear to see. Realizing, to their surprise, the yards they had travelled in such a short space of time, measured against the view from up top, even Ragnarr was impressed. They were now in semi-darkness and torches, held aloft, offered little in the way of light, with their reflective capability being absorbed by the rock. Nikomeades released his staff from his saddle and cast a spell.

'*Illustro, lux lucis meus via.*' The cliff face was bathed in a bright blue glow.

'Show off,' whispered Tartarus, behind him, with a tight smile.
Suddenly, as though waiting for that moment to attack, they were engulfed by a barrage of yellow beaks squawking in front of their faces. White and grey wings flapped frantically, unsettling their horses. The birds, fearful of danger to their nests in the rock face overhead, were going berserk.

'Nikomeades, by Algrim, your blue light has set them upon us,' Ragnarr responded tersely, removing his war hammer from its sheath.

Angus, growling and barking, attempted to scare them off and was jumping up and down. Then, to stop a seagull pecking Pippa, he leaped off the ground and caught it by the wing, locking his jaw. The little girl was gobsmacked when, instead of landing on the trail, he nosedived straight into the sea. As she screamed Cloud panicked and she nearly plunged to her death too. The mare had backed up so close to the cliff's edge that grit and dirt trickled over. However, Brun was alert to the danger and reined his mare in, just in the nick of time, to prevent another tragedy. With things spiralling out of control Nikomeades uttered a spell to dim his orb's glow, which immediately calmed the flock down. However, with moments for recrimination to come later, they continued towards the stream that flowed into the sea below before, unexpectedly, the path veered away from the ocean and passed under a short tunnel through the side of the mountain. The tunnel led to a secluded cove, with mangroves growing alongside the water's edge, some distance upstream away from the sea.
It was a mesmeric view, even by torchlight.

'This leads to the River Tay and Gulf of Bar-da-Shar,' declared Nikomeades sombrely, his voice still tinged with regret at not having been quick enough to save Pippa's pet.

He could hear their mumblings, and after recent events, he agreed with Tartarus it was time to make camp.

'It's about bloody time,' said Nefanial, looking at his tired horses and exhausted men.

Tarquin and Flint were consoling Pippa but were unable to stop her tears. It was heartbreaking to watch their little princess sob uncontrollably.

'He didn't listen to her the first time. He's only got himself to blame,' said Ragnarr, glad to see the back of the pesky mutt. The brothers looked on unimpressed. They unpacked and, after a meal, it was decided Reece would take first watch.

'We'll make Boondreigh by midday tomorrow,' said Nikomeades. However, with most of them too tired to listen, his words fell on deaf ears. He looked up at the stars and then sat in a position of meditation. He was still in doubt, yet had to admit that by their endeavour alone there were signs of potential. In truth, he would have preferred more Alfari warriors than this ragtag group with boys, wet behind the ears. Although he had seen them in action, there was still a big question mark over how they would fare against seasoned fighters, warlocks and ghouls. The elf and the little girl had promise, although she was still too young, and he was sure the grumpy dwarf would stand up tall. The fact still remained that he did not know if he could count on them, as a group, to commit to the hard tasks, to do what needed to be done when the time came, no matter what. He closed his eyes as Tartarus bid him goodnight.

*

In the morning, after breakfast, they resumed their journey. As promised, Nikomeades headed in the direction of Boondreigh. A good night's sleep had rejuvenated everyone and it was tough to subtract from the view they awoke to, with a clash of two realms all around them. Why the most beautiful places on Elohim were also the most dangerous ones was a question Nikomeades continually fought with; was it a process of natural selection or breeding?

Considering they were about to meet the Kelts for the first time, he was surprised by their zeal. Angus's intuitiveness and limitless energy was missed, and for many of the younger members of the group it was like losing a family friend and, just like Pippa, some were still holding on to hopes of their lucky mascot returning. Sitting on Rainbow's saddle, Pippa was unusually quiet. The Daginhale terrier, having saved her life, was more than just a friend. On reflection, she cherished the moments they shared. They had laughed, cried and smiled together, not forgetting the times she had been forced to tell him off, when his adorable face would curl up. There were now pictures embossed in her mind and, although inconsolable, Pippa was determined to keep her spirits up by refocusing on her goals: Kallen's head on a pole, and taking her father's ring back home.

They rode for some time against the summit's base and, as the stream started to narrow for the first time, the wizard slowed them to a crawl.
    'We had better cross here. Any further and we'll need a craft to cross. It opens up again round that bend.' He pointed. 'And nearer the Tay it's extremely treacherous.' On the opposite side was a condensed wooded area of shrubs and trees.

'Treacherous, you say? It doesn't look too clever here,' observed Ragnarr, looking at the choppy stream.

'What does treacherous mean?' enquired Pippa.

'I'll tell you later. First we must cross,' replied Nikomeades with a smile, glad she was emerging from self-imposed exile. Swinging his leg over his saddle he dismounted. The spell he was about to perform was a complicated one, setting the stream against its tide where they needed to cross. It was a spell against nature. He freed his hands from his sleeves and, reciting a chant, summoned his staff from his horse's saddle and it flew into his hand. Then, raising both arms, he shouted, '*Flow of matris flows per mihi EGO postulo suus flow ut subsist, flow of matris flows per mihi EGO postulo suus flow ut subsist, flow of matris flows per mihi EGO postulo is flumen ut subsist*!'

He banged his staff down hard on the bank's muddy soil and his orb flashed. Then, like a parting of the waves, the section of stream calmed enough for them to cross. The group blinked.

'Quickly,' he urged. Led by Tartarus, they thundered across. Amid the splashing suddenly, floating towards them, with his furry face drenched, panting, was Angus. He was paddling away, just barely managing to keep his head above water. The current's strength had prevented him from being able to get a footing on the bank. Nikomeades' spell had briefly put a stop to all that and he jumped onto Pippa, throwing them both into the stream. She didn't care. Crying tears of joy, she screamed.

'You're a bad boy, Angus! Yes you are, yes you are!' She covered him in wet, soppy kisses.

'Get them out of there. I can't hold this spell all day,' ordered Nikomeades. Perplexed, remounting his horse, then aiming his staff at the stream, he charged. Tartarus, Tarquin and Flint helped pull Pippa and Angus out. Rainbow was already on the other side chewing on some shrubs.

'Now, you've got to be more careful, boy,' said Tarquin, with playful pats and ruffles of Angus's fur. He was all too aware of the heartache Angus's absence had caused his sister. The terrier, panting and revelling in the adulation, was immediately fed. Pippa, soaked through, refused point blank to change into the spare clothing Gunn-Hilda had provided. As a treat, in view of her recent torment, Nikomeades used a spell to solve the problem; he felt partially to blame for Angus jumping off the path in the first place. Telling her to close her eyes and stand absolutely still, he waved his staff over her head, willing the orb to life, while once more he whispered words of magic. However, this time, its effect was different and she was covered in pixie dust, leaving her clothes and her boots bone-dry.

'I'll say one thing: he does come in handy,' commented Ragnarr with a firm nod.

They may have only just crossed a stream, but no one was in doubt of its importance now that they stood on Keltic soil, having just crossed the threshold of their western divide. In an entanglement of brambly branches and leaves, they looked at each other with renewed pride. After Goreham and Darrell's veiled threats about the animosity to be expected they were back on high alert and proceeded with caution.

'Thanks for drying me, Nikomeades,' said Pippa, with a probing expression on her face. 'May I ask you a question?' The mage nodded, returning her smile. 'Is war coming?'

'I'm afraid it is, child.'

'Really? I've never seen war before.'

'I should hope not; war is no place for a little girl, Pippa,' he said firmly, though acutely aware she had encountered its devastating effects at first hand. Then, trying not to scare her, he explained the reason war was bad. 'And war must always be the last resort,' he said in conclusion.

'May I ask another question?' she spoke tentatively, while biting her bottom lip.

'Of course you may.'

'What's magic?'

'What's magic?' he repeated, nearly swallowing the words. He looked at the little girl, with freckles on smudged cheeks, riding beside him on what was practically a donkey. He raised a wistful eyebrow. 'Why do you ask?'

'Well, the fairy princess spoke of it and you just used it to dry my clothing, for which I am thankful,' she said, hurriedly.

Nikomeades laughed and imagined what Bellamina would say about her daughter's grubby face and cheeky grin.

'Very well then, the easiest way to explain it is that everything is made up of tiny reactive molecules. Magic is the way in which we channel and manipulate this energy.' He caught a fly in his grasp, mumbled a word and when he opened his hand, a ladybird flew out. Pippa, listening intently, looked on in amazement. 'Some of us are born with these skills, like you and I. Granted, yours has not reached maturity yet, but it will.' He nodded, sure of himself. For once, Pippa was a picture of bewilderment and was left speechless as she tried to figure out what that meant. In many ways it was fortunate Kallen had been so hell-bent on his apprehension, so that her zeal was disregarded and put down to the innocence of her age.

'I felt your life force from the moment we met. Others will too. This is the reason I couldn't leave you with my wife.' He paused. 'Young lady, there's no other way to say this: you are an enchanted.'

Pippa's eyes opened wide in total disbelief. He simply smiled and, with a wink, he placed a finger over his pursed lips.

Tartarus was wondering what they were talking about when, just as Nikomeades had predicted, with a midday sun fast approaching, the Gulf of Bar-Da-Shar came into view and, gradually, the width between the stream's banks widened, altering in shape and size, becoming a torrent of white-water swells and ripples as the two tides collided, crashing against the jagged rocks and boulders that littered its convergence into the Tay. Now, above the collage of leaves, a clear sky, with a solitary cloud, greeted them overhead. Angus, prancing about and foraging, for a moment stood still, surveying the new frontier, as the woodland underfoot gave way to wet sand, covered in a sheet of light snow.

In the distance the Tay's vast expanse of water, between Brigantia and Damgarden, lay in wait. Its auburn colour, from a combination of rich copper deposits and a reflective glare, glowed majestically. On the opposing side, waves lapped against the perpendicular, uneven cliff face of Cariadau Lama, or Lovers' Leap, outlining the rugged landmark's undeniable attraction.

'Do you see it,' said Sid, bringing them down to Elohim with a bump, looking at a medium-sized vessel anchored beside smaller fishing boats in the port's harbour. The knarr, similar to a longship, was a type of cargo vessel used by the Kelts. It was reliant solely on its squared-rigged sail for propulsion.

'I see it,' responded Nefanial.

Up until that moment the notion of our intrepid heroes actually splitting up had been a subject openly ignored. However, with their sights set on Boondreigh, Nefanial's decision to split the group was dolefully confronted and farewell glances were exchanged. Soon some would be leaving, crossing the Tay to Damgarden, and the fishing hamlet of Henthorpe, and eventually arriving home at Irons Keep. Nikomeades ordered the group to dismount, conscious of Keltic customs. Such a large group of strangers riding into port would be regarded as a show of force.

'I'll do the talking,' he warned them, aware of Ragnarr's antagonizing tendencies.

Boondreigh, positioned behind a protective dune belt on the southern coast of Brigantia, centred round a main hall, a gaming house and brothel, a brewery and a draeyplaetsen, where cordage for ships' rigging was made. It was an agricultural area with a fishing port. Boondreigh accommodated thirty stone homes, with thatched roofs, alongside black, wooden smokehouses. The smokehouses were glazed on the outside with creosote, a substance used for a variety of purposes from meat preservation to wood treatment, from an antiseptic to a potent laxative. As was typical of a settlement next to a large river, its compactness was different from rural Keltic encampments, with no spaces set aside for stables, gardens or fields between the homes. With a third of the population usually away at sea, fish stocks remained high. The remaining Kelts employed twenty or so fishing vessels, each crewed by three or four men.

The traditional small boats called yoles, or hookers, were characterized by their clinker construction, with the edges of planks overlapping the hull from helm to stern. Typically, they had a mast with three brown sails, and a tarred timber bottom, blackened by coal or creosote. Still, the Kelts who lived in Boondreigh were not simple folk, who eked a living digging peat from the dunes to produce salt. In addition to trading dried, salted and fresh fish, sold daily, they also participated in acts of skullduggery and smuggling. Yet it was not only beachcombing that facilitated the gathering of luxury items. River Kelts were extremely good traders, boasting commodities such as ceramics, bronzes, walrus tusks, raw uncut pink beryl stone, paradise seeds, grains and peppers, to mention but a few. There was always a scent in the air of fruit from faraway lands and home-made goat cheese on market day.

It was the only reason Nikomeades came to Boondreigh. For him discretion was the better part of valour and in its market place, that condition was met. Having noticed that the fish market was disturbingly quiet, he gave the order and, instantly, weapons were drawn. Huddled together they followed his stride cautiously. The only indication that the Kelts were at home was the slamming shut of window shutters.

A Keltic warrior, with a greying sandy beard, wearing a horned helmet, fur boots and cloak covering a tartan throw, stepped out from behind a smoke shack fifty yards ahead.
    'Volkan,' said Nikomeades, squinting at the silhouette, and having to raise his arm to ward off the sunlight clearing the ridge of Cariadau Lama. The sciplieden, or boat captain, who owned most of the fishing vessels, was a central figure in the settlement. His usual warm welcome

was replaced by heavily armed Kelts, who immediately surrounded them with shields raised, swords drawn and long pikes held firm.

'Who gave you the right to bring these strangers here?' he asked. Although calm, there was a veiled threat in his words and he was unable to conceal his contempt.

'They seek passage to the hamlet,' replied Nikomeades.

'So they seek passage on our hookers?' The Keltic warriors surrounding them treated them to an abrupt chorus of hearty laughter. Then, turning to a clean-shaven warrior with brown braided plats, who held an axe, he asked, 'Is that them?' The warrior nodded gleefully, heightening the tension.

Brun, with his axe gripped tightly, returned the Kelt's stare with a menacing grimace and, as though feeding off his nervous energy, Cloud aggravated matters by making bullish noises.

'What is the meaning of this?' asked Nikomeades. Volkan did not reply but smiled, looking at Brun.

'Are you a blacksmith? We're in need of a good blacksmith.' Brun held his gaze but said nothing.

'They look like the two our king is after. Did you know, old man, that these strangers you travel with are wanted men?' Nikomeades shook his head. Unfortunately, with the mention of Taliesin, he knew these Kelts would fight to the death.

'I'm only their guide,' replied the mage pensively, still squinting. 'We are weary and thirsty, and have no time for this tittle-tattle. Of which two do you speak?'

'Those two.' The Kelt by his side pointed out Ragnarr, then Brun.

'So then, the rest of us are free to go where we please?' asked Nikomeades shrewdly.

'I don't think you heard me, old man' responded Volkan, raising his voice. Flint gave the boat captain a curious look as he steadied his aim.

'You're not taking my brother-in-law anywhere,' responded Nefanial, signalling to his men to get ready. Tartarus, observing the signal, looked at the thirty Kelts surrounding them. They were heavy-set men, and clearly fighting men too; although they were relaxed, the steely glint in their eyes was cold and unapproachable. He could tell his kind were not welcome here as their eyes passed over his features, scrutinizing him as if he were a piece of meat. They took particular interest in his pointed ears. Unfortunately, he had missed a trick but now was not the time to be lifting up his hood. Anyway, who were they to judge him? The Alfari warrior who now returned their gaze poured scorn on their narrow-mindedness as he weighed up the question of whether to attempt an escape or not. The knarr, tied to the pier, looked prepped for a voyage and he knew that if it came to a fight the odds were heavily stacked in their favour, with Nikomeades by their side, so boarding her and fleeing capture was a distinct possibility.

'Ride to Bright-Ling and tell Eldrun we have them. Go now,' ordered Volkan. The braided warrior ran to an awaiting horse, mounted it and rode off. Then, jumping over a small hedge, between two leaning trees, he disappeared from sight.

'It is said this man killed a royal rider.' He looked at Nikomeades then at Brun, quizzically, as though sizing him up.

'So I hope you've been paid for your labour, old man, because the only place you'll be guiding them now is straight to Taliesin's encampment, and if you resist ...' His men moved closer.

'Old man,' whispered Tartarus. 'Don't they know who you are?'

'No,' murmured Nikomeades. Tartarus, itching to use a spell on Volkan's disrespectful tongue, admired the wizard's restraint and humility.

'They lie!' screamed Sid, waving his sword frantically while backing towards his horse. 'They want our gold.'

'Our king's orders were quite clear. Anyone found with these men must be brought before him,' Volkan said firmly.

'He's not my king!' cried Nefanial, all set to fight.

'Hang on, isn't that where we want to go anyway?' said Ragnarr. With his mission in jeopardy, he was here to align with the Kelts, not fight them. Tartarus, Tarquin and Flint conceded that they were of the same mind as they begun to lower their weapons.

'Not I,' responded Nefanial angrily.

'Me neither,' said Sid. Calhoun, Reece and Daniel wore blank, confused faces, standing behind Barnaby.

'Does anyone know a Bollymore, by any chance?' asked Ragnarr.

'You'll see him soon enough. He's our king's companion,' replied Volkan.

Ragnarr dropped his war hammer, lifted up empty hands, and urged Brun to drop his weapon too.

'Your friend is wise to offer up his weapon. You would all be wise to do the same,' he said. Reluctantly, Nikomeades gave the nod and the sound of their weapons hitting snow followed.

'What about our prisoners? These two pillaged our village,' said Rex.

'Did I not say everyone?' replied Volkan dismissively. Rex dropped his sword and relinquished their prisoners as a Keltic pike was pointed at his chest. Gorham and Darrel smiled.

'I wouldn't be smiling if what he said is true. We Kelts take a dim view of attacking women and children,' said Volkan, wiping the smiles off their faces. Not long after, stripped of their weaponry and all their worldly possessions, the group was frogmarched on the Claddagh road to Taliesin's encampment, escorted by the sciplieden and twenty or so Kelts. Watching from a distance was Kallen, who couldn't believe his luck. He transformed his appearance and rode into Boondreigh to get a boat across the Tay.

*

Having traded at the fishing port over a number of years Nikomeades, riding alongside Volkan, was puzzled by his strange behaviour towards him and openly questioned it.

'I did not want to mention it before, but we are on the brink of war and it's your friend here, this blacksmith, that has caused it,' confided the sciplieden. Nikomeades, listening to his account, seemed visibly surprised at how tenuous peace was, although these circumstances were actually perfect to incite war, which was the main reason for their presence in Brigantia. However much Ragnarr would have protested to the contrary, that was the truth. To make a gauntlet of power without the ninety-third element was impossible and far beyond the dwarves' comprehension of the way of things. The answer lay within the scroll, of this he was sure, and for this reason he knew they were travelling in the wrong direction. Nevertheless, he was willing to pander to their whims to keep the group together, or until he could enlist more bodies to his cause. His ideals were to prevent war, not incite it.

After laying down their weapons he had refused to be bound.

'And as for this young lady, she is in my care and has already been through an ordeal. I will not allow her hands to be bound,' he had stated.

'Just as long as you keep her, and that mutt quiet, old man,' was Volkan's response. Tartarus, not entirely at ease with their predicament, stole a brief smile.

'So why do Kelts not call themselves westerners?' asked a bound Calhoun, in the convoy beside Nefanial.

'Because of that stream we crossed. They believe it makes Keltic terrain an island, and therefore makes them different.' Nefanial practically spat out the words, although if this was Keltic hospitality it wasn't as bad as he'd been led to believe. Ragnarr told them both to be quiet.

Taliesin's normally bustling encampment, with so many warriors away, was quiet. Halwn's return was greeted by way of relief, with the settlement low on defensive manpower, but the relief evaporated quickly when they learned that hunts were to be reduced. The prevailing winds of the north were blowing harder with each passing day. Its brisk breath of bereavement wilted all in its path and, just like the fading of plant life, soon the time for hunting would be gone.

Although no news was good news, Taliesin felt his grasp on his reign slipping. Words of war were being bandied about more readily and shortly he would be riding to join his brother on the plains of Asseconia, to reap Anu's providence. Fighting two barons did not concern him. It was the aftermath of the destruction that concerned him and at least a few of the clans felt uneasy with the idea of years of war, as did he.

Taliesin sat on his throne, in the company of Bollymore and Halwn, making his final preparations to hasten his departure. In his mind the battle was already being fought and that was the grim fact. As Halwn was about to leave to carry out his orders, Eldrun burst in and hurriedly informed him that the blacksmith had been found.

'What?' he exclaimed. Finally, he'd been brought the words he'd been longing to hear. Sitting forward in his throne, a contemplative visage was gradually replaced with a broad smile as Eldrun relayed the facts. 'Volkan, you say?' The scout nodded. He was caught up in the euphoria, a dreary evening became a night for celebration and he called for a feast.

'And once we hand over this blacksmith I can continue my search for the ninety-third element,' said Bollymore with an even bigger smile.

'Let's not forget that I may have to hand over his dwarfish companion as well,' teased Taliesin. For a moment Bollymore's grin disappeared.

'You wouldn't?' he said, before his smile returned.

Of course, Taliesin would, especially if it prevented all out war. He looked at Halwn, his rugged loyal warlord of the Claddagh province, brought into his inner circle by Nemetona. He had proven to be an indispensable ally.

'Grab some men, ride to Bright-Ling and escort them in,' he ordered.

With a warm smile Halwn dipped his head and left.

By the time Nikomeades and Pippa, followed by the others, finally entered Taliesin's encampment, led by Halwn and Volkan, under armed guard, the mood was almost celebratory even days after the feast.

'I know this dwarf,' said Bollymore with a quizzical eye, still a little the worse for wear after an evening of drinking. He squinted.

'Ragnarr Morbere, is that really you or are these old eyes deceiving me?'

'Get them to untie me and I will tell you,' said Ragnarr. He left Taliesin's side to greet him.

'It is you.' Bollymore turned and looked at Taliesin, who gave his approval.

'But lock the blacksmith with the beast. I will speak with him later.' Two Kelts dragged Brun away, kicking up snow and dirt.

'We found this.' In Volkan's cold hand was a plain Keltic crown, catching the sun's rays from time to time. Taliesin stopped in his tracks, gobsmacked.

'The crown of legend,' he murmured, flabbergasted. Volkan placed it in his hands and even the hardest of Kelts was unable to contain his emotions. Eyes filled, and a salty tear ran down the sciplieden's cheek, before disappearing into his thick beard.

'The markings are unmistakable, sire.'

'Where did you find it?' asked Taliesin, inspecting the crown inch by inch.

'In his saddlebag.' Volkan, walking in front of the group, pulled out Calhoun from the line. The assistant looked petrified. Tartarus and Nikomeades shared a glance.

'Tell me, young man, how did you come by this?' He held the crown aloft.

'I thought it lost to time itself,' he said, as though reunited with a long-lost friend. The crown of Iden, although only managing to catch flickers of sunlight, now seemed to gleam in his hands, as though acknowledging the connection with Taliesin's bloodline. Calhoun started nervously, but became more confident as he told him about their encounter with the spider queen and how he found the crown while they were trying to escape her clutches.

'Maybe at a later date this colony needs further study,' added Nefanial.

'And who are you?'

'He's my assistant,' said the baker. Taliesin told Calhoun to continue, handing the crown to Nemetona to confirm its authenticity. Within moments she was smiling warmly.

'When were you going to mention that you were in the possession of the Keltic crown?' whispered Nikomeades.

'I did not know we were,' whispered Tartarus, just as bemused. He indicated that he wanted the rope around his wrist removed.

'May I have a word?' asked Nikomeades, clearing his throat.

'And who is this?' asked Taliesin, tired of being interrupted but noticing that his hands were not bound.

'He's an old man we trade with,' replied Volkan dismissively.

'I have no time for old words; these are desperate times.'

'You will hear my words, dear king. Here, before you, stands one of the enchanted.'

'And yet you did not prevent their apprehension,' Nemetona replied, dubious.

The man before her looked more like a conjurer of lyrics and tricks than one of the majestic beings he spoke of.

'What was the point? I wanted to speak with Taliesin anyway.' He smiled as he dismounted; it was time to put an end to this charade. 'These men are all with me, including the blacksmith you've thrown in your stockade.'

'Tell me your name and we can be done with this tall tale,' said Taliesin. Bollymore looked at Ragnarr, who nodded.

'Nikomeades,' replied the mage softly.
Taliesin stepped back, eyes wide open as though he were looking at a ghost. However, he immediately regained his composure; he was a king, not a vagabond.

'If this is true, and with this crown in my hand, my people have wronged you. Come inside my tent; indeed there is much to discuss.'

Nemetona had been only a druid's apprentice when she had last heard the name and she bowed her head. Known to be Elohim's peacekeepers, the enchanted were revered. He nodded to Halwn, who was ordered to untie the rest of them as Taliesin ushered Calhoun, Nikomeades and the others into the warmth of his banqueting tent. He placed an arm on Calhoun's shoulder.

'This young man' –Taliesin paused to savour the magnitude of the moment –'has made my kingdom whole again.' He removed the crown on his head and Nemetona replaced it with the crown of legend. Along its band were the symbols of each Keltic clan, symbolizing their unity. Its aura was more imposing than the crown he was just wearing.

'This will bring total allegiance from all the clans,' she whispered and stepped back.

'Now, when we ride onto the plain of Asseconia, they will see a show of force the likes of which will make all who stand before us quiver with despair and if Brandenburg or Syracuse dare to step foot on Keltic soil, their days are over,' declared Taliesin. His words were greeted with a hearty cheer.

'But we're not travelling to Asseconia,' cried Sid.

'I cannot release your friend until then; war is still brewing,' he reminded them.

He turned to Nikomeades. 'And if you violate that rule, you breach any pact you want to discuss. That said, you may have my ear.'

'Brun has the royal rider's note in his possession and once you've read it I think you'll change that view,' said Nefanial.

'Words cannot always prevent careless actions, but very well.' Taliesin nodded to a warrior, who immediately left. Then, turning his attention back to Calhoun, he tapped the crown that now rested on his brow.

'Name your price. We are not thieves.'

'The blacksmith's freedom,' answered Calhoun solemnly. 'You have your freedom and you'll have to be content with that for now, but ... I know ...' Taliesin clapped his hands twice and his wife, followed by a couple of wenches, walked in. 'Measure him up, and get him dressed in a suit of armour befitting a warrior that has found the crown of Iden.' Before he could object they carted him away. 'From this day forth you'll be known as Calhoun the Fox,' he said proudly.

No sooner had the tent's entrance flap shut, than it opened, the warrior returning with Brun's note.

'Do you believe we can trust these men?' asked Volkan. Taliesin raised a hand. 'I do,' he replied, reading the note. 'It seems that this Edwin is up to no good and plans to supplant his master. Why else would he meddle in things that don't concern him?'

'Agreed,' responded Nikomeades.

'But this won't save your friend; his charges are grave.'

'We also have this.' Nefanial carefully removed the wolf's bane before handing him Bowen's message. 'The barons wish to have Crofton killed.'

'On that score they have already succeeded. Have you not heard he's missing, presumed dead?' Taliesin's eyes rested on the parchment. 'His wife is what? Mmmm, interesting ... this might avert war and save your friend, but come now,' – the king looked at Nikomeades –'for you to have not shown your face until now must mean we have more serious matters to discuss.'

'You are, indeed, correct. These are the darkest of days and it is those of the southern realm that place all our lives in harm's way.' He nodded to Ragnarr, who then explained the reason for their visit. 'My king, Mortfran Weldig wishes that we become allies in this fight –you in the west, us in the east – to rid our land of this illness once and for all.'

Taliesin, listening to his words, remained silent, though the word kromillium lay on his lips. It was worse than he could possibly have imagined. He wasn't expecting this; in many ways he wished Nikomeades had stayed hidden.

'Eldrun, I want you to send scouts to Skara Brae, Kaleköy, Clovelly, Walraversijde and Dunmore. Tell them the time for doubt is over. I wear Iden's crown and I require their warriors on the field of battle to defend it.

'Is that wise? We don't fight in snow,' said Volkan.

'Did you not hear what he just said?' asked Taliesin with fierce eyes. 'If we do nothing there will be no more winters.' Volkan nodded. 'Halwn, when will your Claddagh warriors arrive?'

'Tomorrow, sire.'

'Good. As for your treasure,' – he turned to the group – 'a lock box full of coin is an adequate exchange.'

'Can you split it in half? They're not coming,' replied Flint, standing next to Pippa, who, in the company of so many large men, had remained quiet.

'We'll split it later. I will not walk away from war with the south. This is a day I have lived for. My wife will have to wait a little while longer before she sees my ugly mug,' said Nefanial. The group laughed.

'So what do I call you lot, then?' enquired Taliesin.

'That's easy,' replied Pippa. 'The guardians of the scroll.'

'Well said, little one. And with that settled, we leave in the morning for Asseconia and if Millard wants my help against these southern barons, by Anu, he shall have it.'

'These two prisoners ransacked their village.' Volkan brought Gorham and Darrel forward.

'I am a fair and just king and I believe in giving a man a second chance; you mercenaries have heard what has been said today. My warriors can either take you outside and behead you, or you can earn your freedom on the battlefield. What say you?' Falling to their knees, both men nodded in shame. 'Get them cleaned up, Volkan,' he ordered, 'and stick around. I have need of your services and we have not yet discussed your reward.'

'Reward!' cried Volkan. 'Not for me, king. To serve is our reward, and if you think my lot would walk away from a fight you haven't visited the river lately.' Volkan smiled. 'I know it's not permitted, but I'll have you know we fight on a daily basis.' He chuckled and led the mercenaries away.

'They were not your prisoners to free,' protested Nefanial.

'If we are to win this fight the west must fight as one.' Taliesin knew that the real reason the west had been invaded was because of Iden's murder and their reneging on coming to Ebenknesha's defence, while they awaited reinforcements from Andorra which, he now knew, was connected to Cressida's witch's brew. It gave him a sickening feeling; no one had searched for Iden's remains, believing the body dismembered and the crown melted down. Many had perished because of that decision. The Autocrat fuelled those flames and had pulled the wool over Keltic eyes for far too long. Revenge was a dish best served cold and on the plain of Asseconia, with no notable tree cover and snow falling readily, it would be very cold indeed. Tomorrow they would ride into folklore. In no small measure the fate and destiny of the planet rested in their hands.

*

He knew that building a university would house the books his father had saved from the Autocrat's fires, giving Glen-Neath the status of city that he so desperately craved. It was a standing that his southern rulers seemingly would not allow but, under his watch, he was determined to have the west regain its greatness. Crofton, sitting at the opposite head of a long banqueting table, was accompanied by the newly re-formed Ebenesian Knights and they were discussing matters of state. Suddenly, he suffered from a dizzy spell and the next room he found himself in, with large windows, looked very familiar. He was sure he'd been transported to the fishing village of Abbehale, where he had spent most his formative years. His mother's laughter distracted Crofton's attention and his father walked into the room, calling out his name. An informal greeting quickly developed into a full-blown argument over honour and Crofton, who now knew he was in the recesses of a dream, awoke with a start. He had blurred vision and clammy, perspiring skin. He murmured his wife's name, but, as the dingy cavern became clear, he realized he must still be dreaming, and tried to move.

'Calm yourself. Be still. You've been suffering from a fever and your wounds are still fresh.' Her warm, melodic voice had him lulling back into unconsciousness, before he reopened his eyes and gazed into hers. Receptive, icy-blue pupils looked back at him. He reached for her face. Gently, his hand was intercepted as he winced.

'Careful, you're still very weak.' She smiled, shaking her head. 'You were fortunate; the arrow went straight through.' Crofton, acknowledging his condition, gingerly lay back down. 'Who are you? Are you a merchant? Were you attacked by my people?' she asked, enthralled.

'Do you normally accost your guests in such a manner?' he asked, immediately noticing the c-shaped copper torc around her neck, with an amber stone on each end. It indicated that she was a Kelt.

'Yes, I do,' she replied, sweetly. 'I've waited seven days for you to speak.'

While she counted with her fingers, a thoughtful smile appeared on her lips and Crofton felt like he was shying away as he returned it. Her light-hearted approach, and the fact he'd been well looked after, was winning him over. He didn't even know her name.

'How about I ask you a question, then you ask me one?' he suggested.

'Huh.' She nodded excitedly.

'My name's Crofton. And you are?'

'Lyra.' She poured water into a drinking bowl and handed it to him. 'So were you attacked?' she asked, eager for knowledge. Greedily emptying the vessel to quench a grasping thirst, he passed it back to her for a refill.

'I can't remember.'

'That isn't an answer,' she said, biting her bottom lip. 'But I suppose you have been sleeping for some time, so it's to be expected. I found you by the stream's bank, bloody and bruised.'

'You brought me here all by yourself?'

'Fortunately for you, you were handsome and I was with horse and cart,' she teased.

'I'll say. I'd probably be dead.'

'Mmmm.' She nodded while making his pillow, which was a cloth bag filled with grain, more comfortable behind his head.

'So, do you have kin?'

'I'm Aghamore's eldest daughter,' she replied proudly.

'Is he a chieftain?' he asked, having never heard of him, but the way it rolled off her tongue made the name sound important.

'No, silly,' she said, dismissively, with a tight smile.

While charming enough, her enterprise and astuteness meant he would have to choose his words wisely. Lyra was not to be taken lightly. Her answers, however sweet, actually offered nothing by way of information and he believed that, like all Kelts, she'd be a tough nut to crack. The Kelts were shrouded in mystery and since ancient times their ways had never changed. However much he admired their tactile nature, their secretiveness to strangers was something he could not abide, especially when they were neighbours.

'So, where are your wagons then?' asked Lyra. Crofton responded with a hapless grin, while sizing her up.

'So you looked after me for seven days? Where am I?' he asked.

'Ain't I big enough? And that's two questions, silly.' They both giggled, although Crofton with some discomfort and through gritted teeth. 'You already know the answer to one,' she continued, 'so I'll answer the other. You're in Gulzar forest. I dare not bring you to the village.'

'Gulzar?' blurted out Crofton, lost on the geography.

'It means garden of flowers. It's our special place, my sister and I that is, but she doesn't visit here anymore. She's courting and is to be married.'

'What about you?' Crofton knew he was wasting a question, but his fascination compelled him to ask.

'My husband died, so I will not marry again. That is our way.'

'It may be yours, but it isn't mine.' He realized that they'd had their first disagreement. 'I'd marry you in a heartbeat, but I'm already married.' He showed her his wedding band.

'I'd better watch you. You're a sweet talker, ain't you?' she said, smiling.

Aghamore's daughter was captivating beyond belief, with fair, freckled skin, light yellow hair and a slender figure. Not many women came close to his wife's faultlessness but, immediately, he could tell the lady before him did. Although she hadn't yet gained his complete trust, he felt at ease in her company.

'Was I right? You are a merchant, ain't you?' Crofton nodded; he was not about to reveal who he was just yet. For all he knew his men's heads were outside, standing on sticks, and she was a witch. 'You kept calling for Kennice. Is that your wife's name?' she asked. Suddenly, his wife was in his head and he found himself comparing the two women.

'That reminds me, she wouldn't like the idea of me courting you, even if you did save my life.' Lyra giggled.

'I know you've just awoken, but I've been here a while so I'll have to leave you soon,' she said sadly. Being away too long might arouse suspicion and neither wanted unwelcome attention. Lifting a cloth off a plainly woven basket she revealed bread, cheese, meats, and fruits. 'That should keep you going until I visit you tomorrow.' Her thoughtful smile returned.

Leaving ointment for his wounds, with strict directions on its use, she reminded him that he was still many days away from full health. She then picked up a similar fruit basket and disappeared through the cavern's opening. The vibrancy of the hideaway evaporated with Lyra's departure. Crofton was left to survey his surroundings in more detail. Crude light emanated from a wood burner that radiated a balmy heat. He presumed he was in some type of ancient underground cavern, with rudimentary wall paintings accompanying a smell that consisted of damp and mould. He held it in high esteem because she had called it her secret place. The entrance was probably obscured from sight. It may have been used as a shelter from storms in primitive times. He looked at the basket, which contained a hearty meal indeed, and he reached inside. His blood still stained his hand. He wondered about his men and the Draconians, although he had not dared to mention them. In fact, he wanted to keep the habits of his world away from her

simplicity. Now was not the time to be worrying about search parties. That would come later. Now, he needed his strength.
The arrow had gone, replaced by bandages, and touching his forehead revealed wrapping around his temple. From the jug he poured himself more water to clear his throat before tucking into the food she had provided. He took his first bite and, after the initial soreness in his jaw, got stuck right in.

A dozen more days passed by before Crofton resembled a picture of full health. Fortunately, when Lyra had burned closed the arrow wounds, he had still been in a fever. He considered himself very lucky when he thought of the considerable pain he would have had to endure. Hot metal on skin: he could hardly bear to think about it. He rubbed the scar at the edge of his waist.

That day, Aghamore's return was a source of great rejoicing within the village, only a few leagues from Crofton's position.

'I haven't been gone long. Why such a greeting?' The journey from Brigantia by chariot was a long one in the changing weather and, with the cold seeping through his clothes, the druid lifted his arms wearily, dropping his staff.

'We've missed you, father,' his daughters said in unison.

'Careful, I'm not young in years.'

'Father …' Alastrine said, teasing him. Unlike her sister, she had striking Keltic red hair and, although Lyra was prettier, Alastrine was definitely cuter in her mannerisms.

'Leave father be,' scolded Lyra, picking up his staff. After the family reunion the other villagers joined in.

'So, how is the king?' asked an apprentice from Taliesin's encampment.

'He's well, Durrell.'

'I hear war is brewing. Do you bring us news?'

'War?' cried his daughters.

'There are ladies present. Curb your tongue,' said Aghamore, annoyed. The head of the circle had no allegiance to any chieftain. Gulzar forest was his and his alone, bestowed to the head of the Circle of Druids to harness neutrality. Under Aghamore's leadership the village was also a druid training school, so mingled in with the denizens were a large number of apprentices sent from other encampment. Once he settled, however, he sent search parties out to sieve the stream and comb the forest.

Though the days had been monotonous, Crofton's time with Lyra was anything but. With his strength and mobility restored, he even ventured out for fresh air and firewood. The forest wasn't big enough to hide a whole army, but one man could stay hidden within his sovereignty and serenity for a lifetime. With each passing day he felt less like a baron and more like a free man, if you could feel free while in hiding. In truth, this was the life he had always longed for, although children and the rearing of livestock were missing. He envied a knight's virtuousness where matters of state went hand in hand with tending the land, which was not dissimilar to life within the forest, and he seemed to be a damned sight happier than serving a master from a faraway land. He looked at Lyra. This Keltic angel ignited passions in places he never believed existed, and he enjoyed their colourful exchanges. She returned his gaze.

'Your eyes look sad this morning.'

The words 'if only' had run through his thoughts too many times to mention. It was nothing like the way he loved his wife. In Kennice he yearned for something that she, for some reason, was unwilling to provide. Her attitude and demeanour prevented any warmth from blooming, unlike during his moments shared with Lyra, where the experience was not one of love slowly being suffocated. Through reverence he had stayed true to his vows and would need much more convincing to do otherwise. And to abandon his leadership responsibilities, when they were needed most, would make him no better than his father.

'You can tell?' She nodded. 'I will be leaving soon.' His rehearsed phrase was uttered with no real conviction.

'I know,' she whispered, feeling that in their mutual understanding no more words were needed. She held his hand and he felt her openness.

'You are well now,' she said, beaming, 'and your wife and friends must be missing you, as will I. But it is time for you to leave,' she said, nodding, and kissed him on the cheek. So with the time spent in Lyra's company coming to an end, he swore an oath that he would never forget his heroine. In a matter of days he would be leaving, probably never to set eyes on her again, and the troubles of his world would retake his focus. Still, getting anywhere fast without a horse would be a problem. Lyra assured him she would be able to obtain one, given a day or two. So with the date set, they were both determined to enjoy their remaining time together.

Unfortunately, Lyra's disappearing act was becoming common knowledge. Word reached her sister and the very next day, taking great care not to be seen, she followed Lyra to the cavern and watched her enter. She waited awhile before following her in and immediately heard Lyra giggling. Alastrine was livid. Were the rumours actually true? With her back against the tunnel wall she crept forward listening for that telltale sign which would confirm her worst fears.

The laughter had stopped, though that did not deter her, and as she reached the cavern's opening Alastrine froze. She heard a male voice addressing her sister. Was this the man their father was searching for? Scared of being seen, she quietly retraced her steps. When Lyra emerged from the cavern sometime later Alastrine confronted her, far enough away not to alert the man inside, and in a blind rage she knocked Lyra off her feet, sending the empty basket in her hand flying. Lyra, sitting on the ground, pleaded with her sister not to say anything.

'Have you gone mad, Lyra? He maybe the man father is looking for.'

'No, he's just a merchant.'

'Men lie, Lyra. Men lie,' said Alastrine, with her hands on her hips.

'Promise me you will not tell father. He will be leaving soon,' said Lyra, with tears streaming down her cheeks.

'Do you like him?' asked Alastrine, searching her sister's eyes. Lyra nodded.
'All right, I promise. But he'd better be gone in a couple of days,' she said sternly. Lyra wiped her face and nodded. Alastrine helped her up and gave her a hug.

When they arrived back at the village they both said nothing, remaining tight-lipped.
However, as soon as Lyra made the trek to the cavern again Alastrine, watching her leave, marched into her father's tent to relay the facts.

'She's deluded, father, and she's with him now.'

'Your sister has been caring for a stranger in the forest? 'repeated Aghamore in disbelief. She nodded.
'Guards!' he shouted.

A little while later Aghamore, followed by Alastrine and a number of Keltic warriors, burst into the cavern.

'Lyra!' he cried.

'I told you, father. It is him.'

'Why, Alastrine?' screamed Lyra as she went for her.

'Your sister was right to tell me,' Aghamore said firmly, blocking her path.

'Your father is a druid?' Crofton sat on the makeshift bed and held his head in his hands.

'Yes, he's the leader of the Circle of Druids,' said Lyra as she turned to face her father, embarrassed. Her father wasn't just any old druid. He was a maker of kings, a man who held sway over others. The circle's power was only second to that of the king in the Keltic power structure. Crofton continued to hold his head.

'You wait outside,' Aghamore ordered his guards and Alastrine.

'I want to speak with them alone. We might still avert war, if we leave now.'

He then addressed Crofton. 'We've been looking for you. War is brewing because of your absence. And here you are, under my very nose.' He tapped his staff on the floor. 'Lyra, I will deal with you later,' he said, scolding her.

'I never told her who I was,' responded Crofton in her defence.

'If you've sullied my daughter there will be no peace between us,' warned Aghamore.

'I'm married,' snapped Crofton.

'I know,' retorted Aghamore. 'Barons always are.' Crofton stared at the ceiling.

'Taliesin is nearby.'

'Taliesin!' cried Crofton, shocked.

'Yes, and if I can get you two together maybe we can fix this mess!' He turned and shouted down the entrance.

'Ready my guards. We ride to Talabriga, to Lluddrum's encampment. Lyra, you're coming too.'

'Is your father always like this?' whispered Crofton as the druid turned his back. Lyra whispered, 'Yes.'

*

The trudge through slush was laborious, with tracks being covered as fast as they were made by the relentless snow flurries. Far from leaving it behind, the cruel weather seemed to be overtaking them. Up ahead Eldrun, plotting a path for two hundred men on horseback on a winding trail, could hardly be seen. Tartarus, hooded, riding alongside Nikomeades, could tell something was troubling the mage.

'No one said the trip would be easy but we're nearly there. Why so glum?' Nikomeades just stared back with a blank expression. 'Is it because our direction upsets you?' Each attempt to discover what was wrong was neatly deflected or met with, 'Really, I'm fine.' Tartarus, unmoved, was right to have reservations. The mage seldom suffered from bouts of true anguish. Despite that, in this instance, it was justified. The celestial bond he shared with beings born with the gift meant he felt Ekaterina's passing more than most. Hers was a life force of clarity, immense wisdom, and coherence; Elohim had lost a sister and her forceful insight would be sorely missed. At the very moment her existence on this plane ended, her essence made a final, selfless act and whispered words of encouragement. A tear ran down his cheek, marking her passing.

'If you keep to the path you will prevail. God's speed, Nikomeades,' were her whispered words.

Yet, this would not be shared with Tartarus. He needed the elf to fight bravely in the days ahead and he wasn't sure if her passing would dampen his spirits or toughen his resolve.

'I need to speak with the brothers,' he said absent-mindedly, as though that was the cause of his ailment. Then Nikomeades slowed down his horse's pace until he was in step with theirs. He did not like the idea of holding things back, but, in certain circumstances, it was necessary. Nefanial rode up to take his place. Tartarus greeted him with a nod, trying to remain alert in the dark. Talabriga's fires burned brightly on a hill not too far from their position.

'I'm glad you decided to tag along,' smiled Tartarus.

'The truth is, I couldn't look my Lillian in the eye if I ran away from a fight. She's the same,' he replied contentedly. 'I have a feeling that, in the coming days, our world will change irrevocably and I will not stand on the sideline when that change comes.'

Tartarus nodded; he was a guardian of the scroll, as Pippa had stated, and unless told otherwise he believed his home was gone. Inwardly, he wished there was a sideline that he could retreat to, but knew there wasn't one. Nikomeades had spoken of northern shores and the islands in between. So much to explore yet, but so little time. He wasn't looking that far forward, not when the ringing of steel and glancing of blows lay ahead.

'For too long we have been under their thumb, feeding on their scraps.' Regaining his attention, Nefanial held his gaze. 'I'm glad I met you, Tartarus Leadbottom.'

'And I you,' returned Tartarus. Nefanial handed him a piece of lava bread. The crumbs stuck in the corners of his mouth. He had come a long way since his exploits at the Hogshead tavern; much of his youthful exuberance was suppressed, now replaced by a stern exterior which, in many ways, his experiences in the Black Forest had given rise to.

All the same, he was still hoping to have a swig of ale before going into battle, and he shared those sentiments.

'Aye, and after which I will be happy to fight by your side,' replied Nefanial.

Just like Nikomeades, Tartarus assumed the scroll was where their answers lay. However, unlike Nikomeades, he believed that at some point war would have to be waged to cleanse the land of these beings that had failed it so miserably. It may only be a small dent by way of averting their fate but it was time the forces of good made an impression and sent a message. So as long as his lungs were full and he breathed fresh air, he would strive to make a difference. To succumb to a destiny imposed by others was not an option. Thoughtfully, Tartarus looked at the maker of bread beside him, willing to lay down his life in the defence of his realm, and knew he would do the same. He turned and whispered words of encouragement to Cloud, harnessed to his saddle.

'There, there, he'll be with you soon.'

The rudderless mare, constantly groaning, was missing her rider. Being locked in a cage with the Draconian that had, inadvertently, saved his life was surreal, and for Brun life had just become one big full circle. He was baffled as to why he was actually looking at this beast at all and he was sure Zog would have preferred to meet him on his own terms; it was evident he'd been badly mistreated. He had recognized him almost immediately, even though Draconians were impossible to tell apart. Zog had recognized him also.

'You,' he cried gruffly, before falling back into unconsciousness.

Instantly tinged with guilt, he felt this was his doing and wished he had some food to give this broken beast, who looked like he hadn't been fed in weeks. Captivity was cruelty enough. Was this who Edwin had sent after him, or was it punishment for letting him escape? Nonetheless, he knew what Zog's orders were: to bring him back dead or alive, preferably dead, and some part of the detail would entail his head. How much did this warrior, slumped in the opposite corner, against cold iron bars, actually know? Probably nothing. If the lizard-man had been awake, Brun would have said, 'We keep meeting in unusual places,' even though the first place they met was, essentially, his old barn.

As it was, an exchange of words would have to wait. Although the evidence was irrefutable, Taliesin had refused to release him. Ragnarr, having made enquiries on his behalf, had ridden alongside a few times to keep his spirits up and stated that once Taliesin spoke with Millard, he was certain he'd be freed. Now, housed in a cage on a cart, Brun and Zog had plenty of time to talk while they endured the bumps and ditches together. Zog had complimented him on his ability to remain unseen, while Brun was impressed with Zog's tenacity, having pursued him over two, or was it three, continents. Brun asked him why.

'My dagger,' was the reply.

'Once I'm free you can have it back. You have certainly earned it.'

'What good will it do for me now, Ling?' Zog responded as he turned away. 'No one wants me back, and I've been left here to die.' Brun thought it was only right he knew the truth and shared his suspicions about Edwin and his masters.

'Oi, steady on,' shouted Brun to his jailer as they rode over a hole. Zog laughed.

'Take better care of my friend!' shouted Ragnarr, riding alongside Bollymore and stopping mid-sentence to give the warning.

Since meeting up, Ragnarr and Bollymore had been almost inseparable. Ragnarr got him up to speed with current events as they discussed all manner of things, from Mortfran's orders to Furnus's death. Bollymore shared his knowledge of what minerals he knew the ninety-third element wasn't to be found in and told Ragnarr that, if they could find him, Korrigan was the dwarf to decipher the parchment's text.

'Though he might not choose to help you. I've heard he's fallen in with the wrong crowd.'

'He'll talk,' Ragnarr assured him.

'Now, Algrim's vault ...' Bollymore shook his head. He explained that Gilius was the only man who might be able to shed light on its whereabouts, but that no one had seen the curator in a very long time. 'Your best bet is simply to see where this scroll leads,' advised Bollymore. Reluctantly, Ragnarr nodded. 'I so miss Tuath Farquharson. If it hadn't been for Vilanshaw, I never would have left. Is he still the chieftain?'

'Yes,' replied Ragnarr. Bollymore rolled his eyes.

'I know you haven't asked, but the Kelts will align with us. Don't think Taliesin rude; out of respect, he wants to speak with the clans first. All he need do is convince Aghamore, really. And they're on good terms. Normally, what the circle says, goes, but wearing the crown of Iden puts him above the circle's authority. That crown represents the pledges from all the warring clans, given to Iden at the stone of ages. So, in a weird way we're in uncharted territory,' Bollymore informed him.

Nikomeades, having arrived just in time to prevent the brothers having another heated squabble, got them in a huddle and whispered, with Pippa watching on curiously.

'You must watch your sister, she's very special. When we're not in company I will explain in more detail. Now, I need to speak with Taliesin.' He sat upright, slowed his horse and left their side. Flint and Tarquin shared a glance, having already decided he still needed time to adjust. Behind Rex, Barnaby rode alongside Sid, looking like the odd couple of the group.

'Hey, Flint, we have a lock box of coin. Granted it's back at the encampment, but at least we have something to live for!' shouted Sid with a smile, kicking his heels into his horse.

'True,' replied Flint.

'But if we die, we get nothing,' said Barnaby.

'That's my point,' said Sid, beaming.

'And if we die we'll be heroes,' said Rex reassuringly.

'That's not the point I was making,' said Sid, shaking his head.

'Nothing wrong with being a hero,' mouthed Tarquin.

'I agree,' said Calhoun. 'I think Brun's already a hero.'

'Well said,' added Nefanial. 'Here's to Brun.' The group, raising their weapons, shouted in unison, 'To Brun!'

Before they knew it Taliesin's army was making the long climb up the hill to Lluddrum's encampment. Like Irons Keep, it was a stronghold made from wood and iron. Eldrun rode ahead to inform them of Taliesin's arrival. However, Talabriga's strategic positioning meant it was an act born from custom rather than necessity.

In the shadow of Lluddrum and his son, amidst the wind and snow, stood Druce, waiting to welcome his brother.

'The Asseconian air suits you well,' said Taliesin, embracing his brother.

'Not at all, not at all,' replied Druce. 'I've heard the news. Is it true?'

'See for yourself.' Taliesin pointed to the crown on his head.

'How could I miss that?' replied Druce, stepping back in amazement as his eyes scrutinized his brother's brow. 'Are you sure we can trust these westerners?' he asked discreetly, looking over Taliesin's shoulder at Nikomeades, Tartarus and the rest of the group.

'I do, brother. I believe they speak the truth.'

'Then, today, we plan Iden's revenge,' said Druce, smiling.

'Halwn, take them in. They must be weary.' As ordered Halwn and his Claddagh warriors rode past them, dipping their heads to acknowledge Druce, and Talabriga's chieftain.

'You know Lluddrum, and remember that little runt? Well, look at him now,' said Druce, laughing. Varden bowed, with his right arm across his chest.

'I have news,' Taliesin said solemnly.

'As have I. Plenty has happened in your absence. So if it's bad news, then you can tell me later. Look, Walraversijde and Dunmore, and more arrive each day,' said Druce, pointing.

Down below, on the other side of the hillock, strewn across a plain littered with torch fires ablaze, were pockets of small encampments of different Keltic clans.

'And that's the fool who disobeyed your orders,' continued Druce, turning his attention to a man standing in between two of his warriors.

'A man who disobeys his king had better fight well,' replied Taliesin.

'He does, my king,' interjected Lluddrum. Toran, with his hands bound, looked at the king, then at his own feet.

'Has he been punished?' Taliesin looked for acknowledgement. Druce nodded. 'Then untie him. I'm sure he's learned his lesson. I'll explain later,' he whispered in response to Druce's peculiar expression. Toran nodded, lifting up his wrists, and Varden took it upon himself to do the honours.

'Oh, and before I forget, this is for the leader of my army.' A warrior brought forward a round case and opened it, and Taliesin removed his former crown. 'This is yours, brother.'

Druce, not one for ceremonies, handed the case with crown back to the warrior.

'Put it in my tent, I'll wear it tonight.' He turned to Taliesin with a devious glint.

'And while we're on the matter of bearing gifts, I think you'll find one in that tent. And once you've tidied up,' – he pointed to a suede brown tent within the encampment – 'Lluddrum and I have prepared a banquet in your honour where you can introduce me to your friends. Now, where's that mighty fox?' Taliesin told Calhoun to step forward. 'You're coming with me,' Druce said loudly. 'A warrior of your calibre deserves a drink. I hope you like sylvestris wine and Keltic ale?'

'I do,' replied Calhoun, loving his new-found state of notoriety. His response brought warm smiles to faces that were stiff from the conditions, as the two proudly entered Talabriga.

'Varden, take care of our king's friends,' ordered Lluddrum.

'Of course, father.'

'Bollymore, we'll speak before the banquet,' said Taliesin, remounting his horse and riding through the gates, accompanied by his guards. He dismounted at the tent Druce had pointed out, and peered inside.

'Aghamore,' he said, surprised. 'And who is this?'
'The man we've been searching for. Who else?'
'You didn't?' The tent-flap entrance closed behind him.

Not long afterwards, Crofton, shell-shocked, staggered away from the tent. Dazed and confused, with tears streaming down his face, he wandered aimlessly in the snowball the time he'd waited, hoping she'd return to the woman he'd first met, was all for nought. He felt as though the sky had fallen from a great height, crushing his ability to think clearly. So much so, he just wanted the bottomless pit to open up and swallow him whole. He loosened his tunic to lessen the burden on an inflamed chest. He was a baron, and yet he had never felt so alone. He had to urge himself to breathe, while he questioned his beliefs. All the while, one word, 'why', reverberated around his mind, seemingly elevating her infidelity and giving rise to further revulsion. He staggered a few more paces, looking for a quiet spot, and vomited. Leaning forward, he wiped his lips and recoiled. It was revolting. How could she? How *dare* she? He took a deep breath. A mind trapped in the recesses of reason imploded and he fell to his knees. Dismay turned to anger. Crofton, with burning fists buried in snow, seethed. She'd never loved him, not even at the beginning, not even for a moment. No words could fill that void. In disbelief he shook his head. It had been a cruel plot, a cruel twisted plot, to kill off his bloodline, a bloodline of kings as far back as memory served. There was one thing he was sure of – apart from never wanting to set eyes on her again –this would mean war. He'd feed Syracuse Bargelmir his wolf's bane personally, or run a lance through him, whichever came first. As for Kennice ... His body jerked and he coughed up the bile lining his stomach. He wasn't free from her chains just yet. Suddenly, hearing footsteps, he looked up. Standing in the snow, with her beautiful flowing locks being blown by a gust of wind, was Lyra. Although they couldn't see him, they heard the noise. Taliesin went to follow.

'Leave him be. The only thing that can heal a man's soul in moments like these is the rush of wind against your skin, and time to think. You know this.'

Aghamore looked at Taliesin who, in turn, nodded. 'You've just told him his wife is with child by Baron Syracuse of Daginhale and that she's been plotting his death for some time. No man should have to suffer such indignation,' continued Aghamore with a shake of his head. 'You need to get ready for your banquet and, now you've heard what he said, free the blacksmith.' Aghamore produced a tight smile. 'If you want to keep our new friends on side, I think you should. He's suffered long enough.'

'As always, Aghamore, your words are wise. Of course, I will.' Taliesin pulled a face. 'I could do without this banquet, mind you, but I expect they'll want to see Iden's crown,' he said, exhausted, just wanting a good night's rest.

'A king's duty, Taliesin. Druce's heart is in the right place,' replied Aghamore, amused. Then, on a serious note, placing his hands on Taliesin's upper arms, he said, 'Mark my words, that crown wanted to be found. It's a good omen; use it wisely. I'll wait for Crofton here.' Taliesin nodded and left.

*

'A king's banquet? I've got nothing to wear!' cried Pippa excitedly, clapping her hands, setting Angus on edge.

'We wear what we wear,' replied Ragnarr, his tone flat.

'Just wear Gunn-Hilda's thingamajig,' suggested Reece.

'I'm not wearing that. If I have to wear that I'm not going,' she replied stubbornly. Then, right on cue, under a bright blue moon and star laden sky, a pretty Keltic maiden, standing near to Tartarus, appeared at the entrance.

'I've been told you have a little girl who needs to get ready for the banquet.' Pippa looked up.

'That's me!'

'Steady on there, Pip,' said Tarquin.

'Can I bring Angus?' she asked, clicking her fingers for him to get up.

'No, they might eat him,' said Ragnarr, teasing her. Pippa pulled a face.

'Ragnarr, behave,' Nikomeades warned him. 'This is neither the time nor the place.' He turned to Flint. 'I think you'd better go too.'

Flint was up in a flash. He didn't need telling twice. The lady about to escort his sister had already caught his eye.

'Well, it's nice for some,' observed Sid.

'Very,' said Barnaby, smiling. 'Wake me when it's time for the banquet.' He closed his eyes, his arms folded.

'That boy could sleep through a storm,' said Nefanial, taking off his boots.

'What's that smell?' enquired Sid, waving his hand in front of his nose.

'I think this tent is next to a pigpen,' replied Rex. Sid raised an eyebrow.

'And where's Cal? Shouldn't he be back by now?'

'He's got his own tent,' answered Reece.

'He's got his own tent!' cried Sid, as though he was in need of reminding.

'Inconspicuous, Sidney Barbuckle, that's what we need to be. Have you learned nothing? The beings that will pursue us, once it is known we have this' –
Nikomeades spoke through gritted teeth, waving the scroll – 'will be more devious than you can imagine, and won't stop until they've carried out their master's bidding. Our only chance of survival is written on this parchment. And a raging war may be the only diversion we have at our disposal, to turn our enemies' eye and achieve our goals. That is why I'm here. You? You're free to leave anytime.' Nikomeades' outburst caught them all by surprise.

'He's right, Sid. What are you complaining about? It's spacious enough in here, and we weren't even expected,' said Daniel, defusing the tension.

'Can't you be still, lad,' chipped in Rex. Sid, with a face like a slapped arse, sat back down.

Tartarus wasn't paying attention to their bickering. Sitting at the entrance, looking up at a night sky, he watched the footprint of a falling star shed light on a white undulating blank canvas. Momentarily distracted, he acknowledged Flint and Pippa's departure by dipping his head. He was as mentally drained as the rest of them and, behind sore eyelids, he dared to dream as a cold gust brushed his skin. White winters were virtually unheard of in Ganesha, where the weather rarely varied so dramatically, and in a Keltic fortress, comforted by the bosom of war, for some reason, snow had a calming influence on Tartarus. He marvelled at its effect on the landscape and a challenging frontier did not detract from the serenity, similar to that found in Oaken-

Dale at nights though, admittedly, he could do without the climate's bite. He would have gladly made his excuses and given the banquet a wide berth if Nikomeades hadn't stressed the fact that Kelts viewed this type of gathering as an informal opportunity to counsel and petition allies which, in Keltic law, was given high credence. A pact was a mark on a parchment, whereas your word was your bond. If their plan was to succeed they needed the southern realm to be fighting on two fronts and this was their best, and last, chance of getting the Kelts on-side.

Suddenly, Tartarus was startled by someone approaching from his right. A man wearing a white tunic and black waistcoat stumbled past. Having never met the man before, Tartarus paid him no heed, even when he saw him being sick.

'Better stay away from the broth,' he thought, amused by the anecdote. A woman with blonde hair, wearing a red velvet dress with an embroidered corset, approached the man. By this time, Tartarus's mind was elsewhere, his chin resting against his chest. In another part of Talabriga, Taliesin, accompanied by three guards, was marching at pace.

'Free him,' he ordered a Kelt. The guard was sitting in a chair under a large canopy that housed men in cages. The jailer, having drunk too much, laboured to his feet and burped.

'Now would be a good time,' urged Taliesin impatiently. Sluggishly, the jailer lifted his head.

'And who might you b–?' The jailer suddenly recognized Taliesin and nearly choked. 'Yes, my king,' he said, while fumbling with a bulky, cast-iron key holder hanging from his thick leather belt. He walked promptly over to Brun's cage.

'Come on you, get up,' ordered the jailer.

'Having spoken with Baron Crofton Abbehale, you're free to go,' said Taliesin. 'In fact, he'd like to thank you in person for saving his life. If it hadn't been for your action this plot may never have come to light.'

'That wasn't me.' Brun was no liar. 'It was Tartarus who killed Bowen, not me, and Sid found the note.'

'I admire your honesty but you do yourself a disservice. Without Edwin's message, war may well have still been in doubt, and your life in jeopardy. As it is, these southern barons won't know what hit them.' He then fell silent. It was as though he wanted to say more but couldn't.

'What about him?' asked Brun, looking at the cage next to his.

'What about him?' asked Taliesin. The jailer, opening his gate, urged him to come out.

'I want you to free him.'

'Can he be trusted?' Taliesin asked.

'I think he can,' replied Brun, ducking to get out.

'Well, on your head be it. Get him up.' The jailer banged on Zog's cage. 'Hear my words, beast-man. You either fight for a just cause or die by my sword: the choice is yours.' Taliesin looked into Zog's eyes.

'I'll fight,' replied Zog, just glad of an opportunity to wreak havoc on those who had left him to die.

'Good.' Taliesin turned to one of his guards. 'Take him and get him cleaned up, and find him a bed for tonight.' He then turned to Brun. 'You, you're coming with me.'

'I'll never call you Ling again,' said Zog over his shoulder as he was led away.

In the encampment, carts and wagons, converted into homes, sat alongside large tents erected to accommodate the influx of visitors. With war brewing Lluddrum's warriors, under Druce's direction, had been busy.

'Your friends are over there, in that tent,' said Taliesin, pointing. Brun nodded, but wondered how he could tell the tents apart, they all looked so alike. However, he then saw Tartarus sitting by its entrance and presumed Taliesin had too.

'Crofton had asked me to release Zog too, but now you have his arm, this is good; he knows how the enemy thinks and in the coming days his advice could prove invaluable, if he is proven trustworthy,' whispered Taliesin. 'And before I forget, please tell Aghamore I expect the dwarf to address the clans present at the banquet. And get to the wash wagon. You smell,' he concluded.

'Now, isn't that the truth,' thought Brun, walking towards the tent. 'Wake up,' he said to Tartarus as he approached. 'I think you nodded off.' He shook him by the shoulder. 'Tartarus, wake up.' His words were greeted with a large yawn and a stretch. 'It's nearly time for that banquet their king wants us to attend.'

'Brun!' Tartarus hurried to his feet and gave him a hug, only to instantly jump back. 'Yuk!'

'I know,' said Brun.

Groups from the smaller encampment started to arrive. All warriors of note had heard Taliesin's calling, from the great to the good. They were all present to pay homage to the bearer of Iden's crown. A long banqueting table, weighed down with an assortment of food one could only hope to wish for, greeted guests eager to set eyes on their king's crown. Lluddrum's banqueting hall wasn't, strictly, a hall at all.

The massive tent, centred on a tall maypole linked to four more of similar height, entombed by coarse linen, was used for a variety of activities. To the left of the main seating area a bard conducted proceedings. Musicians were playing hazy Keltic melodies on a harp, fiddle, bagpipe and pibgorn, which was a two-ended horn carved from bone. Nikomeades walked into the crowded space with his group in tow.

Flint and Pippa were already seated, as was Calhoun, though he was sitting at the head table, left of Druce, in between Bollymore and Aghamore. Ronan marshalled them to their seats. The warmth within the tent was a welcome contrast to the cold, dense air they were now acclimatized to. Tartarus's trepidation turned to surprise when he found it wasn't filled with the burly, heavily armed men he had been half expecting. Apart from the guards posted at the entrances, many were in evening wear and were mingling among well-dressed women. Some still wore scabbards with protruding sword hilts. Before they could settle Lluddrum stood up.

'Friends, I would like to welcome you all to my humble Crannog, in honour of Taliesin.'

'Humble, Lluddrum?' shouted a warrior from the seafaring clan of Walraversijde. The chieftain smiled, acknowledging the lavish feast on display.

'The king,' he announced, and everyone got to their feet. Taliesin, wearing the plain gold crown and a tartan cloak with his clan's colours of black, green and yellow, entered. He was led in by a maiden and made his way to his seat, in between Druce and Lluddrum, to cries of, 'Long live the king! Long live Taliesin!'

'This is a great day for those who are Kelts. I can see the clans from Glandomirum, Asseconia and Brigantia all here as one. You represent the best of us and your presence is a mark of our resolve. But this is who we should thank for bringing us closer together: Calhoun the fox, stand up,' ordered Taliesin. Calhoun, wearing exactly the same tartan colours, stood up. 'He and his friends fought off a spider witch to return Iden's crown to us.'

'The fox, the fox, the fox!' rang out as fists banged on the banqueting table.

'Friends, I know we're here to celebrate but, before the merriment begins and we can enjoy this fabulous feast Lluddrum has laid on, I would have this dwarf speak to us. His is a tale we all must hear,' he said solemnly.

Ragnarr relayed the story of his quest. There was silence in the room.

'Who do these southern scum think they are?' said a warrior, unable to contain himself. His outcry received a pat on the back.

'One question. Are we sure it is the southern rulers that are our enemies?' asked Druce. Ragnarr explained that the substance was highly toxic and that small villages seemed to disappear from the landscape without a trace, their villagers never to be seen again.

'This has only happened on southern soil or lands they've conquered. We believe they use an extract from the devil's trumpet, which induces a sleep-like state that allows them to mine without fear of death, though eventually they succumb to kromillium's poisonous affect.' The dwarf paused. 'The south and west have been heavily mined, that speaks for itself.' Ragnarr said nothing of his emotional attachment to the tale. Druce nodded, as did Aghamore.

'I have heard yarns of Nzambie roaming the coastal villages off the southern realm's coast,' said the warrior from Walraversijde.

'Aye, when they're close to death and of no more use, they release them to roam. From what I hear there's no known cure,' added Ragnarr.

'I've heard enough.' Taliesin stood. 'Are we with these dwarves or not?'

'Yes!' came the cry, as if shouted with one voice.

It was decided beforehand that the scroll would not be mentioned in public just in case of spies in their midst. Nevertheless the outcome was a favourable one and, unbeknown to all, Taliesin had already been given Aghamore's blessing.

'Now, let us feast,' he declared, and with the opening of ale barrels and the filling of goblets with wine, they did just that.

'At last,' commented Bollymore, reaching for a turkey drumstick. Halfway through the proceedings a Kelt, in ceremonial garb, banged a large gong. Then Lluddrum, standing up, announced, 'In Taliesin's honour we've arranged a little light entertainment.' He looked at the king and smiled. As the spinning board was brought in Taliesin leaned forward.

'I hear you're good at arrows, young elf?' he teased.

'Who told you that?' replied Tartarus. Taliesin looked at Bollymore who, in turn, looked at Ragnarr.

'I saw you playing it at that tavern, remember?' he said, shrugging. 'I told him if ever there was an elf to bet on, that elf wasn't you. Well, you can't give away trade secrets; you don't know when they will come in handy,' he said with a straight face. The board was larger in diameter than an arrows board and instead of spears or arrows, a Kelt walked in with an unusually high number of throwing axes attached to his belt. Then, with a maiden strapped to it, the board was spun at a furious rate of knots. Blindfolded, he began to throw axes, one after another. The audience was impressed, and showed it. The woman was spinning so fast it was impossible to tell her legs from her arms. At times heads turned away, only to return their gaze in awe at his precision. No one noticed that the three small boxes, laid in a row on the ground as part of the first act, were left as the girl, unmarked, and the board were led away. The crowd was in raptures.

A girl started climbing drapes attached to the roof girders when, slowly, the boxes beneath began to be opened from within by a hand. Then an elegant arm, shoulder and part of the neck were seen. To gasps of amazement three female contortionists exited the boxes while a colourfully dressed man played a furry of notes on a flute, rather like that of a snake charmer. The performers formed unnatural angles with their bodies as the three combined to make vivid images, even getting to their feet to scratch their own noses and balancing vases and sharp weaponry. They finished off by swallowing flaming swords up to the hilt while the young girl, using the two suspended drapes, made death-defying spins with a falling summersault.

'So, these are wonders we've been missing out on, and you said it wasn't a good idea to leave home,' said Flint. Tarquin smiled, totally enthralled. Then Lluddrum clapped his hands and, as the contortionists left, Keltic river dancers took centre stage. The bard changed his tempo and others joined in by clapping their hands.

'Isn't that the girl you and Pippa went with?' asked Tarquin. Flint nodded as she gave him a wink, which he returned.

'That's Verity,' he said with a big broad smile.

'Oh, Flint,' responded Pippa, slapping her forehead while Angus barked lightly. The group laughed.

Dawn was approaching when Tartarus fell asleep on Brun in his makeshift bed, too drunk to be bothered. He slept with his head at one end while Brun's was at the other. The cock's crow, signifying a brand new day, was not a welcome sound. Those occupying Tartarus's tent were suffering from the ill effects of an evening of drinking into the small hours. With the gathering of forces, it was only a matter of time before a scout was sent out by Millard to investigate. That scout came in the form of the raven.

'A royal rider approaches!' shouted a lookout, as her unmistakable black cloak came into view, glistening under a crisp sun, floating from her back. The rider's eyes opened wide as she approached.

'You!' she exclaimed. 'They said you were dead.' Crofton brought her horse to a standstill.

'I didn't think you were one for rumours, Alexandra,' he said, stroking her horse's mane.

'I'm not,' she replied cheekily.

'Well, as you can see, I'm fine although, admittedly, I've lost a bit of weight.' He looked down at his waist proudly, as though he were leaner. 'How was your journey in?'

'Treacherous,' replied Alexandra. 'In places the snow has turned to ice.'

A stableman took her horse, leading it away by its bridle once she had dismounted. By late morning Talabriga was normally up and running but, due to the banquet overrunning, hangovers were plentiful.

'Is it usually as busy as this?' asked Alexandra sarcastically, baffled at the lack of bodies.

'I wouldn't know. I haven't been here that long. But where are my manners? You must be hungry and thirsty. Come, you can wait in my tent while I prepare a message for Millard. I presume he sent you?'

'He did. As we speak, he is preparing to meet the Kelts in battle while Brandenburg and Bargelmir ride to Glen-Neath to claim your title.'

'I wish we were meeting in better circumstances. It seems you've had your hands full.'

'It pays well, baron.' She smiled, then her features softened and, in the tone of a concerned friend, she whispered, 'Come, we need to talk.' Crofton led her to his tent.

A little while later Crofton arranged an impromptu gathering at the banqueting hall. In attendance were the baron, Taliesin, Druce, Bollymore, Nikomeades, Ragnarr, Nefanial and Calhoun.

'We just have to let him know I'm alive,' Crofton stated confrontationally.

'That may not be enough.' Taliesin shook his head. 'We must prevent them from laying claim to your land and, with that, control of your army. If that happens it would be difficult to support you avowedly,' he said. Druce nodded.

'My brother's right. Your north gate is almost impregnable. Believe me, we've checked, and if that happens then we've already failed. Laying siege will just buy them time, time we don't have.'

'I understand his reasoning, but men must see their general.'

'I couldn't agree more, and they will. However, if Syracuse knows you're aware of his plot, this could change things. His army alone outnumbers yours, and the west will need your leadership in the coming days; this war will not be short,' forewarned Taliesin.

'Don't I know it!' Crofton pressed his palms against the banqueting table of veneered wood and looked at the blank parchment, still undecided on what to write.

'The day we ride against them, from all accounts, is the day we start the third Great War. Even more so than its predecessors, this one we must win.'

'Well then, you've heard my counsel. He is a man of peace, not unlike your clergymen, and it makes perfect sense.'

'And I can take a few of my men and inform the keep's chieftain of our plan. I will not leave them in the dark when I can prevent loss of life,' said Nefanial. Taliesin looked at Calhoun.

'What does the fox have to say?' he asked, eager to hear the young hero's words.

'I agree with both of you,' replied Calhoun cautiously. Nikomeades nodded.

'As do I. Few among us have felt the full brunt of the Autocrat's armies. I have and, that day, I lost most of my friends.' He stressed the enormity of their task, and saw it sink in as a picture formed in their minds. 'Taliesin's plan is simple and its simplicity makes it more effective. Others will join our ranks but right now our armies are too small to win without surprise and targeted attacks.' Taliesin remained passive at the acknowledgement; his army wasn't small. 'Although our paths may seem different,' continued Nikomeades, 'our goals are one and the same. No one has exclusivity on intention or valour; to prevail we must pool our resources and, in that regard, my dwarfish friend here speaks the truth. We need to form an alliance with such defiance that we will bring hope where before there was none.'

'Shake their very fabric is more like it,' added Ragnarr, his elbows resting on his war hammer.

'And we must build it quickly,' Nikomeades concluded.

Ragnarr, standing next the wizard, still a little the worse for wear, nodded.

'Edwin must be made to believe he has awoken a hornets' nest, to not return and quell our fires, and keep his forces fragmented,' added Taliesin.

'I can get word to Mortfran to do just that,' said Tumbleweed.

'But can we rely on the east? If they do not fight this will be the shortest war in history, not to mention what the swarm will do when the Autocrat gets wind of our uprising,' said Crofton.

'They will be chasing us once he gets word of my presence, I assure you,' said Nikomeades, 'and with a horde the size Tartarus described, the Alfari will have been routed, though I still have my doubts; the Alfari are, indeed, well-trained fighters. In any case, they would have regrouped at Galatea. Remember, the city still possesses a gauntlet.'

'I like your candour, Nikomeades. And, yes, I was told there were more of you. Where is this elf and the blacksmith, Brun? I haven't thanked him yet,' asked Crofton.

'They're still sleeping,' answered Ragnarr.

'At this time?' Crofton asked, seemingly appalled.

'You weren't at the banquet then?' asked Nefanial.

'Did you mention Brun to Alexandra?'

'I had to. She's a friend and if we want to clear his name it was the only sensible course of action, or your brother-in-law will be a wanted man everywhere he steps.

She said she needs proof, which I said I'd give her when I'm back in my castle.' With it decided that Taliesin's plan had more chance of success than the others discussed, Crofton dipped his quill in ink then, placing his hand over the parchment, narrated the words.

Meanwhile Tarquin, in a panic, was looking for Flint. Having searched everywhere, and with the weather the way it was, he was worried. He was on his way to the only place he hadn't checked. Knowing Flint, he was probably eavesdropping and he would arrive just in time to prevent his brother causing mischief, or so he thought. Distracted, he ran straight into Alexandra waiting outside the banqueting hall.

She looked down at the boy warrior, with his oddly matched armour, sitting on the ground in front of her.

'You're not from around here?' she asked curiously. He didn't seem to be a Kelt; they had a battle-hardened natural ruggedness. This young man, though handsome, looked wet behind the ears.

'How can you tell?' he asked, hoping she'd noticed something distinguished about him.

'You're too weak to be a Kelt.'

'I'll have you know I was brought up never to hit a lady,' he replied, vexed.

'Who said I was a lady?' Alexandra's expression teased.

'You know what I mean.' Alexandra nodded, amused. 'Well, what I was trying to say was that's the reason I'm down here ...Oh, forget it, I give up.' Tarquin shook his head, confused. 'I'm looking for my brother. Dark hair, so high. Have you seen him?' he asked, indicating Flint's height with his hands.

'Is that him?' she asked, noticing a lad, fitting the description, clambering out of a caravan.

Tarquin, figuratively speaking, broke his neck to see Flint standing on the steps, getting a farewell kiss, while pulling up his britches. As he called out to him, Flint ran off like his very life depended upon it, leaving Verity looking as if she done something wrong.

'He's got away with the ladies, then.' Alexandra giggled as she watched Flint attempt to tighten his britches and take a tumble in the snow.

'It's our first time away from home,' Tarquin whispered, trying to alleviate his embarrassment.

'How cute,' thought Alexandra as she helped him up. He felt her strength through gloved hands, and her facial beauty stretched the boundaries of his comprehension, but far from rendering him speechless, Tarquin found he was jabbering.

'Look, I'm here on important business, but it was nice meeting you.' Fun-time was over. He didn't hear her.

'What's your name?'

'Alexandra.'

'Mine's Tarquin, and if you don't mind my asking, what do you do for a living?'
he blurted out, as his mind raced for something to say. He knew he had chosen poorly. 'It's only that … you look like a merchant, and I'm here on important business too,' he boasted.

'Well, don't let me keep you from your important business, master Tarquin.' She smiled, knowing her role meant she'd probably never meet him again, but you never know. He was rather sweet, especially his naivety and the fact that he didn't know who she was. This took some beating and, actually, it was a turn-on. His downside was that he was slightly ham-fisted and Alexandra's preferred type, with no exception, was a man's man, which they needed to be to handle her.

When Tarquin finally caught up with Flint, he explained that he had thought Tarquin was a peeved previous boyfriend, a warrior from the encampment named Toran, who had fallen out of favour.

'Was he at the banquet?'

'No, she would have said.' Then Flint went over his evening, after he had left them at the banquet. Tarquin was too busy thinking about another 'not a lady'. Flint tapped him.

'Where's Pippa?'

'Here,' she answered, popping her head through the entrance. 'I was just taking Angus for a run. Why, what do you want?' Then she looked at Tartarus and Brun, still fast asleep. 'Don't you think they've slept long enough?'

Outside, the banqueting hall's entrance flapped shut behind Crofton, who emerged with a rolled parchment in hand.

'It is done. This is my reply.' He reached out his arm. 'Guard it well.'

'With my life,' replied Alexandra, taking possession and sliding it into her leather-bound tube.

'I have bad news. We have decided that their druid will go back with you, as a show of good faith.'

'What, are you crazy?' Alexandra gave him a tetchy look, as she fastened its buckled lock. 'You jest in poor taste. You know I ride alone.'

'These are testy times. If you were to return without me, Millard may march my army onto Keltic soil and this would breach a condition in the treaty I have lent my seal to.

'I will not ride back with anyone. I am a royal rider: we ride alone.'

'I know, Alexandra, but if Millard thinks this to be a ploy the consequences will be dire.'

'Your message will be fine. Royal riders have diplomatic immunity,' retorted Alexandra, clearly annoyed.

'Silvanus, I note, did not stand by those high standards. Word spreads, and mud sticks.'

'Point taken, baron, though I still have reservations. I could be stripped of my commission if it be seen that I'm one to take sides.'

'You chose a side a long time ago.'

'I know,' replied Alexandra. 'That's what I'm afraid of.'

'Anyway, isn't preventing wars and saving lives what you do?' Alexandra took a moment before she mouthed a response.

Taliesin was having the same difficulties convincing Aghamore.

'She won't take you both. We're going to have a hard enough time persuading her to take you, and you won't go unless with guards.' Aghamore nodded. 'Yet, for all her charms, Lyra's no guard, Aghamore.'

'Your plan is perfect: just one flaw,' said Aghamore.

'And what's that?'

'I will not leave my daughter here. Now, out the way.' He moved Taliesin slightly to the left with his arm then, agile for a man of his age, reached down behind him to pick up an empty sack. 'Give me a hand.' Taliesin held the bag open while Aghamore placed provisions inside for the journey. 'Listen here, Taliesin, I respect you greatly but if you were a snowball you would have a better chance in inferno. I'll not leave my daughter with wanton men. Lyra.'

'Yes, father.'
'Come and help me pack. You're coming too.'

Taliesin looked up at the tent's roof; the best part was that he hadn't yet told him who his escorts were to be. Having decided that Nefanial would be Aghamore's escort, Reece, Daniel, Sidney and Barnaby were picked to accompany him. Sid had wanted assurances that his wealth would be safe, as he seemed to be travelling further and further away from where it lay. The rest of them were at ease with his decision; Nefanial hadn't led them astray yet. Even though they thought it was set in stone that they would all ride to Glen-Neath together, they had spent enough time around the baker to know that plans could change at a moment's notice. After hugs and farewells they were ready. So, with both Aghamore and Alexandra still remonstrative at the decision, the group were waved through the gate.

'Did you see his face when you told him the baker was his escort?' Druce asked Taliesin.

'Well, did you see hers when I told her they were his guards and the girl was his servant?' responded Crofton. The three of them were in stitches while Tarquin, still gawking, needed Flint to help him lift up his chin.

'Thought she was a merchant,' he murmured. Nikomeades pulled Tartarus to one side.

'Taliesin's mens' bravado and Crofton's mens' liberation, after years of oppression, does not make the perfect broth. Compromises will have to be made, on both sides, in the coming days. They will need our guidance. Now, we must prepare for war.'

*

'I'll do the talking,' instructed Alexandra instinctively. Nefanial gave her a peculiar look, as did Sid. The two-day ride, that quickly became four, felt more like six. Aghamore was just glad he had packed provisions for a longer trip, aware of the time snowfall could put on a man's journey. Even so, Glen-Neath was a welcome sight for a man eager to put his feet up and warm his old bones in front of a slow-burning fire, which was what Taliesin had promised. So why had the baker gone and opened his trap? That was a question with no easy answer for the circle's leader, who was used to men following orders. Shaking his head, he looked at his daughter who sat across from him in a gatehouse cell, below ground. The cell was cold and there was an annoying, endless, dripping drone that would be the death of him. Anu, give him strength. He could ring Taliesin's neck. Guards, indeed! The royal rider told him that she would do the talking, but had the baker listened? No. He had to open his big mouth and tell them that he was from Irons Keep and needed to speak with his chieftain, a man named Gwillym. The last words Aghamore remembered hearing were, 'Gwillym's a wanted man and westerners like you, on Keltic soil ... seems fishy to me. Seize them, I think they're spies. Someone get the captain. He's with Lucian. 'Before he could protest his innocence, he was being led down stairs, shouting, 'But I don't know these vagabonds!'

Alexandra, on the other hand, was immediately escorted, under armed guard, to the castle grounds and was, no doubt, now in the comfort and warmth he'd been expecting. He pondered her enviously. Suddenly, the cell door opened and a guard said, 'You two, follow me.'

Led by Crofton's footman, Eric, and four guards, Alexandra entered the stateroom.

'She was with six others, sir.'

'Are you sure? Riders travel alone.' Millard looked at Alexandra curiously as the warrior nodded. 'Where's Lucian?'

'With the prisoners and our captain,' replied the warrior.

'Can you explain this?' asked Millard, tilting his head.

'I don't think she can,' remarked Wilfred. Alexandra returned his words with a look of disgust.

'Crofton–'

'The baron's alive?' interrupted the man-at-arms.

'Yes, Wilfred. It seems you were mistaken to have left him for dead,' she replied with immense satisfaction. 'And, as I was saying, he needs them to speak with a chieftain named Gwillym. The druid is here so that you believe what is written in his message.'

'I trust your word,' Millard replied, confused.

'I told him you would.'

'So where is he then?'

'You need to read this.' Alexandra handed over the leather canister. Millard looked up at Aoibhe as he unbound the buckle.

'You can finish up later.' She curtsied and left with Alexandra's armed escort.

'Eric, wait outside. Wilfred, stay.'

However, as he read the message it became clear why the druid's presence was needed. Even if it was written in the baron's handwriting, spoken in his own tongue, Millard was still having a hard time digesting his orders. He lifted up his arm.

'Release her friends immediately.' Wilfred went to object. 'Just do it,' said Millard, burying his head in the parchment. Meticulously, Taliesin had left nothing to chance and to that end, in part, though ingenious, it was cold and calculating. The captain, continually shaking his head, took his time reading it, memorizing the timing of each command. When Millard got to the bottom of the parchment he was up on his feet.

'Eric,' he shouted, leaving the parchment on the marble table for a moment as he turned towards the door. Alexandra could read the words, 'I declared war.' Her eyes opened wide. Before she could read more, Millard quickly picked it up and, with his body blocking her view, burned its edges by candle flame and then threw it in the fireplace. However, unless her eyes were deceiving her, she had just seen two pieces of parchment. Vellum was translucent and she could see another message underneath. But he had only burned one.

'What is going on?' thought Alexandra, puzzled.

'Here's your fee.' He placed two large pouches, filled with coins, on the marble table, as Eric entered.

'I don't have to check the colour, do I?' she asked accusingly. Millard smiled.

'I still may have need of your services.' She picked up the pouches. 'I'm sorry about your mistreatment.'

'And so you should be.' As Alexandra was leaving, she overheard Millard say to Eric, 'We need to send a scout to Syracuse immediately, and get the southgates' captain here now.'

After moons of hearing nothing, Kennice was shocked at the news that her husband, though badly injured, was actually alive and, in about four or five days, would be well enough to travel. Millard was to continue raising an army in readiness, just in case the Kelts reneged on their agreement. Crofton's message was quite explicit: Kennice was to be fed this false information and, on the third day, which should have given Millard enough time to prepare, he was to go through a southerner known to have Isadora's ear, and inform him that the Keltic druid at Glen-Neath was awaiting Crofton's arrival to sign a pact on the Keltic king's behalf. This was to be a treaty which would ratify Crofton's giving Taliesin permission to use the fort as a base, signifying that a Keltic invasion was imminent, as was a shift in the balance of power if Crofton was allowed to bolster his army with a limitless number of men. Her husband, having declared war on the south, was trying to strategically orchestrate an attack on Abbehale and Daginhale, and could not be as injured as was first thought. No spy worth their pinch of salt could sit on such information and when Taliesin had devised the plan, that is what he had been counting on. So once it reached Kennice, they knew their intent would be met.

'A surprise attack on the barons.' No sooner had she uttered the words, than Kennice's brain went into overdrive. She ordered her chambermaid to go and fetch Wilfred. However, it was Millard who knocked on her door a little while later.

'I've received some disturbing news. Can I read my husband's message?'

'It's been sent to Syracuse,' he replied sympathetically. 'Those were your husband's instructions.'

'So who brought you the message?'

'A royal rider.'

'Did the messenger return with anyone?'

'Yes, with a Druid.'

So it was true. She paused, choosing her next words carefully.

'I am with child and was saving this surprise for my husband, but war is no place to bring up an infant and, with others saying Glen-Neath is about to be overrun by Kelts, I don't know what to think. Is my husband alive or not?'

'He is, baroness.'

'Then where is he?' she sobbed, releasing fake tears.

'There's no need to be fearful. Syracuse's encampment is not far from here if we need reinforcements. And Brandenburg has sent word he'll arrive within a day or so. Once the north gate is closed an army of ten thousand men could not penetrate her or vault her walls. They say that when you're with child your mind plays tricks on you. We'll be fine.'

Although her facial expression stayed the same, Kennice was watching his intently for that sign that indicated he was lying. No twitching eye, no ungainly perspiration, and no telltale movement. Kennice had always known Millard was a good liar, though he couldn't hide the fact that he despised her. Trying to be nice when, normally, he would avoid her was a dead giveaway. Now Kennice knew she needed to get out, if only to warn Syracuse that if he took Glen-Neath now it would put a nail in the coffin of Crofton's plans and prevent the Kelts from getting in.

'I've heard too many rumours to feel truly safe here and, in all honesty Millard, I can't stay here a moment longer. I will not put the health of my unborn child at risk. Isadora is leaving and I plan to ride with her to my father's keep in Angleshore, until it is safe to return or until Crofton calls for me.'

'Very well, if you must. I'll arrange a carriage but in this weather I would not advise it.'

'Your advice has been noted.' She closed the door, pressing her back against the hard wood and cast-iron rivets. Her heart was beating so hard she felt dizzy. She looked at the window with its tapestry curtain slightly ajar. Looking out onto the balcony, her eyes ventured further afield. For all Kennice's scheming, her future lay elsewhere.

'Why else would he declare war, unless …?' Her words trailed off as she still tried to deny the fact her secret was out.

'Unless what?' pressed Isadora.

'Unless he knows about me and Syracuse.' Then she thought about what she was saying: that was impossible. For a moment her frantic panic, which had been gathering momentum, stopped.

'Is that what Wilfred said?' asked Isadora.

'No, it was Millard, and it's what he didn't say that alarmed me.'

'And what was that?'

'When Crofton would be back. Put those in there.' She threw a couple of items of clothing across the room.

'How reliable is your source?'

'Very,' replied Isadora.

Just like clockwork, Eric had spoken to a man at the tavern, a merchant who was known to have Isadora's ear. Over a large tankard of mead Eric had spun him a sad tale about how his leader's reckless actions would put lives at risk and, just like Geneshian whispers, it found its way into Kennice's chamber. She didn't know how he knew, but he knew: she was sure of it. It was the only logical conclusion she could come up with, in a short space of time, that made any sense. She was aware of his resentment of the west's occupation, but surely that wasn't enough to tip him over the edge? She looked at her dithering cousin, packing at a snail's pace.

'Hurry up! We're leaving!' she screamed.

Taliesin, in his wisdom, was right. When word spread that the Kelts were taking over Glen-Neath, the southerners within left without a fuss; a southerner would rather be dead than accept Keltic authority. In among the mass of heads leaving were Isadora and Kennice, in a horse-drawn carriage, riding through a now-deserted market place to the outer wall gatehouse and the plains beyond. As the outer gate creaked shut behind the last of them, in the confusion, no one observed the hooded pilgrims entering the gatehouse, travelling in the opposite direction. However, if someone had cared to oppose their entry they would have noticed that, under dull brown caparisons, they had well-groomed destrier war horses in tow.

Stockpiles of encased elm oil were rolled out ready to be launched by strategically positioned trebuchets; anything, in any direction, within six hundred yards of the outer castle wall was vulnerable. So, needless to say, when Branic, the barbican captain, greeted Tempest, son of one of the nine remaining landowners of Damgarden, phase two of Taliesin's plan was already underway. The man, in his twenties, accompanied by eight others, briefly stopped and nodded while making the sign of peace before continuing up the cobbled path to southgate.

*

A female blackbird, with her protruding yellow beak, brown feathers and speckled breast, was chirping for her mate, but abruptly stopped when a twirling squall of air ripped a rime-covered leaf from a bare branch beneath her. Violently removed from its serenity, ignorant to the turmoil about to unfold, it floated down, eventually falling harmlessly in a downward spiral until it lay upon the ground, only to be trampled by the metal-rimmed wheels of a wooden wagon. A podgy bullmastiff, plodding in the snow contentedly and watching his master's every move, gathered the crumpled leaf in his mouth. Brandenburg's roofless red carriage, with gold trimmings, was pulled along by four Palomino thoroughbreds, each harnessed with red leather trappings who, under the driver's arbitrary whip, crushed a path through the Damgarden wilds, riding in tandem behind the troops.

The baron had only one thing on his mind as Glen-Neath came into view: mines. In all but name, Edwin had promised him the west and, with Crofton gone, its domination was now complete. Having heard rumours to the contrary was of no importance; he hadn't marched his army all this way for nothing. If someone did come forward claiming to be Crofton, the imposter's assertion would be rebuked and his head summarily despatched. The pompous baron's smug expression personified his portentousness and he was delighted when given the news of Abbehale's unfortunate demise. Immediately, he despatched a courier pigeon to Athena, seeking instruction, and once Edwin's plenipotentiary decree was received, he mobilized his army. Finally, the west's egalitarianism would be suffocated from existence. Brandenburg was not expecting resistance; Damgarden had no belly for war. In the intervening years of his stewardship, elected by deed, he had been proclaimed Edwin's main protagonist, upholding the oppressive regime that allowed a defeatist mindset to thrive and fester. The cruelty he imposed left no bitter remnants of resentment and, to his satisfaction, his welcome reward was being a marked man throughout the western realm. Any number of villages would have loved to have added his scalp to their tally against tyranny.

A whole race had endured a lifetime of his brutality and, although his expectation of a quick handover was premature, he still rode out under no illusions, with a formidable force of five thousand men and close-quarters ballista machinery on carts. This impressed upon his subjects the south's strength, while safeguarding his safety, with no need for larger siege weaponry; in the past Azram had been a more than an adequate replacement for such things. Once he entered the fort Crofton's western army were to be disbanded; he had already hand-picked the men to be installed in key roles to cement his position, before re-enlisting the ones released and deemed fit for purpose. Then his favourite activity, the raising of revenue, could commence. Crofton's lax ways and black-market racketeering would cease and, of course, the landowners would be the hardest-hit. A carucate of land represented one hundred and twenty acres. However, one plough could only work half that amount so it stood to reason that, if you had three ploughs and three carucates, you could only work half the land and be taxed accordingly. Not in Brandenburg's tax book; if it was owned or traded, then it would be taxed. That was his law.

The Damgarden was flourishing, even with the restrictions placed on Crofton's movements. With hamlets and villages alongside the Tay there were rich pickings to be had, some of which were earmarked for Edwin's war chest. Being one of only a few in his inner circle, Brandenburg knew exactly what his prince was up to—in fact, it came with his blessing; if

Edwin succeeded it would virtually make him judge, jury and executioner of all western provinces; this was the promise for Brandenburg's obedience. So, not to scupper his objective to supplant Crofton, word was sent to Solom City by barge, the cheapest and slowest way to send news. The unease felt at Edwin's sudden monopoly over the western realm's wealth was propagating anxiety. Even with a signed treaty, the continued occupation was beginning to be raised more and more on the senate floor. King Albeitstein of Solom and Tellick of Angleshore were a constant thorn in the side of Edwin's desires of conquest. Soon there would be a changing of the guard and which side you aligned yourself with was crucial. The emblem of a blue-eyed dragon, flapping in his flag-bearer's hands, told you the side he had chosen. He looked across at a snow-covered landscape, up to the cliff edge overlooking Loch-Neath, expecting his view to be unimpeded but, as Brandenburg got closer, his expression changed from one of devious intent to surprise.

'It seems bad news travels fast,' he said, pointing at Baron Syracuse of Daginhale's green and white banner flying just under Edwin's flag, in an encampment entrenched to the west of their position. Brandenburg looked at his captain, who glanced at his man-at-arms, riding alongside Kallen and Rog.

'What are you looking at? It didn't come from me,' responded Lockwood, looking over the carriage at his captain on the other side. Brandenburg tactfully shook his head and discreetly rested his eyes on the Dökkalfar. His captain nodded before signalling the convoy to stop.

'There's a rider approaching from that encampment,' said a warrior riding alongside him.

'I see Bargelmir has wasted no time,' whispered Azram, arching his neck to see.

'Cuthbert, find out what that scout wants,' ordered the baron. An abrupt nod and the man-at-arms galloped off, only to return with the scout.

'I think he needs to speak with you.'

'And why is that?' asked Captain Elkington, querying why Lockwood had not carried out his baron's orders.

'Crofton is alive, that's why, and has declared war on the south, and has reclaimed his former title, Earl of Abbehale,' answered the scout.

'That's absurd,' replied Brandenburg, overhearing the conversation.

'Well, you can ask his wife. She's over there, baron,' retorted the scout petulantly, pointing back at his encampment.

'Send a couple of scouts to Glen-Neath,' Brandenburg said coldly, leaning back against his seat in the carriage.

'I wouldn't advise that, baron,' ventured the scout.

'Silence! You've said enough.' With a dismissive gesture Brandenburg ordered Elkington to carry out his command. The captain told the warrior beside him to pick two men. 'Tell your baron, if this is true I will attack Glen-Neath at once,' he continued, looking at Syracuse's encampment and siege towers. 'I see your baron is well prepared,' he added suspiciously.

'We were informed of these developments, just as you were,' the scout replied mendaciously.

'Shouldn't we wait?' said Kallen, feeling cautious.

'Baron, I really think you should speak with my baron first. You don't know what you're up against,' added the scout.

'Nonsense, that's Glen-Neath, not the halls of Hockenheim,' said Brandenburg, laughing. 'We can take her in our sleep. If we wait, we give them time to set their stall.'

His words were spoken from experience. Azram nodded in agreement.

'The new outer wall is not completed yet, my lord,' Lockwood informed him.

'Even better. Ready the men.'

A huge horn, calling his troops to order, sounded overhead repetitively. Brandenburg, not blessed with the luxury of Edwin's monstrous horde, had only men's feet and horses' hooves to fall into line. The two warriors picked to check the validity of this so-called declaration galloped across a white expanse dotted with solitary, isolated trees, between them and the barbican gateway, a fortified gatehouse and the main entrance into Glen-Neath. It served, predominately, as a checkpoint when the twelve-foot drawbridge was lowered, and the yeoman of the guard was heard shouting, 'Who goes there?' The barbican's solid stone walls were perforated with a number of arrow loops, front and side. Some were set at the height of a small door, with a palm's breadth, on the external wall, and were virtually impregnable from projectile attack. Behind each of these embrasures were stationed archers with scorpions, small catapults that discharged iron darts. The edifice was linked by a walled, cobbled passageway – called 'the neck' – to the market place further up the hill. In times of war it was known as a killing field, because of the clear line of sight from southgate's elevated position. On either side of the barbican, imposing merlons, with cross-shaped slits, added additional firepower to the walls' defences, offering archers better shelter than firing their arrows from crenels. Below, covering the circumference of the fortified outer walls, unfilled and unfinished, was a dry moat, twenty feet deep, that gave the wall extra depth.

'You won't see those two again,' Syracuse's scout told Lockwood.

As they watched the warriors get closer, off in the distance the regimented clicks of a trebuchet's mechanism winding up was just audible before the sound of it propelling a missile skywards could be clearly heard. Then the whistle came, a low hum getting louder as it inched closer. Some even managed to make out an animal hide with a flame seemingly trailing it. Eerie screams echoed downwind just before it landed on its intended victims. Momentarily, a fierce blaze arose and black smoke billowed. When the snow settled a small crater, with smouldering charred remains, was left.

'I told you,' said the scout, and nodded.

'Impressive,' added Elkington.

'You can say that again,' said Lockwood in disbelief, but it was the scout who spoke next.

'I told you so,' he reiterated.

The baron, clearly flustered, was sitting forward staring at the spot where man and horse had been burned to dust. With enraged eyes, he turned and looked at the scout.

'Tell Syracuse that once I've made camp, I will meet with him. My men will signal when I'm ready. Now go.' The scout nodded. His captain acknowledged his statement by riding off to make camp. Lockwood followed.

The campaign tent was the first to be erected and it wasn't long before a bustling encampment was surrounded by an abatis, erected with the sharpened boughs facing outwards. Fires burned freely under guinea fowl, with men replenishing their strength, before the call to arms. It was decided that the baron, Azram, Lockwood and Kallen would meet with Baron Syracuse of Daginhale and, in the dwindling sunlight, escorted by four warriors, they left camp.

'What's he doing here?' Syracuse looked at Brandenburg. 'This isn't a wizard's convention.'

'I see you've left yours at home. Why, does my mage frighten you?'

'No, not at all,' replied Syracuse, a tall, handsome, dark-haired man in a brown fur cloak, a velvet tunic and matching britches.

'How is Mephistopheles? Does he still have Gilius under lock and key?' Azram asked. Everyone knew that the newly acquired abilities of Syracuse's mage were down to the historian.

'None of your business,' he said, in a heated manner. 'Read this.' He handed the parchment Millard had sent him to Brandenburg.

'It is in Crofton's hand, granted,' he acknowledged, while digesting the message. 'But it says here that he has set a trap to capture the Keltic King Taliesin and charge him with treason.' He looked up at Syracuse doubtfully.

'Capture the Keltic king? Baron, you've been duped,' said Kallen, laughing. His outburst received a royal grimace.

'I know,' Syracuse replied reluctantly.

'Did you really fall for this westerner's egregious tongue?' asked Brandenburg, battling with the fact that there must be more to it than the brief given. He handed back Crofton's vellum.

'Yes,' replied Syracuse in disgust, before introducing Kennice.

Her arrival received a frosty reception; her charms bounced off a man whose liking for young boys was renowned. He was all too aware of her trifling agenda. Kennice explained that there was a Keltic druid at Glen-Neath, awaiting

Crofton's mark to join forces with the Kelts and then attack their fortresses.

'Preposterous!' exclaimed Azram. 'The reason the Kelts didn't fight last time is the same reason they will not fight this time; they believe Iden wasn't granted passage through Glen-Neath and was murdered where he stood.'

'What's the name of this druid?' asked Brandenburg. Though he and his mage professed otherwise, they knew the truth.

'Aghamore,' replied Kennice, at which point Brandenburg spat out the words 'the Circle of Druids', before taking centre stage and telling them all they needed to know about this conjurer of herbal remedies.

'If he signed that pact Edwin will have us replaced,' conceded Syracuse. Kallen, listening intently, connected all the dots. Having already come across the blacksmith and dwarf twice, he wondered what part they played in this plot. He revealed parts of what he knew.

'You say you saw this blacksmith on Keltic soil?' asked Brandenburg.

'He was under Keltic guard, baron, the last time I saw them, and when I enquired where they were being taken, I was told that they were going to Taliesin,' said Kallen.

'I first came across them on Black Forest Summit: they and twenty others cornered me and killed Patch. I barely manage to escape with my life.'

'Well then, Prince Edwin will soon have his renegade,' said Brandenburg.

'Remind me again why you were even there?' said Azram.

'I was pursuing the elf I believe is in possession of an item your prince wanted me to procure,' Kallen replied firmly.

'And what of this wizard the villagers of Irons Keep spoke of?' Azram pressed.

'The villagers were mistaken,' Kallen retorted vehemently. 'How would they know what I am up to?' Brandenburg raised an eyebrow, and Azram took the hint; the matter wasn't to be taken further.

'We must attack immediately. He knows about us.' Syracuse looked at Kennice.

'About you two?' Brandenburg said, baffled. 'I thought she was here because she's a loyal southerner!'

'I gave Bowen a very special message for Kennice to give her husband, the type of message you don't walk away from,' said Syracuse.

'You damned fool, you've just given him a reason to align with the Kelts,' said the red-faced baron, about to blow a blood vessel. He looked at his equal with utter contempt. 'I hope this ill-conceived plot was not your bright idea. If that pact is signed we won't just be replaced. Not long after, we'll be deceased. Now get her out of my sight,' said Brandenburg aggressively. 'The rest of you wait outside.'

Syracuse nodded to his dark-haired female captain, Rangda, who was smartly dressed in a dark-brown leather tunic and britches. She escorted Kennice out, shadowed by her counterpart, Astaroth, along with Kallen, Lockwood and Azram. His adviser, Daedalus, from the race of taller men, was the last to leave. As soon the tent flap shut, a shouting match ensued.

'How dare you speak to me like that in front of my men?' Syracuse cried.

'How dare you put all our lives at risk for the sake of your libido! Have you no shame?'

'She is with child!' shouted Syracuse. The tent fell deadly silent. When they exited the tent, to everyone's surprise, they were both calm. Syracuse looked at his captains.

'We attack at the end of light. Ready the men.'

'Take me to our encampment,' ordered Brandenburg, boarding his two-wheeled chariot. Lockwood flicked the reins and they moved off. The main reason behind him choosing to get cleaned up when they had returned to Glen-Neath with Wilfred, was to pinpoint its weak spots and find a route into the fort other than using the main gates. Having fashioned a daring raid, he put forward a proposal.

'That's an excellent plan, Cuthbert,' said Brandenburg.

*

The barons' encampments were a hub of frenetic activity. Rows of light cavalries, with a thirst for blood and black visors firmly shut, stood thirty across and a thousand riders deep on both flanks. They flew their baron's ribbons, but were dressed in black chainmail and Edwin's regalia. Their orders were clear and concise: draw covering fire. Dry fists clenched, and grips tightened on reins and bows in anticipation of the cry, 'To war!' Behind them were the infantry, with aggression levels raised and armed to the teeth, some at the front carrying ladders. Their baron's hunger burned deep in their eyes.

Since the killing of their compatriots there had been no sign of life on the outer wall. A ghostly calm was heightened in that moment when night forms; steeped in a net of mist, covered with a panoramic spectrum of colours from the sun's dying rays, Glen-Neath had a majesty rarely seen. However, with trebuchets moving within range, ready to discard disease-ridden carcasses, fetid garbage and large boulders over the wall, all that was about to change. Having decided that they would not integrate their armies the barons, within the relative safety of their encampments, on a windswept early evening, stood ready.

In days to come it would be known that Elkington and Astaroth's roar started the Third Great War. Standing beside their respective barons, as it would be written, they gave the order simultaneously and, with their words still reverberating, the sky blackened with covering arrows and with catapults and siege towers on the move. The battle to topple a baron had begun. Leading Brandenburg's charge with Lockwood was his nephew, Sprague, a sergeant, the rank below man-at-arms.

Although Glen-Neath's crenellations were not completely finished they still held the higher ground which, defended properly, would not be easy to take. Two of the six turrets, built into the four-metre thick walls at regular intervals, were still under construction and were of special interest, having been targeted as weak spots. Accordingly, being on either end of the wall meant the defenders would be stretched.

Suddenly, with fire bells ringing, the border town came alive.

Then, to Brandenburg's surprise, the drawbridge was lowered as a screeching portcullis was raised and riders of Glen-Neath rode out to meet the challenge laid. Their chrome helmets were a shining beacon of a town's aspirations against the offset of remaining light; they sallied forth. Leading the charge was Lucian. His orders were to cause disarray and prevent them from setting fire to the battlements. He was followed, stride for stride, by a meagre seven hundred and fifty men on horseback facing the might of two thousand well-oiled invaders, bolstered by infantry. The distance between the opposing factions decreased rapidly as they travelled towards that crunch where bones are broken and metal, crushed out of shape, is strewn and slides to a stop across the battlefield. Among a stampede of hooves, the clash and ring of steel, accompanied by screams and howls of death, echoed and chimed, while raring war horses, unnerved by the boom of the drums, charged again.

It was a scene of chaos, with continuous volleys of arrows in flight in both directions. It was hard to distinguish aggressor from defender amid exploits of gallantry and acts of cowardice. A bloody awful sight would be one way to describe the disembowelled and horrifically bludgeoned bodies that lay departed on both sides. Lucian blew his horn to get his remaining men to regroup, but the command fell on deaf ears. The sound was lost in a melee and in sequences of fast-moving events. A swoosh from a weapon too close for comfort and the hipparch took evasive action, managing to duck while delivering an underarm blow which caught his attacker in the chest. The warrior's release of breath, and anguished expression as the blade ploughed deep, was an instant relief. The rider slumped forward before sliding unceremoniously from his saddle, and their intimate moment was over. No time to inhale. In the same moment that the iron-hilted blade was removed and the cracking of bone ceased, the familiar hum of metal arose as Lucian and another warrior locked horns. Off to the right of his position, where the screams of his men were the loudest, a freak of nature was leading the charge of the baron's left flank. He had heard of Bargelmir's fastidious warrior woman but, as yet, had never set eyes on this female captain whom men would gladly follow anywhere. However, only by fighting on the opposing side were her ferocity and thirst for battle truly felt.

The pleasant views for warriors in her path were copious visions of wishing they were somewhere else, which normally coincided with them uttering a final prayer.

Lucian, managing to elude the next warrior with a firm kick, blew his horn again.

This time its trumpet achieved the desired effect and men rallied to his cause. A spear, flung from behind, pierced the chest of the warrior he had kicked from his horse, not a moment ago. In the midst of condensation rising from warm crimson trails of splattered crowdedness, magnified on a blanket of snow, Lucian raised his stained sword. The thrill for a warrior is in the not knowing, relying on instinct, though trained for that moment and hence, when it is relied upon, remaining intuitive while all around confusion is rife. Overcoming that adversity is what the name of hipparch embodies, and he immediately bolstered their belief with words that spoke volumes.

    'The hour has passed when we cower in the dark. We fight for more than just a fort. We fight for our earl and for our way of life. Now, hold firm your sword and fight by my side.' Pointing at the breaches in his defensive lines he charged, followed by troops now galvanized by his words. Unfortunately, with the infantry arriving to swell Sprague and Rangda's ranks the tide had already turned. Syracuse, standing next to Kennice and Daedalus, watched the onslaught with immense satisfaction. His cavalry, led by rakish Rangda, were running rings round Crofton's men with their sheer weight of numbers and tactical nous beginning to show. Little did he know that her loyalties lay elsewhere.

Kallen, standing beside Rog, felt vindicated that he had deliberately withheld the fact he had seen Nikomeades. One mention of such a powerful mage would have had both barons heading back to their fortresses on a forced march. There were rumours that Azram and Nikomeades were once friends. However, that was none of his business and he could not care less about his inaccurate report. Kallen needed his copy of the scroll deciphered, at all costs. He did not intend returning to the Kalfar High Council empty-handed. He had been on his way back to recruit more men when, as luck would have it, he and the baron had crossed paths. Brought up to speed with current events, the prospect of a disposable army that could be manipulated filled Kallen with nefarious glee. His original intentions were to go back to Irons Keep and pick up the group by following Nikomeades' scent. While still looking forward to keeping his word by questioning Pippa's brothers, he still had no knowledge of who the ring bearer was.

Although he had no conscience, Patch's death still left a gaping hole and he was partly to blame, having wrongly presumed all the Alfari were dead. Kallen wouldn't have believed it unless he'd seen the elf with his own eyes, standing before him with throat intact, so sure was he that his arrow had hit its mark. It was the first time he had missed a target, a slip he would immediately rectify if they crossed paths again.

However, now knowing that Syracuse's note had reached Crofton meant the men he sought were probably with this baron and, if he could capture one of them, he'd find out if Nikomeades was worth pursuing. Kallen did not expect the mage to lend support to a battle of such little importance and the worst part of his misfortune was that he was convinced the ruby ring he now possessed would reveal missing symbols and activate a chart by sunlight, in correlation with the gold-rimmed scroll. He was sure the archaic text was actually a map of a vast pool of ancient knowledge, or the ultimate power, though, in theory, he believed it to be the latter, so was willing to risk Edwin's wrath.

With the need for surprise gone, arrows were lit and the sky was awash with flames headed towards a thatched compound which was already under bombardment from boiling tar and all manner of foul substances pitched over the wall. Thatch is usually slow-burning, but the settlement – built mainly from wood –had various waxes, used in construction, and oils lying around; they did not stand a chance as sparks set alight the incendiary accelerants. There were sporadic plumes of smoke and howls from the injured. Men were in uproar. The siege towers rolled on, heavily marshalled by battalions running alongside, ready to scale the gauntlet of the outer walls.

Brandenburg knew that without the Kelts coming to their aid this battle would be little more than a pathetic exercise, especially with Azram by his side, although he was conscious of the fact that dark magic had to be used sparingly.

Suddenly, his eyes were transfixed by a bright burst of light as a tower, engulfed in flames, exploded. Another followed, before a catapult was completely obliterated as the wall's defences started to hit their mark. The cheers on the battlements echoed the trebuchet's achievements and could be clearly heard through the walls within Glen-Neath castle's stateroom, bringing relief to the pensive faces of the eleven who sat in prayer with the head of the clergymen, around a long banqueting table.

The hail of arrows intensified, homing in on the invaders. Lucian, in the thick of the action, boosted by the destruction, again rallied his troops.

'Protect the remaining towers!' ordered Brandenburg, frantic at seeing the co-ordinated attack beginning to unravel. The mage closed his eyes and summoned a protection spell, as a boulder tore through the battlements, killing many. Out of the five siege towers only the two under Azram's protection had nearly made it to the moat. Lucian sounded his retreat and the drawbridge was lowered. Archers ran out to cover their withdrawal.

From the cruel smile on Brandenburg's face, you could tell Azram's spell was working, with the retreat of Crofton's cavalry and the drawbridge closing shut. However, his smirk quickly evaporated when a tower, reaching the moat's bank, lost its grip on the icy soil and slid out of control, smashing into bits against the outer wall. Each attempt to gain entry with ladders was repelled. The strain on Azram, redoubling his efforts, was clearly showing, with the lines on his brow deepening and his closed eyes projecting a fiery orange glow, as did his staff.

The second tower reached the slope, attempted the same manoeuvre, and re-enacted the previous tower's fate. It rolled halfway down the moat's bank before falling horizontally against the solid stone walls although, far from falling to pieces, it remained intact.

There is always a solitary blink of an eye that no one remembers, when your mind questions the truth, a crossroads where all things still remain possible when, in reality, that opportunity to change your future has already gone. For those who inhabited Glen-Neath that luxury of limbo, vivid tranquillity's saving grace, was all they had to cling on to as warriors poured out of the leaning siege tower like a mob of fanatics, baying for blood. Even when weapons were relinquished the outcome was identical. With no quarter given, in no time at all, the defenders on the battlements were overrun.

'Seek refuge behind southgate!' shouted Lucian, seeing the barbican fall as he sat in his saddle in the middle of a riotous mad dash to the fort's gate. The drawbridge was released from its latch, but this time it was Rangda that stood in the middle of their barbican gateway, one hand on her sword hilt, the other on her hip, ushering them in.

'Where's Lockwood?' asked Elkington.

'Inside with the beast,' she replied, referring to Rog.

Once all resistance was put to bed and the battlements were secure, Brandenburg and Azram entered on horseback.

'I see your baron has stayed behind our forward lines,' said Brandenburg.

'Who said we were safe?' retorted Rangda, looking up at the baron.

'We're safe,' replied Azram casually. Brandenburg ordered his captain to find Cuthbert. A little while later his man-at-arms was standing in front of him with Rog.

'They've sabotaged the trebuchets so we can't turn them on the fort,' he reported.

'I didn't call you for that! It's nearing dawn and I think it's time you retrieved me that high-value target we spoke of,' said the baron. Lockwood produced a warm smile.

'She's pretty handy at close quarters,' Brandenburg said admiringly. 'I think you should take her too.'

Lockwood, having fought alongside Rangda when taking the outer wall, knew what she was capable of and immediately agreed with his baron's wise choice.

'Remember, at dawn we attack southgate,' ordered Brandenburg. So, having been given their instructions, Lockwood and Rog, accompanied by Rangda and two of her men, left.

'I don't like this, baron. We should continue the attack,' urged Kallen. Brandenburg shook his head.

'No, that neck is a killing field and that's what they're counting on. We'll wait until we've regrouped. Anyway, if Lockwood is successful I have a feeling we won't have to worry about the Kelts entering any battles.' Brandenburg's lopsided smile returned as he looked at Azram, who nodded. 'And Syracuse has a little surprise in store for them.'

'Baron, if it is the blacksmith they're after, don't you think I should go?' asked Kallen.

'Why?'

'I believe they handed Crofton the note. Needless to say, Edwin will not take kindly to anymore mishaps.'

'I see where you're going. From all accounts these individuals are very resourceful so maybe you're right. Having seen the faces we seek, you have my permission.'

'A wise decision, your grace.'

Kallen kicked his heels and rode off along the outer wall to join Lockwood, who was on foot.

'I don't think you should trust this dark elf; he speaks half-truths,' said Azram, voicing a niggling suspicion.

'And what made you think I do?' said Brandenburg, smirking. 'But think, Azram. How else am I to find out what he's really up to unless I give him a short leash?' He looked at his bullmastiff and reached down to give him a pat, before pulling himself upright. 'Unlike Edwin, I do not suffer fools gladly. Elkington, have my army ready. We attack at first light.' His captain nodded.

'As you wish.'

Brandenburg was right. The southgate's captain had enlisted archers to man the murder holes, as well the turrets and walls. Pitch and oil were winched up to the battlements and villagers were told to put support beams against the entrance's frame to buttress the gate. The captain stood on the curtain wall looking out over the parapet, staring into darkness, half expecting their second wave. His orders were crystal clear: he was to hold the south gate at all cost, until help arrived. He looked at Millard who, having left the castle, was standing next to Lucian and Drake, the captain of Crofton's heavy infantry, going over their defensive frailties. Millard dipped his head, glad that the endless battle drills he had put his men through seemed to be paying off. Hopefully, Crofton's delaying tactics had given them a fighting chance.

He had been disappointed at the barbican's capitulation and when he looked into Lucian's eyes, and those of his hipparch, he knew Branic was dead. He went to inform the others of his passing. Branic was an Ebenesian Knight.

The hill fort and southgate were a different proposition. Compact and built for defence, the imposing gate was two metres thick and, with insurmountable rocky terrain on either side, a frontal attack was the only option though, in truth, Glen-Neath was never built to defend against invaders attacking from the west. Its original function was to keep the Kelts out and, to that endeavour, it had served its purpose.

Lockwood, reaching a culvert duct to an underground sewer, which was virtually a dirt hole in the ground covered with an iron grid, threw his torch in. It landed with a splash, although not in water, remaining lit for a moment before its flames were drowned out. It gave him just enough time to see a familiar burgundy pouch, bobbing on a cesspit of slush, unable to pass a wooden mesh at the base of an adjacent entrance. Medieval towns were a space where smells and odours were commonplace, but nothing could have prepared them for the rank smell they had stumbled upon. Even Kallen, not perturbed by a rancid scent or two, was the first to reach out his hand as Lockwood handed the group a tin of smelling salts. However, Rog, dumbfounded, wondered what all the fuss was about.

One by one the group climbed down. Rog went first, Rangda last. Lockwood lit a torch and quickly checked his footing. The light shone on a gangway that would eventually bring them out by an abbey, still under construction, away from prying eyes.

*

The sun rose, breaking night's stranglehold, and another inhospitable wintry day approached. On a half-burned sundial in the middle of the area known as the neck, with a stretching, moving shade on its face, dawn was marked at five in the morning.

With southgate's wall sentries keeping watch, the barons were ready for their final assault. Taking deep, measured breaths, their archers stood poised, keeping to the shadows.

This time the numbers were bolstered by Syracuse's battalion of taller men, thick-set tribal barbarians. With fur cloaks and boots they seemed oblivious to the cold. Some, underneath, were pushing the dreaded scarab, a battering ram completely covered from top to bottom with protective plates on a steel mesh, lined with linen soaked in a fire-resistant liquid. For some, it was a thing of exquisite beauty, though for the keeps that felt its full destructive force, it was a fearful sight. Standing eight feet tall and six feet wide, the object did not have a ram's head but, with two humongous spikes, each the circumference of a yard, it could wreak havoc. Brandenburg smiled and signalled to attack. The fog over Glenn-Neath was dissipating and a bright sun now would only be to his advantage because it would impair the enemy's view.

'Hold, hold!' the southgate's captain shouted as the spikes thudded against the gate, while villagers below added extra support to buttresses.

'They're in our arc of fire!' shouted an archer, using the term as a warning that their arrows were useless.

Boom …Boom …Boom …The south gate held firm, though its two-metre thick gate was, literally, taking a battering.

'Pour the pitch over and light the hot oils. We'll burn them out,' ordered the captain. Unbeknown to Kallen, using a spell to cover Glenn-Neath in fog on exiting the sewers was the signal that Crofton and the Kelts had been waiting for. It had alerted them to the baron's presence. Brandenburg never travelled without his mage. They had managed to get into the fort and, after the two men standing watch were quickly disposed of and replaced by one of Rangda's men, Kallen used a spell to transform the group, making them look like clergymen. Now, with their targets in potato sacks, unconscious, and it getting lighter, Kallen removed the fog spell and, to his surprise, witnessed the Kelt's silent arrival in the evaporating mist.

Lockwood was just as shocked as he saw Crofton wearing his familiar long sheepskin coat, riding by on his kidnapped white charger en route to his castle.

Zog, riding in the convoy, noticed something suspicious about one of the hooded men, walking in a group carrying sacks. For some reason, he associated it with the way that Draconians move and he gave Brun a nudge, as the group disappeared by the abbey. Flint, always curious, followed too. Zog turned the corner to see Kallen removing the manifestation. Brun, on his heels, watched in amazement as Rog's features and complexion returned while Rangda, standing beside him, turned back into a woman.

'I knew it!' exclaimed Zog, looking at the men that had abandoned him. He threw a dagger, then drew his sword. The projectile just missed Lockwood, the man-at-arms giving him a cheeky wink as he disappeared down the hole. Brun told Flint to go and fetch the others but, for some reason, he seemed in two minds on whether to leave him with Zog, while staring down at the creature that had killed his parents.

'Go now,' ordered Brun. If he was ever going to give this beast his complete trust then now was a better time than any; maybe a leopard can't change its spots but not giving it an option to try is the true injustice. Anyway, he knew none of them was capable of dealing with the

Dökkalfar. Flint ran off shouting, 'Its Kallen!' at the top of his voice.

'Deal with them,' commanded Kallen. 'He's the one Edwin wants.'
'With pleasure,' replied Rog, who was standing guard at the shaft's exit, as Kallen disappeared down it too.
'Kill this Ling and we can go home.'
'This man saved my life!' shouted Zog.
'Why are you wasting time?' said Rog.
'Like the time I wasted on Keltic soil?' Zog hissed. Rog drew his sword.
'If you won't, I will.'
'Sorry, Rog, but it is you who are about to die.'
'So, it has come to this, brother.' Rog smiled at his former captain.
'You're no brother of mine,' replied Zog, as they clashed swords and glared at each other through crossed blades, each almost tasting the other's breath. Then, suddenly, they were three feet apart and arms were flung back from other jaw-tangling collisions. The swordplay, displaying both strength and speed, was filled with poise, passion and self-belief, and acts of uncertainty were not entertained. Blood was drawn on a number of occasions. Each deflected swings worthy of an honourable kill, as blade ran against blade and sparks flew. Even a ducking position was used to launch an attack.

Zog kicked up some snow, in an attempt to gain an advantage, which Rog nimbly avoided. There was little to choose between them and the contest was perched on a knife-edge. Brun, with his orks' axes gleaming in hand, had decided to let them fight it out. In many ways he believed the Draconian needed this so, unless it started to look bad for him, he would not intervene. However, if he was in any doubt before about the dragon-man's oath, Zog dealt that ambiguity a crippling blow. Their clash was still raging when Flint arrived, with Nikomeades and the others.

'I'm telling you, he was right there,' said Flint. Tartarus took aim, as Angus growled.

'No! He's mine!' shouted Zog.

'In the company of Lings you have become weak,'said Rog with a well-placed kick that made Zog spin on his heels.

'Better to be weak than dead,' replied Zog as he continued the spin, and then delivered a blow across the neck and chest from right to left. The metal cut deep and Rog fell to his knees, dead. Brun patted Zog on the back.

'You're sure you don't want your dagger back? Your aim was slightly off-centre.' Zog shook his head.

'I'm sure. I was aiming for where I thought he'd move to.'

'Shouldn't we pursue?' asked Tarquin. Nikomeades shook his head.

'No, it maybe a trap. Remember, he still has the ring,' he replied.

'Exactly,' whispered Flint. Although he disagreed with the decision, Tarquin, giving Nikomeades a quizzical look, nodded. However, Tartarus understood.

On exiting the shaft, Lockwood made a conscious decision that it was each man for himself: there was no way to defend against the army he'd just seen. So, with a large hole through the outer wall offering them a fortunate escape route, they bundled the sacks over saddles and headed toward Syracuse's encampment at a pace. Rangda was greeted by Syracuse and Daedalus at the encampment entrance.

'We must leave at once, my lord. Crofton's amassed a Keltic army the likes of which ...' She hurriedly dismounted and gave a quick shake of the head.

'Are you sure?' asked Daedalus. 'My kin are up there.' She nodded.

'With my own eyes.'

'Then we must sound the retreat,' agreed Syracuse.

'No time, my lord.'

'No time?' Syracuse replied, baffled. All five nodded their heads.

'And, baron, I have a gift that should keep them off our coat-tails,' added Lockwood, patting the closest sack. A terse grunt was heard.

'Well, whatever you've decided you'd better do it quickly,' prompted Kallen.

'Impertinent,' thought Syracuse, as he asked why.

'Because I think you're about to be attacked,' observed Kallen, amused.

Covering the ground at a rate of knots were warriors charging towards their position.

'They look like rabble, my lord,' advised Daedalus

'I can see that. Get Kennice and Isadora now,' Syracuse replied coldly.

'We're leaving.'

Candlelight, repeatedly covered then revealed, coming from a window within Glen-Neath's castle, was the signal for the keeps to attack. Eric, having seen the signal, was already on his way to the stables to inform Millard. In the midst of an unorganized, chaotic dash, Sid, Barnaby, Reece and Daniel were riding behind Nefanial, who was matching Gwillym's stride. Beside them, others ran on foot towards Brandenburg's encampment, armed with pitchforks, axes, swords and spears. Their cries were ones of freedom as they covered the snow. Brimstone's chieftain was co-ordinating his attack on Syracuse's camp. Brandenburg's force was haemorrhaging infantry, with Keltic archers shoring up the southgate's defences.

'I need reinforcements,' he shouted, knowing his cavalry were ineffective until the gateway was breached. He watched another man fall to his death from a ladder.

'Our encampment is under attack, uncle, but I can take my battalion toward them off.

'No, ride to Syracuse. Tell him we've got some silly commoners attacking our flank and we need reinforcements.'

'But–'

'But what, nephew?'

'So, you haven't heard. Syracuse has fled and whatever you told Lockwood to get from Glen-Neath is now en route with the baron to his fortress.

'What? You must be mistaken,' said Brandenburg, turning green. He had planned to have the druid paraded in front of the south gate.

'No, I'm not. See for yourself.' He handed his uncle a stargazer. True to Sprague's words, he could just make out a caravan, sporting Syracuse's colours, about to leave the horizon. It was indicative of a prevailing wind, and Brandenburg knew the game was up even before the south gate swung inwards and, for as far as the eye could see, warriors were mounted on horseback.

For Tartarus, the word greenhorn, in essence, meant battle-shy and, indeed, it would be his first battle. But he welcomed this fight with open arms; shy was the wrong word. He felt so angered by what the south represented: greed, fallow lands, devastation and misery ... he could go on. However, he tightened his grip on his reins. Willow gently reared his head. Tartarus knew the telltale sign back to front; his stallion was ready.

Druce banged his shield to get his warriors' attention and Taliesin spoke.

'From the rocks of Skara Brae to the hills of Clovelly, and let's not forget the forests of Kaleköy' – he smiled then, with his war face in place – 'It's about time we Kelts joined this battle once and for all. For Iden!' he cried. The Keltic warriors banged their shields. Tartarus, agreeing with his sentiments, added his own whispered words.

'This is for my holy mother, for Eolande, for Jacob and for all my elven brethren, past and present.' Then he drew his sword just as Brun, on Cloud, unclipped his axe. Crofton sat in his saddle and thought back to a previous conversation with Nikomeades, a conversation that had been playing on his thoughts.

'I'm aware my father betrayed you and I will not do the same,' he had told Nikomeades.

'Crofton Abbehale, I do not suffer empty words lightly. The hour has not yet come when you have proven your worth. Fortunately for you, that time still exists.' He had smiled then, though he pondered the mage's words now. Betrayal ran in his family. He recalled the meeting when Taliesin told him to face the fact that his wife was a spy and should be dealt with appropriately. She had been, and it was time to reap the rewards, though it tasted bittersweet.

'Why so glum?' asked Tempest. 'Haven't you seen our insignia on your white mare?'

Beneath them, his courser and Tempest's destrier were wearing ancient armour with chainmail wrapped around their mane and fixed to a criniere, shielding the neck, and connected painstakingly to a peytral and champron, designed to shield the face. Hinged plates protected the cheeks and shell-shaped flanges covered the eyes, extending from ears to muzzle, engraved with Ebenesian ornamentation and a small spiked embellishment centred on their brow. The emblematic colours of the Ebenesian Knights' coat of arms adorned their horses from nose to tail, finishing just short of the ground.

Crofton nodded, then pulled down his shiny visor with a sword arm free of armour. Millard and Wilfred did the same. This was a day his whole being had yearned for. Wearing the regalia of the fallen order, although there were only twelve of them, the Ebenesian Knights rode into the fold, closely followed by Tartarus, Ragnarr, Brun, Flint and Tarquin, Calhoun, Druce, Taliesin and his Kelts in full voice. Picking up the slack were Lucian, with his light cavalry, and Drake, with his heavy infantry. The noise as they covered the ground was deafening and, in an instant, it was over, like a huge wave consuming all in its path and claiming the filth that had besieged it.

> When men go to war …
>
> A family's love is torn, when a warrior dons his helmet and picks up a sword.
> Don't shed a tear: I defend my homestead, our green grass of home.
> In doubting our actions, we pour scorn on the fruits of our loins.
> I beat my chest at the sight of death and gallop, with unerring finesse, into folklore.
> Like a herd of wild boars among the screams and roars, contained within an iron-cast breast, entwined with the taste of man's sweat, my blue blood runs cold,
> For a man is at his destructive best …
>
> When men go to war.
>
> Gilius.

Brandenburg was left speechless in face of an avalanche of men and horses coming towards him. He knew the battle was lost. Azram looked up and saw Nikomeades on the battlements.

'It can't be ...'

'What?'

'Nikko, Nikomeades,' he blurted out.

'But weren't you his apprentice, and isn't he an enchanted?' In the shade of the barbican, Brandenburg realized what he was saying and mouthed, 'Get us out of here, now.'

However, having heard the clamour from the Kelts, banging their shields, Elkington and Sprague hightailed it once southgate opened. Astaroth wasn't given that option. With the entrance about to be broken in two, severely fragmented in its centre by the scarab's non-stop bombardment, he was directing his men further up the path and, like his men, he was swallowed up in Crofton's stampede. Before Azram could fashion a response to his lord's request, a dark cloud was already forming overhead. Nikomeades told Pippa to close her eyes before speaking the last part of his spell.

'Ala-car-zam!'

A booming rumble shook Glen-Neath's foundations, with the cloud's thunderous energy being released. One massive bolt of lightning shot down, splitting Azram's hat and parting his hair but not his head, as it proceeded to fry his brain. His eyes popped out, looking like poached eggs, as he fell on his face with steam rising from his temple.

'What was that all about?' asked Rex.

'Don't ask,' replied Nikomeades abruptly, before adding, 'Bad blood.'

'Can I open my eyes now?' asked Pippa, not waiting for a response and looking over the parapet. 'So, was he treacherous then?' she asked sheepishly. Nikomeades nodded. Pippa smiled, glad she had got its meaning right.

Crofton, leading the charge, with Tartarus by his side releasing arrow after arrow, had been overtaken by Druce and Calhoun on a rampage, culling their victims with a sword and axe. The barons' forces were routed and, in the ensuing confusion, Brandenburg lay dead. No one knew who had landed the fatal blow; he was simply thrown on a funeral pyre with the rest of his men's bodies. However, Druce had found a new pet, with the baron's bullmastiff being fed by the burly Kelt.

'You should be a knight,' insisted Tempest

'No, I think you'll find that the fox is already an honorary Kelt.'

'Well, let's just agree to disagree,' replied Tempest.

Calhoun, silent, glowed under the adulation of the seasoned campaigner. On reaching Syracuse's encampment Taliesin, now with Calhoun, Crofton and Tempest, commended the assistant's efforts. They were met by Varden and Ronan, holding a scout with a black domed helmet. Varden informed him that the scout had information.

'I've been told to tell you, King of the Kelts, that if you pursue Syracuse your druid and his daughter will be put to death.' Taliesin ordered his men to release him.

'You've given me your message. Now go. Tell your master this isn't over, but his wishes will be adhered to.' The scout got to his feet and ran to a nearby horse, mounted it and galloped off.

'Isn't that the girl you mentioned earlier?' asked Tempest. Crofton nodded, seething. 'Why did you let him go?' Tempest looked at Taliesin.

'So that Syracuse believes we won't pursue.' He then turned to Varden and Ronan who were awaiting instructions. 'Find Nikomeades and tell them to meet me at the castle.'

'What are you up to?' asked Crofton, removing his helmet. With Syracuse gone, the battle was over.

'Maybe we can kill two birds with one stone,' said Taliesin, smiling, though inwardly livid; it was his plan that had put Aghamore in harm's way.

After the fighting had died down, some of Tartarus's group were on a nearby hill.

'Where do all these people live?' asked Pippa, looking back across the battlefield. Tartarus looked at her and thought it was a good question. Flint went to hazard a guess, but simply smiled.

'I don't know why you're all looking at me. Can we go now?' said the dwarf, tapping the hefty amulet inside his pocket. It was left to Nikomeades to explain the enormity of Elohim. The group stood in the snow waiting for the mage to speak.

'As you can see, my heart still beats within me.'

'What?' asked Brun.

'Oh, I'm sorry. I was thinking about what I'm going to say to Gunn-Hilda. I have been away an awfully long time.' The group laughed. 'But I do have something to say.' Nikomeades cleared his throat. 'I, for one, will look back on this day and say that, this day, the Third Great War against tyranny began.' Angus barked.

'Well said,' added Ragnarr. Brun nodded. 'Now all you've got to do is fix this' –he produced Arachna's cracked ruby –'and I can give it to Crofton, to protect Glen-Neath, so then we can continue our quest,' added Ragnarr. Brun smiled, acknowledging the gesture.

'An inhibiter. Of course I can,' replied Nikomeades, taking possession of the item.

'Ragnarr Morbere, you are full of surprises.'

A rider rode up to them.

'Nikomeades, you're wanted. Syracuse has kidnapped Aghamore and his daughter, Lyra.'

'I told them it was a bad plan,' muttered Nikomeades as he walked back to Glen-Neath.

'What plan?' asked Pippa, with Rainbow following. Tarquin and Flint shook their heads behind her.

Although they were celebrating, the wailing women and children told another tale, and it reminded Tartarus that victory only comes through great sacrifice.

'It's beautiful, even in the winter, isn't it?' said Rex, looking at the still lake.

'Yes,' replied Tartarus.

'Hey, aren't you two coming?' called Brun, walking off with Zog and Ragnarr.

'We're going to meet Nefanial, Sid and the others.'

'In a moment,' said Rex.

Tartarus was proud of what they had already achieved. A tight smile masked his true feelings; he, too, was looking over the cliffs at Loch-Neath. He would face sterner tests; the road ahead was paved with anguish and despair, still. The smile widened.

Flashes of joy were to be relished, just as times of sorrow would be endured. After all, Tartarus Leadbottom was a guardian of the gold-rimmed scroll.

The Gauntlets of Power
Guardians of the Gold-Rimmed Scroll

Epilogue

A mesmerising, complex mosaic floor greeted Queen Cressida. Arrogantly, her white pupils, set in red eyes, acknowledged a Svartalfar and Greymon, leader the Order of Anarchists. Admiringly, they returned her gaze. Her long black hair was as exquisite as she was venomous. Cressida told her pet to stay. The Nameless One, standing on his tower's balcony, revelling in his autocracy bestowed from the masses below, continued to receive their adulation.

'So, this is what you use it for. But soon they will be hungry,' she whispered, walking up behind him, an elaborate dark headdress lengthening her slender form.

'And soon, they will be fed,' he replied, turning his gaze on the horde below.
'What brings you to my lair?'

'It's been awhile since you've visited my bed chamber,' she said, unashamedly.

'I take it your puppet still amuses you? I would have thought you'd have tired of him by now,' he said, referring to her short attention span.

'Edwin serves his purpose,' she retorted stubbornly.

'No doubt,' he responded doubtfully.

A Draconian courtier walked in, stopping just short of the floor's patterned centre, and he looked down at Cressida's pet sheepishly. The human-headed manicore, with the body of a lion and a deadly scorpion's tail, was fast, powerful, and known for its hunger for human flesh.

'There's been a revolt, my king, and there is word that one of the enchanted has resurfaced.' Abandanon's eyes opened wide and he turned away from his worshipping hordes.

He walked back into the chamber and sat on his backless, black metal throne. Two rows of iron skulls were positioned as armrests. The chair was just one of many wondrous and ornate objects residing in the autocratic king's majestically decorated throne room.

'Where?' he growled.

'In the west,' his courtier replied.

'Fetch Scallion.'

'At once, Autocrat,' said the courtier, before walking back down the long corridor directly opposite his throne chair. Abandanon look at Cressida.

'You're not above my disapproval,' he snarled. The witch, producing an awkward smile, stroked her manicore's mane. It purred like a cat.

A gentle hum preceded one solitary fly. Then, suddenly, the chamber was filled with a swarm that took a humanoid form, though the millions of transparent winged flies still seemed to be constantly on the move.

'What is your bidding, my lord?' Scallion hissed with his forked tongue.

'I want you to hunt down an enchanted. Find out what it is up to, but do not kill it; it may lead us to others.'

'And where should I look?'

'In the west.'

'As you wish.' Scallion bowed his head and then, in a cyclone of flies, the creature was gone. The swarm maintained his authoritative presence. Soon, all those who stood in his way would be...Abandanon smiled.

Acknowledgement

To all my family and friends who help me in this endeavour, without your support this would not have been possible.

W. E. JAMES

Printed in Great Britain
by Amazon.co.uk, Ltd.,
Marston Gate.